"HAS ALL THE MAKINGS TO BE THE NEXT
DA VINCI CODE."*

"DAN BROWN MEETS TOM CLANCY."†

From its heart-pounding opening scene to its hair-raising
last, internationally bestselling author Glenn Meade's
acclaimed and controversial new thriller will knock you
off your feet.

PRAISE FOR *THE SECOND MESSIAH*

"A plot that screams, a controversial edge, and characters with
attitude and something to prove." —*Publishers Weekly**

"Nonstop action." —*Booklist*

"Reads at a breathtaking, frantic pace from beginning to end. . . .
A daring work of fiction that will have people talking."
—*Fresh Fiction*

"Thriller readers will love this book." —*Midwest Book Review*

"Written in the mold of *The Da Vinci Code, The Second Messiah*
keeps readers on the edge of their proverbial seats with multiple
plot twists." —*Charisma*

"Glenn Meade sure knows how to get your pulse racing. I
was gripped from page one. . . . *The Second Messiah* is a roller
coaster of a thriller that lifts the lid on the inner workings of the
Vatican and leaves you wondering just how much of the fiction
is actually fact." —Stephen Leather, author of *Nightfall*†

GLENN MEADE

THE SECOND MESSIAH

A THRILLER

POCKET BOOKS

New York London Toronto Sydney New Delhi

Pocket Books
A Division of Simon & Schuster, Inc.
1230 Avenue of the Americas
New York, NY 10020

This book is a work of fiction. Names, characters, places, and incidents either are products of the author's imagination or are used fictitiously. Any resemblance to actual events or locales or persons, living or dead, is entirely coincidental.

First Pocket Books paperback edition July 2012

POCKET and colophon are registered trademarks of Simon & Schuster, Inc.

For information about special discounts for bulk purchases, please contact Simon & Schuster Special Sales at 1-866-506-1949 or business@simonandschuster.com.

The Simon & Schuster Speakers Bureau can bring authors to your live event. For more information or to book an event, contact the Simon & Schuster Speakers Bureau at 1-866-248-3049 or visit our website at www.simonspeakers.com.

Manufactured in the United States of America

10 9 8 7 6 5 4 3 2 1

ISBN 978-1-4516-7283-1
ISBN 978-1-4516-1188-5 (ebook)

FOR MY SON, NEAL,
WHO ALREADY KNOWS THAT
LOVE IS THE MOST IMPORTANT
PART OF LIFE'S STORY

ACKNOWLEDGMENTS

As always, there are people to thank. In Israel, archaeologist, author, and scholar Hanan Eshel.

In the United States, John Wood, in Knoxville, who patiently answered my many questions and always pointed me in the right directions. Aramaist and author Douglas Stuart. Jeff Fisher for kindly sharing his memories of his time at Qumran. Author Bart Ehrman. Claudia Cross, my agent at Sterling Lord Literistic in New York. And not to forget Elizabeth Lacy and Marion McDonald—a promise kept.

In Italy, the Vatican Press Office. And a list too long to set down here of experts who gave of their time and help. My sincere thanks.

I'd love to be able to continue that great authorial tradition of buck-passing by saying that all errors that may appear are theirs, not mine, but that's not so. However, I'll try to cover myself by saying that some may be theirs, and some mine.

Ancient Rome's remains and underground passageways mentioned in this book exist, as do the biblical settlement at Qumran and the town of Maloula. The Atbash code is a real cipher. It was discovered in a number of the Dead Sea scrolls by one of their most eminent translators, who believed from the coded evidence he had unearthed that the material would one day bring to light a prophecy or revelation of immense significance to humankind.

Sometimes the past is best left buried. For with the bones of the dead can lay some dark and very dangerous secrets.

—JEAN PAUL CADE

What we have found in these Aladdin's caves is a true treasure trove. It appears that a large number of the scrolls may date from the time of Jesus. We will carefully translate all that we can but the work will be painstaking. For who knows what important messages are hidden within these ancient parchments? Who knows if their contents may some day astonish the world?

—FATHER ROLAND DE VAUX,
INTERNATIONAL TEAM LEADER
WORKING ON THE DEAD SEA
SCROLLS, DISCOVERED AT
QUMRAN, ISRAEL, 1947

PART ONE

THE PAST

EAST OF JERUSALEM
ISRAEL

Leon Gold didn't know that he had two minutes left to live and he was grinning. "Did anyone ever tell you that you've got terrific legs?" he asked the drop-dead gorgeous woman seated next to him.

Gold was twenty-three, a tanned, good-looking, muscular young man from New Jersey whose folks had immigrated to Israel. As he drove his Dodge truck with military markings past a row of sun-drenched orange groves, he inhaled the sweet scent through the rolled-down window, then used the moment to glimpse the figure of the woman seated next to him.

Private Rachel Else was stunning.

Gold, a corporal, eyed Rachel's uniform skirt riding up her legs, the top button open on her shirt to reveal a flash of cleavage. She was driving him so crazy that he found it hard to concentrate on his job—delivering a consignment to an Israel Defense Forces outpost, thirty miles away. The road ahead was a coil of tortuous bends. "Well, did anyone ever tell you that you've got terrific legs?" Gold repeated.

A tiny smile curled Rachel's lips. "Yeah, you did. Five minutes ago, Leon. Tell me something new."

Gold flicked a look in the rearview mirror and saw sunlight igniting the windows and the glinting dome of a fast-disappearing Jerusalem. There was only one reason he stayed in this godforsaken country with its endless friction with the Palestinians, high taxes, grumbling Jews, and searing heat.

The Israeli women. They were simply gorgeous. And the Israel Defense Forces had its fair share of beauties. Gold was determined that Rachel was going to be his next date. He shifted down a gear as the road twisted up and the orange scent was replaced by gritty desert air. "Okay, then did anyone ever mention you've got seductive eyes and a terrific figure?"

"You mentioned those too, Leon. You're repeating yourself."

"Are you going to come on a date with me or not, Private Else?"

"No. Keep your eyes on the road, Corporal."

"I've got my eyes on the road."

"They're on my legs."

Gold grinned again. "Hey, can I help it if you make my eyes wander?"

"Keep them on the *road*, Leon. You crash and we're both in trouble."

Gold focused on the empty road as it rose up into sand-dusted limestone hills. Rachel was proving a tough nut to crack, but he reckoned he still had an ace up his sleeve. As the road snaked round a bend he nudged the truck nearer the edge. The wheels skidded, sending loose gravel skittering into the rock-strewn ravine below.

Alarm crept into Rachel's voice. "Leon! Don't do that."

Gold winked, nudging the Dodge even closer to the road's edge. "Maybe I can make you change your mind?"

"Stop it, Leon. Don't fool around, it's crazy. You'll get us killed."

Gold grinned as the wheels skidded again. "How about that date? Just put me out of my misery. Yes, or no?"

"Leon! Oh no!" Rachel stared out past the windshield.

Gold's eyes snapped straight ahead as he swung the wheel away from the brink. A white Ford pickup appeared from around the next bend. Gold jumped on the brakes but his blood turned to ice and he knew he was doomed. His Dodge started to skid as the two vehicles hurtled toward the ravine's edge, trying to avoid a crash. The pickup was like an express train that couldn't stop and then everything seemed to happen in slow motion.

Gold clearly saw the pickup's occupants. Three adults in the front cab, two teenagers in the open back—a boy and a girl seated on some crates. The smiles on their faces collapsed into horror as the two vehicles shrieked past each other.

There was a grating *clang* of metal striking metal as the rears of both vehicles briefly collided and then Gold screamed, felt a breeze rush past him as the Dodge flew through the air. His scream combined with Rachel's in a bloodcurdling duet that died abruptly when their truck smashed nose-first into the ravine and their gas tank ignited.

Fifteen miles from Jerusalem, the distant percussion of the massive blast could be heard as the army truck's cargo of antipersonnel mines detonated instantly, vaporizing Gold's and Rachel's handsome young bodies into bone and ash.

The Catholic priest was following two hundred yards behind the pickup, driving a battered old Renault, when he felt the blast through the rolled-down window. The percussion pained his ears and he slammed on his brakes. The Renault skidded to a halt.

The priest paled as he stared at the orange ball of flame

rising into the air, followed by an oily cloud of smoke. Instinct made him stab his foot on the accelerator and the Renault sped forward.

When he reached the edge of the ravine, he floored the brakes and jumped out of his car. The priest saw the flames consume the blazing shell of the army truck and knew there was no hope for whoever was inside. His focus turned to the upturned white Ford pickup farther along the ravine, smoke pouring from its cabin. The priest blessed himself as he stared blankly at the accident scene. "May the Lord have mercy on their souls."

His plan had gone horribly wrong. This was not exactly what he had intended. If the pickup's occupants had to die, so be it—the priceless, two-thousand-year-old treasure inside the vehicle was worth the loss of human life—but he hadn't foreseen such awful carnage.

He moved toward the pickup. A string of deafening explosions erupted as more mines ignited. The priest was forced to crouch low.

Seconds later his eyes shifted back to the upturned Ford pickup. He could make out the occupants trapped inside the smoke-filled cabin. One of them frantically kicked at the windshield, trying to escape. Nearby the sprawled bodies of a teenage boy and girl lay among the wreckage.

When the explosions died, the priest stood. His gaze swung back to the burning pickup. The desperate passenger had stopped kicking and his body had fallen limp. As thick smoke smothered the cabin, the priest caught sight of the leather map case, lying wedged inside the windshield.

He knew it contained the ancient scroll that had been dis- covered that morning at Qumran, and that the pickup was on its way to the Antiquities Department in Jerusalem with its precious cargo. But the priest was desperate to ensure that the scroll never reached its destination.

His orders from Rome were clear.

This was one astonishing secret that had to be kept hidden from the world.

Flames started to lick around the map case. "Dear God, no."

He scrambled down the rocks toward the wreckage.

PART TWO

THE PRESENT

TWENTY YEARS LATER

2

ROME

It began with an omen.

Some said the bizarre event in the Sistine Chapel that midnight had been prophesied by Nostradamus, that it was a sign destined to happen.

There were other signs.

The Eternal City had an air of stillness, as if a storm were about to break, but that evening the sky was clear, a soft wind blowing from the west. Rome's usual aggression and bustle had become a hushed calm.

On the main roads and along the Tiber, drivers occasionally pulled in, switched off their headlights, and turned on their car radios. Around a densely crowded St. Peter's Square, the media crews' satellite dishes pointed skyward, as if seeking celestial guidance.

Powerful television arc lamps illuminated the Sistine Chapel, while in the seedy pickup bars of the city's red-light district, even the prostitutes took time out from their evening's work to listen to the media coverage chattering from televisions and radios.

After all, whoever was elected pope was predicted to be the last—the man who would supposedly face Armageddon— and hundreds of millions of people all over the world were anxiously awaiting news of his election.

The previous pontiff had been dead for twenty-eight days. After the ancient rituals had been observed, his body embalmed, his papal seals broken, and his burial completed, a solemn procession of 120 cardinals of the Sacred College, dressed in red hats and red silk robes, had filed into the Sistine Chapel to choose a replacement to fill the Shoes of the Fisherman.

After twenty-nine secret ballots, they had failed to elect a new pope. When the clock struck twelve and a candidate had still not been chosen, the church would face its fifth week without a leader.

Among Rome's anxious clergy agreement was clear. By midnight, a decision had to be made.

Cardinal Umberto Cassini thought he was about to have a heart attack. A small, scrawny Sicilian with watery brown eyes who usually smiled a lot, Cassini wasn't smiling now. Beads of perspiration ran down his face. His pounding chest ached with stress pains.

The air in the magnificent fourteenth-century Sistine Chapel reeked of sweat. Every window and door was locked and the lights were on. The temperature was up to a humid eighty and the tense atmosphere was expectant. Cassini glanced at the wall clock: 11 P.M.

Seated at his wooden table in the ancient chapel, Cassini shifted his eyes toward Michelangelo's powerful wall painting depicting the horrors of the Apocalypse. Umberto Cassini was experiencing his own terror.

The history of papal elections was a stormy one. Cassini recalled a troubling fact—the conclave of 1831 had lasted fifty-four days and in the process the indecision had almost ruined the church. Tonight it seemed another nightmarish tempest was unfolding. As camerlengo, the head of the conclave, Cassini was the man on whose shoulders rested the task of ensuring a papal successor was chosen.

But the twenty-ninth ballot had been completed two hours ago and had failed to produce a pope. Cassini dabbed his brow and thought, *Has God deserted His church in its hour of need?*

Of the three main candidates, none had the eighty-vote majority required to win the election. It had been like that for nearly two weeks, the voting almost equal among the candidates, and it had proved impossible to break the deadlock. It was obvious that the conclave was in turmoil.

Cassini had prayed that the voting would reach a conclusion by midnight. Hoping to break the impasse, one of the Curia had proposed yet another new compromise candidate to join the other three contenders: the American, Cardinal John Becket. The strategy was obvious—that Becket might split the voting pattern and break the deadlock. Cassini nervously licked his lips. Sixty minutes remained to midnight and the tension was killing him.

He glanced over at John Becket, sitting at one of the tables opposite. He was an imposing figure. Tall and lean, with fair hair and gentle, honest blue eyes, the American was almost Christlike in appearance.

His face was deeply tanned and his hands had the rough calluses of a laborer. The kind of tough hands that might have built this very chapel. And yet there was something strangely regal about him.

Anyone in his company would at once have been aware of his incredibly powerful physical presence. Those who knew Becket spoke of his unique personality and charisma. The son of a Chicago lawyer, he had proved a learned, devout priest who had chosen to shun the many comforts of his American homeland for a deeply religious life.

An outsider, Becket had initially been considered a touch too young for the papacy at fifty-seven. This time, Cassini wondered which way the vote would go.

The Conclave of Cardinals had retreated to pray and seek further inspiration from the Holy Spirit. They had returned and placed their folded voting slips, first onto a golden platter, then into a gold chalice, to signify they had completed a sacred act. Then they had filed back solemnly to their individual tables and chairs and waited for the three scrutineers seated behind the platter and chalice to examine the slips and count the votes.

Now Cassini fidgeted nervously with his pectoral cross as the minutes ticked away. He saw the counters finish their work. One of the scrutineers approached him with the piece of paper bearing the result.

As he anxiously unfolded the slip of paper and read, Cassini felt absolutely stunned. *Cardinal John Becket—81 votes.* It certainly wasn't the result Cassini had expected. Becket had not only completely changed the voting pattern, he had won. Despite the surprise result, Cassini felt overwhelmed with relief. He sighed deeply, felt the pains in his chest ebb away.

The scrutineer made the announcement. "Cardinal John Becket, eighty-one votes."

As the remaining votes of the other candidates were read out, it hardly seemed to matter, for the tension in the chapel had been miraculously broken. All eyes had turned to John Becket, who simply sat there looking shocked, like a man who sensed danger all around him and saw no way of escape. He closed his eyes and his lips seemed to move in silent prayer.

Umberto Cassini rose majestically, despite his puny size.

Accompanied by the master of ceremonies and the three scrutineers, he approached Becket. As tradition required, he asked the question in Latin that the elected pope was required to answer.

"Do you, Most Reverend Lord Cardinal, accept your election as Supreme Pontiff, which has been canonically carried out?"

Becket was silent and his eyes remained closed. Cassini nervously repeated the question. "Do you, Most Reverend Lord Cardinal, accept your election as Supreme Pontiff . . . ?"

John Becket didn't reply.

Cassini felt the tension rise in the chapel.

Very slowly, Becket's eyes opened. He stood up from his chair, towering above Cassini and the others. Sweat glistened on Becket's upper lip.

"Camerlengo, I am deeply moved by my brother cardinals' faith in me. Words cannot express how humbled I feel. I honestly did not expect this result, which comes as a great surprise." Becket paused as he took a deep breath. "I will accept my election, Camerlengo. I will accept in the name of—"

Becket's voice faltered and his piercing blue eyes watered with emotion. "Forgive me, please. But before I continue, before I choose a papal name, I must explain something important to all present. Something deeply private that I have told no one until now. A secret in my heart that I feel must be revealed."

Becket's unexpected words had a stunning effect. An astonished hush settled over the chapel, as if all present expected a frightening confession. Cassini's eyes flicked nervously to the bewildered faces of the cardinals seated around the chapel, then over at the wall clock—it was approaching midnight—before he looked back at Becket. "With respect,

John, the rules make it quite clear. Your acceptance must proceed as protocol demands—"

"I am aware of the rules, Camerlengo. But I feel compelled by the Holy Spirit to speak. And once I speak, I fear some of my fellow cardinals may wish they had not elected me as their pope."

The chapel was deathly silent. It seemed as if someone had pulled the pin on a grenade and everyone was waiting for the explosion to go off. Cassini, his heart again beating faster, drew in a worried breath. "And what is it that you wish to explain?"

For a time, John Becket didn't speak, and then he looked out at his audience. "Long ago as a priest I made a promise to myself. A promise that if I was ever called to fill the Shoes of the Fisherman, I would do my utmost to fulfill certain personal goals. Those goals have been my lifelong ambition."

Every pair of eyes in the majestic chapel focused on Becket. The fact that he was an American, born and brought up in Chicago, was only evident when he spoke. His Italian was reasonably fluent but America was there on his tongue like a visa stamp.

"The church is a rock, and I am well aware that rock isn't malleable. But I made a pledge to myself that I would seek a new era of honesty, of truth within the church. If ever I was chosen as Vicar of Christ, I promised that my papacy would mark a new beginning, one that would require your help and support."

The chapel was terribly still.

"Tonight, as we sit beneath Michelangelo's vision of the Creation and the Flood, as we witness his frightening images of the Apocalypse, I am certain that what I propose may be seen by many among you as a threat. But I want to assure you it would not be so. It is something I am convinced Christ would have wished and which the church desperately needs. My promise was this: there would be absolute openness and honesty. There would be no more lies. No secrets kept from our flock or from the world. The church belongs to us all, not only to those who control the Vatican."

A wave of disbelief spread through the astonished crowd.

"What exactly are you suggesting?" asked one elderly cardinal, ignoring protocol. "That we open the Vatican's doors to public scrutiny?"

"That would be one intention of mine," Becket answered firmly. "Nothing would be concealed. Even the darkest secrets hidden in our archives would be made public."

There was a gasp from the audience and then silence. Cassini, standing in front of Becket, felt his chest about to explode. *Never* in the history of the church had *anything* like this ever happened.

Another cardinal asked, "And the Vatican's finances?"

"Made public also."

There was a murmur of disbelief from the listeners. Then Becket's voice carried firmly over the hot, crowded chapel. "Did Christ want lies told? Did He want secrets kept? Did He want those of us in authority to behave like secretive, petty bureaucrats and banking officials? I cannot believe that He did. Above all, Christ believed in truth, as we should."

Another elderly cardinal spoke up. "John, there are some things too dreadful for the world to know."

Becket looked at the speaker, but his words were addressed to everyone present. "You mean there are some things the Vatican would not *want* the world to know. Things it has kept secret by design, unpleasant mistakes it has made that its flock should never know of. But they *should* know. Not just Catholics, but Christians everywhere. Our archives will greatly concern them too. Christians all over the world share a common purpose, and they have a right to know the dark secrets that have been kept in Christ's name."

Becket stared out at his audience, his arms held wide as if in pleading. "We ask our flock to confess the error of their ways yet we refuse to confess our own sins. How can this be right? You have chosen me and those are my intentions upon accepting the papacy. It will mark a new day, a new beginning that will return all of us to the ways of Jesus Christ. I have spoken."

Some of the older cardinals looked deeply shocked, as if the devil himself and not the pope had spoken in their midst.

But most were profoundly moved, for it seemed a fresh blast of wind had suddenly blown through the musty Vatican corridors with the force of a hurricane. Every one of them knew he was in the presence of a man who radiated charisma and authority.

Umberto Cassini was quite dumbfounded and suddenly fearful. He looked up at John Becket, who settled his piercing, honest blue eyes on his audience.

"As for your fears, I will ask only one question. Have you no courage, my friends? The Lord may give us the burden. But He will also give us the strength to carry it. I accept my nomination as Supreme Pontiff. *Ego recipero in nomen of verum.* I accept in the name of truth. And the name I choose will be Celestine."

3

The ancients believed that the spirits of the dead lingered near their tombs. Jack Cane wanted to believe in that too as he drove toward the gravesite.

The Toyota Land Cruiser bumped over the desert trail and where it ended Cane cut the engine, jerked on the handbrake, and climbed out.

The grave stood near the curve of a ridge, four miles from the Dead Sea. It had a neat stone border filled with gravel chips and was a peaceful resting place. A ravine below and only the gritty wind and the occasional hawk soaring overhead.

Life had taught him a cruel lesson: grief is the hardest cross to bear.

Today, more than any other, he needed to talk to his ghosts.

Cane stepped toward the rear of the Land Cruiser, the white-hot sun of the Judean desert beating down on him. He was thirty-nine and had a confident, boyish look that some women found appealing. It was a look that hid a tough streak.

His tanned body was no stranger to backbreaking physical labor. His archaeologist's getup—dusty cut-off Chinos and worn leather boots—were testament to a grueling day's site work. But instead of physical exhaustion all he felt was a powerful sense of elation. Today of all days—the anniversary—he had discovered an astonishing treasure.

Cane raised a hand to shield his eyes from the fierce sun and surveyed the landscape. The desert ridge looked toward Jerusalem, sixteen miles away. The ancient city shimmered in a heat wave, its famous golden Dome of the Rock glinting like a mirror.

I've waited a long time for this day, but I never believed it would happen.

Cane unlocked the Land Cruiser's rear door. Lying on the backseat was a bunch of white lilies and a plastic liter bottle of drinking water. He carefully removed the flowers and bottled water and turned again to face the grave. His eyes moistened.

Not a day passed when he didn't reflect on the tragedy of his parents' deaths. How the powerful loss of their passing had changed him forever. And today, of all days, he had important words to speak.

Do the ghosts of the dead hear the words of the living? I want to believe that mine do.

Overcome by emotion, Cane strode toward the gravesite.

4

MEDITERRANEAN SEA
TWO MILES OFF THE TEL AVIV COAST
ISRAEL

It was a yacht fit for a Saudi king but the man who owned it had been born a pauper.

Sleek and white, sparkling with polished chrome, the vessel had anchored off the Israeli coast just after midnight. A $50 million yacht equipped with the latest technology, a helicopter pad, two bars, a ballroom, and a dozen luxurious cabins to pamper its guests.

That noon, a trio of bright red Kawasaki Jet Skis roared around the vessel, churning up the warm blue Mediterranean. The three muscled bodyguards who manned the Jet Skis were part of the ship's three-dozen-strong crew, which included a top French chef lured from a famous Paris restaurant.

The special weekend guests were three beautiful, bikini-clad women who sunbathed by the stern's turquoise swimming pool. One was a stunning Playmate, the other two were highly paid Paris models, their faces more beautiful than Botticelli angels. The man whose generosity they enjoyed stood alone by the pool.

Hassan Malik wore a linen suit and stared up at the sky. He had the quiet stillness of a man completely in control of his body and his emotions. His strong, lived-in face and quick, intelligent eyes seemed to miss nothing.

·   At that precise moment they were focused not on his three beautiful companions but on the skyline, as the yacht's Bell helicopter sped in from the Israeli coast.

Hassan Malik was at home in a dozen capitals of the world—in his New York Trump Towers penthouse, two more residences in London and Cannes, and in his palatial villa outside Rome—but he felt at ease in none of them. His soul belonged in the parched deserts of his Bedouin ancestors that lay beyond Jerusalem. He had grown up in dire poverty but that same poverty had lit a fire under him, brought him riches other men could only dream of.

He heard the clatter of helicopter blades as the Bell banked sharply and came in to land. It hovered above the stern deck before it touched down with a bump.

The passenger door was flung open and his brother Nidal stepped out. He was twenty-eight, his boyish face drawn, almost sickly looking. He wore a dark Armani suit and a white silk shirt, open at the collar, and his beard was neatly trimmed. His angry, olive green eyes seemed to regard the world with distrust.

·   Hassan Malik waited until his younger brother came over and then he kissed him fondly on both cheeks. "Well?"

Nidal said, "Cane has left Qumran and is headed toward the gravesite. Our pilot has arranged permission from Israeli air traffic control to overfly Jerusalem."

"Good." Hassan Malik strode after his brother to the helicopter, climbed in behind him, and slammed shut the door. The pilot raised the aircraft into the hot blue sky. Hassan consulted his watch: 5 P.M.

Fifteen more minutes and I will face my ghosts.

What was it his father used to say? *We can never escape our past.*

Hassan Malik didn't want to. He wanted to remember his past because it felt like a stiletto in his heart—a wound that screamed out for vengeance.

And he knew exactly how to avenge that wound.

First, I'm going to use Jack Cane.

Then I'm going to kill him.

The powerful GE engines thrust the helicopter forward and sped its passengers in the direction of Jerusalem's golden dome.

5

Jack Cane sat on a boulder facing the gravestone. He placed the flowers in a parched, sponge-filled oasis within the neat stone border, filled with gravel chips. Opening the water bottle, he drenched the oasis until it was soaking wet. He lay the empty plastic bottle by his side and his gaze swept over the chiseled granite marker that inscribed his pain.

> *In memory of Robert and Margaret Cane,*
> *who died tragically at this spot.*
> *Rest in peace.*
> *Miss you always, love you forever.*
> *Your son, Jack.*

He still missed them, always would. Their passing had left such a deep sorrow, a terrible ache. He removed a worn leather wallet from his pocket and flipped it open. He kept the tattered, twenty-year-old photocopy of the newspaper clipping in a cracked plastic sheath and he unfolded the page. He knew the words by heart as he stared down at the page:

JERUSALEM POST
RENOWNED AMERICAN ARCHAEOLOGIST
AND HIS WIFE KILLED IN TRAGIC ACCIDENT

Five people were killed yesterday afternoon and another two badly injured on a remote stretch of road near Qumran.

Jerusalem police report that two men and one woman suffered fatal injuries when their pickup collided with an Israel Defense Forces truck and crashed into a ravine. The three were respected New York archaeologist Robert Cane, 69, and his wife Margaret, 58, along with local Bedu digger Basim Malik. Two teenage passengers traveling in the back of the pickup—Lela Raul and Jack Cane, both age nineteen—are being treated for injuries.

Police also confirm that the two deceased occupants of the military truck, which exploded carrying a munitions cargo, have not yet been named.

It is believed that Mr. Robert Cane was working on an international dig at Qumran. He and his Bedu helper had only that morning discovered several fragments of an ancient scroll and were traveling to Jerusalem to show their find to the Israeli Antiquities Department when the fatal accident occurred. Police fear that the ancient parchment may have been destroyed by fire.

Father Franz Kubel, the Vatican-appointed coordinator of the Qumran dig and a colleague of Mr. Cane's, was reported to be shocked by the deaths. "This is dreadful news. Robert Cane was a wonderful man and a highly respected archaeologist. He will be sadly missed."

Local driver Basim Malik leaves behind a wife and three children.

Jack folded the cutting and shut his eyes. The dream often came to him when he visited the grave and it came to him now.

He was seventeen again, standing in a camp at Qumran, a warm spring day, watching his parents sweating as they dug on a hill above the ancient ruins. In his dream, he ran up the hill to join his parents. They saw him, waved, and opened their arms to greet him. But the closer Jack got, the more the image of his parents faded. He blinked, felt his eyes moisten.

He knew why the dream came. He had loved his parents deeply. His father was a patient, good-humored man with sharp blue eyes and an infectious laugh, always ready to share his enthusiasm for archaeology. His mother had blond hair and a beautiful face with high cheekbones. Jack remembered a cheerful woman with a warmth that could lift the gloom of any day.

A college buddy once told him, "All families are screwed up and dysfunctional. But some are even more dysfunctional than others."

That had never been Jack's experience. His childhood had been incredibly happy. As he accompanied his parents on digs to South America, Egypt, Rome, and Israel, by his sixteenth birthday he had traveled half the world with two people who never ceased to both love and fascinate him.

He closed his eyes once more and he was nineteen again and the past washed over him . . .

6

He could never forget the day. It was seared into his mind as if with a branding iron.

His parents and their Bedu driver, Basim Malik, were traveling in the front cab. Jack sat in the open back of the pickup, chatting and laughing with Lela Raul, an Israeli girl he had got to know in the last three months since her police sergeant father had been posted to the nearby kibbutz. Lela was smart and kind, with chocolate brown eyes, a sensuous mouth, and long black hair, and she'd made a big impression on a gangly, awkward nineteen-year-old.

Suddenly the vehicle veered out of control and Jack remembered the screams of the passengers and the sickening sensation as their pickup skidded across the road, plunged into the ravine, and rolled over.

A massive blast erupted from somewhere and he was thrown violently from the back of the pickup along with Lela, who lay sprawled nearby, and then the vehicle exploded in flames.

Jack tried desperately to stand but his left leg was shattered, blood gushing from a nasty gash below his knee. He couldn't hear, for there was a painful ringing sensation in his ears. Helpless and in agony, he crawled toward the wall of flame to reach the upturned pickup, but already it was too late.

He saw the horrific image of his mother clawing wildly at the window, her blond hair on fire. His father yanked frantically at the passenger door as the cab was engulfed in smoke. The last thing Jack heard before he lost consciousness and everything faded was the muted sounds of his parents' tortured screams.

When he came to he felt groggy and saw a Catholic priest kneeling over him, slapping his face. "Can you hear me? Wake up. Please wake up."

Jack recognized Father John Becket but he could barely hear him. He was one of a small number of Catholic clerics working on the dig. Nearby, he saw that Lela was propped with her back against a boulder, unconscious, her head lolled to one side. Another priest tended to her, a red-haired man with a strong, sculpted face. He was small and wiry, with the build of a jockey. Jack remembered him as an archaeologist with the Catholic delegation.

Becket said, "The young lady's concussed but she's breathing okay. That's Father Kubel. He was driving by the accident scene too. Father Kubel is skilled in first aid, he can take care of your friend. He thinks she'll be fine. Do you understand me?"

Jack nodded and saw the wiry little priest patting Lela's face, trying to wake her. "What—what about my parents?" Jack asked.

Father Becket looked toward the wreckage. The stench of burning flesh seared Jack's nostrils and he stared in horror at the pickup. Someone had tried to force open the door but without success, and the windshield had been partly shattered, the dashboard turned to melted plastic, black smoke pluming out. He couldn't see his mother or the driver but his father's body was nearest the door, his flesh burnt like charcoal.

The priest's ashen expression said it all. "I—I managed to force open the door a little but the oxygen only made the cabin fire worse. I'm truly sorry. They're all dead."

And then Jack's head swam, his eyes flickered, and he drowned in darkness.

He awoke in the intensive care unit of a Jerusalem hospital. Sergeant Raul, Lela's father, was seated next to him. He was a tall, fit-looking man with a tanned face and dark, sensitive eyes. "How are you coping, Jack?"

I'm not. Jack found it difficult to reply. He had lost the two people who had mattered most in his life and his grief seemed bottomless.

Sergeant Raul said gently, "You've been out of it for the last three days with a concussion. But thankfully your hearing's recovered after the blast and the doctors tell me you ought to be up to talking. Do you feel like talking, Jack?"

"I don't know how I feel."

"That's understandable, you've been deeply traumatized."

"My—my parents couldn't be saved?"

The sergeant said grimly, "I'm afraid not, Jack. Basim Malik, their driver, died too. It's a terrible tragedy. I've examined the accident scene and the skid marks suggest that the army driver was on the wrong side of the road. Once the fire in the cabin took hold, your parents and Basim were trapped inside."

Jack looked away, racked by anguish.

Sergeant Raul patted his arm. "Lela asks after you. She's in another ward, doing fine. She's been checking on you the last few days but you've been sleeping for most of it. I know she'd like to see you as soon as you're up to it. I hear you two have been good friends. I know Lela thinks highly of you."

Jack simply nodded. He could hardly speak, his heart as heavy as steel.

"It seems you and Lela owe Father Becket your lives, Jack. Luckily he came along when he did. And Father Franz Kubel too." Sergeant Raul paused, then added delicately, "About the scroll your father excavated. Lela said it was in a map case in the front cabin."

"That's right."

"I couldn't find it. And forensics found no remains of the case. But the windshield had been partly shattered. I wondered if you recall seeing the map case after the accident, Jack?"

"No, I don't. Father Becket told me he'd tried to force open the door to free my parents. He must have shattered the window as well. I'm sorry, Sergeant Raul, but I'm really not up to talking right now."

"Of course. But I need to inform you that your father's colleagues have suggested erecting a grave memorial where the tragedy took place. It's a particularly beautiful spot, looking toward Qumran, which your parents loved."

"Y-yes, of course."

"I also understand that your parents expressed the wish to be cremated in the event of their deaths. They wanted their ashes scattered in the Holy Land where they spent so much of their time. Sadly, your parents' bodies were so badly burned there was little left but ashes. Perhaps I can arrange a symbolic gesture to help you carry out their wishes. I can arrange that an urn be filled."

Jack was overcome, fought back tears. His body felt scarred by wounds but the scars inside him were the hardest to bear. "I—I appreciate that."

"The grave memorial will be looked after, I promise you. Arabs and Jews have great respect for the dead. If only we had the same respect for the living." The sergeant stood briskly, then said, "One final question, Jack, and then I won't trouble you any longer. Do you know if the pickup had any maintenance work carried out recently?"

"Not that I know of. Why?"

Sergeant Raul pursed his lips thoughtfully. "You're sure about that? There was nothing mechanically wrong with the brakes, for instance?"

"I—I don't think so. Why do you ask?"

The sergeant considered, then shook his head. "No reason. Keep a firm grip, you hear? Try to stay strong, Jack. Your parents would have wanted you to."

Two days later, Jack was sitting in a chair outside his hospital room, his leg propped up on pillows, as he stared out absently at the parched hills beyond Jerusalem.

As he sat there, numbed by grief, he heard footsteps and turned. A priest—small, wiry, with thinning red hair—stood there, carrying a brown paper bag. It was Father Kubel, the archaeologist who had tended to Lela. He placed the bag on the table. Jack noticed the man's fingers were stained brown, the sign of a heavy smoker.

"Some fruit," the priest said awkwardly, his accent German. He looked upset. "I—I just came to say how sorry I am about your parents. They were good people. Your father was a fine archaeologist. It was an honor to work with him."

"That's kind of you to say."

"I wanted you to know that Father Becket and I tried our best to rescue your parents. In fact, I've been asked by my superiors to write a report about the scroll's destruction and the tragic accident. It will be an internal church document, of course, not meant for public consumption. But my superiors are anxious to know what happened. Your father's work was a great asset to the dig." Kubel hesitated. "I'm so sorry. If Father Becket and I could have done anything more, we would have, I assure you."

Jack fought back his emotion. "I'm grateful for what you both did."

Kubel placed a hand firmly on Jack's shoulder. "I know it's little consolation, but we will always remember your parents in our prayers."

Four days later Jack was discharged from the hospital, hobbling on a crutch until his leg healed. He made the final arrangements for his parents' burial. It was to be a brief affair, yet more than two hundred people turned up, huddled in prayer along the roadway overlooking the ravine where Robert and Margaret Cane had died.

A commemorative marker had been erected, and when the prayers finally ended Jack numbly shook the hands of mourners. Sergeant Raul waited until the crowds had driven away, then he touched Jack's shoulder and handed him a metal urn containing a few handfuls of his parents' ashes. "At least you can have a private moment to do what your folks would have wished, Jack. Someone wants to say hello, so I'll leave you alone."

And then Sergeant Raul was gone and a voice said, "Hello, Jack."

He turned, saw Lela Raul. A white gauze patch covered

her forehead, her pretty face bruised and drawn. It was the first time Jack had seen her since the accident and his heart lifted a little. "Lela, it's good to see you."

They hugged and she kissed him on the cheek. "I don't know what to say, Jack. I'm still in shock too. I wanted to come see you in the hospital but they wouldn't allow you visitors for the first few days. I had to peer in at you through your door whenever I could." Her voice broke off as she stared at the urn in Jack's hands, then she reached out, her fingers touching his. "It must be so difficult for you. I just want you to know that you've got a friend."

Jack looked into her face, her chocolate eyes pools of concern. "How are you, Lela?"

"I've felt a lot worse."

"How about Basim Malik's family? They must be distraught that they've lost their father."

"It's thoughtful of you to ask. My dad says they're just about coping, like we all are." Lela's expression changed, as if there was something she was going to add but she fell silent.

"Can you do something for me, Lela?"

Her eyes lifted to meet his face. "Of course. Anything."

"Borrow your father's car and drive me away from here."

"To where?"

Jack felt overcome. "Anywhere. There's something personal I need to do but I'm just not ready to do it yet."

Five minutes later, they were driving on the dusty roads toward Qumran, Lela steering her father's blue Escort.

"Did you think about what you're going to do in the near future, Jack?"

"I have to put my folks' estate in order. Estate—that's a joke. It's just a small house at the end of a dirt road in up-

state New York. My folks didn't put much store by possessions. Their career never paid much but it meant everything
to them."

"The house is where you grew up?"

"More often than not I traveled with my folks. I got most
of my education on the hoof. I guess I'd feel more at home in
Qumran than in upstate New York."

"What will you do?"

He had a lost look on his face as he said quietly, "Right
now, I don't know, Lela. Maybe go back to the States and finish my education."

She reached across, held his hand. "Am I allowed to say
that I'm worried about you?"

"I'm worried about me too."

"Will you write to me? Please?"

"Sure."

"You don't sound very convincing."

He looked at her. "I'm sorry, Lela, I guess my mind's all
over the place right now."

"Did my dad explain that the scroll may have been destroyed in the blaze? The forensics people found no remains
of the leather map case."

"He told me."

"He asked Father Becket and Father Kubel if they'd seen it
lying among the wreckage but they claimed they didn't. Dad
questioned a few other drivers who arrived at the accident
soon after but no one knew anything."

Jack frowned. "Are you suggesting that your father thinks
someone may have stolen it?"

"No, but like most cops my dad's just suspicious by nature.
He's got no proof that the scroll was completely destroyed in
the inferno and it bothers him."

"Why did he ask me if any repair work had been carried out on the pickup? I almost got the feeling your father thought the crash was sabotage."

Lela's face darkened. "I—I don't think he's sure of that, Jack. Certainly he's got no evidence."

"What's wrong? Is there something you're not telling me?"

"No. I told you, my dad's just naturally suspicious. It's the same with every case he works on. He'd really hoped forensics might have found at least some remains of the map case."

"My parents and Basim Malik were burned beyond recognition. What hope would a leather map case have?"

"You're right. I guess we'll never know what the scroll contained."

"Right now, somehow, that doesn't even matter. Though my dad would never have forgiven me for saying that. He was so excited about his discovery. He had high hopes it might have amounted to something. Can you turn back to the ravine now, Lela? I think I'm okay."

"Of course." Ten minutes later she pulled up to the edge of the ravine and killed the engine. The afternoon sun was still hot, the sky cloudless, a strong breeze caressing the desert. Qumran lay beyond, stunning in the fading light. The pickup's wreckage had been removed from the gully but the blackened stains from the fire were still there. Jack shivered.

Lela asked, "Are you okay? Do you really think it's such a good idea coming back? I don't want you to torture yourself, Jack."

"For some reason I feel closer to them here, where I lost them. Does that make any sense?"

Lela touched his hand, looked into his face. "Can I tell you something? When my mother died I learned that grief can be a very private thing. One day the person you love walks out the door and you never see them alive again. It can leave so many loose ends, so many things unsaid, because it can be all so sudden and unexpected. Sometimes it's so very hard to come to terms. We clam up, can't talk about it. But if ever you feel the need to talk, or you just want somebody to listen, you only have to say, Jack."

He gripped her hand, wanted Lela to hold him, to feel her comforting embrace, but this wasn't the time. He clutched the urn and went to climb out of the car. "Can you excuse me a minute?"

"What are you going to do?"

"Something that my folks would have wanted."

Jack faced toward Qumran and the Dead Sea. He was dreading such a final act of farewell. He opened the urn and tilted a single handful of ashes into his palm, allowed them to trickle through his fingers and scatter into the soft breeze. They swirled, eddied away, toward Qumran's tangerine hills.

Jack thought, *Is this all that remains of the two people I loved? My life and theirs simply turned to dust?*

When the last of the ashes blew through his fingers, he held up his dusty gray hand and smeared it on his face. Why, he didn't know, except that for some strange reason, and just for that brief moment, it made him feel closer to his parents. Overcome, his body convulsed in a fit of sobbing.

All he remembered after that was Lela appearing by his side, her arms going round him, holding him wordlessly. And so he stood there, clinging to her, both of them swaying in the desert breeze, as if at that moment each was all the other had in the world.

Jack opened his eyes, let the past wash away. He looked out over the vast dusty landscape toward Jerusalem. *Lela, where are you now?*

A hawk circled overhead, its shriek interrupting his thoughts. The months after his parents' deaths were a reckless time when he'd done things he never should have, just to bury his anguish. It was a time in his life he just wanted to forget.

He stared down at the grave marker. *Dad, Mom, I finally hit pay dirt and found a scroll. Everyone on the dig's thrilled. Professor Green, our director, thinks it could be a pretty important discovery. I'm excited about it. I want you both to know that.*

Jack thought: *I sound like a child.* It was as if he were trying to impress his parents with his exam results. But he had such a powerful need to communicate his excitement with the two people who had shared his life.

A memory came to him.

A sunny winter's day outside Cairo on his fifteenth birthday. Helping his father dig near some old burial sites at the Cheops pyramid, they had stopped to brew coffee, talk, and eat lunch. About that time Jack began to really feel the powerful allure of a career in archaeology. Ancient tombs, cryptic inscriptions etched in stone or onto papyrus, valuable coins, bits of jewelry, human bones, and broken pottery—this was the stuff adventures were made of.

And as they sat and talked his father spoke about the Egyptians' unshakable belief in an afterlife. It almost seemed to Jack that his father was suddenly conscious of his own mortality as a parent.

At fifty, Robert Cane had come late to fatherhood. The experience had awed him. He adored his son, loved him with a depth that was sometimes frightening in its intensity. He was an emotional man, and his bright blue eyes had a hint of tears that day. "I want you to know that I love you, Jack."

"I love you too, Dad."

"You know what I believe, Jack? I believe love never dies. It's the sole reason why we're all here. To create love and to nurture it. And I believe the Egyptians were right, just like so many other civilizations that put their trust in an afterlife. There's a dimension that as humans we can't even begin to perceive, call it heaven or Nirvana or whatever you want, but it's a dimension created by God, where we all meet again and renew our love. Do you understand what I'm saying, Jack?"

"I think so."

"You know what else I believe?"

"What, Dad?"

"That once we depart into that dimension there's no coming back. We can no longer be part of this earthly life and the loved ones we've left behind. But we can observe them, at least be with them in spirit until we join with them again."

Robert Cane looked out over the mighty splendor of the Cheops pyramid, and his voice filled with emotion. "The ancients believed that the spirits of the dead lingered near their tombs. I sometimes get that feeling when I'm here. The hairs rise on the back of my neck. It makes me feel as if I'm touched by something powerful, something magnificent and unearthly. It's almost as if the dead can touch us."

"You mean physically?"

His father smiled. "No, not in that sense, Jack. But I believe the spirit world can induce feelings in us, like intuitions and emotions, or invoke unnatural phenomena. You hear people talking about guardian angels, that they feel there's something supernatural watching over them. It's that kind of feeling. A chill down your back that's more than an intuition, that might warn you something bad's going to happen. A feeling of a presence in an empty room. A sudden gust of wind, yet there's no wind nearby."

"Those things have happened to you, Dad?"

"Sometimes. I once remember sitting by my own father's grave. It was a difficult time for me. I had problems to deal with and no one to turn to. That day I strongly felt his presence, sensed him near me in spirit. It was uncanny, but I was sure I felt his hand touch my shoulder, just the way he used to when I was in need of comfort. He'd look at me and say, 'Bob, whatever it is that's on your mind, I want you to share it with me and let me bear some of the burden.' And I would, and he always did. I felt that same feeling that difficult day."

His father paused and met his son's stare. "Jack, you're at an age when you'll start to question your beliefs, your future direction, even the reasons for your existence. It's all part of growing up. But trust me on this one—there's an afterlife."

Robert Cane put an arm around his son, hugged him close, and winked. "So promise me something? Someday when I'm gone I want you to know that even though I won't be here in flesh, I'll be here in spirit. You can still talk to me. Anything you want to say, anything you need to discuss, come sit by my grave and talk. Same with your mom. We'll be listening, okay? You won't see or touch us, but we'll be standing next to you. Don't ever forget that, Jack."

Years later, Jack wondered if his father had spoken those words simply to provide his only son with a small blanket of comfort—a touchstone to lessen the pain of loss after his parents had gone. Jack never knew the answer, only that talking worked. Some people talked to their dog, or to their image in the mirror. He talked over his parents' graves and afterward felt the better for it. *So long, Dad, Mom. We'll talk again.*

And yet, despite his belief that he was being listened to in some unearthly dimension, always the questions came that were tiny seeds of doubt. *Do we really meet again? Does the love we nurtured on this earth go on forever, beyond this universe, for all eternity?*

When he had finished his final words to his dead, he picked up the empty water bottle, stood, and turned toward the Land Cruiser.

He heard a noise, looked up. Not a hawk this time but a sound like a metallic wasp—a distant helicopter, a speck in the sky. Shielding his eyes, Jack stared at the speck and then the noise faded and it was gone.

7

Five thousand feet in the air Hassan Malik sat in the Bell helicopter and watched the Land Cruiser depart. He nodded to the pilot and ten minutes later the chopper touched down near the graves with a flurry of sand.

The swish of the rotors died and Hassan climbed out, followed by Nidal. The scorching heat of the late afternoon ripped the air from their lungs, but they had known this desert furnace all their lives.

In the distance, Hassan saw the faint plume of Cane's Land Cruiser disappear toward Qumran.

Hassan stood there, hearing the light murmur of the desert wind, as if he were listening for something, he wasn't sure what. But for a moment, he could almost hear the ghostly echo of voices carry on the wind. In one of those flashes of recall, he was fifteen again, a poor Arab boy wearing cheap jeans and a pair of his father's worn sandals, digging among the ruins of Qumran. And from that to now, so much in between.

Hassan stepped over to the gravesite. He stared down at the lilies lying on the tomb, within the neat border filled with gravel chips. His own parents were long gone, buried in the chalk earth, his father dead on the same day as Jack Cane's.

He would never forget that day. *Never.*

That same night his mother had traveled to her cousin in Jerusalem and never came back. The police told Hassan that she had hung herself. Hassan knew why. His Bedu mother would rather endure death than the indignity of a barren life without a husband or an income. His brother, Nidal, and his sister, Fawzi, were inconsolable. Hassan too, but after the numbness wore off a fierce determination blazed inside him. He was not going to leave little Nidal and Fawzi to the fate of an orphanage. They were all going to stay together.

First Hassan had buried his parents, and then he had buried his dignity, begging on the streets of Jerusalem, putting barely enough food in their bellies to keep from starving.

He and Nidal and Fawzi had slept in filthy doorways, searched for scraps among garbage in rat-infested alleyways. In winter, he kept his little brother and sister warm by giving them his own filthy coat, while he himself froze from the cold.

Nidal was always a weak child. Living malnourished on the streets had not helped, and his bouts of sickness had more than once brought him close to death. But somehow Nidal had survived, as if his small body had fire in its belly.

All of it happened a long time ago, but what was it his father liked to say? We can never escape our past.

Nor can we rewrite it, Hassan thought. *But we can change our future. And in changing our future, we can right the wrongs of our past.*

Nidal touched his arm, taking him from his reverie. "We are late for our appointment, Hassan."

"Right now, *this* is our most important appointment."

Nidal noted his brother's voice was very quiet, but as always infinitely dangerous, his dark eyes glittering with purpose. "Of course, Hassan. It is as you say."

"Go back to the helicopter. I'll join you in a moment."

Nidal retreated without a word. Hassan watched his brother walk back toward the chopper. The sight of Nidal's rake-thin body always brought out a protective streak in him.

He heard a bird cry overhead, looked up, and saw a hawk circling. He tried to focus, knew that this moment was important. Not one to be rushed but savored. *What happened in Rome had changed everything, he felt sure of it.*

Now Hassan turned to stare down at the graves of Robert and Margaret Cane. He stared for a long time until a wave of fury exploded inside him. Without a word he violently crushed the lilies with his shoe until they were a trampled mess of green stalks and white flowers. He stamped and kicked, scattering the gravel chips. All control gone now, Hassan hawked a mouthful of saliva and spat upon the graves.

Then he wiped his lips with his sleeve and strode back to join his brother.

8

QUMRAN
DEAD SEA
ISRAEL

"It's pretty incredible. Take a look for yourself. I wanted you to be the first to know, Jack. You're the one who found it, after all."

Jack Cane, wearing a pair of white latex gloves, steadied the magnifying glass in his hands. "Are you sure about all this, Professor?"

His excitement mounting, Jack studied the faded images on the two-thousand-year-old parchment. It lay partially unrolled on the table, the scroll edges sepia brown, fragile from centuries of lying buried in an earthenware jar. They were in Professor Green's tent, a stand-up affair cluttered with boxes of reference books, a cot, a table, and folding chairs.

Jack tried to read by the light of an overhead butane lamp and using the magnifier. Faded lines of ancient Aramaic characters had been exposed in the unraveling. "I mean, really sure?"

Professor Donald Green frowned. "Sure about all what, Jack?"

"Your translation."

Green's delight was replaced by a tone that bristled with

irritation. "Of course I'm sure. Yasmin and I stayed up working on it after everyone went to bed. Once I managed to unravel another three inches of the parchment, which was about as much as I could without causing damage, I went to work deciphering the exposed text. I wouldn't have had Yasmin fetch you from your bunk if I hadn't been certain."

Jack rubbed his gritty eyes, tried to focus on the ancient writing in front of him and ignore Green's annoyance. It was, after all, past 5 A.M. "I'm glad you did, Professor. I was half awake and couldn't sleep either."

Professor Green was a bear of a man, bristling with energy. Distinguished-looking with gray hair, he wore a khaki tropical shirt with epaulettes, one of them hanging loose and missing a button. He removed his half-moon glasses and gave an excited nod. "Okay, go ahead. Translate lines three and four."

"Give me a chance, Professor. My Aramaic's pretty basic and not up to your standards, and here and there the writing's faded." Jack's mind felt sluggish, despite his elation. Like most of the other forty-strong crew he had stayed up late, drinking beer to celebrate the scroll's discovery in one of Qumran's caves. He'd only climbed into his cot two hours before being woken again by Green's niece.

The professor hovered at his shoulder. "Let me tell you again what it says—"

"It's okay, I think I've got it." Jack studied the faded parchment symbols and his voice was hoarse with shock. "You're right. It's incredible."

Green said excitedly, "Of course I'm right. No scroll like this has ever been discovered at Qumran. We both know with absolute certainty that this scroll's unique."

Jack knew that Green was right. In 1947, two hundred

yards farther up the valley of Qumran, the first of many hundreds of the famous Dead Sea scrolls had been discovered by Bedouin tribesmen. Most of the finds dated from between 250 B.C. and 70 A.D. and had been hidden by the Essene community. They had remained hidden for thousands of years.

The discovery was to rock the world.

The leather parchment, papyrus, and copper scrolls documented the life of the Essenes—an austere Jewish religious group that had been in existence during the time of Jesus Christ. Copies of parts of the Old Testament, as well as unknown New Testament records, were also found.

The restoration and translation of the scrolls was directed by Father Roland de Vaux, director of the Ecole Biblique, a French-Arab theological school in Jerusalem. Dominated mostly by Catholic priests, the process had taken decades and became mired in controversy.

It took almost fifty years after the discovery for the Vatican to finally claim that all the contents had been made public. But the slow pace of de Vaux's work and its extreme secrecy fueled a theory that some senior Vatican churchmen wished to suppress damaging information revealed in the scrolls. The theory was never proven, but the Dead Sea caves produced such a rich mother lode that digs were ongoing, even after more than six decades.

And now he, Jack Cane, had uncovered another ancient scroll. But one that was very different from all the others that had been discovered.

Yesterday afternoon, digging in one of the many cave recesses that dotted the Qumran landscape, in the southern part of the location known as Area A, he had found a two-foot-long sealed terra-cotta pot. Breaking the seal, inside the pot he discovered a single rolled leather parchment wrapped in frayed linen. The scroll appeared fragile but reasonably intact. Cane was elated.

Judging by its material condition and its written language, Aramaic, Jack believed it came from the same period as those already uncovered. When Professor Green unrolled the first two inches of the leather—as much as he dared risk at first without causing damage—they saw that it had already suffered partial destruction.

Portions of the inked parchment were obliterated, leaving holes and frayed gaps in the parchment. However, it was still possible to decipher several word clusters. Two in particular—faintly visible on the second line—leaped out and made Cane's pulse race:

Yeshua HaMeshiah

Yeshua HaMeshiah—Jesus the Messiah. Jesus Christ. Jack knew that the presence of that name was remarkable, for one very simple reason.

The Dead Sea scrolls that had already been discovered in the last sixty years were mostly Jewish documents. They had almost nothing Christian in them. Jesus' name was never mentioned once in the 870 scrolls and the tens of thousands of scroll fragments found—not a single reference made to him or to his followers. *Until now.*

Green said, "Do you have a knife handy?"

"Sure." Jack unfolded a well-worn four-inch Gerber folding pocketknife. The sharp-tipped titanium blade was his favorite implement for picking away any fine debris, and he handed it to Green. "Be my guest."

The professor's enthusiasm rose as he used the tip of the

knife to raise the edge of the parchment. "Take a look at the sentences that comprise the first lines. You can just make out the words. There's definitely something very odd going on here. You see?"

Green's left index finger hovered over the first faded words of Aramaic.

דנא דבר על נברא ישוע משיחא וכענת

באתר די אול מן קיסריה לדורא קריא די שמה חשיב סניא בה

לא כהל תמה כלל לרפיה עוריא ובאישיא

אף על גב אמר די יכהל לרפיה יתהם

אחרי דנה אחדו בה רומיא די תמה בדורא

והתיו לה לדינא ואשם השתכה בה

ואמרו די להוא מתעבד מות מנה

Green added, "The entire literal translation of the first lines reads, 'This story concerns the man known as Jesus the Messiah. Having traveled from Caesarea to Dora, where his name had become well-known, he failed miserably to cure the blind and the sick, despite his promises to do so. Soon after, he was arrested in Dora by the Romans, tried and found guilty, and sentenced to be executed.'"

Green wiped a patina of sweat from his forehead as he finished reading, put down the knife, and looked up at Jack.

"Which is bizarre. Because so far as history records there's no mention of Jesus ever having visited Caesarea or Dora, or being arrested and sentenced there to be executed. He's recorded to have traveled to places in Egypt, Jordan, Israel, and Lebanon, but never to Caesarea or Dora, which are on the Mediterranean coast, in the northwest of Israel."

"You've no doubt about your biblical history?"

Green grinned, stuck a hand in his pocket, and held up a BlackBerry. "As technology is my witness."

"You checked."

"I may be an expert on the period, but even I still double-check. I consulted a couple of excellent online Bible study sites to be absolutely certain."

"What did you learn?"

"Jesus was known to have frequented a fairly small stomping ground in Judea. Caesarea and Dora were Mediterranean coastal towns, about sixty miles away. Dora at that time was in a Roman-controlled province of Syria. Its population wasn't Jewish. In fact, it feuded with the Jews. Caesarea was in Samaria province. And as for failing miserably to cure the blind and the sick . . ." Green spread his hands and gave a dramatic shrug. "Like I said, it's bizarre. None of it makes sense. It's certainly going to confound the Bible scholars."

Jack rubbed his eyes, stared at the scroll's writing once more, and shook his head. Green was an Aramaic language expert, so Jack discounted any possibility of a mistake. "It sure is a puzzle, Professor."

Green tossed his reading glasses on the table in a gesture of defeat. "One that's got me stumped for now, I'm afraid."

Jack removed a worn leather notebook from his Chinos pocket. "Do you mind if I copy down the text in my notebook?"

"Feel free, you're the one who found it. Here's hoping that the rest of the scroll reveals more information and helps us put the words into context. But to tell the truth I did manage to get the scroll open just a fraction more before I gave up and decided to let things be. The text I saw had me confused."

"What do you mean?"

"It read like gibberish. The Aramaic characters all looked legible, apart from a few holes in the parchment, but the few words that I saw didn't make any sense. Like they were jumbled or written in an alien language." Green tried to rub the sleep from his eyes with his thumb and forefinger. "It's probably my own exhaustion. It's been over twenty-four hours since I last slept. My eyeballs feel like they've been smacked around a pool table."

Jack put down the magnifying glass. "You went as far as you could go with it tonight. We'll get expert help to unravel the rest of the parchment. We don't want to continue and cause damage."

The professor let out a sigh. "That's what I thought. All in all, it's been an astonishing find. The name Jesus Christ is not mentioned once in any of the scrolls and fragments already found over the decades. Yet here it is, clearly legible. You've found a truly unique document, Jack. One that may cast significant new light on Jesus himself. You deserve a big pat on the back." Green slapped Jack's shoulder heartily.

"Thanks, Professor."

"Most importantly, this find will serve to confirm the very existence of Jesus. That kind of solid evidence is hard to come by outside the Bible. I think this calls for another celebration."

Green crossed to a scuffed leather trunk by his cot. "The rest of the crew are going to be even more amazed when they hear this news. You'll join me in a drink? Of course you will."

Jack finished writing and smiled tiredly. "Mind if I pass, Professor? I had quite a few beers already. Tomorrow's another long day."

"No way, we can't let a moment like this pass." Green grabbed a bottle of Wild Turkey and two glass tumblers from the trunk. "Don't force me to twist your arm."

"Maybe just one." Jack stuffed his notebook in his breast pocket.

Green pulled off the corked top on the Wild Turkey bottle with his teeth, spat it out, and splashed a generous measure into their glasses. "Get that down you. You deserve it, Jack."

He swallowed a mouthful of liquor. "Thanks."

"What's the bet that the parchment's going to cause a sensation among the scholars? Who knows, it may contain information that challenges or even refutes established traditions, perhaps even something compromising? In fact, I'd like to propose a toast."

"To what?"

Green smiled, clinked their glasses. "That whatever else this find of yours contains, it knocks their socks off."

9

A moment later the tent flap opened and a striking young blond woman came in. She looked as if she had Arab blood in her veins with her amber eyes and long black lashes, but everything else about Yasmin Green was westernized. She wore khaki shorts that bared her slim, tanned legs, her shirt tied in a knot above her waist, exposing her smooth belly. She smiled, then said in an American accent, "Aren't you two going to get some sleep? You must be exhausted, Uncle Donald. You too, Jack."

Green, still bubbling with excitement, stared back at his niece as if she were mad. "Sleep? Who can rest after this find? Have another drink, Jack." He splashed more Wild Turkey into their glasses.

"Go easy, Professor."

"Yasmin?"

"Not for me. I've just spent the last half-hour picking up empty Heineken cans after the crew. Crew like me, who are not lucky enough to be archaeologists, just mere interested amateurs, always seem to get stuck with the housework."

She tapped her watch at her uncle. "I know you told me this is the most incredible discovery you've ever been involved with, but it's also well after five A.M. The rest of the crew bedded down hours ago. If you want to be in the full of your health when the Israeli Antiquities Department visits tomorrow, you ought to get to bed."

Jack finished his drink in one swallow. "Yasmin's right, Professor. I think I'll hit the hay."

The professor grinned. "That's it, chicken out just when a guy's beginning to enjoy himself."

Yasmin winked at Jack. "Try and convince my uncle to get to bed, will you? I'm going to finish tidying up and hit the sack. Congratulations again, Jack." She gave him a final smile as she went out, her blond hair and amber eyes an arresting combination.

Jack watched her figure retreat into the dusk. Green noticed his stare and closed the tent flap. "She's a good-looking young woman, isn't she, Jack?"

"She sure is."

"My brother's Lebanese wife was always something of a beauty, which explains Yasmin's looks. The union of the Middle Eastern and the Western can produce quite an exotic mix. And of course, Yasmin's had the benefit of a Western education, which can make her all the more alluring." Green gave a tight smile, then knocked back his liquor, put down his glass, and filled it again from the bottle. A sudden, irritated edge crept into his voice. "I've always had a soft spot for the opposite sex, as you probably know. Three marriages and a weakness for a pretty woman wearing a short skirt say it all. However, can I give you a friendly word of advice?"

"What's that, Professor?"

"I promised my brother I'd watch over his daughter like a hawk while she was working on the dig." Green took a gulp of Wild Turkey and made a face, as if the alcohol suddenly tasted nasty. "But maybe I should just tell you the truth and be done with it . . ." His words trailed away, as if he'd instantly regretted them. "Never mind, forget it."

"What truth?" Jack asked. "Forget what?"

Green appeared embarrassed. "I guess what I'm trying to say is that most of the guys working on this site are a bunch of skirt-chasers. Me included. Not that I'd be inclined to count you among them, Jack. I've known you too long a time to suggest that."

"Thanks for the vote of confidence, but I have my moments."

Green smiled weakly. "Haven't we all where women are concerned? But I don't want Yasmin being taken advantage of in any way. You understand?"

"Yasmin's what . . . twenty-five, Professor? I'd have thought she was old enough to make up her own mind about whatever it is she wants."

"Well, sure, but—"

Jack put down his glass, too tired to take it any further. "Why don't you cork that bottle until another day and get some rest, Professor? Me, I think I'll take a walk to clear my head before I turn in."

Green sounded a little drunk as he slapped a hand on Jack's shoulder. "Okay, but I wanted to say well done, Jack. I know your parents would have been proud. It's just a pity they're not here to witness this moment. It's hard to believe it's twenty years since they've gone. I still miss them."

"We both do."

Green's hand fell away. "Good night, Jack."

"Good night, sir." Jack pulled back the tent flap but Green's voice stopped him.

"By the way, I guess you've been too busy to hear the news?"

Jack looked back. "What news?"

Green drained his glass. "The American priest who worked at Qumran at the time your folks died."

Jack nodded. "John Becket. What about him?"

"He's got himself elected pope."

10

In the beginning, there was only darkness and then God created light.

As the sun's blush peeked above the horizon, Jack climbed up a rocky slope, his solitary figure silhouetted against the dawn's orange glow. He was thinking of those ancient words, how they seemed so appropriate to the moment.

But since he was feeling a buzz after drinking Wild Turkey, those other words of a stand-up comic he'd once heard in New York also came to mind: In the beginning there was nothing, and then God created light. There was still nothing but you could see it a lot better.

That always made him crack a smile. When he reached the top of the slope, he paused to stare at the view of the Judean desert toward Jordan and get his breath. His chest pounded, not from exertion but the exhilaration that sped through his veins.

The rising sun was lost behind the mountains of Edom. Jack shivered. The desert air was still cold after the night and he looked out at rust-colored rock and parched stony mountains, Bedouin camps in the distance, dotted with camel and goatherds. Past a palm-fringed wadi, he saw that a ring of massive rocks that formed a boundary with the surrounding desert were stained by the sunrise.

I love this land. Love its mystery, its coppery light, its incredible history.

He sat cross-legged on a huge boulder, breathing slowly. At dawn, the Dead Sea valley, at more than thirteen hundred feet below sea level, was tranquil. A desolate landscape, but strangely it was where Jack felt closest to God. Not that he was deeply religious. More spiritual.

As his father used to put it, sometimes religion is for those who are afraid to go to hell, but spirituality is for those who have been there.

Except here in the Holy Land, it seemed easier to understand belief. History was like a scent in the air. You breathed it every time you sucked in a lungful. Here was the land of Abraham and Jacob, and where Christ was born, the sky he slept under, the soil he was crucified upon. To the north lay Jericho. And twenty miles behind him, to the west, Jerusalem's gilded temple.

Jack heard a clatter of stones and turned, seeing Yasmin Green's figure moving up the slope from down in the camp, her long blond hair tinted by the amber rays. He was pretty sure every man on the dig had been having the same fantasies about Yasmin Green since she had joined the excavation two months ago. She saw him, waved, and called out, "Hi, Jack!"

He waved back, his heart beating a little faster, and waited for her to join him.

She reached the top and sat next to him on the boulder, curling her bronzed legs. She carried two cans of Heineken and handed Jack one. "The last two. I thought you might like to join me in one final nightcap?"

"I guess I may as well be hung for a sheep as for a lamb."

She giggled. "I know I told Uncle Donald to rest but I couldn't get to sleep. You?"

Jack took a swig of the chilled Heineken. "I'm still on a high since our discovery. I wanted to take a little exercise to help me unwind."

"Me too. You seem miles away. What are you thinking about, Jack?"

"Honest?" He looked out at the view. "Twenty years ago when I was nineteen my father worked on a dig not far from here, and I sometimes sat on a hill much like this, with a pretty girl by my side. Her name was Lela Raul." Jack nodded toward the horizon. "She used to live in an Israeli settlement, over there. Her father was a local police sergeant."

"Do you know what became of her?"

"It was a long time ago, Yasmin. But the last I heard she was a cop, like her father, though they're long gone from the settlement."

"I heard you went to visit the place where your parents died. Is that what got you thinking about the past?"

"Probably."

Yasmin put down her beer, touched his arm a moment. "Your friend Buddy's always spoken very highly of your parents. And my uncle Donald does too. You must miss them?"

"There were only the three of us. I guess we were extremely close."

Yasmin bit her lip and her lipstick glistened. "I saw you come up here and thought I'd join you. I hope you don't mind. Or maybe I'm intruding on your thoughts?"

Mind? The sight of her only added to Jack's elation. He could smell her subtle perfume. He glanced at her exquisite skin, golden in the dawn light. She was one of the few women on the dig who bothered with her appearance. Two of the females on the excavation were Orthodox Jews and wore long, modest dresses while digging.

The other women, students and college grads of various nationalities, none of them afraid of wielding a shovel, forgot about makeup and wore loose clothes and scruffy old work boots. But somehow Yasmin always managed to look good even after they had spent the day cave-crawling and scooping dirt out with *gufas*, homemade rubber buckets made out of half tires. She was a magnet for men's attention.

Jack said, "To tell the truth, I'm glad to have the company."

"Has Donald finally gone to bed?"

"I hope so. But he was still up when I left him."

Yasmin smiled, put a hand out, and touched his arm. "You must be thrilled. Donald said that for centuries archaeologists have been searching for concrete proof of Christ's life, with no success. He said that's why Christians placed great significance on things like the Turin Shroud and relics from the cross. But he's got a gut feeling that the scroll may turn out to be a groundbreaking historical document. How do you feel?"

Jack was aware that her hand lingered on his arm. "As if all my lottery numbers have come up."

Yasmin reached into her pocket, took out a wristband made of leather and polished steel, holding it in her palm. "I hope this doesn't seem too juvenile, but this is for you."

"What is it?"

"Something silly I bought in a Jerusalem market. They inscribe them to order. Read what it says."

In the dawn light, Jack could just make out the wristband's indented letters: ARCHAEOLOGY ROCKS. He put down his beer, slipped the band on his wrist, and smiled. "It'll remind me of you. Thanks, Yasmin."

She patted his arm playfully. "Hey, I'm not playing the dig groupie just because you're the man of the moment. But I wanted to say that I think you deserve whatever fame and lecture tours come your way after this." She leaned across and kissed him on the cheek. "I really mean that. You work so hard."

Jack put a hand to his face, felt the ghost of her lips. "Now I really do feel like I've won the lottery."

Yasmin giggled and brushed a strand of hair from her face.

Jack thought, *She's over ten years younger than me. Or does it really matter?* He wanted her to kiss him again and knew it wasn't just the alcohol. There had been women over the years, some that mattered, and some that didn't. None of them yet the right one. He didn't honestly know if Yasmin Green could ever be that, but he had been a long time without female company, and he hungered for the softness of a woman's touch. But then a thought struck him.

"You've gone very quiet. Are you okay?" Yasmin asked.

"Did Buddy Savage put you up to this? The dawn visit. The kiss."

"Buddy? Why on earth would you say that?"

"He's a prankster. Sometimes he'll dare people to do things for a joke. Once in a Mexican bar during a Mayan dig he got me drunk and tried to shave off my eyebrows."

She laughed. "You and Buddy are close?"

"At times he sounds like he's my old man. That's when I call him Pops."

She reached out and took his hand between her palms. Then she bit her lip and said quietly, "No one put me up to it, Jack. I can prove it."

She leaned in close and kissed him on the mouth. Jack felt

the sensual press of her lips. His pulse raced, and then Yasmin drew away, smiling. "Convinced now? I like you, Jack Cane. If that's okay with you."

"Can I be honest? I sensed something between us in your uncle's tent. When I left, I was hoping you'd still be awake, that we'd meet and talk. But Donald seems a little overprotective."

Yasmin traced a finger across his lips, kissed his mouth softly, her voice husky. "Who cares about Donald?" Yasmin picked up the Heineken cans, stood, and winked at him. "You've made a tired girl very happy, Mr. Cane. But it's time we both slept."

Jack rose to his feet. "Will you tuck me in, or is that asking too much on a first date?"

"You just never know your luck. Watch your step on the way down."

Jack felt her soft, slim fingers mesh with his and it felt good. He dusted his Chinos but before he started down the slope after Yasmin he suddenly saw Josuf, the chief Bedouin digger, scrambling up the rocks, clutching the hem of his gown. "Mr. Cane, Mr. Cane—I have been looking everywhere for you."

Jack and Yasmin waited until Josuf reached them.

The man's cheeks were puffed after the climb, his chest heaving. "Please—Mr. Cane, you both must come with me. Something terrible has happened."

The Bedouin went to clutch at his arm to drag him, but Jack said, "Calm down, Josuf. What the heck's so important?"

Josuf's words came tumbling. "It's Professor Green, Mr. Cane. He's been murdered and the scroll is gone."

PART THREE

QUMRAN
ISRAEL

The Bell helicopter with Israeli police markings descended with a swirl of dust as it came in to land.

As the swish of the blades died, Inspector Lela Raul climbed out of the passenger seat. She was in her late thirties with chocolate brown eyes, her dark hair tied back in a ponytail.

She noticed a group of journalists gathered nearby, a couple of TV camera crews among them, all of them being herded back by the police.

Three police Fords were parked a short distance away and half a dozen officers from the local police station stood around, chatting and smoking cigarettes. Lela Raul walked toward them, slipping on a pair of Ray-Ban sunglasses. A herd of Bedu goats grazed on a distant slope and all around her were parched cliffs and craggy hills.

A second later an Israeli Air Force F-18 screamed up the valley, then shot skyward and climbed like a bullet, sending out a shock wave followed by a massive clap of thunder. It scattered the distant goats and echoed through the surrounding Dead Sea cliffs. Air patrols were common this close to the Jordanian border.

Lela looked back toward the journalists and camera crews. She saw that one of the policemen talking with them was a plump sergeant with a beer gut. He had a pencil clenched between his teeth and a notebook in his hand. He peeled away from the crowd, took the pencil from his mouth, and tipped his cap respectfully. "Inspector Raul, thanks for coming."

"Sergeant Mosberg. I see the media jackals are already picking over the carcass."

Mosberg smiled. "Bad news is always good news for some. There's a lot of interest, even a few foreign correspondents drove out from Jerusalem. Murder and archaeology don't often go together, I guess. The body's over there, in the nearest tent."

A hundred yards across the landscape, Lela saw a collection of canvas walk-in tents. Two policemen stood guard outside the nearest. Off to the right, two SUVs and a blue Opel passenger van were parked beside a pair of temporary portable cabin buildings and toilets, a row of shovels and picks stacked against one of the walls. Lela saw a group of civilians of mixed ages standing outside one of the cabins, watching her arrival.

Mosberg said, "In case you're wondering, they're all part of the archaeological team. You probably know our forensic pathologist, Yad Hershel. He's almost finished his examination. Are you familiar with this area, Inspector?"

Lela nodded. "I think you could say that. I lived in a nearby kibbutz and grew up trudging these hills. Tell me about the victim."

"Your chief didn't tell you?"

"Most of it, but I want to hear it from the horse's mouth."

Mosberg took a pipe from his pocket. He cupped his hands, lit the pipe with a cheap plastic lighter, and took a couple of puffs. "The stiff's an American professor named Donald Green. He was the director in charge of this archae-ological dig."

Lela followed the sergeant as he walked toward the tents. "How did he die?"

"A little before six A.M. he was found with a knife buried in his chest."

Lela asked, "Anyone's knife in particular?"

"Turns out it belonged to one of his fellow crew, an Ameri-can named Jack Cane. He claims he loaned it to Green when the professor was examining an artifact that Cane discovered."

Lela raised her eyes. "What kind of artifact?"

Mosberg pointed across the valley. "He found a leather scroll contained in a clay vase right over there, near the bot-tom of the cliffs, to the south of the dig location known as Area A. Qumran is sectioned into areas. The campsite is in Area B3, for example."

Lela nodded. "I know what you're talking about. Con-tinue."

"It seems when Green found out about Cane's find, the professor was so excited he almost wet himself. He reck-oned it was an important discovery. First century A.D. Lots of scrolls have been found in this area. All the Dead Sea stuff that caused so much controversy over the years. It seems that this newly discovered scroll may be a major find, or so Cane is suggesting."

"How come?"

"I think he can best tell you that himself, Inspector. I'm no expert, so I don't know what the fuss is about."

As Lela and Mosberg approached the civilians standing outside the portable toilets, Lela scanned their faces. "Is Jack Cane our killer?"

"That's where it gets murky. He claims not. He says that at about twenty minutes before six A.M. he left Green alive and went to climb that rise over there to the east of the camp to see the sunrise. Green's own niece, Yasmin, says that she joined Cane on the slope, at about six. She says that she saw her uncle still alive just over twenty minutes earlier, still studying the scroll Cane found."

"At five-forty A.M.? I didn't know archaeologists worked a night shift."

"Like I said, Green was excited about the find. The team had been up late celebrating."

"Is the professor's niece an alibi for Cane's movements?"

"Not quite. I figure Cane had about fifteen minutes unaccounted for before Yasmin Green spotted him up on the hill. Cane says that he wandered around the camp, thinking about his find before he decided to climb the summit. All of which sounds a bit convenient, if you ask me."

"Do we have a motive?"

"Not yet. But the consensus is that Green was brash and didn't always see eye to eye with the crew. Catch him in the wrong mood and he could treat you like dirt. *Arrogant* was a word used. *Abrasive* was another. There's a whole bunch of other words I heard but I'm in a lady's company so I'll skip them."

"Abrasive enough to warrant being stabbed to death?"

Mosberg shrugged.

Lela said, "Was there professional rivalry between the professor and Cane?"

Mosberg scratched his head. "I've been told that the two sometimes argued like cat and dog about archaeological matters. But not over the scroll, apparently. Green was thrilled about the find."

"Told by whom?"

"A few of the other dig members."

Lela counted more than two dozen civilians over by the johns. "Who are all the crew?"

"It's an international dig hosted by the Israeli Department of Antiquities. Forty crew in total, thirty men, ten women. Eight are Israelis, the rest Americans, German, British, Italians, and French. There's even a Palestinian and a Lebanese and about a dozen local Bedu are helping with the donkey work. Everyone's in shock."

"What about the Bedu?"

Mosberg shrugged. "I know of many Israelis who say our government has got a lot to answer for because of the way we treat some of the Bedu and Palestinians, confiscating their lands and building settlements on them."

"You can say that again. Go on."

"But all that being said, the tribes in this area are usually a well-behaved, decent lot who keep to themselves. No arguments or disagreements with the crew. No motive to go sticking a blade in someone, from what I hear."

They arrived at the tent. Two officers on guard stood to attention.

Lela saw a couple of plastic sheets pegged over several patches of sand, as if to preserve evidence. "Okay, let's see if we can find out what the professor did to earn a knife in the chest."

12

"I couldn't have done a better job of it myself. A single stab wound. The blade went straight into the heart." The forensic pathologist stood in the center of the tent. Yad Hershel was a small man with a goatee beard and a permanent grin that seemed to suggest he found death amusing.

In front of him, Green's body lay on the ground, partly covered with a bloodied white sheet, one end of which was held up by Hershel. "Of course death would have been quick, but very painful."

Lela studied Green's corpse. Big and fleshy, the American professor was tall, about 250 pounds, with a mane of gray hair. His eyes bulged, a shocked look on his face as if his own death had come as a complete surprise.

Lela examined the Gerber folding knife planted to the hilt in his upper chest. Channels of dried blood radiated out from the wound. Lela looked away, taking in the expansive walk-in tent.

A camp bed lay in one corner, a storage trunk in another, a tier of bookshelves stacked with books and ledgers by the bed. Nearby was an old desk, and on top of it what looked like a rolled clump of rotting material. An ancient-looking clay urn sat on the ground.

Lela nodded. "I've seen enough. What else can you tell me, Yad?"

Hershel replaced the sheet. "Death happened sometime between five and six A.M. The knife hilt had been wiped clean of any prints. We found four sets of footprints leading to the door, but from the wipe marks I found on either side of them I reckon they came after the killer left. The floor had been scrubbed, probably just after the killing. I wish my wife was as clean."

"What else?"

"A couple of partial bootprints to the right outside the tent—we'll try and match those. As for fingerprints, we'd be busy for another year just trying to document them all. On the bookcases, the storage trunk, even part of the ground sheet. This was the professor's office, after all. All of the crew came in here at some stage. We took at least twenty sets of prints off the center tent poles alone."

Lela noticed a dried crimson spatter on the dirt floor, knelt, touched it with her fingertip, and placed the tip to her nostrils. Hershel grinned. "It's a coffee stain. I checked."

Lela brushed her hands and stood, turning her attention to the desk and the rolled clump of rotting material that lay on top. "What's this?"

"The linen cloth the scroll was found wrapped in. It was inside the urn. We'll take a look at those for prints too."

Lela leaned over to study the linen and inhaled. It smelled ancient, infused with must and soil. "Any prints on the desk?"

"A lot." Hershel picked up a plastic evidence bag and showed it to Lela. "We also found these scattered on the floor."

Lela examined the bag and saw slivers of sepia-colored material that looked like faded newspaper, a couple of inches long. "What are they?"

"I suspect they're flakes of ancient parchment. They probably came from the scroll."

Lela said, "Do you think there was a scuffle of some kind?"

"There isn't much evidence of that. But we'll analyze the material. We can even have it carbon-dated just to prove the age of the parchment."

"So when will you have something for me, Yad?"

"Like I told Mosberg, I ought to have the autopsy done by tonight. The other stuff sometime tomorrow."

Mosberg said, "I've sent out a couple of my men to talk with the local Bedu, hoping we might pick up something. So far we've drawn a complete blank."

"Any witnesses? Did anyone see anything, Yad?"

"The trouble is, everyone claims to have had a few drinks too many and crashed in their tents, except Jack Cane and Yasmin."

"Are they involved with each other?"

Mosberg shrugged again. "Nobody's saying that, but the two were talking on that hill at six A.M. I'm thinking it couldn't have been just social. Buddy Savage says he was woken by the sound of Professor Green's tent entrance flap cracking in the wind at about six A.M. He claims the noise kept him awake and that when he went to investigate he found Green unconscious with the knife in his chest. Mr. Savage woke the others. Later it was discovered that the scroll was gone."

"What do you mean, gone?"

"Stolen, disappeared, whatever. I had my men search every tent, porta-potty, and office trailer. There's no sign of it in the camp."

"Do you think the scroll's theft might be the motive for Green's death?"

Mosberg scratched his neck. "It seems likely. My men are still interviewing the crew. It's going to take some time to get through them all and make any conclusions."

Lela flicked a nod at Hershel. "Thanks, Yad."

"Pleasure." Hershel grinned and went back to work.

Lela said to Mosberg, "Have you interviewed this Buddy Savage?"

Mosberg nodded. "His story seems to fit. I've got an interview room set up in one of the office trailers. You can talk to whoever you think you need to."

"We may as well start now." Lela followed Mosberg as he moved outside the tent into harsh sunlight.

There was commotion as a stocky, red-haired man approached the guards. He was pushing sixty and wore a khaki military shirt, grubby sneakers, and a pair of knee-length combat trousers. A baseball cap was tilted back off his head, NYPD in dark lettering on the front. He seemed irritated as he said in an American accent, "Hey, Mosberg. You mind telling me how much longer we're going to be hanging around in this dang heat? Everyone's wilting. You've got all our statements, haven't you?"

Mosberg said, "We'll try not to keep you much longer, Mr. Savage. But Inspector Raul here may want to go through your statements with you, as well as everyone else. So don't wander off."

"Who's wandering? We need to sleep, not wander."

"This is Inspector Raul, she'll be in charge of the case."

The American looked Lela over and offered his hand. "Pleased to meet you, Inspector. Or maybe not so pleased. We're all still shocked about what's happened here."

Lela saw dark rings under Savage's eyes. "You're Mr. Savage, who found the body?"

Savage took a swig from a can of Coke he clutched. "You heard right, and it was pretty unsettling. Professor Green was a longtime friend. The name's Buddy, by the way. Do you guys have any idea yet who killed him?"

"Not yet."

Savage crushed the empty can in his hand and tossed it carelessly in the sand. "Listen, Inspector, I told Mosberg everything I know, just like everyone else did. You really need to talk again with all of us?"

"Yes, I probably do, Mr. Savage."

Savage sighed tiredly, took off his baseball cap, and ran a hand through his thinning red hair. "Then can you do us all a favor and do your best to move this thing along? With all respect to the professor, most of the crew didn't sleep much last night. They're fit to collapse."

"I'll do my best, Mr. Savage."

"I'm going to hold you to that." Savage tugged his cap back on and wandered back to the crew.

Lela said, "So that's Buddy Savage."

"Yes, and he's got a point. We've held everyone here for the last four hours, and they were up most of the night. They're exhausted."

"Then let's try and move things along." Lela looked over at the crew. This time she saw a tanned man wearing cut-off Chino shorts step out of one of the tents. He didn't look in her direction but spoke with one of the other crew. Mosberg said, "That one's Jack Cane."

"Yes, I recognize him."

Mosberg frowned. "You two know each other?"

"From another life, a long time ago." The sun came out again and Lela slipped her shades back on. "But it's probably a lousy time to be renewing an old friendship."

13

The room had a scratched table and a couple of odd chairs. In one corner was stored a pile of archaeological site maps. In another, open wood crates were filled with a selection of label-tagged clay pots, pottery shards, and animal bones that the crew had unearthed.

Lela was alone and she tapped her fingers on the table. Jack Cane was next on her list of people to question. While Mosberg continued questioning other members of the crew, Lela had spoken with Yasmin Green and Buddy Savage. Yasmin was a stunning woman, with a figure that would stop traffic. She also guessed from the undercurrent of the conversation that Yasmin liked Jack Cane. She wondered how deep their relationship went, and just as quickly forced the thought from her mind. Unless it factored into the case in some way it was really none of her business.

Buddy Savage was a different specimen. He reminded her of the kind of man she'd sometimes seen hanging around in bars with a more attractive male friend, in the hope of latching on to any spare women that happened along. Behind it all, Lela figured that Savage was sharp as a barb.

As for Savage's and Yasmin's account of their movements, she'd consider them later, when she had gathered all the case facts. Her interview notes were in front of her but she barely studied them as she leafed through her notebook. She had an odd feeling in the pit of her stomach, a mix of suspense and excitement.

She remembered where exactly she had said her final good-bye to Jack Cane: at Tel Aviv airport twenty years ago. Footsteps sounded outside, the handle rattled, and her heart skipped a beat as the door opened.

Jack stepped in. He wore a cotton shirt with epaulettes. His camel-colored Chinos were cut short, his desert boots covered with a film of sand. He looked fit and tanned, older but handsome. Gone was the teenage face that she remembered. Age and fine lines and a few sun wrinkles around his eyes had matured his features, and his hair was flecked with silver. "Hello, Jack."

He smiled and shook his head. "Lela Raul, well I'll be darned. It's been a long time. When I spotted you earlier I couldn't believe my eyes. I know this sounds weird considering that this is a murder investigation, but it's wonderful to see you again."

Lela stood and they shook hands warmly. "It's good to see you, too, Jack."

He put a hand on her arm, held it there. "You look well. You look—"

"Older?"

"I was going to say great. You're a cop now. An inspector no less. I'm sure your dad's proud. How is he?"

"Living in a retirement home outside Jerusalem. He's still in good health and refuses to slow down. They'll probably have to shoot him on Judgment Day."

"Did you marry?"

"Divorced, no kids. Jack, I'd love to talk some more. There's a lot to catch up on, but first I have a job to do. I need to ask you some questions. Go over what you spoke about with Sergeant Mosberg."

Jack slowly let go of her arm and took a step back. "Sure, I understand. But I told Mosberg everything."

"Humor me, Jack. I need to hear it again, for myself. You know what I imagine? That a discovery like this could bring out the worst in people. Make them jealous, envious of the professional admiration it would bring. It could cause rows, arguments."

Jack's face clouded. "I'm not sure what you're getting at. But you're right. Except that Professor Green and I didn't argue about the find, Lela. Just in case you're wondering, I didn't kill him either. I can give you the reasons why not. Number one, I doubt I could kill anyone. Number two, a find like this, it's the dream of every archaeologist. The equivalent of winning the Oscars. It'll attract a lot of attention, media, academic, the works."

Lela looked toward the window and where the journalists and TV crews were gathered. "I can see that it's got the media rattled already."

"Lela, it's the kind of discovery that I've worked hard for. It'll probably be the pinnacle of my career, something I'd almost want inscribed on my headstone. Why would I ruin it all by murdering Green?"

Lela considered the reply before she again looked past the window toward the parched hills, then turned back. "Living near here, seeing all the digs take place, I learned enough about the scrolls to know that they were a remarkable discovery. But what's so spectacular about the scroll you found?"

Jack's voice sparked with excitement. "You've no idea,

Lela. It may be one of the most dramatic finds of this century. Or any century, for that matter."

"It's that important?"

"We found the name of Jesus Christ written in the scroll, which is simply incredible. You know why?"

Lela picked up her notebook. "No. But how about you show me where you made the discovery and you can tell on the way?"

14

"You know what most people don't understand? The Dead Sea scrolls are mostly Jewish documents. They have almost nothing Christian in them." Jack's boots crunched on gravel as he led the way along a footpath toward a distant cliff face, carrying a heavy-duty electric torch in his hand.

"Apart from some copies of parts of the Old Testament and a number of unknown New Testament records, they mostly tell us about a Jewish religious community called the Essenes living in and around the same time as Jesus and in about the same place."

Lela nodded. "Sure, that much I know. And that the manuscripts found here include biblical texts, psalms, poetry, commentaries on daily life, even prophecies and apocalyptic visions. Plus miscellaneous texts that don't fit anywhere."

"That's right." Jack smiled, followed the rise of the land, enthusiasm braiding his voice. "You remembered. But what's so remarkable is that in all the other Dead Sea scrolls, Jesus' name isn't mentioned once. There's not a single reference to him or to his followers in any of the documents."

"But there is in the scroll you found."

"Precisely. It's a bombshell."

"Tell me how you found the scroll."

"It was just after noon yesterday. Yasmin and I were digging near a cave in field fourteen, in Area A, which is up there." Jack pointed to a weathered sandstone cliff face they were headed toward. "The entrance had been covered by a rockfall, which some of the crew had cleared away. You know what's kind of ironic?"

"What?"

"It wasn't all that far from where my father made his own discovery, or from where many of the original scrolls were found over fifty years ago."

"How did that make you feel?"

"To be honest, it felt special, Lela. Really terrific. As if somehow I'd managed to carry on where my father left off all those years ago, if that makes sense."

"You must still miss your parents."

Jack smiled. "Of course. Pretty much every day I visit their resting place. I sit awhile, talk to them. And hope, as always, that they're listening. I'd like to think that they do. That there's something greater beyond all this. Even if on a bad day I get the hollow feeling there isn't."

Lela touched his arm and nodded. "Go on."

"We were about to finish for lunch but Yasmin suggested that we open just one more hole for the heck of it, so we did."

"But Yasmin's not an archaeologist, is she? Just an interested amateur?"

"Like some people on this dig. The professor said she's helped on a couple of excavations since high school, working with other members of her family. She's worked as hard as anyone on the site, and with as much passion."

"She's an American, right?"

"Her passport's American. Her father's from New York but her mother was Lebanese."

Lela kept up with Jack's stride. "Keep going."

"I'd found very little during the dig. We've been here since late January and done a lot of hard digging but mostly all we had to show for it were some ibex bones and pottery vessels and shards dating from the first century. My high point until today had been an ostracon I discovered—a piece of a broken pottery jug with what looked like an ancient grocery list written on it. That was normal practice at that time—people used junk broken pottery like slips of notepaper."

"But this find was different?"

"You said it. I'd dug about a half a yard of soil when my trowel hit something hard. I saw immediately that it was the neck of a clay jar. Most of the important scrolls found in this region were stored in clay jars or urns, so I got excited. Sure enough, I'd struck it lucky. Inside the jar I found a linen wrap containing the scroll."

"Could you tell how old it was?"

Jack nodded. "I'd examined other material found in the area and figured it had to be at least a couple of thousand years old. Carbon dating would have pinned it down more precisely."

"Our forensics people found some flakes of parchment on the floor of the professor's tent. It's likely they came from the scroll, seeing as it was the only one found on this dig. But we'll have the flakes analyzed and carbon-dated."

"Good. Like so many of the scrolls found in this region they're beyond monetary value, even if some dealers manage to put a price on them."

"Which dealers are you talking about?"

Jack wiped his brow from the heat as they followed a track that led up an incline and toward a narrow chasm fifty yards away. "The ones who trade in stolen artifacts and parchments.

There's an entire industry that deals in plundered historical objects, even Dead Sea scrolls. I'm sure you know that."

"Are you including the Bedu tribes?"

"Of course. They're the ones who discovered many of the scrolls in this area. Some Bedu like to treasure-hunt for booty. They'd use some of the same indicators that we use to find buried artifacts."

"What do you mean?"

"Like burrow holes, for instance. When wild creatures tunnel into the ground, they can leave pieces of pottery and coins behind them in the soil mound, which can be a good indicator that it's worth digging in that location. Sometimes that's how we find our material. So the Bedu pitch their tents out in the valley and under cover of night they'd dig down into the burrow holes. Sometimes they'd get lucky and find valuable objects. Then they'd fill in the holes, dismantle their tents, move on, and no one's the wiser."

Lela nodded. "I've heard about such practice."

"They sell their more important finds to dealers, rich private collectors, or church representatives. Stuff like pottery, Roman or religious artifacts and documents. You name it."

Jack slowed as they stepped up a rocky incline, then went on. "You might call it theft, but the Bedu would argue that they didn't steal anything in the first place. These lands have been their stomping grounds for thousands of years, since way before Christ. They consider their finds to be rightfully theirs."

"Do you think that the scroll's theft could have been a motive for killing Professor Green?"

"Hey, you're the cop, Lela. The professor's dead and the scroll's disappeared. It's simple deduction that theft's the motive. Why else would anyone kill him?"

"Have you anyone in mind?"

"No. But I can't imagine any of the dig crew stabbing their director to death, no matter how much of a moody guy he was."

"What about thieves who specialize in valuable artifacts?"

"Maybe. But how could they have learned so quickly that we'd made a valuable find?"

Lela considered the reply, then said, "Let's get back to the contents. You told Mosberg that Green managed to translate some of the text."

"The scroll seemed in remarkable condition and written mostly in Aramaic. Green didn't unravel it entirely because of the risk of damage. But the first inked lines were legible and mentioned the name *Yeshua HaMeshiah*, Jesus the Messiah, Jesus Christ."

"What exactly did the text say?"

Jack halted, removed his notebook, and flipped it open.

"This story concerns the man known as Jesus the Messiah. Having traveled from Caesarea to Dora, where his name had become well-known, he failed miserably to cure the blind and the sick, despite his promises to do so. Soon after, he was arrested in Dora by the Romans, tried and found guilty, and sentenced to be executed."

Jack looked up. "Green thought the text bizarre and so did I. There's absolutely no historical or biblical mention of Jesus ever having visited the towns of Dora or Caesarea, never mind being arrested in either. Jesus Christ was principally known to frequent a fairly small area in Judea. Dora and Caesarea were in different Roman provinces, over sixty miles away. We didn't understand the reference to not curing the blind and the sick either. Like I said, it's bizarre. Had we been able to fully translate the text, it may have shed new light on established biblical events."

"Do you mind if I copy down your translation in my notebook?"

"Help yourself." Jack showed her the note.

Lela copied it. "Do you think the text could have been significant historically? Perhaps even extremely valuable as well?"

"I think so, Lela."

"Are there any other Aramaic experts on site?"

"Buddy Savage isn't an expert but he knows enough. There's a German guy, Wolfgang, who's pretty hot on Aramaic but he was away in Munich. A couple of the Israelis are Hebrew experts. Why?"

"Did the professor consult Savage?"

Jack raised an eyebrow. "Are you kidding? He wouldn't have even consulted Buddy about which shirt he ought to wear for dinner."

"Why?"

"With respect, Green could be arrogant. He believed his own intellect was superior to everyone else's and he rarely consulted anyone."

"Sounds like he wasn't the ideal team leader."

"He raised the funds to cover the cost of the dig in the first place. He's the one who got our sponsors, so Green was the boss."

"Who are the sponsors?"

"Wealthy benefactors in the United States. I don't get into the politics of it but I believe they've sponsored lots of digs in this area in the past. And don't ask me who they are or why they do it. I think some of them may have wanted to remain anonymous. Buddy Savage may know more. He often helped Green with his paperwork."

"What about religious convictions?"

"What do you mean?"

"Are many of the team here because of any particularly strong religious beliefs?"

Jack shrugged. "I guess about half are interested in religion, whether it's the Christian, Jewish, or Muslim faith. The other half are here just to learn and appreciate the dig. But some among them, being young and carefree, are just here to party and have fun."

Lela smiled. She removed her Ray-Bans as they came to a cliff face that rose at least a hundred feet in the air. At the bottom was a scattering of massive limestone chunks, once part of the cliff that had long ago collapsed. Jack led the way into a six-foot-wide chasm on the right. Twenty paces later their path ended at a cave mouth. Limestone debris had been moved to a mound on the right, a rockfall that had been cleared away.

"This is where we found our treasure. Do confined spaces bother you, Lela?"

"If you mean am I claustrophobic, the answer is . . . sometimes. It depends how small the space is."

"Not too small, but maybe you better hold on to me. There are some holes where we'd been digging." Jack held out his hand to her. "Ready?"

Lela's eyes met his. "When you are."

Jack winked at her, a tiny smile flickering on his lips, and then she took his hand, held her breath, and let him lead her inside the cave.

15

Lela saw that inside the cave several holes had been dug into the ground. Jack stepped around them, leading the way, shining the torch. He halted when he came to a hole that was about a yard wide and the same deep. A mound of clay was piled behind it.

"This is where we found our trove." Jack's voice echoed inside the cave.

"You found only one scroll inside the jar? Is that usual?"

"Sometimes scrolls have been found singly, or sometimes we get a whole bunch of them in one place. It could be just a single page consisting of twenty lines, or dozens of pages all rolled together. There's no rule."

Jack shone the torch as Lela knelt to examine the bare, three-feet-deep rut in the ground where the jar had once lain. She plucked a handful of the gritty dirt, let it run through her fingers, then dusted her hands and stood. "Tell me when you last saw the professor."

"We'd all had a few drinks to celebrate, then everyone began to head to bed between three and four A.M., me included, while the professor carried on examining the scroll. I was asleep when Yasmin woke me to say her uncle wanted to see me at once, that he had found something in the text he wanted me to look at. I stayed talking with Professor Green until five-forty A.M."

"How did he seem?"

"Like he was walking on air. That's the only way to describe it. He was thrilled."

"No arguments?"

Jack raised an eyebrow. "Are you kidding? What was there to argue about? The professor believed that the find would help confirm the existence of Jesus Christ. Despite what you might think, archaeological evidence of that fact is thin on the ground. There's the Bible, sure, but outside of that and the historian Josephus's account of Christ, there are few ancient documents that actually corroborate his life. Finding a scroll like this one, mentioning Jesus and specific deeds relating to him, would be pretty powerful confirmation if proven to be genuine."

"You really believe the parchment is genuine?"

"Yes, I do. It's also truly remarkable. Archaeology has never produced anything that is a clear contradiction to the Bible. But this scroll does."

"Did Green try to claim any credit for the discovery?"

"No, Lela. He seemed happy I'd hit the jackpot, and was full of praise."

"You sound very sure you left the professor at five-forty."

"I checked my watch as I left Green's tent. I was trying to make up my mind if I'd go straight to bed or watch the sunrise. I was still excited."

"Did you see anyone else in the vicinity of Green's tent at that time?"

"Not a soul. Everyone appeared to have gone to bed."

"Except Yasmin."

"Obviously."

Lela said quietly, "I heard that you and the professor had your differences."

"Green could be a difficult guy sometimes. Temperamental, even aggressive. Sure, we had minor clashes. But I didn't kill him, Lela."

"The professor was found dead at six A.M. You were the last to see him alive."

"So?"

"Mosberg said that one of the crew who arrived at Professor Green's tent soon after you and the others had already got there claimed that you had blood on your hands, Jack."

"So did everyone else who helped try to stop the bleeding from Green's wound."

"You mean Yasmin and your friend Buddy?"

"Not Yasmin; she blacked out. The sight of blood gets to her, apparently. Her uncle's bloody torso must have been too much. But Buddy and I tried to resuscitate the professor. We weren't a hundred percent certain that he was beyond help so we decided to try to restart his heart."

"Who decided?"

"I did. But the knife kept getting in the way and we were too afraid to pull it out or touch it in case we did more damage. So the resuscitation was a pretty awkward attempt and we all got blood on our hands and clothes."

"It was your knife."

"I loaned it to the professor when he called me to his tent. He used it to delicately raise the parchment while he read the text. I was so tired I guess I forgot to take the knife back."

"We found no prints on it. Not even yours. The hilt was wiped clean."

"My prints are probably everywhere else. I was in the professor's tent pretty much every day."

"What were you doing before you headed up the slope to watch the sunrise?"

Jack said, "Wandering round the camp, finishing a beer, smiling to myself, disbelieving my luck."

Lela, deep in thought, looked down at the gaping hole in the soil. "I've talked with your friends, Buddy and Yasmin. They both back up your story. But Mosberg tells me he's walked from the professor's tent to the top of the slope. He didn't rush and it took him just under ten minutes."

"So?"

"What time did you start to climb the hill?"

"Five-forty-five, I guess."

"That means you got to the top about five before six. Yasmin says she joined you at six. I estimate there could be at least a fifteen-minute time gap when your whereabouts can't be accounted for. Mosberg has suggested that those fifteen minutes could have been used to kill Professor Green, and he has a point. You were the last person we know of who saw the professor alive."

Jack's jaw tightened. "I hear what you're saying, Lela. But I'm innocent. I'm telling you the truth."

Lela took one last look around the cave. "I've seen enough for now, Jack."

He led the way out into sunlight.

Lela glanced toward the tents and cabins, then turned to face Jack. "I wanted us to get away from Sergeant Mosberg and the others so that we could talk alone."

"Why?"

Lela regarded him intently. "Because we're old friends, Jack, and I wanted you to be aware that we haven't interviewed everyone yet, so we may still turn up a decent lead as to who killed the professor and for what motive. We'll also put out a bulletin to Interpol for police agencies everywhere to be alert to anyone trying to sell ancient documents or scrolls. We'll try to cover all the bases. That's the good news."

"And the bad?"

"Right now Sergeant Mosberg thinks you're his strongest suspect."

16

ROME

Behind the Vatican Library, near an open courtyard known as Cortile del Belvedere, is a sturdy granite building surrounded by high walls. It has no nameplate at its entrance. Those select few who have business there know it as L'Archivio Segreto Vaticano, the Secret Archives of the Vatican, whose vaults contain a vast collection of historical treasures and countless secrets of the Catholic Church.

It was just after two that afternoon when the cardinal stepped through the solid oak doors. Moving past the discreetly armed security guards, he entered a marble hallway. He ignored the custodian seated at a large oak table, bare except for the book that every visitor was supposed to sign before proceeding beyond this point. This visitor hadn't signed the book in all the years since he had become a cardinal. Nobody had ever dared challenge him.

He had first come here as a young American priest, when he worked at the Pontifical Gregorian University in Rome and had to study the records of ancient judgments stored in the archives. In those days the furniture was medieval but now it was modern, complete with photocopiers and computer terminals, Coca-Cola dispensing machines and coffeemakers that gurgled all day.

He kept his head down, but he was conscious that the sudden entrance of a cardinal of the Curia made those who worked in the building nervous. Many were quite young and casually dressed, clerical scholars and custodians who presided over the most clandestine archives in the world. Here, in this same room, with its great clock and carved throne, was where the prefect of archives sat watching his assistants silently fetch and carry records for the few privileged scholars who were granted permission to inspect them, and only within the confines of this room.

Even then, there were limits to what they could see. Certain ultrasensitive files required the special consent of the pope before they could be opened. The cardinal ignored the passing stares and moved toward the rear of the building.

The Vatican Archives was a storehouse of astonishing secrets.

Thirty miles of shelves were filled with books, parchment, and paper manuscripts of the greatest historical importance. Here were slips of paper detailing long-forgotten sins, broken promises, indulgences, and special exemptions from ecclesiastical law. Here were records from conclaves since the fifteenth century. And more, much more: documents from the Inquisition, thirteenth-century intelligence about the Mongols, church reports about Joan of Arc—correspondence that helped have her burned as a witch—and a vast repository of papers that ran from Napoleon to Hitler, from Luther to Calvin.

There were registers that contained nightmarish drawings of the world's end, of devils and vampires and women with the bodies of nymphs and the faces of beasts, dating from the days of Innocent III. Files to do with UFOs, religious sightings and revelations, demonic possessions and exorcisms. Steel boxes containing extraordinary church secrets and prophecies.

The cardinal also knew of the remarkable holy relics and artifacts that the Vatican jealously guarded, and on which the church's faith was built: a sliver of walnut wood, part of the headboard of the cross on which Christ was crucified, the skull of John the Baptist, the robe of Jesus, the Virgin's cloak, Mary Magdalene's foot, and even part of the foreskin of Jesus Christ, said to be the only known remains of the Savior, kept in an emerald- and ruby-studded casket adorned by two solid silver angels in a safeguarded shrine in Calcate, north of Rome.

The cardinal moved on, carefully picking his way through the corridors of shelves into the heart of the building, knowing exactly which route to take to avoid most of the cameras, and past the small private chapel of the infamous Borgias. He crossed the high-roomed cavern called the Hall of Parchments, filled with tens of thousands of documents, many of them tinged with a violet-colored fungus that defied even the most scientific of treatments. It was a musty place and eerily reminded him of a funeral vault. But he knew the Secret Archives were more than the storehouse of a dead past.

Contained here were highly sensitive records of the church's contemporary involvement: its business dealings, banking and financial affairs, its numerous investments— some of them highly controversial and illegal, which in several cases had involved the Mafia and had led to criminal prosecution and even murder. The cardinal knew all too well these hidden secrets: for five years he had occupied a senior position at the Vatican Bank. It was a dangerous time and they were black days he would rather forget.

Finally he had reached his destination, a small room at

the back of the building protected by double oak doors, blackened with age. A plastic sign on the door said in Italian, ACCESSO LIMITATO. Restricted Access. The cardinal removed a bunch of keys from beneath his burgundy cassock. Selecting one, he inserted it in the lock and turned the key.

The door creaked open and he stepped into a room that looked forgotten by time. Paneled oak walls, dusty shelves, and two walnut desks with brass lamps. He moved into the room and flicked on one of the lamps. He knew exactly what he was looking for and when he found the cardboard box he plucked it down from one of the shelves, took it over to the desk, and placed it under the lamp.

Inside, on top of a collection of files, was a manuscript, bound with red twine and a wax seal the size of a large button. He broke the seal, and pieces of the wax scattered everywhere. He carefully picked them up, placed the fragments in his pocket, and opened the file's hard cover. Inside on the first typewritten page it said:

REPORT INTO THE UNDISCLOSED SCROLLS
AT QUMRAN.

It took only moments to scan through the headings on the next page, for he knew them well:

1. List of Qumran scrolls and parchment fragments kept secret.
2. Disturbing revelations contained within these scrolls (with accurate translations, and references to known historical and archaeological data).
3. The dramatic revelations concerning the Second Messiah and the significance of the original scroll discovered by Mr. Robert Cane.

4. Steps the church must take to prevent the publication of controversial/harmful scroll material in the future.
5. Conclusions and recommendations.

The cardinal slowly closed the manuscript again, puckered his lips, and sighed, as if a great weight were pressing on his shoulders. Then he quickly opened the buttons on his cassock and tucked the manuscript inside.

Theft of any item from the Vatican Archives was tantamount to a grave sin. But he was wedded to the church since those early days in the Catholic orphanage when he had sought and found God's protective embrace. His pious loyalty had helped him rise from a meek orphan to a respected American cardinal, a prince of the church, and in return this was one sin he had no regrets about committing. No one could know what the manuscript pages contained.

Not ever.

The cardinal flicked off the brass lamp. Then he left the room as silently as he had entered, closing the door after him and turning the key in the lock.

17

Buddy Savage eased on the brakes and the Toyota SUV halted in a cloud of dust. As it settled he studied the clusters of tents and coarse brick huts that passed for the village named Nazlat, then said back over his shoulder, "Okay, you can get up now, the coast looks clear. It always beats me how these people live like this."

In the backseat, Jack raised his head, sat up, and grabbed a pair of binoculars. "Like what, Buddy?"

Buddy took a drag on his Marlboro Light and nodded to the rambling collection of tents and huts. "Sure, they're mostly nomads and it's a way of life that's gone on for thousands of years, but it's Trashville. No running water, no utilities, and when it rains the sand turns to mush."

Jack aimed the binoculars toward Nazlat. "Think of the upside. No property taxes, no utility bills, no lawn mowing."

Buddy took another drag on his cigarette. "What about having to take a shovel out in the desert every time you need to use the john?"

"You're starting to get crabby in your old age, Buddy, you know that?"

"Hey, listen, after thirty years digging holes in the sand

without much to show for it but calloused hands and a lousy back, I'm learning to appreciate the small comforts in life. Like electric light, a flushing john, ice-cold beer."

Jack scanned Nazlat. He saw no police, only a scattering of grazing goats and camels. He spotted two dusty, battered Nissan pickup trucks, one red, one white, packed with worn plastic water containers.

"So how'd you get on with the inspector?" Buddy probed. "You still like her?"

"Lela and I were friends a long time ago, Buddy."

Buddy grinned. "It's about time you took more of an interest in women. For years you've been burying your head in work. Now all of a sudden you've got a couple of hots on the horizon. Talk about striking it lucky."

"Lela's here to do a job, not renew old friendships."

"So what happened between you and her back then? C'mon, you can tell papa."

Jack lowered the binoculars. "Give me a break, Buddy. It was twenty years ago and we were just a couple of teenagers. We've got more important things to think about."

"Hey, quit worrying, there's no way you or anyone else in the crew killed Green. The cops will figure that out sooner or later."

Jack put away the binoculars. "Somehow I don't think Mosberg shares that sentiment."

Buddy said, "Then the guy's got to be a dummy. What precisely did you and the inspector talk about?"

"We didn't exactly cover old ground from A to Z since we last met. It was more businesslike, to do with the case."

"So Mosberg thinks you're the main suspect? What about Lela?"

"She said nothing. Which worries me even more. Somehow I'm going to have to convince her that I'm innocent."

Buddy arched an eyebrow. "So that's why you had me hide you in the back of the SUV. A guilty man would never do that, right?"

Jack snapped open the rear door. "Funny. I asked Yasmin to talk with the Bedu to see what she could learn. You know that the Bedu keep their mouths shut around the police. It's like the Mafia's omertà, the code of silence. But I'm hoping they might tell us anything they know."

Buddy shrugged. "If you really think it's worth a try."

Jack climbed out of the Toyota. "If anyone asks after me back at the camp, tell them I'm catching up on some sleep. If it's the inspector, hold her off until you can call me on my cell."

"You're sure you don't want me to stay?"

"If all three of us vanish, Lela and Mosberg will get even more suspicious. I'll fill you in when I get back. That's a promise, Buddy."

Savage shifted the Toyota into gear and tipped his forehead in a mock salute. "Watch yourself, you hear?"

"There you go again, Pops. Sounding like my old man."

The Toyota drove away and Jack shielded his eyes from the sun as he strolled down the unpaved street. He passed a herd of goats cropping at the sparse desert grass. Half a dozen barefoot village children appeared and crowded round him, calling for money. "*Salaam! Baksheesh! Baksheesh!*"

"*Salaam,*" Jack answered, and he patted them on the heads, dug a hand in his pocket, and tossed a fistful of coins into the sand. The children scattered after the coins. He saw Yasmin come out of one of the large tents made of goat hair which he knew belonged to Josuf, the foreman in charge of the Bedu workers. Yasmin waved her straw hat and hurried over to him.

"Thank God you got here, Jack."

"What's up?"

She took Jack's hand, leading him toward the tent. "You better hear for yourself. Josuf has some information that he didn't want to share with the police. And you're not going to believe what he has to say."

18

QUMRAN
ISRAEL

The Arab woman was at least in her nineties, with faded tribal tattoos on her wrists. Dressed in black, she was bent almost double with arthritis. She placed a bowl of ripe figs in front of them, and then poured piping red tea into glass cups. As she left the tent she cackled something to Josuf, seated cross-legged on a red carpet next to Yasmin and Jack.

Josuf wore a white dishdash gown, and a silver tooth flashed in his mouth when he spoke. "My mother remembers your parents with fondness, Mr. Cane, and the day of their deaths with great sadness."

Jack sipped his hot tea and placed a hand over his heart. "I am touched by her kind words."

Josuf fell silent. With his gray stubble and dark walnut skin, the Bedu chief looked close to seventy but rumor had it that he was only in his fifties. Other rumors suggested that he had eight wives and forty children. Judging by the number of his "sons" who worked on the dig—at least six—Jack was tempted to believe it.

The goat-hair tent that Josuf and his family lived in was scrupulously clean. On a low pinewood table, flower petals floated in bowls of water, and a lit amber-colored candle gave off a fragrant smell of honey.

Out of courtesy to his host, Jack burst open a fig and sucked on the red flesh. With the Bedu, you had to be patient. "What news do you have, Josuf?"

The Bedu chief helped himself to a fig. "I did not want the policewoman to know what I am about to tell you. To help the Israelis is not the way of my tribe. There are those among the Bedu who despise the Israelis for confiscating Arab lands."

Jack heard the cluck of women's laughter and children's conversation off in another wing of the huge tent. "Tell me what you know, Josuf."

The Bedu chief adjusted the folds of his gown, craning his neck to make sure that his mother was gone. "You are aware of the many valuable finds made in the Dead Sea area by Bedu tribes."

"Of course."

"We both know that some Bedu have found objects and sold them to private collectors for large amounts of money, without telling the Israelis. My people consider these lands to be theirs by birthright. That any objects they find rightfully belong to them."

Jack nodded. He knew that the Israeli authorities could never hope to put a stop to illegal digging. "Where's this leading, Josuf?"

"I have heard that the Israelis suspect you of being a killer, Mr. Cane."

Jack figured there wasn't much that Josuf didn't hear about in his locality. But the speed at which the news had traveled surprised even him. "How did you know?"

Josuf waved the question away as if it were a fly. "I know

that you are not a killer, Mr. Cane. It's not in your blood. Such an accusation is unjust. That is why I want to help you. My youngest daughter knows something, Mr. Cane."

Jack sparked. "Knows what?"

The Bedu chief clapped his hands together. The old woman returned, opening the tent flap, and Josuf said, "Bring Safa."

19

The girl was no more than ten and her cocoa brown eyes were strikingly beautiful. She wore a simple cotton gown and gauze headscarf and she bowed to Josuf. "Father."

"Sit beside me, Safa. Tell my friends everything you saw."

The girl sat by her father. When she hesitated, her father squeezed her hand. "Tell them, Daughter."

The girl looked at Yasmin and Jack and spoke softly in Arabic. "Today I woke before sunrise with two of my brothers to tend to my father's goat herds, as we always do. It is my job to tend to one of the herds that graze beyond the Red Rocks. This morning I saw someone leave your camp and walk past the rocks toward the desert."

Jack knew where the girl meant. The Red Rocks were a half ring of massive rust-colored boulders that formed a natural boundary where the desert began.

"Go on, Safa," her father prompted. "Who did you see?"

"I could not tell if the person was a man or a woman. The light was not good. But whoever it was they stopped just beyond the rocks where two men stood waiting by a car. The person gave something to the two men and then quickly returned to the camp. Then I saw the two men drive away."

Jack felt a flutter of excitement and flicked a look at Yasmin before he said to the child, "Are you positive about this?"

"Yes, I am certain."

Josuf interrupted. "It wasn't the first time that my daughter saw the two men from the car, Mr. Cane."

"What do you mean?"

Josuf nodded to his daughter. "Explain, Safa."

"My uncle Walid knows the two men."

Before Jack could ask Josuf to explain, the Bedu patted his daughter's arm. "Leave us, Safa. Go back to your mother. I will explain the rest."

"Yes, Father."

The girl bowed and left. Josuf said, "What I have to say next is not for my daughter's ears, Mr. Cane."

"I don't understand."

"I have a confession to make. You do not know my brother, Walid. He lives not far from here. Over many years he has found small pieces of ancient parchment in these hills. However, Walid never told the Israelis. Instead, he sold the fragments of parchments to a Syrian black-market dealer."

When Josuf hesitated, Jack inclined his head. "I'm listening, go on."

"The two men my daughter saw sometimes came here from Damascus to buy Walid's fragments."

"How do you know that?"

"From Safa's description of one of the men, and the old white Mercedes they drove. My daughter ducked behind some rocks as the car drove past. She managed to see the passenger's face. He was a middle-aged man with a gray beard. He wore a broad white Panama hat with a black band around it. It sounds like one of the men I often saw Walid deal with. He usually drove here in a white Mercedes."

"Who are the men?"

"Criminals, from the Syrian underworld. They sometimes buy artifacts from the Bedu, to sell them in turn to wealthy collectors for a profit."

"Are they Bedu?"

Josuf nodded. "Settled Bedu. They bribe border guards to help them cross frontiers."

Jack said, "Do you know who they were working with?"

"No one from among my people, I am certain. I phoned Walid. He is in Jerusalem, visiting friends. He believes either these men came of their own free will to steal the scroll or that they planned it with someone working on the dig. Walid says that the men are ruthless enough to have killed the professor."

Jack let the Bedu's words sink in. Then he said thoughtfully, "How can your daughter be so certain they're the same men? The light couldn't have been great."

"My daughter told me that the man with the hat had a lame walk and a withered hand. That fits the description of one of the criminals Walid dealt with. You see, many years ago this man stepped on an Israeli land mine. He suffered serious injures to a hand and foot. In Arabic, he's sometimes called by the name Slow Foot, because he drags his leg behind him. But he calls himself Pasha."

Yasmin said, "You have to tell all this to the police, Josuf. For Jack's sake."

Josuf shook his head, his face troubled. "I can tell them nothing. My people would curse me as an informer."

Yasmin met his stare. "Even if it meant an innocent man being imprisoned for a murder he didn't commit?"

"It could also mean my throat being cut. But I want to help you find these two men. They are the real criminals. And I think I know where they can be found."

"Where?" Yasmin asked.

"Walid told me of a Catholic monastery called St. Paul's, near Maloula, outside Damascus."

Jack considered. "I've heard of Maloula. It's a mainly Christian town that dates from the fourth century. One of the few places in the world where Aramaic is still spoken."

Josuf nodded. "The same language that Jesus spoke. The same language that's written in many of the scrolls discovered at Qumran."

"Go on."

"Walid heard that an elderly priest there has worked translating scrolls and fragments for these black-market criminals. A religious man should have nothing to do with murder. Perhaps if he learns of the crime these men may have committed, his conscience will cause him to help you. For your sake, I hope so. I do not believe you are a killer, Mr. Cane. However, if you are to make the Israelis believe it, then you must go to Maloula and find out more about these men. It would take a half day's journey across the desert through Jordan and Syria, no more than that."

Jack said, "I have a visa that allows me to cross into Jordan from when the team visited Petra. But I'd be wasting my time trying to get into Syria. I have an Israeli border stamp on my American passport. There's no way the Syrians will issue me a visa. They hate Israel and anyone who's even been there."

Josuf replied, "You forget that the desert has always belonged to the Bedu, Mr. Cane. No borders will prevent my tribe from traveling where they want. But you will both need your passports for part of the passage if the lady means to travel with us. And it will not be a journey without its dangers."

Jack frowned. "What are you saying, Josuf?"

"I know a way to get you to the monastery at Maloula."

20

Lela was at the desk in the office trailer, reading through her notes, when Sergeant Mosberg knocked on the door. "My apologies for disturbing you, but you said you wanted to speak again with Jack Cane, Inspector."

"That's right."

"He's gone."

"What do you mean, gone?"

Mosberg blushed. "I've checked Cane's tent and the rest of the camp and he's nowhere to be found. I've even sent some of my men to search the hills but no one's seen him."

Lela jumped to her feet. "What about Savage and Yasmin Green?"

"Miss Green drove to Nazlat a couple of hours ago in her SUV. She returned for about thirty minutes and left in that direction again. One of my men tells me that Savage visited Nazlat soon after Miss Green and later returned."

"Did anyone check the vehicles before Savage and Green left?"

Mosberg said sheepishly, "No, Inspector. No such orders were given."

Lela angrily stuffed her notebook in her tunic and moved to the door. "Keep looking for Cane, Sergeant."

Lela stormed toward Savage's tent. When she tore open the flap, the American was lying on his bed flicking through a magazine and sipping from a can of Heineken. He lazily got to his feet. "What can I do for you, Inspector?"

"Where's Jack Cane?"

Savage shrugged. "Hey, you got me there. Last time I saw him was over an hour ago in his tent. Why, what's up?"

"Where is Cane, Savage? And don't play me for a fool."

"Hey, I don't know what you're talking about, Inspector."

At that precise moment, Lela heard the clatter of a helicopter descending. The tent material rippled as the rotor blades whirred and then died. Seconds later the tent flap was thrown open and Mosberg appeared. "You have an important visitor, Inspector."

As Lela stepped outside Savage's tent she saw her boss, Chief Inspector Danni Feld, climb out of the helicopter and duck his head under the dying blades. He hurried toward her. Feld wore civilian clothes, not his usual crisp police uniform, which suggested that he'd been summoned unexpectedly. As he reached Lela he stood upright and gave her a wave.

"Inspector Raul."

"Sir, I thought it was your day off."

Feld vainly patted down a raised flap of graying hair. "So did I. How is the investigation going?"

"I'm still gathering evidence."

Feld scratched his head as he studied the Dead Sea landscape. "It must be a very interesting case, Lela, that's all I can say."

"Sir?"

Feld turned to stare at her. "I got an urgent call from the head of Mossad, no less. He wants to see you straightaway. Says it's a matter of grave urgency."

Lela was puzzled. Israel's national security agency had a reputation as one of the best and most secretive intelligence organizations in the world. "I'm in the middle of a murder investigation. What does Mossad want with me?"

Feld jerked his thumb toward the helicopter. "I wish I knew. But I've a feeling you'll get your explanation in Tel Aviv. You're to fly there immediately."

21

ROME

The sleek black Mercedes bearing Vatican diplomatic plates and a fluttering gold and white pendant turned into the Via della Conciliazione with a gentle squeal of brakes.

Sitting in the back of the chauffeured limousine that afternoon was a large, beefy, red-haired man with a pale complexion and bright green eyes. Sean Ryan removed his monsignor's black biretta from his head and ran a handkerchief over his damp brow. It was only April but already the temperature was up to a cloudless seventy, the trees along the banks of the Tiber in full bloom.

Two thousand years of history lay around him, a ragged sprawl of ancient crumbling monuments and temples, and at the heart stood the famed Colosseum and the Forum. To the tourists, Rome seemed rather grand and noble, but Ryan knew it was also the most sordid and sinful of cities, and that some things had changed little in two thousand years.

On the Via Claudia, homosexual men dressed as women still solicited as prostitutes, much as they had during Emperor Caligula's time. Immigrant black girls as young as fourteen had sex with their customers in city lanes and park bushes, just as their predecessors had during the time of the Caesars.

Once the girls had been freed black slaves; now they were impoverished refugees from Africa.

As the Mercedes glided silently down the Via della Conciliazione toward the Vatican, Ryan glanced idly out of the window.

The broad street that led up to the magnificent St. Peter's Basilica was lined on both sides with gaudy souvenir shops and kiosks, cafés, and currency exchange bureaus. Ryan didn't appreciate the cheap commercialism that was permitted to exist a stone's throw away from the burial place of St. Peter, crucified and tortured on a whim of the Emperor Nero, and his broken body dumped in a pauper's grave on the ancient Roman hill that was now the symbol of Christianity. But this morning Ryan had other things to worry about.

His meeting with Cardinal Cassini was scheduled for noon. Ryan was Chief of the Corps of Gendarmes, with command of the Directorate of Security Services, responsible for protecting the pope and the Vatican State. He wondered what was so important that the head of the Curia had summoned him to his office.

Ryan's personal history was an outlandish mix. He had at various times been a police detective with the Irish police, An Garda Síochána, an amateur heavyweight boxer, a champion target shooter, a gambler, boozer, and a womanizer until, at age twenty-eight, the car he was driving recklessly while he was over the alcohol limit had caused the deaths of his pregnant young wife and their two-year-old son. After that, there seemed nowhere for Ryan to deliver himself but into God's hands. Soon after came the priesthood.

Ryan looked up as a flock of pigeons scattered in front of the car when it approached St. Peter's Square, and he replaced the handkerchief in his pocket.

The Mercedes didn't go through the Vatican front entrance—that was for the pilgrims and tourists—but instead veered right. There was a barrier down, three blue-uniformed Swiss Guards on duty. Ryan thought the young men looked blatantly ridiculous in their medieval uniforms, their private parts bulging through their skintight pants.

But of course, the real security was more discreet—inside the gate and off to the right was a long, gray brick building where a heavily armed plainclothes unit of the Vatican's security services was stationed. At that moment, one of the doors to the security building opened and a man with a mustache stepped out, a holstered Beretta clipped under his leather jacket, his eyes cautiously scrutinizing the Mercedes' occupants.

Ryan recognized Angelo Butoni at once. He was one of the young detectives with the security office, and Butoni waved when he saw Ryan roll down the window.

"Monsignor Ryan, always a pleasure to see you."

"Angelo, it's yourself. Keeping busy, I hope?"

Butoni raised his eyes in mock despair. "As always. You'll be glad to know we've improved the security patrols, just as you ordered."

Ryan smiled. "No trouble to you, Angelo me boy, and that's the truth of it. Keep up the good work."

One of the Swiss Guards lifted the barrier and Ryan's Mercedes passed into the Vatican.

22

Cardinal Umberto Cassini was seated behind the ornate desk made of dark Brazilian mahogany in his office overlooking St. Peter's Square, working through some papers, when the floor-to-ceiling oak doors opened softly and a young prelate in a black soutane appeared. "Monsignor Ryan has arrived, Your Eminence."

Cassini looked tired as he threw down his eighteen-karat-gold pen on his desk blotter. "Good. Then let's not keep the man waiting. Send him in."

The prelate bowed and withdrew.

Cassini stepped over to a bookshelf behind him. He pressed on a red leather-bound book, there was a soft click, and the entire shelf swung open on hinges. A short hallway was revealed behind the bookcase. Cassini pulled a string and a light sprang on.

A stone spiral stairway led up and down, part of the maze of ancient stairways and tunnels that honeycombed the Vatican. In a recess was Cassini's private safe with an electronic keypad. He punched in the code and the safe door opened.

Inside was a brown leather briefcase with an elaborate se-curity chain. He removed the briefcase and lay it on his desk, then crossed to the open French windows and looked out over a stone balcony.

Since he had presided over the election of the new pope, life had been hectic indeed, so many pressing things on his mind, and Cassini anxiously fingered the cross around his neck. He turned back as the door opened and Sean Ryan entered.

He looked younger than his fifty years, with a boxer's broken nose and a rugged physique, and he smiled as he stepped into the room. Cassini was aware of a man of considerable, hearty charm. But he also knew that behind the charm lurked a brain as sharp as a stiletto and a temperament that didn't suffer fools gladly, traits that had served Ryan well as head of the Security Office.

Cassini came in from the balcony as Ryan crossed the room, knelt, and kissed the cardinal's ring. "Your Eminence."

"Sean, thanks for coming so promptly. There's coffee on the table if you want some."

Ryan got to his feet. "No, thanks. I'm still a tea man myself, Your Eminence. The Romans may have conquered half the world but they still haven't mastered the art of a good cup of tea."

Cassini gestured for Ryan to sit in one of the red leather wingback chairs opposite. "No doubt you're wondering why I asked to see you."

As Ryan looked across, he saw dark rings underneath Cassini's eyes, as if the man had been up half the night. He also couldn't fail to notice the bookshelf ajar, the secret passageway beyond, and the brown leather security briefcase lying on Cassini's desk.

As head of security Ryan had offered Cassini advice on the choice of safe he had installed many years ago, but not its location behind the hidden bookshelf—that had been Cassini's choice. Ryan knew that the little Sicilian cardinal seemed to take great enjoyment flitting between various floors and offices using the Vatican's maze of secret passageways, as if he were a child playing at some elaborate game of hide-and-seek.

"It had crossed my mind," Ryan suggested.

Cassini pushed the bookshelf with his hand and it floated back into place with hardly a sound, except a tiny click to register that it had locked in place. "Before we get down to business, there's something I must ask of you."

"Your Eminence?"

"The conversation we are about to have, and what I am about to show you, *must* remain totally confidential. That is of the utmost importance. I think you'll understand why afterward."

"Of course, as Your Eminence wishes."

Cassini nervously fingered the cross around his neck, glanced at the locked briefcase, and sighed. "Good. You are aware that the Holy Father has made known his intentions in regard to the future course the church must take, and in particular his plan to make public all files held in the Vatican Secret Archives."

Ryan nodded. The word had spread like wildfire, and nothing else was being whispered about in the Vatican's offices and corridors. "A brave step, Your Eminence."

From his desk, Cassini picked up a beautifully made letter opener with a silver blade. The bone handle was hand-carved from deer antler, a gift from the last pope. Inscribed on the gleaming blade were words Cassini treasured: *"With great affection, to a loyal and dutiful servant of God."*

Cassini pointed the blade at Ryan. "A brave step indeed, Sean. Not to mention the fact that he has taken the name

Celestine the Sixth. Celestine, from the Latin, meaning 'supremely good,' or 'angel.'"

Ryan said, "Am I right in saying that the last Celestine was the only pope in history ever to have resigned? He was certainly a strange character—a thirteenth-century dreamer, prophet, a healer."

"And a reluctant pontiff if ever there was one, at least if we're to accept church history. It's said that he believed there was no meeting place between the pursuit of power and riches and the worship of God." Cassini raised an eyebrow. "Indeed. I have heard whispers that already some are calling our new pope the 'second messiah,' because he promises to return the church to the true ways of Christ. And because he appears to have intimated a belief in some kind of broad religious unity by opening our secret archives to all Christian religions. At least it sounded that way to me. It's certainly a noble belief, but if history is anything to go by, I fear its fruition is highly unlikely."

Ryan nodded. "I must admit I've heard the rumors. Including a few outspoken ones that even dared to call him an Antichrist."

"Not all in high office will agree with the Holy Father's plans but he is one of the few absolute monarchs remaining and his word is law. He refuses to change his mind despite the strong advice of some of the Curia."

"So when exactly will the archives be made public?" Ryan inquired.

"The Holy Father intends to make an announcement from St. Peter's Square. He hasn't yet said when, but I have a feeling it could be soon, certainly within a week or less."

"And may I ask what all this has got to do with me?"

Cassini sighed, and threw down his letter opener. "Quite

simply, I fear the intentions of His Holiness may put his life in danger."

Ryan said, "How exactly?"

"No doubt you can imagine that some of these secret files contain information on historical and supernatural matters so highly sensitive that they have been deliberately kept from public knowledge. Without meaning to put too fine a point on it, some of the material will be quite shocking. And to be blunt, there will be those who wish certain of our more sensitive Vatican files were not revealed."

Ryan said, "Who might that be, Your Eminence?"

Cassini raised his hand. "We'll come to it later. As you well know, I number myself among those of authority within the Vatican who are privy to certain of its secrets. And few organizations keep secrets better. Our archives are perhaps the most securely guarded in the world. But now we must prepare to obey our Holy Father's wishes."

"But why exactly should his life be in danger?"

Cassini looked uneasy as he picked up the leather briefcase and the chain lock rattled. He opened it with a key from his cassock, then slid out a thick, red leather folder with a wax Vatican seal that had already been broken. The bundle was tied with wax cord.

Cassini tapped the folder. "You'll understand once you read the pages inside this file. It's a list of some of the material from the Vatican Archives that will be released. I am invoking my protocol to have the list available for you to examine, which is within my power to do. The keeper of the archives— who knows nothing of this—believes I am simply studying the documents on the Holy Father's behalf."

Ryan licked his lips. "What sort of material is in there?"

"Highly confidential, the sort I spoke about. Considering

that you're in charge of the Holy Father's security, you ought to be aware of the stakes in this matter. And I think you'll agree that once you've read what's inside, they are very high stakes indeed."

Cassini smiled bleakly, then continued. "Normally, what's inside this folder would never—and I mean *never*—be made known to the outside world. The reasons will become obvious. Some of the matters dealt with go back a long time, even to the time of Christ, while others are more recent. And now you, Sean, are about to have the unpleasant privilege of knowing some of those secrets."

Cassini moved the leather folder to the center of the desk. He lifted the glinting steel letter opener by the bone handle and with an expert flick of his wrist, slit the wax cord.

Ryan said, "Now there's a man who knows how to use a blade."

Cassini smiled tightly as he slid the folder across. "It must be my Sicilian blood, Sean."

Ryan looked uncomfortable as he hefted up the bundle with a beefy hand. "Why do I have a bad feeling about this?"

Cassini nodded to the papers. "For now just read, Sean. Then we'll talk."

23

Ryan closed the folder in Cardinal Umberto Cassini's office. His hands were trembling as he looked up, ashen-faced. The Irishman looked stunned, overcome by a deep sense of turmoil. Over fifteen minutes had passed but he had not felt the time go by. "*My God,*" he breathed. "Everything I've read is *really* true?"

Cassini said quietly, "Every word is fact. Now you understand the seriousness of the situation we find ourselves presented with."

Ryan was too dismayed even to nod. Finally he managed to speak. "Holy Mother, it's dreadful. Truly dreadful."

"Does it shake your faith?"

Ryan put a hand to his brow. "Why, n-no. I've been too long a priest, my faith too ingrained, but I *am* truly shocked. This frightens me deeply."

"And now you must also understand why the Holy Father's life may be in danger."

"Has he been made aware of that fact?"

Cassini replaced the documents in the folder. "Of course. I told him so after his election. But he remains firm. He considers this matter a personal crusade."

Ryan shook his head, still ashen. "Now you have me really worried, Eminence. Some of that stuff will be sensational."

"Which is why we must ensure the pontiff remains alive before and after he makes these secrets public." Cassini tucked the folder into the briefcase and locked it. He again pressed the red leather-bound book and the bookshelf swung open. Stepping into the secret passageway, he returned the briefcase to his private safe and extinguished the light after him.

"You can be assured the security arrangements I've put in place are more than adequate. But I'll certainly consider any improvements you might think of," Ryan said.

Cassini pressed shut the bookshelf and heard it click into place. "That's exactly why I summoned you here. There's a saying I'm sure you've heard. Do you know what makes God laugh?"

"People who make plans," answered Ryan.

Cassini nodded, unsmiling, and took his seat. He neatly replaced his treasured letter opener at the top of his desk ink blotter. "True. But I'm a man who likes to make plans. I don't just want security watertight, Sean. I want the Holy Father hermetically sealed. It's no reflection on your professionalism, but I'd like to go over your security arrangements, just to be certain. I'm convinced that the days ahead will be especially fraught with danger. We're all aware how easy it was for that lunatic assassin, Mehmet Ali Agca, many years ago."

"I can assure Your Eminence that our security measures have improved immensely since then."

Cassini sat forward. "Yes, I'm quite certain they have. But we can't allow room for error. Especially under these worrying circumstances."

Ryan frowned. "What circumstances would those be, Your Eminence?"

"There may be those among our clergy who speak reverently of our new pope, who almost see him as a Christlike figure. I've mentioned that some among the Curia, elated by his intended reforms, even talk of him in terms of a 'second messiah.'"

"Yes, I've heard it said."

"John Becket is certainly an unusual man. By all accounts, those who have known him since he was a young priest say he always had an unearthly air about him. People could never fully decipher him. They got close to him, but never close enough that they could admit they knew him completely. He played his cards close to his chest."

Cassini sighed and slapped a palm on his desk. "However, there are two things that you never mentioned in your reference to history, Sean. For one, the last Pope Celestine was murdered by hired assassins. Which almost seems like an unwelcome bad omen."

"Omen?"

"Don't you recall the famous prediction of your Irish St. Malachy, Sean? Our John Becket is prophesied to be the world's last pope."

Half an hour later, Sean Ryan was seated behind his desk in a small, cluttered office on the third floor of the Umbria building, just inside the Vatican walls. The view faced a small square and was rather pleasant, were it not for the loud traffic noise that vibrated through the double glazed windows—a noise the Romans called the *tufa*.

The door opened and Ryan's secretary appeared. A tall Italian Jesuit with a dour face, he carried a silver tray bearing a cup of steaming hot chocolate and a small plate of sugary biscuits. Under his arm was a bunch of newspapers and a clutch of classified security files. He placed both on the desk.

"The Nut File you requested, Monsignor, and the daily publications."

"Anything interesting?"

"The usual coverage you'd expect about the new Holy Father." The secretary smiled bleakly. "It seems the press have nothing else to talk about."

"Thanks, Guido."

The priest withdrew and Ryan sipped the hot chocolate, ignoring the biscuits and the clutch of newspapers and magazines. The usual reports of violent death and destruction in the media would only depress him. The secret documents Umberto Cassini had shown him had disturbed him enough.

Ryan got up, crossed to the window, and stared down at the cobbled square below, manned by two Swiss Guards. The Vatican's security services consisted of just over two hundred men and two dozen women. In times of high security, Ryan considered the women particularly useful. As they were often dressed as nuns, it amused him to think that they mingled so easily with the crowds near the pontiff, high-powered pistols concealed under their habits.

Ryan patted his left side and felt a gentle bulge. He pulled back his jacket.

He wore a snug, inside-the-pants Galco leather holster, in suitable clerical black. It neatly concealed the subcompact Glock 27, .40 caliber he always carried. He removed it from the holster. An ultrareliable weapon, the black Glock semiautomatic pistol had been altered to his own requirements: Ryan had added titanium night sights for low-light conditions, an extender magazine, and a Pearce Grip to accommodate his bulky hands and to give him a couple of extra rounds. He also had a spare clip in a leather magazine holder he carried in his pocket.

He saw no contradiction in being a priest and carrying a loaded weapon. The gun was to help defend the pope's life. Ryan had always been a keen shot but he abhorred killing, and had never once shot an animal, not even a gutter rat.

Still, he could punch a tight group into the center of a standard silhouette target at twenty-five yards, which was impressive enough. And the Glock's .40-caliber round packed a massive punch, could do almost as much damage as a .45. He tucked the Glock back in the holster.

Many of Ryan's security officers were former Italian police detectives and carabinieri, others were security professionals specially hired for the job, but all were dedicated professionals whose task it was to protect the pope and the Vatican, and safeguard its many priceless works of art and religious artifacts.

Ryan had gone over his security arrangements in detail with Cassini, and the head of the Curia seemed more than happy. He felt certain that Cassini was simply trying to reassure himself that everything was in order.

Ryan turned back to his desk, sat down, and studied the Nut File, so called because it contained details on every crazy and deranged person who had threatened to kill or harm the various popes over the last forty years. There were hundreds of letters, mostly anonymous, but a few were signed. Some threats were blatant, promising certain death, others more veiled, the mad, dangerous intent hidden between the lines, and quite a few came from oddball religious groups and sects throughout the world in whose warped minds the pontiff was marked for assassination.

All the letter writers' identities that could be traced and verified were recorded, along with reports from the relevant country's police and intelligence authorities who had copies passed on to them for investigation—the Security Office liaised with most of the Western intelligence organizations—but Ryan's office kept the originals.

Ryan read through the files again. They came from America, Europe, Asia, and the Middle and Far East. Most of the writers were quite obviously mad. It was amazing to think that anyone would want to kill a pontiff, but there you had it.

Ten minutes later, Ryan had just finished reading when there was a knock on his door and his secretary returned, looking worried. "Monsignor, I've just phoned the papal office to confirm your appointment at three P.M."

"Good man, Guido." Ryan had a raft of security issues he wanted to thrash out with his new boss.

"I'm afraid the Holy Father decided to cancel your meeting at the last minute and gave no reason. Now it seems there's a major security problem."

Ryan jumped to his feet, alarmed. "Explain."

"The appointments secretary tells me the Holy Father isn't in his rooms. He's searched the entire building and phoned all the Vatican offices but he's nowhere to be found. I've never heard the secretary so distressed."

"What are you saying? Out with it, Guido."

"It appears Pope Celestine has vanished."

24

At that same moment, less than two hundred yards away, a man dressed in a simple white gown stepped into the cool vaults of the Sistine Chapel.

There were no throngs of tourists admiring Michelangelo's ceiling or Botticelli's angels, for the Sistine was closed to pilgrims that morning. Just inside the chapel doors a young attendant was putting the finishing touches to an array of fresh flowers on the altar. When he looked round he saw a tall, imposing figure with the hood of his gown up, his face half covered.

The attendant frowned. "I'm sorry, but the chapel is out of bounds right now."

The man in the habit pulled back his hood and smiled. It was a smile of great warmth and charm, a smile that could melt the coldest heart. "I thought the chapel might be empty. My apologies."

The attendant flushed with embarrassment. "H-Holy Father. Please forgive me. I didn't recognize you."

The pope said gently, "It is I who should be forgiven, my son. I had thought I might visit the chapel. But I'm sorry if I've disturbed your work."

"No, of course not. The chapel was merely out of bounds while I tidied the altar. Please stay, Holy Father."

The pope nodded. "I wanted some time alone to say some prayers. Half an hour, no more. Would that be okay?"

"Of course. A great pleasure, Holy Father."

The pope nodded modestly as the attendant knelt to kiss his ring, then the man left, the chapel doors closed with an echo, and John Becket was alone.

The Sistine Chapel never ceased to amaze him, a testament to the mad genius of Michelangelo. A man who had spent ten years of his life lying on his back, hand-painting the murals and ceilings, for no payment but his board and lodging. John Becket glanced up at the vivid ceiling.

He always marveled at the way the many colors and images all came together to create an incredible whole. And it always reminded him that there were too many coincidences in this universe. The way it dovetails, fits together, the way physics so finely balances nature's existence.

In the seminary he had rediscovered what the Jesuit thinkers discovered long ago when they began searching the skies from their Vatican observatories, looking for answers. That whatever begins to exist has a cause—that the universe began to exist and has a cause. That this earth wasn't the product of some random unguided nature. How could it be when each single cell in the human body contained more information than entire volumes of an encyclopedia? We were not monkeys, not freakish mistakes of nature, not accidents. We were made deliberately and for a purpose by God.

John Becket believed that with all his heart.

Since his election, he had wanted to come here again, to pray alone. He was about to kneel in front of the altar when he felt something brush against the inside of his habit.

He remembered what it was. The envelope had been delivered to him by one of the Vatican secretaries. *"A letter for you, Holy Father. The lady who brought it said it was urgent, that its contents were private, meant for your eyes only. She said you would want to see the letter at once."*

Becket removed the plain white envelope from his habit. His name was handwritten in blue ink—*Holy Father, Pope Celestine VI*—and in the top left corner, the words *Personal and Private*. He tore open the envelope with curiosity. Inside was a single handwritten page and a folded newspaper clipping. As he read the page's contents, his face turned ashen. His hands shaking, he then unfolded the cutting from an Italian daily newspaper, dated two days previously. An article was headlined in typically dramatic Italian style:

MYSTERIOUS TWO-THOUSAND-YEAR-OLD SCROLL FOUND IN ISRAEL VANISHES AFTER BRUTAL MURDER

For a long time Becket stood there in deep shock, reading the article and the sheet of paper, his eyes devouring both with a look of utter disbelief on his face. Then he refolded the papers with trembling fingers, replaced them shakily in the envelope, and tucked it under his habit.

He felt struck by his own hypocrisy.

I insist that the church reveal its darkest secrets, while I keep my own dark secret to myself. One that could destroy not only me but also the church.

He was sweating despite the coolness of the chapel and he put a hand to his brow. There was a hint of agony in that simple gesture, and then slowly he lifted his garb and sat cross-legged on the floor. In moments like this, there was only one refuge that always gave him comfort.

He stretched out his body and prostrated himself in front of the altar, lying on his stomach, pressing his sweating face against the cold marble floor. He closed his eyes and began to pray, remembering the words of St. Augustine, *There are secrets in my heart that only You can know, my Lord.*

When he finished minutes later Becket heard a bell ringing in the Vatican grounds. He knew what he would have to do. Raising himself from the marble tiles, across the chapel he saw an ancient wooden door. He recalled that it led out through the gardens, toward the Vatican's east gate.

He crossed the floor, lifted the door's latch, and found himself in a familiar hallway that served as a cloakroom for the religious who toiled in the Vatican's gardens. Along one wall was a row of frayed gowns and friars' habits hung on garment hooks, below them pairs of muddied work boots.

The pope removed his own gown and changed into one of the brown habits. Then he covered his face with the hood, opened the door, and stepped out.

25

Five minutes later he walked toward the gate's security hut, his head down, his habit flapping about his legs. A pair of nuns passed him, their faces bowed in whispered conversation.

Becket smiled to himself as he imagined them both armed with pistols under their habits. He had heard that Vatican security used female officers dressed as nuns. He also heard the joke among the religious in Rome that it was impossible to purchase a new habit or clerical suit, because Sean Ryan's personnel had bought them all up so they could dress as priests and nuns for security purposes.

He approached the east gate, where a pair of Swiss Guards and a plainclothes officer manned the exit. Becket was hoping that it would be easier to get out of the Vatican than to enter it, and sure enough the guards said nothing as he went past them. The Holy City was full of clerics and he was just another one. He strode out into the bustling streets of Rome, filling his lungs with deep breaths as if to celebrate his freedom.

After the hushed walls of the Vatican, the city's bustle and traffic noise hit Becket like a brick. The air was warm and dusty, the streets alive with pedestrians and cars. He always considered Rome the most insane city on earth. Every driver was a lunatic and every car appeared to have at least one side mirror missing while their drivers tried to maneuver in the narrow backstreets.

Impatience and testosterone crackled like electricity in the air. But whether he liked it or not it was his city, too, for it belonged to him now, to Peter's successor. He kept walking east, crossing a bridge. Plunging his way through the crowds, he thought how absurd it was—here he was, the most protected man in Rome, and yet he had escaped his protectors. It neither alarmed nor amused him, no more than it did that no one in the passing crowds realized his true identity.

He walked for a long time and passed a pair of young men hanging out on a street corner. When they saw him they sneered and made the sign against the evil eye. He knew of this old Roman custom: its citizens either loved or hated the Vatican's clerics. Soon he left the crowds on the Via Cavour behind and when he turned into an alleyway he saw the young woman.

She was leaning against a wall, wearing high heels, clutching a white handbag, a cell phone pressed to her ear. Dark-haired and pretty, she was dressed in a short black skirt, a denim jacket, and a tight white top that displayed her bosom. The handbag had Gucci written on it but Becket imagined it was probably a cheap fake, the kind you saw touted by poor African immigrant vendors who plied the tourist backstreets. She saw him, put away her cell phone, and sashayed toward him. "Hello, Father."

"Hello, my child."

"Would you like to spend a little time with me, Father?"

Becket stopped in his tracks. He wasn't shocked by the prostitute's offer. But close up he saw that her left jaw was badly bruised. The damage was masked with thick makeup but it was still unmistakable.

She forced a smile, as if the effort was difficult. "What do you say, Father? I have an apartment nearby. We could have a good time together. I'll give you the best experience of your life. It'll make your eyeballs roll."

Becket knew that the fact the young woman was touting a clergyman for business spoke for itself. Priests were human. Some perhaps too human. He looked into the young woman's eyes and said gently, "What is your name, child?"

"Maria. What's yours?"

A powerful anger rose in Becket's chest as he studied the woman's bruises. "Who did this to you? Who hurt you?"

She fell silent. Becket was certain his question had touched a vulnerable nerve. He went to put up a hand to gently examine her face but she drew back. "Don't touch me," she said, suddenly defensive.

"You need medical attention, my child. Your jaw—"

"Do you want to spend time with me or not?" the woman snapped back.

Becket wasn't struck by the direct language—he had heard much worse—but by the irony of the situation. Here he was, the pope, being propositioned by a young woman.

"Please understand, I simply want to help you."

"Then how about you buy me a drink? There's a café around the corner. Even a coffee will do."

"I have no money, child. Please, let me see your face."

When she realized that she was getting no customer, the woman glanced up and down the alley and said, "Listen, I don't need your help. If the pimps around here see a goody two-shoes trying to interfere on their turf they'll do the same to you. Now get lost, and I'm saying that for your own good, Father. Beat it." She went to lean against the wall and light a cigarette.

"But you really need to see a doctor," Becket called after her.

The woman drew on her cigarette. "I'll be fine. Didn't you hear me? It's a dangerous place around here. Get lost."

Two young men entered the alleyway. The woman named Maria forced another smile as she went to approach them. "Hey, you guys want to have a good time?"

Becket suppressed the ire in his heart. He stared up at the alleyway's nameplate for directions, committed it to his memory, and hurried on.

He came to a littered side street and stopped in front of a terraced house. The double front door was painted blue, its crumbling sandstone walls at least eighteenth century. He yanked a bellpull and a tinkling noise echoed somewhere inside. Moments later he heard bolts being slid. A double door opened and a woman stood there. She was middle-aged, with a buxom matronly figure. She smiled at her visitor. "Yes?"

Becket didn't speak but lifted his head. When the shocked woman saw his face beneath the hood she put a hand to her mouth. "John—"

Becket's brow glistened with sweat. "I got the letter. We need to talk, Anna."

The woman glanced up and down the empty street to make sure no one had seen them and then she ushered him inside.

PART FOUR

26

Jack sweated inside the Ford pickup. They had entered Jordan over a hundred miles ago and Josuf was speeding along a stretch of open desert road, the dusty windshield spattered with dead flies, the late afternoon sun hot as a furnace.

"The air-conditioning *kaput*," Josuf told them, cursing the weak stream of cool air that flowed from the cabin's dashboard. They had left the windows open but still it was blistering hot. Endless sand plains stretched across either side, broken only by the occasional palm-fringed wadi or the rusting wrecks of abandoned vehicles littering the side of the road.

Yasmin sat between Jack and Josuf, the pickup cabin cramped. A pair of furry dice dangled from the rearview mirror, the dashboard jam-packed with stuck-on pictures of Josuf's extended family.

The Bedu kept a firm grip on the steering wheel and his foot to the floor, the Ford chewing up the desert road. "From here on it gets more dangerous. Entering Jordan was easy, but where we cross the Syrian border there are often army patrols. If we meet one, please let me do the talking."

"If you say so." Jack felt the tension rise in the cabin. For the last half hour there had been no road signs and it amazed him to think that Josuf could navigate without maps or a GPS system. But then it stood to reason that the desert's geography had to be in the Bedu's blood.

"Don't worry, Mr. Cane, you and the lady will be safe. My cousin is serving with the Syrian army and has promised to guide us over the border."

"You're sure he won't let us down?"

"Not Faisal. He's as reliable as the dawn."

Jack tried to relax but found it impossible. If they were caught illegally crossing the Syrian border, they could spend years in prison.

Josuf said proudly, "The Syrian military likes to enlist the Bedu, as do the Jordanians, and even the Israelis. They make excellent soldiers. Faisal is an officer."

"What happens after we meet him?"

"He'll lead us to Maloula."

"Tell me about the monastery."

"All I know is that it was once part of an Arab fort, built over a thousand years ago. The monastery is still in use and is a place of Christian pilgrimage."

Jack wiped sweat from his brow. They had crossed the Is-raeli–Jordanian border at the Allenby Bridge. For the last two hours they had driven across a ribbon of coarse roads through endless desert. Before they had left Qumran, Josuf had sent Yasmin back to the camp to pack. On the floor between Jack's feet was an overnight bag that Yasmin had stashed with a clean change of clothes, underwear, and toiletries for both of them.

Josuf depressed the windshield-wash button but when a few miserable squirts hit the dusty glass, he pulled to the side of the road and kept the engine running.

"What's up?" Jack asked.

"I must fill the windshield bottle with water. I have a plastic container in the back." Josuf reached under his seat and plucked out a set of number plates, along with a screwdriver. "I need also to fit Syrian license plates. Not false, but genuine. My vehicle is registered in three countries."

"Do you pay taxes in any of them?"

Josuf laughed, flashing his silver tooth. "I try not to, Mr. Cane."

"When do we cross the border?"

"We crossed it five minutes ago."

27

Josuf went to raise the hood and Jack said to Yasmin, "You look distracted. Are you okay?"

"I'm trying not to think what might happen if we get caught. I've heard scary stories about the Syrian secret police. People getting locked up for years without trial, and even being tortured."

Jack felt the furnace heat of the desert fill the cabin and took a slug of bottled water. "Don't dwell on it. Have you ever heard of this St. Paul's Monastery before?"

"Never."

"If we had a signal around here, maybe we could try the Internet?"

"I'll try." Yasmin plucked out her cell phone, flicked it open, and after a few moments said, "No, I can't get a signal."

Outside, Josuf finished under the hood. The Bedu slammed it shut and began using the screwdriver to attach the number plates.

Jack looked at Yasmin, struck by her near-perfect features, her almond eyes and bronzed skin. "By the way, I appreciate you coming along."

Yasmin smiled and touched his arm. "I think you're starting to bring out the maternal instinct in me. Besides, you needed someone to keep you company aside from Josuf."

Jack felt that same familiar stab of electricity as she touched him. She wasn't wearing shorts now but a black Arab hijab that covered her entire body, except the face veil was left open. The hijab had been Josuf's idea so that she wouldn't attract attention. "You could be right."

Josuf came back and climbed into his seat. As he stashed away the old number plates he suddenly said hoarsely, "I think we have company."

Jack peered beyond the windshield and felt his heart skip. A huge dust trail plumed behind two canvas-topped trucks painted in desert camouflage as they streaked across the sand. They were clearly police or military vehicles and Jack saw that each had a machine-gunner standing in the back. "Tell me we're about to meet this military cousin of yours."

Josuf's face drained of color as he shook his head. "This looks like a Syrian border patrol."

The vehicles turned toward them, the canvas tops rippling as they picked up speed. Jack said desperately, "Can't you reverse and drive back over the border?"

"It's too late for that." Josuf sounded desperate.

"Try, for goodness' sake," Jack urged.

Josuf reversed the pickup, revved the engine, and turned in a half circle, just as a heavy-caliber machine gun erupted and the desert to the right of them kicked up sand. A second later another loud volley smacked into the road ahead of them, gouging out chunks of asphalt.

"Hey, they mean business!" Jack exclaimed.

The Syrian trucks roared closer. Two of the vehicles cut out in front of the pickup. Josuf slammed on the brakes in the middle of the road as half a dozen soldiers armed with Kalashnikov assault rifles jumped down, cocking their weapons. One of the soldiers screamed an order.

Josuf's face was drenched in sweat. "They want us to step out and keep our hands in the air."

"Is your cousin among them?"

"No, Mr. Cane."

"Terrific."

28

A fresh-faced lieutenant stepped down from one of the trucks. He brandished an automatic pistol and shouted in Arabic, "Step out of the vehicle and keep your hands high."

Josuf climbed out and obeyed, followed by Jack and Yasmin.

The lieutenant stepped closer and studied them suspiciously. "Who are you? What are you doing on Syrian soil?" he demanded.

"A mistake, sir," Josuf pleaded. "I realized the moment I saw your patrol. I'm lost, sir."

The lieutenant was wary. "The road is well signposted. How are you lost?"

"I can't read, sir," Josuf replied.

The lieutenant pointed his pistol at Josuf's face, then swiveled the weapon toward Jack and Yasmin. "Let me see your papers. Search all of them and their vehicle," he ordered his men, then pointed his weapon at Yasmin. "You, hand over your papers."

Sweat beaded Jack's forehead. He saw Yasmin stricken with fear as two soldiers came forward and searched him and Josuf. Another kept his Kalashnikov trained on Yasmin as she fumbled to hand over her passport.

The lieutenant scrutinized their documents. His eyes

sparked when he saw Jack's American passport. "So, you are an American?" he said in English.

"That's what the passport says."

"You speak Arabic?"

"A little."

The officer's eyes narrowed. "Your passports have Israeli stamps. What are you doing in this area?"

Jack said, "It's like the driver said. We got lost."

"But you speak Arabic. You could have read the signs."

Jack shook his head. "I guess I don't read the language all that well."

In an instant the lieutenant slapped him across the jaw.

Jack felt the raw, stinging blow and clapped a hand to his cheek. "Hey, I told you the truth. I didn't notice any signs that said we had entered Syria."

The lieutenant aimed his pistol at Jack's head. "Liar. We'll soon see if you're telling the truth or not, American."

"Lieutenant Farsa."

A major stepped out of the second truck. Jack had been so preoccupied that he hadn't noticed him in the passenger seat. The man wore a crisply pressed uniform. His dark eyes and pencil-thin mustache gave him a dangerous look. A cigarette was balanced delicately between his thumb and forefinger and he studied his three captives. "I am Major Harsulla, of the Mukhabarat, the Syrian secret police. Who are our guests, Lieutenant?"

The major's voice was surprisingly gentle. The lieutenant handed him the three passports. "The old one's a Bedu, his passport's Jordanian. It seems the vehicle belongs to him. The woman's Lebanese, the man's an American."

The major's eyebrows rose with interest and he flicked away his unfinished cigarette. "American, you say?"

"Yes, sir."

The major grinned. "Well now, isn't that interesting?" He studied the passports zealously before looking at Jack and Yasmin. Finally, his gaze shifted to Josuf. "You say you got lost, old man?"

"Yes, sir, we got lost, certainly. This is all a terrible mistake."

The major closed the passports and tapped them in his palm. "Lost? I doubt it somehow. You Bedu know these deserts better than a blind camel."

Josuf pleaded, "Please, sir. What I say is true, as Allah is my judge. I wouldn't lie."

"We'll soon find out. You're all under arrest."

One of the soldiers finished searching the pickup and came back brandishing several pairs of license plates, along with a curved Arab dagger in a sheath. "We found these under the driver's seat, sir."

The major examined the plates, then angrily tossed them on the sand. He held up the curved Arab knife. "What's this for, Bedu? Picking your teeth?"

"It's a tradition for my people to carry knives. The major must know that."

"And false number plates too?" The major struck Josuf across the face. He staggered back, blood on his lip.

The major removed his pistol and sneered. "Your lies will cost you your life, you old fool." He cocked his pistol and aimed at Josuf's head. For a second or two it looked as if he really meant to shoot, then he grinned and released the hammer, decocking the weapon. "Perhaps I'll keep the pleasure of beating the truth out of you and your friends back at headquarters." He replaced his pistol in its holster and snapped his fingers at one of the soldiers. "Put them on board the truck. Have one of the men follow in their pickup."

"Yes, sir."

The major barked at the lieutenant. "Continue with the patrol. Search the area in case there are other intruders."

"Yes, sir." The lieutenant snapped off a salute and went to join his men in the first truck.

The major turned to Jack. "For your sake, I hope your presence here can be explained, American. Do you have anything more to say?"

"I'd like to talk with a U.S. consul, if there is one."

The major grinned. "I doubt it. But even a consul couldn't help. All of you could be spies. And the penalty for spying against the Syrian state is death." He snapped his fingers at his men. "Put them all in the back of the truck. If any of these vermin try to escape, shoot them."

29

The helicopter carrying Lela Raul touched down at Ben-Gurion Airport with a clatter of engine noise. When she stepped out of the cabin she saw a small, cheerful-looking man wearing a flowered beach shirt, waving from the tarmac. He came over to join her. "Good to see you again, Lela. How've you been?"

"Ari, what are you doing here?" Lela was surprised to see Ari Tauber. They had known each other since serving together with the Jerusalem police force, until several years back, when Tauber had somehow ended up in Mossad. And as colleagues, it had transpired that both their grandfathers had even served together in the same Jewish partisan group that fought Nazis in Ukraine.

Ari took her arm warmly and led her toward the terminal. "I could ask you the same question, but I'd be lying if I said I didn't know the answer. Come on, I've got my car outside."

Minutes later Ari drove them in his blue Ford toward the whitewashed sprawl of Tel Aviv. Lela asked, "How are the wife and kids?"

"Sharon is still working as a medical secretary. And Nathan's nine now, if you can believe it. Geli is hitting fourteen and as beautiful as her mother. And if I needed proof I've got a procession of pimple-faced teenage boys knocking on our front door every ten minutes, smelling of cheap aftershave."

Lela said more seriously, "What's the story, Ari? Why does the head of Mossad want to see me?"

Ari shook his head. "I'm afraid you'll have to wait until my boss talks with you. I'm under strict orders to keep my mouth shut. I was on my day off, enjoying a family barbecue and a few cold Heinekens when I got the call from headquarters."

"But you know what it's about?"

Ari's cheerful expression changed to a serious look. "I'll have to refuse to answer that question on the grounds that it might incriminate me. Relax, you'll know soon enough, Lela. Now, tell me how life's been treating you."

Fifteen minutes later Ari pulled into the private grounds of a concrete building in Herzliya. The blue and white flag of Israel, the Star of David in the center, fluttered on a flagpole above Mossad's headquarters. Two uniformed armed guards stood at a barrier gate and when they checked Ari's papers and Lela's ID, the car was waved through.

The Ford drew up in front of the building and a guard came forward to open the car doors, a machine pistol draped across his chest.

Lela stepped out and Ari said, "Ever met the head of Mossad before?"

"Never."

Ari grinned and clapped a hand on Lela's shoulder. "Then you're about to join the ranks of the chosen few. Come on, I'll take you up to the top floor to meet God himself."

30

Julius Weiss looked like a harmless enough eccentric. A stocky man with cold eyes and an intense stare, his abiding obsession was the security of Israel. With the title of *HaMemuneh*, or responsible one, he held the military rank of general, but as Mossad chief he never wore a uniform, preferring instead the anonymous garb of open-neck shirt and worn leather sandals.

Weiss was seated behind his desk that afternoon, reading a file, when Ari Tauber led Lela into the office. Weiss greeted her with a stare, then shut the file and came round from his desk to shake her hand. "Inspector Raul. How was your trip?"

"It would have been better if I'd known why I'd been summoned."

A smile flickered on Weiss's face. "Go grab a coffee, Ari."

"Yes, sir." Tauber withdrew, closing the door after him.

Weiss indicated a chair. "Take a seat, Inspector. My name is Julius Weiss, and I'm the head of Mossad. I have an interest in a case of yours. The murder at Qumran of an American archaeologist named Professor Green. Would you care to fill me in on what's been happening in the case?"

"With respect, sir, the case is a police matter."

Weiss arched a bushy eyebrow, as if unused to being questioned. "And now I'm making it Mossad's business. An ancient scroll that was found at Qumran has also been stolen, correct?"

"Yes."

"Any artifacts discovered on Israeli soil are the property of the state. In these circumstances, such a theft from the state is my responsibility. I have already spoken with your superior and he assured me of your full cooperation. I believe he told you as much?"

Lela said defiantly, "Yes, he did. But that doesn't mean I have to like Mossad sticking its nose into police business."

Weiss picked up his telephone handset and bluntly offered it to Lela. "Maybe I should call your boss again and ask him to repeat his recommendation to you."

Lela met Julius Weiss's laser stare. "What exactly do you want to know?"

Weiss slapped down the phone, his authority established. "Everything, Inspector, and leave nothing out."

Ten minutes later, Lela finished telling Weiss everything she knew. He considered thoughtfully, studying her notebook open on his desk, reading the translated portion of the text that Jack Cane had given her. Finally, Weiss looked up and said, "Just to be clear, apart from these seemingly bizarre lines of text and the reference to Jesus Christ, nobody knows the full contents of the scroll, correct?"

Lela nodded. "Cane said they couldn't risk peeling open the fragile leather further because it might cause damage. But he said the professor believed the document would serve as a powerful confirmation of the actual existence of Jesus Christ. Apparently, such evidence isn't easily come by."

"I take it he didn't have time to estimate the scroll's likely age with carbon dating."

"No he didn't. Our forensics people will carbon-date the parchment flakes they found. But Jack Cane had seen other scroll examples from the first century A.D. and seemed certain that it dated from then."

Weiss sighed, placed his hands behind his head, and sat back, resting one of his ancient sandals on the desk. "And now the scroll's gone and a man's been murdered and the chief suspect has disappeared. Not good, is it?"

"No." Lela thought that the worn, upturned soles of the Mossad chief's sandals looked badly in need of repair.

"By the way, I knew your father, Inspector. We served together during the Six-Day War. He was a very brave and honorable soldier. I admired him greatly."

"Thank you."

Weiss stood, crossed to the window, and said without turning back, "If you're even half the person your father was, I want you to remain on the case. But from now on, this is not just a police investigation, Inspector, it's also Mossad's domain. Cane's discovery may have grave repercussions for the state of Israel."

Lela frowned. "Can you explain?"

Weiss nodded. "I will. But at a time when I decide it's appropriate. For now, just accept my word that the inquiry will almost certainly turn out to be a lot more profound than a simple murder."

"I'm not sure I like the idea of being kept in the dark about any aspect of a murder case."

Weiss came back from the window and said forcefully, "What you like or don't like is immaterial. I still want you on board, working alongside Mossad. Not only because I believe you're an excellent investigator but because you know Jack Cane."

"Who told you that?"

"My people spoke to Sergeant Mosberg. Do you think Cane's involved in this murder?"

"It's too early to say, but I know his character. He's a good man. Not someone who'd be easily driven to commit homicide."

Weiss raised an eye. "A good man who's gone on the run after a murder in which he's a chief suspect. Such a man is either very stupid or very guilty, don't you think? When was the last time you saw Cane before this morning?"

"When I was nineteen."

"Forgive me, Inspector, but people change."

Lela didn't speak.

Weiss said, "You know the suspect, which ought to help us hunt him down. You've also worked with Ari Tauber, I understand."

"We were partners in Jerusalem Homicide."

"Ari's a good man for you to work with. The scroll is an artifact of immense historical and religious importance that belongs to the Israeli people, and I want it back." Weiss crossed to his desk. "I wish you the best of luck on your journey."

"Journey?"

"You're about to have an interesting trip. Mossad has gotten a tip that Jack Cane and Yasmin Green will attempt to illegally cross the desert into Syria sometime this evening, in the company of a Bedouin guide. Their destination is an old Catholic monastery at a place called Maloula, near Damascus. A priest there has a reputation for translating black-market parchments."

Lela was amazed. "How do you know all that?"

Weiss tapped the side of his nose. "My secret for now. The Bedu may know the desert like the backs of their hands, but

Cane's an American with an Israeli stamp on his passport. My fear is, if he's caught, the Syrians will either shoot him or throw him in jail, and then we'll never get our hands on him. Worse still, he may have the scroll in his possession when the Syrians find him. And then they would never hand such a document back to us."

Lela said, "Why not simply stop him from crossing into Syria?"

"I want to know what Cane's up to at Maloula and if he can lead us to the scroll. Simply stopping him wouldn't help us with that objective, now would it?"

"Why would he cross into Syria?"

"I'm hoping you and Ari will find that out." Weiss stood and adjusted his trousers. "A special forces military helicopter is waiting to take you from a nearby air base and drop you at a desert location inside the Syrian border. Ari will explain all the rest. What's the matter? You look concerned, Inspector."

"There's the slight matter of Syria's ban on Israeli citizens entering that country. If I'm caught I risk being charged with spying."

Weiss smiled. "True. But if I'm any judge of character, you'll take that risk. You want to get to the bottom of this case involving your old friend Cane as much as I do. Syria's certainly a dangerous place and its secret police are first-class. But Ari will have false passports with visas for you both, along with a cover story, expertly provided by Mossad. You also speak fluent Arabic, I believe?"

"Yes."

"Good; so does Ari. He's waiting outside, ready to get this mission under way. Any questions?"

"When do I leave?"

"You already have. Good-bye, Inspector."

31

ROME
7 P.M.

The restaurant known as L'Eau Vive is on the Via Monterone, a narrow backstreet near the Pantheon that the tourists tend to ignore. Owned by the Vatican, from the outside it looks quite ordinary, almost drab-looking, but inside the restaurant the walls are hung with expensive paintings, and the plush candlelit tables sparkle with silver and crystal.

Although open to the public, almost all of the clientele that afternoon were senior clergy, powerful businessmen, and bankers conducting important dealings with the Holy See. L'Eau Vive's prices are much too steep for a humble parish priest.

Ryan noticed that the restaurant was quite full as he entered. A nun approached him. She was strikingly beautiful in an elegant long gown and her face had a look of studied piety. "Have you a reservation?" she asked politely.

Ryan smiled charmingly. "Monsignor Sean Ryan. I believe I'm expected. One of the private rooms."

"Ah, yes." The nun was immediately deferential. "Follow me, Your Grace."

Ryan was led past a large statue of the Virgin, standing in its grotto in a corner, to a discreet alcove at the back of the restaurant. When the nun pulled back the thick red curtain, the room was almost dark, lit only by two candles set in silver holders on the table. The sole occupant was a man, his face in shadow. Ryan slipped inside, the curtain closed, and he found himself facing Cassini, wearing a clerical black suit with a gold cross in his lapel. "Sean. It was good of you to come on such short notice."

"My pleasure, Your Eminence."

"What will you have to eat? I can recommend the saltim-bocca, or the duck filet in Grand Marnier. Both are always excellent."

Ryan picked a modest fettuccine, served with a crisp side salad. Cassini ordered the wine. An expensive Barolo, as befitted his status. "So, Sean. What news do you have for me?"

"Security has been stepped up in all areas. I've had extra guards stationed everywhere, uniformed and the plainclothes variety. No one will get in or out of the Vatican's restricted sectors without proper papers, I can promise you that. Even the zones open to tourists are being patrolled with extreme vigilance."

"Excellent. As always, your professionalism puts me at ease." Cassini looked genuinely pleased but noticed Ryan's face suddenly crease with anxiety. "You look troubled. Is there something on your mind?"

"I think you could say that, Your Eminence. A worrying development, as they say."

Before Ryan could speak further, there was a rustle of the curtain and the wine arrived, served by the nun. When Cassini nodded his approval with the first sip, the nun filled both their glasses. A waiter arrived with their food, serving them from silver platters. Their tasks completed, the nun and waiter silently withdrew. Cassini waited to be certain they were gone, regarded the food on the china plates with obvious relish, and then offered Ryan the briefest of smiles. "Grace first, I think. Then we talk."

Cassini joined his hands, lowering his head as Ryan did likewise. *"Bless us, O Lord, and these Thy gifts . . ."*

32

The cuisine was delicious, as always. Cassini was a man who relished his food and he wasted no time tucking into his meal. "So, Sean, what's bothering you?"

"I asked the Holy Father to curtail his movements and agree to wear a bulletproof vest under his garments at all times, at least for the next few months."

"And what was his response?"

"He refused point-blank. Looked me in the eye and said, 'I trust in God.'"

Cassini speared a piece of tender saltimbocca with his fork, popped it in his mouth, and washed it down with a mouthful of Barolo. "Knowing John Becket, I'm hardly surprised. He's a remarkable man who doesn't scare easily."

"Such bravery is all very admirable, Your Eminence, as is his faith, but it's my job to protect him. And despite what most people think, assassination of a public figure isn't such a difficult thing."

"Explain."

"Take the slaying of Israeli prime minister Yitzhak Rabin. Or Jack and Bobby Kennedy. Or even the attempt on Ronald Reagan's life. High-profile political leaders, all tightly protected. But still each of them got hit. Why? Because no matter how careful the planning or how stringent the security cordon around them, all their assassins needed was the tiniest chink in the armor."

"What are you saying, Sean?"

"That there are no guarantees. No matter how tight a ring of steel we put around the pontiff, history will tell you there's always a chink: a window of opportunity when an assassin can strike, when he'll have surprise on his side. He doesn't even have to be particularly intelligent or an expert marksman. All he has to be is lucky."

Cassini sighed. "Please, go on."

"Ali Agca is a classic example. They might have called him 'the jackal,' but he wasn't particularly bright, a mentally disturbed Turkish peasant really. Yet despite the fact that there were thousands of Rome police, carabinieri, and security officials in the vicinity of the pope's cavalcade that day, he managed to get off five shots, three of them hitting their target."

"But Agca was trained by the KGB in Libya. He was a skilled assassin."

Ryan, only half his fettuccine eaten, pushed aside his plate and shook his head. "Trained he might have been, but he was never more than a zealous amateur, like most would-be assassins. And the proof is that he failed to kill his target and got caught."

"What's your point?"

"That I dread to think what chance we'd stand against a real professional. And there's always another jackal who could come from anywhere."

"Where, for example?"

There was noise beyond the curtain, a discreet pause, and then the waiter arrived to clear away their plates. "Dessert, Your Eminence?"

Cassini consulted the menu, chose a rich banoffee, followed by coffee laced with fragrant amaretto, and for afterward, a special reserve cognac. Ryan ordered the simplest dessert on offer: fresh fruit salad, drizzled with lavender honey, and tea to follow. They waited until their desserts and refreshments arrived, and when the waiter left, Cassini savored a mouthful of banoffee. "You were about to tell me from where this jackal might come."

"Virtually any camp you'd care to mention. Catholicism, like any faith, has its own fair share of dissidents, fanatics with their own agendas, and insane people with grudges or deranged minds. Even terrorists like the Red Brigades, who plagued Italy for decades and were more than once suspected of attempting to kill the then Holy Father, were mostly right-wing Catholics."

Ryan ignored his dessert and spooned two sugars into his tea and stirred. "And then there are the ultratraditional, secretive lodges within the church, notorious for conspiring, which see any kind of change as a direct threat to their power and influence. Or the lunatic religions on the fringe, who believe the pope's some kind of Antichrist and want to see him dead. And I haven't even mentioned the many different Christian churches in America that are deeply suspicious of the Roman pope. The source of the danger could come from any one of those quarters, as you suggested."

"I know, and it's depressing me, Sean," Cassini said gloomily as he pushed aside his dessert plate. "Speaking of worrying developments, I've had my own."

"Your Eminence?"

Cassini reached inside his black suit jacket and produced a letter and envelope, kept in a clear plastic bag. "This turned up with my morning's post. Whether it was delivered deliberately or in error, I cannot say. My secretary showed it to me at once. I found it disturbing. I took the liberty, Sean, of placing it in a plastic bag." Cassini shrugged. "Don't ask me why, but I've seen certain detectives do it in films. What do they call it—an evidence bag?"

Ryan accepted the letter. Behind the clear plastic he saw that individual letters of the alphabet had been cut from newspapers to construct a message that was pasted onto a sheet of plain paper. The message read:

THE POPE IS THE ANTICHRIST. HE IS AN INSTRUMENT OF THE DEVIL. HE WILL RUIN THE CHURCH WITH HIS REVELATIONS AND MUST BE DESTROYED.

There was no signature, not that Ryan expected any. He raised his eyes. "No one else touched this, apart from you and your secretary?"

Cassini shook his head. "Not that I'm aware of."

Ryan carefully folded the letter and placed it in his inside pocket. "I'll need to have it checked out. It may be necessary to take the fingerprints of both you and your secretary, to eliminate you from any we might find on the evidence."

"I understand."

"May I ask if you informed the Holy Father?"

Cassini took another mouthful of the delicious Barolo. "No. I thought I'd leave that to you. You seem troubled. Is there something else on your mind, Sean?"

"The Holy Father disappeared this morning for at least two hours."

"Disappeared?"

"Left the Vatican walls. Where he went I have no idea.

When he showed up his secretary expressed anxiety that he couldn't find him. The pontiff simply brushed aside any concern."

Cassini shook his head vigorously. "That can't be allowed to happen again. It's absurd."

"This is why I propose that we place the Holy Father under surveillance. I would like your approval, Your Eminence."

Cassini finished the last mouthful of dessert, dabbed his lips, and tossed aside his napkin. "Of course. The pontiff's safety is paramount. But it must be discreet. I'd prefer if you handled it personally, Sean."

"You mean you want *me* to follow the Holy Father?"

"You're the head of security. Who else would be better qualified to keep an eye on him? Besides, you're trained in self-defense, and if the rumors from the security office are to be believed, you're an excellent shot."

Ryan raised an eye. "I'm a little rusty in both those departments, but if you insist."

"I do. This is a very delicate matter."

"Very well, but perhaps you'll talk with the Holy Father, Your Eminence? Try and convince him to at least curtail his movements and wear the bulletproof vest? After all, the church needs a pontiff, not another martyr."

33

The army truck slowed to a halt with a squeal of brakes. In the back Jack raised himself from the floor and helped Yasmin drag herself up. Beside them Josuf struggled to his feet and peered out beyond the canvas flap. "It seems we've arrived."

It was growing dark and they had halted beside a clump of palm trees next to a wadi. Ahead of them was a bustling town built at the foot of a sheer mountain. Some of the squat, whitewashed houses looked centuries old and hewn out of the mountain rock, others rose up steeply in tiers toward the summit. Windows were lit with the glow of oil lamps and the markets and food stalls in the narrow streets thronged with people. Jack saw a handful of Orthodox nuns among the crowd and noticed several church domes, one with a blue-painted cross on top.

The four armed soldiers in the back of the truck came alert as they heard the doors of the front cab open, the sound of feet hitting gravel. A moment later the Syrian major tore back the canvas flap. He grinned up at his captives and said in Arabic, "This is the end of the line. I'm sorry if it was a bumpy trip, but these desert roads are not exactly the best. How are you all?"

Jack jumped down, followed by the others. "It could be worse. We could be on our way to a prison cell in Damascus."

The major grinned and slapped Josuf on the back. "My performance wasn't bad, now was it?"

Josuf rubbed his jaw. "That slap of yours hurt, Cousin. You are the mongrel son of a mangy camel, but I forgive you."

The major laughed heartily. "A little pain is a small price to pay. You're still alive, aren't you?"

Josuf said, "At first when I didn't see you among the uniforms I thought we were finished. What kept you, Faisal?"

"My men and I bumped into the lieutenant's patrol. He insisted on joining us because of some minefields in the area. Still, it all came right in the end."

Jack said, "Won't the lieutenant get suspicious when he finds out that we're not in custody?"

The major grinned again. "How would he find that out? No junior officer with half a brain would question the secret police. As for my men, they're all from my tribe and I trust them with my life. Follow me."

He escorted them to Josuf's pickup, where he yanked open the driver's door and barked an order at the soldier behind the wheel. The man jumped down, first removing the Ford's ignition keys, before he tossed them to Josuf.

The major snapped off a salute. "I'll leave you here. You haven't far to go; just carry on past the village and you'll come to St. Paul's Monastery."

"My thanks, Cousin." Josuf and the major embraced and kissed each other on both cheeks, Arab style.

The major shook hands with Yasmin and Jack and offered them a map. "Take this, just in case the old goat that's driving you gets lost on the way back in the dark. The roads around here are poorly marked."

Josuf started the engine, and Yasmin climbed into the pickup, followed by Jack. "We appreciate your help, Major."

The major slapped the roof twice with the palm of his hand. "Drive carefully, and may Allah go with you."

34

The Black Hawk is a robust helicopter, one of the most successful ever built, with powerful twin GE turboshaft engines and a top cruising speed of over 150 knots. The one that Lela and Ari Tauber flew in that evening was a well-used special ops transporter, its mission ferrying them both to a rendezvous near the monastery of St. Paul.

Lela tried to ignore the noise as she and Ari sat on a couple of bucket seats up near the cockpit, the chop of the blades a constant throb in their ears. Five feet away, standing near the flight crew, was a small, balding man with a mustache and cautious eyes who held a map and a pencil torch in his hand and talked with the crew via a communications headset.

Ari said above the rotor noise, "Saul's our dispatcher. He's going to make sure the pilots drop us at our rendezvous and not on some dung pile in the wrong part of the desert."

"Have you ever done this kind of thing before?" Lela shouted above the din.

Ari smiled. "I better not answer that on the grounds it might incriminate me."

"Where are we now?"

The man named Saul must have overheard the question because he removed one of the headset cans from his ear and smiled over at Lela. "We've just crossed the Jordanian border. Another forty-five minutes will have us at our target. Sit back, relax, enjoy the ride."

The man named Saul turned back to talk with the flight crew. Lela said to Ari, "What about the Jordanian or Syrian radar and their air defenses? Couldn't we get shot at?"

Ari grinned. "What radar? It doesn't operate at low altitudes. We simply keep to under a thousand feet. As for air defenses, Saul tells me that we'll be keeping well away from the established Jordanian and Syrian patrol routes." He shrugged. "Don't ask me how Mossad knows the routes, but intelligence collected by American satellites probably plays a big part."

Lela peered out of the nearest cabin window. At a dusky, moonlit seven hundred feet all she could see was endless desert, dotted with the dark outline of an occasional gnarled tree. The Black Hawk buffeted in a gust of wind, and then settled. "What if we encounter a technical problem and have to land short of our drop?"

"No problem, Lela. We've got another Black Hawk flying shotgun three minutes behind us that'll pick us up."

"Your boss seems to have thought of everything."

Ari smiled. "Did you get a load of his sandals? They look like something he stole off a dead monk. Speaking of footwear, I've got something for you." He opened a couple of black canvas bags at his feet and removed a pair of plain, flat black shoes for Lela. Next came undergarments, then black jeans, a cotton top, and a female Arab gown, a black hijab, which would cover her completely from head to toe.

Ari said, "The clothes are all Syrian made and you can change into them now but keep the hijab handy. Slip it over whatever you're wearing if there's a chance we might be stopped by a Syrian patrol. That way they're less likely to search you. They're generally respectful toward women. You remember our cover story?"

"We're traveling to Damascus for our wedding anniversary to visit relatives."

Ari nodded. "Just stick to the bare bones of the story and let me do the talking. A Syrian patrol wouldn't expect the woman to do much of the explaining. These are your documents."

He handed Lela a Syrian passport. She flicked through it and saw what looked like the actual snapshot from her own passport, but in the photograph she was wearing an Arab headdress with her face exposed. Even her passport signature style matched, and her birth date, but the document was in the name of a woman named Melina Rasifa.

Lela marveled at how authentic the forgery looked. "How did Mossad get my photograph?"

"Our forgers had to work fast so they pulled the copy held at the passport office. They had less than three hours once Weiss decided he wanted you on board. They did a pretty good job, don't you think?"

"The headdress looks so realistic. Did they doctor the shot by computer?"

Ari nodded. "Forgers can do wonders these days with technology, and Mossad's guys are the best in the business."

"Your boss said we'd have help. What exactly did he mean?"

"Two of our agents in Syria will be waiting on the ground, ready to give us whatever assistance we need." Ari consulted his watch. "They ought to be at the rendezvous by now. I'm hoping we can wrap this up quickly but then you never know. There's just more thing, Lela."

Ari took two compact Sig 9mm automatic pistols from

one of the bags. One pistol had a black leather hip holster, which he took for himself, and the second weapon had an ankle holster, complete with Velcro straps. "You better take one of these. You might prefer the ankle holster. Are you familiar with this make of firearm?"

"Yes."

"Good." He handed the second Sig to Lela, along with three spare loaded magazines and a matte black silencer, then added with a smile, "You know what they say: The best gunfight is the one that doesn't happen. Hopefully, we won't get involved in any trouble. But these are for what our American cousins like to call in English, JIC. Just-in-case."

The dispatcher named Saul shouted above the din. "Max fifteen minutes to the drop, you guys!"

Lela tensed. It was almost impossible to believe that she was in a helicopter flying over the Syrian desert, risking her life and hunting down Jack Cane as a suspected murderer and thief. She felt her chest tighten and her heart quicken. "What does the Qumran scroll contain, Ari? It has to be something remarkable for Mossad to go to all this trouble. And why all the secrecy?"

Ari's smile vanished abruptly. "That's a subject I can't discuss, Lela. Now, we better go over our cover story one more time, just so we're clear."

35

"We are here," Josuf announced.

Darkness had fallen, the heat still oppressive as the lights of Josuf's pickup turned onto a narrow desert track. Five hundred yards outside Maloula, silhouetted against the full moon, Jack saw the outline of an old fortress with Arab-style turrets, not a single light on inside. The track led past a cluster of ruined yellow sandstone outbuildings.

Yasmin said, "Are you sure this is the place? It looks abandoned."

"It is here, madame. My cousin assured me." Josuf drove along the track until they came to a cobbled square in front of the fortress. He halted the pickup and rolled down his window to get a better look. In the wash of the headlights they saw a citadel with mustard-colored walls. Set in the middle was an archway with a pair of oak doors, studded with rusty nails. High above the archway was a wrought-iron crucifix. Jack said, "Do you have a flashlight, Josuf?"

The Bedu reached behind the cabin and produced a scuffed industrial flashlight made of sturdy yellow plastic.

Jack took it and stepped out of the car. "Let's take a look."

The others followed as Jack flicked on the flashlight and walked over to the oak doors. The ancient wood was split by wide cracks. A square view-hole in the door was protected by a metal grille, a bellpull next to it. Jack shone the powerful beam through one of the cracks and saw a lush courtyard garden beyond, silvered by lunar light, a stone fountain bubbling away.

Yasmin asked, "What do you see?"

"Take a look for yourself," Jack answered.

"It looks deserted," Yasmin said, peering inside, and then Josuf did the same.

"Let's find out if anyone's home." Jack yanked the bellpull and a tinkle sounded somewhere in the darkness.

When no one appeared, he pulled the bell again until finally they heard echoing footsteps scurrying toward them. A bolt scraped, the view-hole opened, and Jack's torch lit up the face of a young monk wearing a worn white habit. He said hoarsely in Arabic, "Yes? What do you want?"

"We've come to speak with one of your priests."

"Who are you?"

"My name is Jack Cane, and this is Yasmin Green and Josuf Bin Doha."

The young monk frowned. "There is only one priest here: Father Novara. The rest are brother monks."

"Then I guess it must be Father Novara we need to see. We have important business to discuss with him."

The monk was reluctant. "What business?"

Jack said, "It's private, for his ears only. If you could please tell the priest that we need to talk with him urgently."

The monk glanced out warily at their pickup. "You must wait," he answered, and closed the view-hole. They heard his footsteps fade away but they returned after a few minutes and the view-hole snapped open again. This time it was a much older, gray-bearded monk wearing a white habit. He had a broad, intelligent-looking forehead and his face was full of strength, firm and pious. He spoke perfect English with no trace of an Italian accent. "I am Father Vincento Novara. What do you want here?"

Jack said, "It's complicated, Father. But if you could spare us a little of your time we promise to explain everything."

"You're not Syrians. Where are you from?"

"We've traveled a long way to find you, Father. I'm American, Josuf here is Bedu, and—"

"I'm very sorry, but it's late." The priest interrupted impatiently. "And I am about to start evening prayers. Come back tomorrow."

"Father—"

"Please respect my wishes."

The priest turned to go, but Jack said, "I believe you've translated a number of ancient scrolls for certain Syrian friends of yours, Father."

The monk's jaw dropped in response. "Who—who told you this?"

"Let us in and I'll explain everything. Otherwise, I'll have to involve the police."

The priest turned ashen. "Let me see some identification."

They handed their passports through the grille and the priest's face disappeared for a few moments, but they saw his features illuminated by the flicker of an oil lamp as he scrutinized their documents. Father Novara frowned as if trying to make up his mind, then he fumbled for something. They heard a rattle of keys, a bolt was slid, and the gates opened into a beautiful stone-flagged courtyard, decorated in the Arab style, full of bubbling fountains and water features.

Father Novara stood there, a tough, gnarled little man with a powerful physique and a head too big for his body. His frayed white habit had a knotted cord at his waist from which hung a cross. He carried an oil lamp and a bunch of keys in his hand.

"It seems," he said bleakly, "that we need to talk."

36

Father Novara led them across the fountained courtyard, his habit flapping as he walked. They moved under a darkened archway and came to a solid wooden door. The priest held up the oil lamp as he ushered them through the door. "This way, please."

They entered a room with whitewashed walls. A table and a couple of benches were set in the middle, the floor covered in worn stone slabs. Novara seemed uneasy as he closed the door.

Jack tried to draw him out. "You speak excellent English, Father."

"I ought to, it's my native tongue. Despite my surname I was born in England, of Italian parents. I studied archaeology and ancient languages at Cambridge many years ago, before I came here."

"It seems an interesting old monastery."

The priest shrugged as he used his lamp to light another that hung from a nail in the wall. "It was an Arab citadel until the ninth century before becoming a Catholic monastery, though nowadays there are only a few of us monks left. But that's not what we're here to discuss. Tell me exactly why you came."

Jack said, "We're interested in a couple of black-market Syrian dealers. One in particular, a man with a withered hand. He's known to us as Pasha. I believe he's a friend of yours."

A muscle twitched in the priest's cheek. "Who told you this?"

Jack said, "That really doesn't matter. But we need to find him."

The priest put a palm to his forehead as if in deep thought, and let it rest there a moment, his intelligent eyes studying each of his visitors in turn before his hand fell away and his gaze returned to Jack. "You are merely fishing for information, aren't you? Trying to find out what I might know. But I really don't know what you are talking about. You have been misled."

Yasmin said, "I don't think so, Father. We know that you've helped this man translate stolen Dead Sea parchments."

Father Novara looked indignant. "That's preposterous. A total lie. I helped no one do such a thing."

"Maybe you'd like to reconsider, Father? Josuf's brother once did business with the man, sold him ancient scrolls. He knows that you helped to translate them."

The priest's face muscle twitched again but he was steadfast. "He can say all he wants but I deny it."

Jack took out his cell phone. "In that case, you won't mind if we call the police."

The priest was defiant as he held up their passports. "Perhaps you can tell them what three people with Israeli stamps on their passports are doing in Syria. Like me, I'm sure they'd be interested to know."

Jack started to punch in numbers on his cell. "I think

they'd be even more interested to know that you're involved in a brutal homicide, don't you, Father?"

"Homicide? Don't be ridiculous."

Jack stopped punching the keypad and fixed the priest with a stare. "Early this morning a man was stabbed to death at Qumran, in Israel. His name was Donald Green and he was in charge of an important archaeological dig. He was also my boss. A valuable scroll I unearthed was stolen during the murder. There's an international police alert already under way to help solve the crime. But if you don't want to help us, it might be better if you deal with the police. After all, you could be an accomplice to murder."

Father Novara's eyes widened, his confidence vaporized, and he grasped Jack's wrist to prevent him using his cell phone. "No, please, wait. I'm an accomplice to nothing."

Yasmin urged, "Father, we need your help to find these men."

The priest nervously bit his lip, then moved to open the door. "I—I must ask permission from my abbot to talk further. Please wait here."

"How long?"

"Five minutes, no more," Novara said, and closed the door after him, his footsteps echoing out in the stone courtyard.

At the end of the courtyard Father Vincento Novara came to a winding granite staircase. Using his lamp to guide him he climbed up one floor. He was trembling, his legs barely able to carry him. He reached a landing with a stone archway. He stepped through and entered a large room with vaulted wooden ceilings that served as his private office.

Crammed with bookshelves, the room also held a simple wooden chair and desk set against one wall. Novara's eyes were drawn to the desk, the wood shiny with age. On top lay a foot-long pinewood box. It was fitted with secure metal clamps that held a hinged lid in place. He stepped over to the box but paused beside the rows of bookshelves, stacked with leather-bound books and rolls of ancient parchments, some of them centuries old.

Novara knew those musty books and parchments as intimately as he knew his own life. His was a life dedicated to scholastic research ever since as a young priest he had studied to become an expert in ancient Aramaic and Hebrew documents. These were reference works to aid his research, and samples of ancient script that went back thousands of years.

Novara placed the oil lamp on the desk and felt a bead of sweat drip from his brow. He wiped his face with the back of his sleeve and noticed that his hands trembled. Next to the pinewood box was a lab microscope and a magnifying glass with a cracked ivory handle. He anxiously licked his lips, released the metal clamps on the box, and lifted the hinged lid.

Inside was an unraveled, sepia-colored scroll.

Using scissors, he had cut out a pair of thin Perspex sheets, which now sandwiched the scroll for protection. Some portions of the parchment were worn and patched with holes, but it was still in reasonably good condition and most of it legible.

He had translated so many manuscripts in his lifetime, but in truth none was as intriguing as this ancient scroll that he had finished translating an hour ago. It was truly astonishing.

But then so was the arrival of his three visitors.

Novara closed the pinewood lid and snapped shut the clamps. He moved across the room to another door, opened it, and climbed some stone steps onto a large roof battlement. He lifted his habit, removed a Siemens cell phone, and flicked it open. Twenty feet away was a miniature satellite dish to ensure that he always had a signal. And up here on the roof the signal strength was best. Novara punched the cell phone keypad and called the number in Damascus.

37

"Father Novara seems to be taking a long time." Jack stepped over to the door and listened.

Yasmin said, "Tell me more about these collectors who buy ancient artifacts. What do you know about them?"

"They're usually wealthy individuals who get a kick out of possessing rare and precious artifacts all to themselves. Some pay millions for the privilege. And they couldn't care less if the artifact's been stolen because no one's ever going to see it except them. That's what gives them their big thrill."

"Do you know of any collectors who might want your scroll?"

"I'm sure there are lots." Jack turned to listen at the door again. "There's not a sound out there. I wonder where the heck Novara's got to."

Yasmin said, "Do you ever get a chill on the back of your neck when something isn't quite right? I get the same feeling about Novara."

Jack nodded. "You might be right. I wouldn't count on him telling us the truth either. I think he may know a lot more than he's saying."

Josuf said, "Maybe I should get my knife from the pickup?"

Yasmin said, "Why?"

"To loosen the priest's tongue."

Jack moved to the door, opened it a crack, and listened. "No, stay here, Josuf. Take care of Yasmin."

"Why, where are you going?" Yasmin asked.

Jack stepped out into the deserted courtyard. "To take a look around for Novara."

Jack walked to the end of the courtyard. The monastery appeared deserted, the only sound his own echoing footsteps and gurgling water from the fountain. Overhead, stars burned silver in the desert night, the air clammy.

He came to a granite staircase that wound upward into darkness. He peered up, listened, but heard nothing. He moved up the staircase, pressing his hands to the side of the smooth stone walls to keep his balance, and came out into an enormous, sparsely furnished chamber.

The room looked to be a private study or office, an oak door at the end. The air had a dank smell. A crucifix was nailed high into one of the bare stone walls. He approached a wooden chair and desk set against a wall. On top lay a pine-wood box.

Jack startled when he thought he heard a faint voice in the distance. He listened again. Silence, except for the faint creaking of the floorboards.

Nearby, a long row of wooden shelves sagged under the weight of leather-bound books and rolls of withering parchments. Some were obviously many centuries old. Below the shelves, a clutch of what appeared to be parchment scrolls were laid out on a broad table, each under a sheet of Perspex.

A magnifying glass lay nearby. It looked as if the parchments were being studied for some kind of comparison. Jack's heart beat faster as he eagerly moved closer. All the parchments appeared to be written in Aramaic. He didn't waste time reading the complete texts but scanned them.

His heart sank. None was his Qumran scroll.

He turned back to the desk and the pinewood box lying on top. It was fitted with a pair of sturdy-looking metal clamps to keep it securely shut. A lab microscope, a desk lamp, and an ivory-handled magnifying glass lay next to the box.

A slim pile of notes and papers were stacked on the desk. Jack flicked through them and frowned. Some of the papers had what looked like jotted combinations of Aramaic words and letters, some of them scratched out, as if the writer had been trying to decipher words. Jack shuffled through more pages. On one he found a legible sentence, written in English:

> When the messiah's corpse was removed from the cross, it was placed in a tomb in the burial caves outside Dora, on the road to Caesarea.

The sentence jolted Jack. His pulse raced. He didn't understand the words' significance but knew he had stumbled upon something remarkable. He read the sentence again to be certain he'd read it correctly. Then he checked the next page and found a pen-and-ink drawing—it was embellished with vivid, dramatic images of animals, monsters, and sylphs.

He frowned again. Something about the drawing looked familiar. He racked his mind but couldn't put a finger on it. Jack slid open one of the desk drawers. Inside was a jumble of pens and pencils, rubber erasers, and paper clips. He pulled open another drawer and discovered bottles of different colored inks, from black to purple, and copper brown. He eased shut the drawers, his attention drawn back to the pinewood box. Looking closely, he noticed it had a hinged lid. He fiddled with the clamps, pressing hard on one until it snapped open. His curiosity aroused, he snapped open the second clamp.

Very carefully, he touched his hand to the lid and lifted it back.

Inside the box lay the Qumran scroll.

Well I'll be darned. Jack felt his heart race. *I've found it.*

Someone had gone to a lot of trouble to unravel and protect the ancient parchment, placing it in a two-layer sandwich of what looked like foot-square plastic or Perspex sheets. At the very bottom was a layer of straw. The plastic sheets were held in place by spring clips. Unrolled, the sepia-colored scroll was less than a foot long.

Portions of the parchment were worn and eaten with holes but most of it appeared to be in legible condition. He noticed something odd. Two sharp lines cut about an inch into the top right edge of the scroll, as if someone had attempted to slice away small portions of the parchment with a knife or scissors, then changed their mind.

Despite the cuts, none of the inked words in that part of the parchment appeared missing. Jack switched on the table lamp and the scroll's coppery sepia tones came alive.

He could hardly contain his excitement. His mind was on fire; his palms felt sweaty. He lifted the magnifier from the desk and held it in focus over the parchment. The words in the first paragraph leapt out at him: *Yeshua HaMeshiah.*

With his excitement came a stab of fear. He knew he could be disturbed at any minute. He urgently tried to figure what to do next. A thought came to him and he replaced the magnifier and fumbled for his cell phone.

He flicked on the built-in camera and pointed it down. The screen blinked and came alive with the image on the desk in front of him. Aiming the lens at the scroll, he directed the desk lamp to neutralize the glare. When he got the distance just right, it allowed him to read a portion of the scroll with a crisp enough image.

He managed to shoot off seven photographs before he heard footsteps beyond the far door. He had a powerful instinct to grab the scroll and run but he suppressed it. Instead, he took out his notebook and pen, flicked off the desk light, and slowly lifted the clips at the edge that held the Perspex in place . . .

A little later Jack heard the door creak open and Novara appeared. He looked as surprised as Jack. "What are you doing in here?" the priest demanded.

Jack plucked down a book as he stood in front of one of the bookshelves. "I thought I heard footsteps. You took so long I came to look for you. Why?"

Novara let the door close behind him and raised his hand. He clutched a deadly-looking steel-blue automatic pistol. "Move away from the shelves, Mr. Cane, and do exactly as I tell you."

"Did you hear that?"

Josuf rose from the table. "Hear what, madame?"

"It sounded like footsteps." Yasmin heard a noise beyond the door and it opened suddenly. At the sight of Jack standing there, she let out a breath and said, "You had us worried for a minute. What's the matter?"

They both saw Father Novara appear in the doorway, armed with a pistol. He pushed Jack into the room and closed the door after him.

Yasmin, alarmed, took a step back. "What—what's going on?"

Novara brandished the pistol. "Sit still and be quiet. Otherwise I'm liable to kill you all."

38

The Black Hawk powered through the darkness. The dull chopping of the blades seemed to throb in unison with Lela's pounding heartbeat.

Ari said, "This chopper's got a FLIR system fitted to its belly—that's forward-looking infrared to you and me. Along with telemetry units, they'll help the pilot get a precise fix on our contact's ground transmission."

"Who are the people meeting us?"

"A couple of Mossad's agents working out of Damascus. They'll make sure we don't get lost."

The helicopter banked sharply, its speed slowing. Saul said, "Approaching target now, better ready yourselves."

Lela, wearing the jeans and top Ari had given her, grabbed the bag at her feet containing the hijab gown. Nervous excitement fluttered in her stomach. Staring out the window she saw total darkness as the chopper leveled out again.

Ari reached for his bag. "Forget the window view and take a look into the cockpit. Near the center of the console you'll see a small TV with a green screen. That's for the passive thermal imaging equipment fitted to the chopper's belly. It's scanning the road and the immediate area for any human activity. With any luck, you ought to see our welcoming committee."

The Black Hawk began to hover, its nose swinging gently left and right in a sweeping motion. Lela peered into the cockpit, past Saul and the busy crew. She noticed a miniature TV in the center console, the screen filled with thermal images in different shades of luminous green and black. Lela could make out the vague shapes of what looked like a car and a human figure standing near the vehicle, the image shot from a high angle.

"You see that? Our contact," Saul told them, smiling. "The wonders of modern technology."

"Target directly below," the pilot called out, maneuvering the joystick as the Black Hawk descended. Moments later the chopper's struts hit the ground with a gentle bump. Saul yanked open the door and a blast of warm desert air swirled into the cabin.

Lela felt a wave of anxiety as the dispatcher ushered them out. "Go, move it, quick as you can."

Ari jumped out first and then held out a hand to her. Lela jumped and her feet hit a hard tarmac road. She followed Ari out under the whirling helicopter blades. A car waited in the vastness of the empty desert. A woman stood by the vehicle, waving at them.

Behind Lela, the Black Hawk was already lifting off again. It rose into the air and sped toward another Black Hawk hovering two hundred yards away, its lights extinguished. The two aircraft powered away, their dull chopping noise fading into darkness.

Lela and Ari reached the woman. She waited beside a gray Volvo station wagon. She appeared young and wore an Arab hijab, a coil of cheap bangles dangling from one of her wrists.

Ari exchanged words with her, then the woman said to Lela, "I'm Rasha. Come, we have no time to lose."

The Volvo's rear door was already open and she ushered them inside.

Lela climbed in first, followed by Ari, who shut the door as the woman jumped into the passenger seat. A middle-aged Arab sat behind the wheel. He wore an immaculate suit and shirt, and he offered his hand and grinned. "I'm Uday."

Lela noticed that the driver clutched what looked like a palm-sized transmitter, which he'd used to guide down the Black Hawk. He stuffed the transmitter into his pocket, started the Volvo's engine, but left the headlights off.

"I'd say welcome to Syria, my friends, a wonderful country, except it's a one-party police state that really stinks. Better fasten your seat belts, from here on we may have a bumpy ride ahead of us."

39

At least thirty minutes had passed, the heat in the small room oppressive. Jack wiped sweat from his forehead with the back of his sleeve. "What's going on, Novara? Maybe it's time you explained why a man of the cloth is threatening us with a gun."

Novara's grip tightened on the pistol as he turned toward the door, and they all heard the sound of a car approaching. "You won't have to wait much longer to have your question answered."

The engine noise came closer, then idled for a few seconds and died. Novara took the bunch of keys from his belt and opened the door. "Escape is impossible. The door is locked and I have the only key. I'll be back with someone who wants to meet you."

"Who?"

"You'll see." Novara stepped out, closing the door, then a key rattled in the lock and he was gone.

Jack moved over to the door and heard Novara's footsteps fade. "It sounds as if he's heading in the direction of the main gate."

Yasmin joined him. "Do you think it's Pasha who's arrived?"

"Who knows? But I saw the scroll."

"Where?" Yasmin said, as she and Josuf stared at Jack.

"In a room upstairs. From the looks of things Father Novara's been working on it. Give me a hand trying to open the door, Josuf."

Jack turned the door handle and tried pulling. When that didn't succeed, he and Josuf took turns heaving their shoulders against the wood but it didn't budge or splinter.

"It's rock solid. We need something to try to lever it open." Jack grabbed the oil lamp and scoured the room but he saw nothing, the chair legs too flimsy and the table legs too thick to wedge into the doorjamb.

"Wait, listen," Yasmin said.

Footsteps sounded out in the courtyard. Jack replaced the lamp as a key rattled in the lock and the door was pushed open. Novara appeared, the gun still in his hand. Behind him stood two men.

One was gray-bearded, in his fifties with dark, restless eyes. He wore a crumpled Panama hat, pale linen suit, and a silk cravat. His left hand was badly scarred and looked withered and twisted. In his other hand he clutched a polished walking cane.

His companion was younger, with a muscular torso that bulged under his lightweight suit. His coarse face had a violent, brutal look.

Novara stepped into the room, followed by the men. The one in the linen suit limped in front of the table and doffed his hat. "My apologies for keeping you, Mr. Cane. Please sit, all of you."

Jack and the others sat at the table. The man held out his good hand to the priest. "Give me the gun, Vincento."

Novara handed over the pistol and the man said, "Now bring me the box."

"You want it here?"

"Yes. Now."

Novara frowned. "Why, Pasha?"

"Don't question. Just do as I say."

Novara seemed to know better than to argue and he left, his footsteps fading in the corridor. The man named Pasha studied his captives, his eyes settling on Jack. "So, the priest says you told him you found out about me through the Bedu's brother. Before you answer my questions I would suggest you tell the truth. Unless you want my bodyguard here to show you what a callous brute he can be, Mr. Cane. The priest also tells me that it was you who found the scroll."

"That's right."

"You're a very lucky man, Mr. Cane."

"You could have fooled me."

The man named Pasha smiled. Novara's footsteps returned. He carried the pinewood box reverently in his hands, as if it contained something precious. Pasha carefully took it from him. "The translation?"

Novara removed a sealed white envelope from under his habit, his face alive with excitement as he silently handed it to Pasha. "It's as I said, truly remarkable."

Jack said, "Any chance of hearing the translation?"

Novara gave him a stern look. "The scroll is destined never to be seen, along with the others."

"What others?" Cane asked.

Before the priest could answer, Pasha put up a hand for him to be silent. "You have said enough, Vincento." He turned to his bodyguard. "Take care of our problem, Botwan."

The bodyguard removed an HK automatic pistol from his pocket, along with a silencer, and screwed it onto the tip of the weapon.

Father Novara looked horrified. "You can't kill them *here*. This is a house of God."

"We do what we must. How many of your fellow monks are in the monastery—three, four?"

"Four, including myself. But that's not the point."

"I'm afraid it is the point," Pasha said.

The bodyguard aimed the pistol at Father Novara. The priest's mouth opened in alarm as the weapon coughed twice. Two rounds thudded into his chest. He was flung back against the wall and collapsed in a heap onto the floor.

Yasmin screamed. Jack held her and shouted at Pasha, "For God's sake . . ."

Pasha said, "You're right. Unfortunately, God has everything to do with it."

Blood pooled around the priest's body as Pasha knelt, felt the man's neck for a pulse. Finally he stood, brandishing the priest's weapon, and said to the bodyguard, "You know what to do, Botwan. I want no trace of us left behind. I'll deal with these three."

40

Jack clutched Yasmin's hand as Pasha pulled up a chair, sat opposite, and kept the pistol aimed at them. The minutes passed but he didn't speak. Jack said, "Are you going to kill us?"

Pasha shrugged indifferently. "It comes to us all in the end, Mr. Cane. I have learned that whether any of us live or die is really of no great consequence except, of course, to those whom we love."

"Then how'd you like to do us all a favor and shoot yourself?"

A grin spread on Pasha's face. "It's good that you have a sense of humor, Mr. Cane. I like that." He touched Novara's limp body with the tip of his shoe. "Men like the priest here, dry as a stick, they give me a headache."

Pasha removed his Panama hat, placed it on the table, and lit a cigarette. "The monk had a great academic mind but in the end he was a stupid man. What is it they say? He who sups with the devil must have a long spoon. I'm afraid his spoon was not long enough. He mixed with the wrong company."

"You mean you, obviously."

Pasha gave a vague shrug.

"Who do you work for?" Jack asked.

"It's unimportant." Pasha gestured toward the door. "You know what's going on outside as we speak?"

"I could take a good guess.".

Pasha grimaced. "This ancient monastery whose history stretches back for centuries is about to go up in flames and its inhabitants executed. And all because of your incredible stupidity, Mr. Cane. What do you say to that?"

"I'd say there's a good chance you need psychiatric help."

Pasha laughed aloud. "I like you, Mr. Cane. But had you left well enough alone, this would not have happened, believe me."

"You're killing everyone and razing the place to the ground and you're blaming *me*?"

Yasmin said, "Why do this?"

Pasha looked at her. "Because every truth has a price, dear lady. And this particular truth has a high price indeed."

"What's that supposed to mean?"

Pasha steadied the gun. "None of you should have come here. You should not have interfered. And this old Bedu goat who brought you should have had more sense."

Josuf said bitterly, "My brother told me you were a ruthless man."

"You should have listened to him and kept your nose out of this, old fool—"

Jack suddenly lunged at Pasha. Despite his lame foot the Arab was quick up off the chair and in an instant he brandished the weapon. "Don't be an idiot. Or you'll end up like the priest. Now sit, Cane."

Jack sat. Footsteps sounded. The bodyguard returned, carrying a can of gasoline, his silenced pistol tucked into his belt. "It's done," he said calmly in Arabic. "We must leave, the blaze is spreading."

A strong smell of burning gasoline wafted on the warm air. Pasha nodded and limped back toward the door. "Move out to our vehicle, Botwan."

Yasmin was ashen. "What now? Are you going to kill us?"

Pasha gestured with the gun. "We have a saying here: The less you know, the less is your burden." He nodded to the bodyguard. "You know what to do, Botwan. If they try to make a run for it, kill them."

41

"I've never seen so many priests and nuns." Ari Tauber stared out of the Volvo as they drove into Maloula's busy streets.

Lela saw that the ancient town was a bizarre blend of the Christian and Muslim traditions. Every few hundred yards was a convent or monastery, the narrow alleyways thronged with nuns, priests, and monks wearing religious garb, mixed in with locals in Arab dress, all out strolling in the balmy evening.

Middle Eastern music blared from tiny shops that sold Arab gowns, worry beads, and trinkets, alongside icons of Jesus and Mary. Vendors sold kebabs and *koftas* cooked over smoking hot charcoal, the spiced aroma of fresh food wafting into the car.

The driver had a map open on his knees. "The monastery shouldn't be far from here." He steered the Volvo out of town and onto a potholed desert road that twisted through a rocky creek, no traffic in sight except for a couple of elderly Arab goatherds. Two miles farther on Lela saw a signpost that said in Arabic and English: "St. Paul's Monastery."

"Do you see that light up ahead?" She noticed a crimson

glow on the horizon. It looked at first like the remains of sunset but then she realized that the glow was a blaze. "It looks like there's a fire."

"I think you're right." Ari tensed and slapped the driver on the back. "Put your foot down."

━━━

Father Novara grunted in agony.

His eyelids flicked and he was barely conscious. The room's white walls were a blur, the pain in his chest excruciating. It felt as if a red-hot poker had pierced his heart. As he lay on his side on the cool tiles he knew that he was dying. He coughed and spewed up a gob of crimson phlegm. His mouth tasted salty. When the shots struck him in the chest with the force of hammer blows, he had been unable to move, traumatized by his wounds. And so he had lain there in the growing pool of his own blood, pretending to be dead. How long he had lain he didn't know but the pain became unbearable, and then the voices of the others in the room had faded and Novara had passed out. Now he had become conscious again, but he felt weak, his senses failing.

Novara grunted, louder this time, but no one answered. He had no idea if his colleagues were still alive, or what was happening, but he feared the worst. He was a fool to have trusted Pasha. His mind floated as his brain released its chemical cocktail to blunt the pain of imminent death.

Novara raised his right hand, touched his fingers to his chest, then drew them to his face. His fingertips dripped blood. He coughed up another gob of crimson. Death would claim him soon but anger flared inside him. He wanted to extract a payment from his killers for their sin.

Novara tried to focus on the walls that stared him in

the face, the whiteness blinding, almost heavenly. He felt his senses ebbing fast. He reached out to touch the wall.

He failed, his hand falling away in a weak attempt.

Novara groaned, made a supreme effort, and stretched out his bloodstained fingers once more, trying to reach the wall.

42

As the driver pulled up outside the monastery, Lela jumped out.

Mustard walls surrounded a centuries-old Arab fort that, unusually, had a crucifix set high above the arched entrance.

Ari moved behind her, followed by the Mossad agents. One of the archways' oak doors was wide open, revealing a splendid courtyard garden with gushing ponds. Lela saw thick plumes of smoke billow from the building's upper floors, orange flames licking the roof. "The blaze looks out of control."

Ari turned to the woman named Rasha. "Stay with the car. Do you have a flashlight?"

"Right here." The woman reached under the Volvo's seat and produced a rubber-encased light.

Ari grabbed it and beckoned the driver. "Come with me. You too, Lela. Everyone keep their eyes open. There could be trouble waiting inside."

Ari reached for his Sig. He ran toward the entrance, the driver and Lela following, clutching her pistol. They stepped into the courtyard.

It looked deserted.

Without a word, Ari pointed two fingers of one hand to his eyes, and then pointed toward an archway across the courtyard. They swung their weapons left and right, covering each other as they moved toward the monastery, silent as phantoms.

It became apparent to Lela that something was wrong. The monastery was too silent, the rooms empty.

She expected to hear screams and shouts for help, frantic monks carrying water buckets as they fought the fire.

There was no one. Not a soul. Except for the background crackle of blazing wood, the monastery was eerily deserted, hollow as a crypt. After five minutes of searching the rooms, Lela saw it first.

They had moved into the main building and found the fire quickly spreading, engulfing the building. Roof timbers crashed and furniture was ablaze. As they climbed the stairs they were beaten back by a fog of smoke. Ari gave the order to retreat and they moved back down the stairway, along corridors untouched by the blaze. In one of the corridors, they found the monks' sparse cells.

Lela froze as she stepped inside the first cell. The body of a young monk lay sprawled across the bed from the force of gunshots to his head and chest. His threadbare white habit was stained with damp crimson. A single round left a blossom on his chest and drilled his forehead. Lela had seen death many times but she choked back a cry of disgust.

Ari stepped up behind her.

Lela reached out to feel the man's lifeless wrist. "He can't be dead long—he's still warm."

Ari examined the wounds. "One shot to the heart, one to the head. A double tap, the sign of a professional hit."

The Mossad agent joined them. "I saw two more bodies across the hall. The same signature as this one, one shot to the heart, one to the head."

They crossed the hall and saw the bodies of two elderly monks. Ari said, "We can do nothing for them. Fan out, see if you can find any evidence of Cane and his friends." He leveled his Sig and they moved back out into the hall. "Go carefully. Whoever pulled the trigger may still be here."

They searched the remaining cells along the corridor but found them empty. The blaze was spreading, the smoke like a fog, and they covered their nostrils as they found their way back toward the courtyard. Lela noticed a door ajar at the end of an archway.

Ari saw it too. "Stay here and cover us, Lela."

He and the driver moved toward the door. Lela tensed as she watched both men linger outside the door and listen, then Ari shoved in the door and rushed in, followed by the driver.

Lela waited, her pistol at arm's length in a two-handed grip, ready to fire.

Almost a minute passed. Nothing happened. Lela began to worry. *What's keeping Ari?*

Her pulse hammering in her temples, she stepped along the archway and kept her Sig aimed toward the room. As she approached it, Ari suddenly stepped out through the door, his pistol by his side.

Lela's heart skipped. "Ari! I could have fired. What kept you?"

Ari's face was ashen. "You need to see this."

Lela stepped into the room. It was sparse, with a wooden table and chairs, the floor covered in worn terra-cotta tiles. The Mossad driver was kneeling beside the corpse of an elderly gray-bearded monk. His white habit was bloodied from a massive chest wound and he lay on his side, his right arm outstretched, his fingers stained crimson. It appeared as if he had tried to write something on the wall with his bloodied fingers.

To Lela, it looked like the image of twin crosses, side by side. The upright stem of the cross on the right trailed off in a bloody tendril. The monk's dead fingers pointed skyward as if he had died in the process of finishing his work.

Lela heard a strange whirring noise and startled.

Ari was aiming an electronic camera and the flash popped. The camera whirred again as he photographed the bloody artwork on the walls and the victim's body from at least a dozen angles. When Ari finished, he stared across, his face still pale. "What the devil does it all mean?"

Lela stared back at him, lost for an answer.

Five miles away, a strong desert wind had started to blow, tossing flurries of sand against the Mercedes' windshield.

Jack stared out worriedly beyond the glass, past the fog of gusting sand, while next to him in the driver's seat Josuf slowly negotiated a narrow desert road. The weather was turning, a sandstorm blowing, and Jack was having difficulty seeing the pickup fifty yards ahead of them. Yasmin was driving the Ford, and the man named Botwan was covering her with his weapon.

In the rear seat behind Jack, Pasha reached forward and prodded Josuf in the back of the neck with his pistol. "Stop here. Honk the car horn, then slowly pull off the road and cut the engine," he ordered.

Jack felt his heart hammering in his chest. He peered out into the desert but saw nothing but sand and a coarse, rocky track. For the last ten minutes Pasha had remained ominously silent as he kept his gun trained on them. Jack feared the worst.

"I said honk the horn and pull in," Pasha barked.

Josuf obeyed, slapping the horn, causing three sharp blasts, then eased the Mercedes off the desert track. Immediately the Ford in front slowed and pulled up, its red taillights illuminating in the fog of the sandstorm. A moment later Yasmin climbed out, followed by Botwan brandishing his pistol, both of them covering their faces with their arms to shield themselves from the gritty gusts.

"Get out of the car," Pasha ordered.

Jack was forced to obey, followed by Josuf, as Pasha clambered out after them, keeping his gun at the ready, covering his mouth with his sleeve as the sand flurries stung their faces.

"Move over there." He gestured with his pistol for them to move at least thirty feet out into the desert. Jack braced himself as Yasmin moved beside him, and he could feel her hand shaking as she gripped his. "Are—are you going to kill us?" she asked Pasha.

Jack's heart sank as Pasha racked the pistol slide and chambered a round, ready to fire. "It comes to us all, young lady," the Syrian said matter-of-factly. "But I'll give you time to say your prayers."

Josuf said valiantly, "Please, there is no need to kill them. I'm the one who's responsible for bringing them here—"

Botwan struck him a blow across the face with his pistol. The Bedu reeled back, blood on his lips. "Kneel, all of you," Botwan ordered.

They knelt in the sand and Jack's heart jackhammered as he desperately sought a chance to escape, but the situation was dire, both Pasha and Botwan aiming their guns.

Yasmin's voice quivered as she begged, "Please . . . can't you let us go? We promise we won't tell anyone what happened."

"Tell it to the devil. I hope you've said your prayers, American. Because you're first to die."

Jack couldn't answer. He felt his body shake as Pasha stepped forward, clutching his pistol. Then Jack suddenly went rigid with shock as the Syrian brought up the weapon and aimed it at the middle of Jack's forehead. Jack tightly closed his eyes, his heart pounding with dread, everything happening so fast he could hardly think, let alone pray.

The pistol exploded.

43

Cardinal Umberto Cassini stepped through the Belvedere Courtyard and entered the sturdy granite building that housed the Vatican's Secret Archives.

Moving past the security guards, Cassini ignored the custodian seated at the large table, bare except for the visitor book he guarded. Like many cardinals of the Curia, Cassini hardly ever signed the book. Besides, he had more urgent matters on his mind.

He entered a sparsely furnished chamber, empty except for a couple of earnest young clerical scholars working at their desks. Cassini ignored them and came to a small room at the back of the building, protected by double oak doors blackened with age. He took a deep breath and let it out slowly, trying to mentally prepare himself for the difficult task that lay ahead.

He rapped twice on the ancient wood and waited.

The doors opened and a tall, handsome priest wearing a black soutane stood there. Father Emil Rossi was a respected archivist, a guardian of some of the most sensitive records in the Vatican Archives. With his high forehead, fine nose, and slender aristocratic hands, his chiselled face was made for sculpting. Rossi bowed in a slight, effeminate manner. "Your

Eminence. It is good to see you." He limped back to admit his visitor.

Cassini stepped into a large chamber with pale, colored walls. It was crowded with at least two dozen priests who sat at metal tables placed around the room. Cassini knew that each man was specially chosen by John Becket for his impeccable trust. Piled high beside the priests were boxes of indexes, documents, and files. Some of the documents looked musty with age, others were more recent. But one thing Cassini noticed: they all bore the papal seal, which meant they had been removed from some of the Vatican Archives' most guarded vaults. The clerics pored over them with scrupulous attention, taking notes as they worked, so eager that they barely looked up as Cassini entered.

"I was informed that the Holy Father was here," Cassini told Rossi in a hushed voice. "But obviously I was misled."

Rossi, who had the solemn air of someone entrusted with dark and dangerous secrets, shot a disapproving glance at the other priests in the room, as if upset that his personal territory had been invaded. "No, Your Eminence. He has been here all day with his examiners."

"And how goes it?"

"We have been working around the clock. But no one complains of being tired. All the priests are deeply impressed by the Holy Father. He energizes them."

"I'm delighted to hear it."

"They feel a sense of importance that their work will help to reinvigorate the church. Indeed, I have heard some of my fellow priests claim that their faith has been refreshed by the pope's election. In the words of one, it's almost as if the messiah has again come among us."

"Invigorating words indeed. Where is the Holy Father now?"

"We all shared a simple lunch and prayers afterward, before he stepped out for air not ten minutes ago. He said he would be back."

"Where did he go?"

"I would try the gardens. He said he needed some time alone, to think."

Cassini turned to leave but hesitated, looked back at the handsome priest, and whispered, "How did the Holy Father seem?"

"I'm afraid he looked worried," Rossi hissed back, his face darkening. "Yes, worried. That is the only way to describe him, Your Eminence."

Cassini nodded solemnly and headed in the direction of the gardens.

44

Cassini followed the path through the Vatican Gardens, past the lawns and flower beds. Situated within walls first extended in the sixteenth century to defend the sacred city, the gardens had become disorderly with the years, a mishmash of orange groves, conifer trees, and shrubbery cluttered with religious statues and gurgling fountains. Cassini halted at the Fountain of the Rock, with its figures of dragons and tritons.

John Becket sat beside the stone fountain. He was very still, the only movement a wisp of his hair ruffled by a stray breath of wind. He stared at the splashing waters, his face a solemn mask of concern.

Cassini noticed that since his election, the pontiff had chosen not to wear papal garments. Instead he wore a simple wooden cross around his neck and a plain white cassock, but without the zucchetto, the small white skullcap the pope usually wore. Cassini moved closer and realized the pope wasn't staring but praying as if transfixed, the set of rosary beads in his hands passing silently through his long, slim fingers.

Cassini waited, expecting to be noticed, but when he wasn't he coughed quietly. "Pardon, Holy Father."

John Becket turned to face him. The solemn look vanished, a smile came instantly to his lips, and the gentle blue eyes regarded Cassini warmly. "Umberto. It is good to see you."

Cassini bent his knee and kissed the pope's right hand. "Your Holiness."

"Sit. Join me."

Cassini sat by the fountain. "I hope I did not disturb your prayers."

"My prayers are completed."

"I went to the archives, believing I might find you there. But Father Rossi suggested you came here, to the gardens, to have some time alone. My apologies if I have invaded your privacy, Holy Father."

"No matter, Umberto. I am glad of your company." John Becket's smile widened at the mention of Rossi. "Father Rossi seems a remarkable man. I never told him I was going, yet he appears to know everything, not just the archive secrets he is a guardian of. I hope he is not upset that we have invaded his territory."

Cassini nodded. "Your examiners are certainly keeping him busy, but nobody seems to complain. By all accounts, everyone has only good words for you. They speak of you reverently, with the deepest of respect, Holy Father."

"They are far too kind, Umberto. And such hard workers."

"May I ask of your progress?"

"These are early days yet. But for now, the records and files my examiners are most interested in relate to matters about which I consider our flock has an immediate right to know. Papers that have to do with the Vatican's more recent past. Subjects of historical importance that have been shrouded in secrecy until now, yet endlessly speculated upon."

Cassini looked faintly anxious. "Could the Holy Father be more specific?"

"Religious revelations and prophecies, for one. Also, the Vatican's financial affairs and its investments. These are subjects that have caused more speculation and scandal than most. My examiners will report to me when their work has been completed. We shall proceed from there." Becket paused. "Is that why you came to see me, Umberto, to inquire about their progress?"

"No, Holy Father. If I may be honest, I have two concerns."

"Tell me your concerns."

"One has to do with your personal safety. The other to do with your pledge to open the archives to public scrutiny. I simply wonder if you still think it wise to abide by this pledge, Holy Father."

"And why should I not, Umberto?"

Cassini sighed, then said as delicately as he could, "I have heard of anxious whispers among Curia members who seem to think that it will destroy the church, and be the end of our religion as we know it. That your desire to embrace other Christian churches in your mission of truth is a step too far. They say your new beginning could really be an ending. I hate to even say this, but some have wondered aloud if this could be your true intention. The question I heard was, 'What if he's a devil in lamb's clothing?'"

"Are you among them, Umberto?"

The unexpected question caught Cassini off guard. He flushed, the first time he had done so in many decades. Fifteen years of curial office had taught him to readily answer any question, never act surprised, but the directness of the query unsettled him. "I—I am merely voicing concerns that I have heard. We both know there are secrets within the archive vaults that could shake the church to its core. Many among the Curia believe those secrets would be best forgotten. Some of my colleagues have voiced certain questions."

"What questions?"

"Do we really want to ignite the flames of controversy? To heap trouble upon ourselves? To unsettle the world by our supreme honesty?"

"I seem to recall our Savior did exactly that. In regard to other Christians not of our church, belief in Jesus' words are truly what matter, and is the glue that unites us. Christ believed in unity, but for too long, through our own pride and arrogance, I fear so many churches have ignored that belief. Perhaps we can begin by forsaking our own pride and reach out to them, Umberto. The simple truth is that deep in our hearts, all believers are more alike than unalike. We believe in the same creator."

Cassini flushed again. "Of course, but we are shepherds of the flock, responsible for the people and the church's continuation. The foundations of the faith may be at risk."

"Do you really believe this, Umberto?"

"I believe such concerns are genuine," Cassini answered diplomatically.

John Becket paused, closed his eyes. For a moment his fingers toyed with the rosary beads in his hands, and then he opened his eyes again. "Do you know why I chose the name Celestine, Umberto?"

"No."

"Celestine was a very simple man. But he had an honest wisdom we can all learn from."

"Holy Father?"

"He knew that while many popes have called themselves servants of God, few of them behaved with the humility of servants. Sadly, when the Curia conspired against him, Celestine resigned and soon after he was killed."

The pope paused and fixed his visitor with a gentle stare.

"Know that I intend to be an honest servant, Umberto. The church is built on love and truth. They are the real foundations of our faith and are among our most important obligations as priests. Out of love for my flock I intend honoring my obligation to truth, come what may."

"But—"

"No buts, Umberto. For years our flock has called for a new papal leadership, one that functions less as a monarch, more as a friend, a pastor. On the night I was chosen I promised that I would be an instrument of that change. I see no reason to alter that promise."

"And your personal safety, Holy Father, is that of no concern?" A trace of argument crept into Cassini's tone. "The forces of darkness may wish to destroy you, as they have tried to destroy other popes. The church has many secretive groups who may even plot your downfall because of your intentions. There has been hate mail containing veiled threats. Monsignor Ryan has voiced to me his fears."

"Christ was threatened also, but did not succumb. We must follow his example, Umberto."

Cassini persisted. "Then will you at least change your mind about Sean Ryan's recommendations? A bulletproof vest. Extra personal security?"

Becket stood, his tall figure towering. "I place my safety in God's hands. I know He will not fail me, Umberto."

There was unshakable strength in the reply, a power to its belief that made Cassini feel humbled. At that moment, the blue eyes that stared back at him were piercing, and Cassini felt himself almost wither under the unyielding intensity of Becket's gaze.

He knew why the Curia had ultimately picked this man, aside from the fact that he had all the qualifications desired of a pope: a long career within the church, ten years spent in Rome, almost twenty as a devout missionary in Africa and the Middle East, where he was as much admired for his pastoral work as his diplomacy, an ideal attribute for any pontiff—from the Latin, the word meant "bridge-builder."

But Cassini knew that John Becket was more than the sum of his parts. There was a powerful solidness to him, an incredible mystical integrity that made you feel you were in the presence of a truly extraordinary human being.

Cassini said quietly, "The last Pope Celestine was killed at the hands of assassins. He, too, placed himself in God's hands. Yet God failed him."

"He does not always do as we ask of Him. As a priest, you know that. But I am resigned to whatever fate He chooses for me. And now, please excuse me. I have important business to take care of, Umberto."

Cassini nodded silently. He knew his audience was over. He knelt, kissed the ring.

John Becket turned to go, but hesitated. "There is something perhaps you should know. A worrying discovery made by one of the examiners."

"Holy Father?"

"Some of the archives' documents are missing."

Cassini looked stunned. "I don't understand. How is that possible?"

"A question I asked myself. It appears several files are unaccounted for. Some relate to the church's financial dealings. Others to the findings in the Dead Sea scrolls. Either they have been deliberately removed, or they are mislaid. Which, is not yet clear."

"This is a serious business."

Becket nodded. "Father Rossi seems at a loss to explain.

However, my examiners assure me they intend to get to the bottom of it."

"Of course, Holy Father. I'm sure they will."

"Bless you, Umberto." The pontiff left, his white cassock flapping about his legs.

Cassini watched him retreat and felt a tremor of concern. He was bitterly reminded of a saying among the cardinals—elect a man as pope on one set of assumptions, and you will find he does something completely different. In this case he realized with certainty that at least one assumption of the cardinals had been misguided: John Becket may have been a compromise candidate, but he was not a compromising man.

Cassini knew that argument had failed him. He would have to rely on other means to change the pontiff's mind.

45

Exactly thirty minutes later, seated in his Vatican office, Cardinal Umberto Cassini was sipping a cup of espresso and attending to a pile of letters, slicing them open with his bone-handled letter opener, when his Nokia cell phone buzzed. He checked the number that appeared on his cell. It was Ryan. Cassini answered his phone. "Sean, any news?"

"I've been busy watching our uncle, as agreed."

Cassini was unused to hearing the pope referred to as "uncle." Ryan had suggested using that term when discussing the Holy Father over the phone, in case anyone eavesdropped on their conversation. Cassini said, "I just left him an hour ago."

"I know. But he's on the move. He exited through the Vatican's east gate."

Cassini put down the letter opener and sat up as he heard a clatter of street noise in the background of Ryan's call. "Did you follow him, Sean?"

"I'm on his tail as we speak. He's walking fast, as if he's in a hurry. You'll never guess what: he's dressed in civilian clothes and wearing a hat to mask his face."

"Where are you?"

"About fifty yards behind him. I don't think he's seen me tailing him yet. I'm wearing civilian clothes myself."

Cassini rose excitedly from behind his desk. "Whatever you do, stay on him. Which direction is our uncle walking?"

Ryan said, "Toward the red-light district."

"What?" A shocked Cassini stabbed the tip of the letter opener into his desk.

"That's why I called. He's just this minute heading near the railway station, where the brothels are."

PART FIVE

46

The luxury villa looked as if it had been built for a Roman emperor, all lush gardens and gushing ponds. As the sleek black Alfa Romeo drew up outside the wrought-iron gates, the Serb removed his Ray-Bans. He had a broad, brutal face, with high cheekbones and a broken nose.

Beyond the gates, two men in suits came forward and peered at the vehicle, then one of them flicked on a walkie-talkie and began to speak into it.

Bruno Zedik, 240 pounds of muscle and seated in the Alfa Romeo, brushed a fleck of dirt from his suit and turned to the tarty-looking girl beside him in the passenger seat. She wore a tight black Lycra skirt and a low-cut top.

Zedik, a former Serb army commando, smiled. "This is the kind of villa I want to own one day. My own pool, servants, a view of the sea."

"That's if you're still alive, Bruno," the girl said moodily. She pouted, her arms folded. "Still, I suppose as long as you know what you're doing."

Zedik sighed. He often wondered why he tolerated Regina Rossini but he knew the answer to that question immediately. During the hour's drive from his apartment the trouble had started when he told her who he was going to visit.

Zedik pushed the Ray-Bans back on his broken nose. "Did anyone ever mention you're hard to please?"

"You do, all the time." Regina sulked. "Now can we just get your business done with and get out of here? This boss of yours gives me the creeps."

"You ought to show more respect."

The girl flicked her mane of dyed blond hair. "You ask me, the guy's got to be a gangster, Bruno. And in case you didn't know it, gangsters kill people. You do wrong by people like that you'll get your dinky cut off. It happened to one of my relatives in Palermo."

Zedik scoffed. "You see too many American films. Some of those Roman and Greek statues on the villa grounds, they're genuine, thousands of years old. My boss is a respected international businessman and art collector."

"I'm supposed to be impressed?"

"Behave yourself, Regina. He's not mafia."

"If he's just a businessman, I'm still a virgin." The girl pouted. "And don't tell *me* how to behave. No one tells Regina Rossini how to behave."

She was starting to get on Zedik's nerves. *Stupid woman.* "You've got a really big mouth, you know that?"

She grinned wickedly. "How come you never complain about it in bed?"

The guard behind the gate put away his walkie-talkie. The second guard gestured for Zedik to drive forward as the gates whirred open.

Zedik snorted, his muscled chest straining under the suit as he suddenly lashed out and struck Regina Rossi a stinging blow across the face.

She reeled back into her seat with the force. A steely look that always lurked just beneath the surface erupted coldly in his eyes, a dangerous stare that told her she had pushed him too far and it was time to shut up. She whimpered. "I—I'm sorry, Bruno. Don't hit me again, please."

Zedik grabbed her savagely by the hair and gritted his teeth. "Just stay out of the way when we're inside the villa. Understand? Now shut up and try really hard to behave like a lady."

The gardens were dazzling in the sunshine. Beds of roses and frangipani ran along one side of the turquoise swimming pool, and the whole place had an air of luxury.

Zedik inhaled the sweet scent as the butler escorted him past the pool to a small garden. There was an amazing collection of exotic flower beds and a well-trimmed maze. A man stood among the flowers, pruning scissors in one hand, a solid gold Patek Philippe watch on his wrist. He had the kind of powerful aura only wealth can bring. His face was rugged rather than handsome and he wore an old pair of designer jeans, crisp linen shirt, and scuffed moccasins. "Bruno. Thank you for coming."

Zedik shook his hand. "Always a pleasure to see you, boss."

His boss gestured to his flower beds with obvious pride. "Well, what do you think of my garden? You like my new roses?"

"They're terrific." Zedik smiled. Personally, he could tell zilch about flowers, and each one smelled the same to him, but his boss was a passionate gardener and Zedik always tried to stay on his good side.

He pointed with the pruning scissors and said to Zedik,

"I've got a Spanish variety in the corner. Very rare. If I'm lucky, it will finally bloom after three years of hard work."

Who could have the patience to wait three years for a flower to bloom? Zedik thought. Only his boss had that kind of staying power. Zedik looked at the roses admiringly. "I'll have to get some slips from you. One of my sisters is crazy about roses."

His boss looked at Zedik as if he were an errant wasp. "All my flowers are rare and special. I never give slips, Bruno, you ought to know that."

Zedik laughed nervously. "It's just a joke, sir."

A tiny smile flickered on his boss's face. "I hear you brought the same girl with you as last time. The one with the mouth as big as her bust."

Zedik grinned. "I'm afraid so, boss. I left her back in the villa."

His boss put down the pruning scissors. "Let's sit by the pool. We need to talk some serious business."

"Whatever you say, Mr. Malik."

47

The butler brought them espresso and sweet almond biscuits. They sat at a table by the pool under the shade of a huge sun umbrella. Zedik admired the rolling lawns. He put down his cup. "What's so important, Mr. Malik?"

"You like this place, don't you, Bruno?"

Zedik nodded. "I love it, boss. Someday I'd like to own a place just like it."

Hassan Malik looked out at the immaculate gardens. "Ever since I was a small boy I wanted such a house. But my family were poor goatherders with only a filthy hovel for a home. I had a brother and sister. We all slept in the same room as my parents. My father died and then my mother. I was fifteen."

"That's tragic, Mr. Malik."

"I begged, I stole, did anything to earn a crust to feed my brother and sister. Sometimes, to forget about my hardship, I used to ride a bus into Jerusalem and walk past the villas of the rich with their splendid gardens. I used to tell myself that I would have such a house one day. It wasn't easy, but I did it."

"I can imagine, Mr. Malik."

Malik shook his head fiercely. "No, you cannot imagine.

You can't know what real poverty is. To never have enough food in your belly or money in your pocket."

Zedik reckoned his boss didn't seem like himself today. Normally he was direct and to the point. He hardly ever spoke about his past or stuff like that but this morning the man seemed distracted. "Mr. Malik, I apologize—"

Malik raised his hand, a serious look on his face. "Let's get down to business. I have a job for you." He reached in his shirt, plucked out an envelope, and placed it on the table. "You have always been loyal to me, Bruno. And that is why I am going to tell you a secret. It will help you understand why I have asked you here today and how important the job is. But I must be certain of your discretion."

Zedik said, "You know you can count on me, sir."

"Good. Because if a word of this ever leaks out, I assure you, Bruno, I will kill you. Slowly, painfully. It hurts me to have to make the consequences so clear to someone I trust, but I don't make such a threat lightly."

Zedik saw icy danger in Malik's eyes. In the ten years he had known his boss he had committed a catalogue of unlawful deeds on Malik's behalf—some of them brutal—but Zedik had never once heard him utter such words. He swallowed. "Mr. Malik, I'd never break my word to you."

Malik smiled gently, tapped Zedik's knee, and leaned closer. "Of course, I know you wouldn't but I've got to make the rules clear. And a wise man should always know the rules of the game." The smile vanished. "Especially a game as dangerous as the one about to begin. Take the envelope on the table, Bruno. It's a sign of my trust."

Zedik picked it up. "What's in it?"

"A check. Think of it as a bonus. When your work is completed to my satisfaction, you may cash that check."

Zedik opened the envelope and saw the generous amount written on the check. He turned pale. "Mr. Malik, I—I don't know what to say."

"Say nothing. Just take it. But against my advice my brother insists on being involved in this enterprise. Nidal can be hotheaded. So I want you to watch his back, Bruno. Make sure he doesn't get hurt. I have trust in a man like yourself, a man well versed in violence, able to take care of himself. You have always served me well."

Zedik slipped the envelope into his pocket. "Sure, Mr. Malik, I understand. You and Nidal are really close. But what exactly do you want me to do?"

Hassan Malik met the Serb's stare. "There is an ancient scroll, a precious artifact that has gone missing. You and Nidal will retrieve it for me."

Hassan Malik sat alone by the pool, sipping an espresso. Nidal stepped out onto the patio and removed his sunglasses. He wore an Armani dressing gown over his reed-thin body and he strolled to the poolside table and eased himself into a chair. "Has Bruno gone?"

Hassan Malik was used to regarding the world with angry contempt, but the sight of his younger brother never failed to elicit a protective feeling in him. "Yes, Nidal. He has gone."

"Have you told him everything, Hassan?"

"No. But enough so that he knows he's a player in a dangerous game and that I will require him to do unpleasant things, perhaps even kill."

Nidal stroked the neatly trimmed beard that covered his delicate features. "What happens next?"

Hassan sipped his espresso, then put down his cup.

"Bruno will help you find the scroll. You will use whatever means you have to."

Nidal's boyish look was suddenly gone, replaced by a kind of angry madness that erupted in his dark eyes. He slipped a frightening, curved Arab dagger from inside the pocket of his gown. "When the time comes, let me do the killing for you, Brother?"

"That's our father's knife. Put it away, Nidal."

Bitterness flashed in Nidal's face. "Is it not rightful that I use it? These people deserve to die, Hassan."

"Put the knife away, Brother. There will be time enough for spilling blood later."

Nidal reluctantly replaced the knife inside his gown.

Hassan stood. "Promise me you'll be careful, Nidal? No taking risks. Leave those to Bruno, it's what he's paid for." He touched his palm to his brother's face in a tender gesture. "I simply want no harm to come to you, ever."

Nidal's face sparked, and then he smiled boyishly. "Trust me, Hassan. I'll be careful. And I'll get the scroll for you, just wait and see, my brother."

48

ROME

John Becket strode into the narrow streets of the red-light district.

He was free again and this time he wore a plain dark suit and white, open-necked shirt. To avoid being recognized he'd pulled his broad-rimmed hat down over his face. He paused at a corner store window and looked back, his heart pounding.

Behind him, reflected in the glass, he saw the figure of a man rounding the corner. He was well built, wearing jeans, sneakers, and a dark jogger's rain slick. He wore a woollen hat pulled down over his head. Becket reckoned that the man had been following him since he'd left by the Vatican's east gate.

Too far away to get a close look at the man's face, Becket felt certain there was something familiar about him. But instinct told him that he was being followed by a member of the Vatican's security services.

Becket stood there, catching his breath, considering what to do next. Dark alleyways veined off the side street, sprinkled with seedy pickup bars and sex shops, the pavements bustling with crowds. There were women everywhere, prostitutes mostly. Some of them were beautiful as only Latin women were beautiful, and wearing the shortest skirts. Here, in the backstreets, you saw life at its rawest, the poverty and despair that drove men and women to crime and wrongdoing.

"Do you want to have some fun, mister?"

John Becket turned. A young woman, jittery with nervous energy, greeted him with a manic stare. She had dyed black hair, painted red fingernails, and bad skin. "No, thank you, my child."

Her smile vanished. "Suit yourself but you don't know what you're missing."

She whirled on down the street, pirouetting like some frenzied dancer. Becket guessed she was high on drugs.

At that exact moment, he saw the man following him. He was fifty yards behind, his woollen hat pulled well down on his head, his eyes staring at the pavement as if he was eager not to be recognized.

Becket saw his chance. He ducked down a crowded alleyway and plunged into the dark heart of the red-light district.

━━━

After five minutes of running through the backstreets, Becket slowed his pace and looked back. He saw no sign of the man. He took a deep breath and his chest felt on fire. He was out of condition, his legs trembling.

"Hello, Padre. It's a small world."

His heart jolted and he looked round. It was the young woman with the fake white Gucci handbag he'd encountered the previous evening, Maria. She was seated at a nearby café, smoking a cigarette, most of the empty tables spread out along the pavement. She wore a low-cut blue dress—revealing more bust than was decent—and high black leather boots. The bruising on her jaw was less noticeable, and still covered with heavy makeup. "Maria."

She seemed in better form as she stood and playfully

wagged a finger at him. "Out on the prowl two nights in a row, Padre? The church mustn't be keeping you busy. And this time you're dressed up for the town, I see."

"How are you, Maria?"

"Not so busy that I couldn't let you buy me a coffee."

"How is your jaw?"

She put a hand to her face and despite the bruising she smiled. "Hey, sorry about the other night. My pimp was giving me grief. He smacks me one now and then when I don't earn enough cash to keep him happy. Well, what do you say about that coffee, Padre?"

Becket scanned the alleyway for any sign of the man. Instinct told him to get far away from here as fast as possible but Maria plucked him by the arm and guided him to her table. "You're not going to hurt my feelings twice in a row, now are you?"

"Maria, I—"

"I could do with the company. I haven't even made the price of a cup of coffee all evening."

Becket needed to escape, not linger outside a café. *What if the man following him caught up with him? What if someone in the café recognized him?* He felt his heart thump and sweat dampen his brow.

Maria frowned. "Why do I get the feeling you look sort of familiar, Padre?"

Becket wanted the ground to open up and swallow him.

Maria whistled at a passing waiter. "Two cappuccinos, Marcelo. And while you're at it bring a couple of Camparis and soda for me and my new friend here."

49

Monsignor Sean Ryan was drenched in sweat.

Dressed like a jogger—in a zip-up dark blue nylon Windbreaker, blue nylon jog pants, a stupid-looking dark woollen hat pulled down over his red hair—Ryan felt like a second-rate private detective in a bad movie. But that was the least of his worries.

He was having a difficult time trying to keep up with John Becket. After running for eight blocks, Ryan figured that his boss could jog with the best of them. Then, much to Ryan's relief, he saw Becket stop outside a café, fifty yards away.

Ryan halted beside a corner store window and winced. A sign above said Madame Sin. The store was in darkness, which was just as well—Ryan saw that the window was filled with scantily clad female mannequins wearing erotic underwear. He was, after all, in Rome's red-light district.

Ryan felt as jittery as a truant schoolboy. He was pretty sure that John Becket had already spotted him and realized that he was being tailed. Ryan could do nothing about that except try to remain well back and out of sight. But the store window allowed him to observe a reflection of what was happening in the café down the street. Sweat dripping from his brow, he focused on the reflection in the window and what he saw shocked him, so much that he risked a look back at the scene.

The pope was drinking and talking with a brassy, attractive blond woman wearing a short skirt and boots. Ryan asked himself, *Am I seeing things?*

There were no two ways about it: the way the woman was dressed in such a neighborhood said *prostitute*. He dreaded to imagine the field day that the rag tabloids would have if the pope were recognized, drinking outside a café bar with a *hooker*. The pictures would end up on the cover of every newspaper in the world. Worse, it seemed that the pope was actually enjoying himself. He saw John Becket smile in the young woman's company.

Ryan shook his head. *This is insane.* Popes were not known to venture into red-light areas to talk with prostitutes. At least not since the debauched reign of Borgias in the fifteenth century, when Pope Gregory liked to frequent Rome's brothels.

Ryan tried to convince himself that what he was witnessing was perhaps harmless. That the pope was making social discourse with the less fortunate of society. But he knew he was simply making excuses. His mind screamed out that something about all of this was *very* wrong. Not only that, this unsavory neighborhood could also be dangerous.

Ryan felt for the reassuring bulge on his left side. His subcompact Glock 27 was tucked in his inside-the-pants holster.

Just in case.

Confused, Ryan forced himself to turn back to the storefront window. Staring at the reflected images of the pope and the prostitute, Ryan's mind was assaulted with a single, worrying thought: *What in the name of heaven is happening here?*

"Italian men think we should be paying *them*. They're all peacocks."

"You think so?" Despite himself, Becket found himself entertained by the young woman's shameless, working-class honesty. She was a breath of fresh air after the stiff formality of the Vatican.

Maria said, "I know so. All they think about is sex, just like all men. Let me give you a good example of the typical Italian male. Have you heard the story about Luigi?"

"No. Tell me."

"His young wife dies and at the funeral he's sobbing his eyes out. As they lower her coffin into the ground, Luigi's friend puts an arm around him and says, 'Don't worry, someday soon we'll find another nice girl for you to settle down with.' And a sobbing Luigi says, 'That's all very well, but what about tonight?'"

Maria giggled and slapped a hand on her leather boot. "Well, not bad, eh Padre?"

John Becket realized he was smiling. "Not bad. If I racked my brain I could probably tell you a joke or two but tonight I'm preoccupied."

Maria sipped more Campari. "By what?"

Becket flicked a nervous look across the street. "Too many things to mention, Maria."

"You speak good Italian but you're not Italian, are you, Padre?"

"No."

He didn't offer any further explanation and she didn't ask as she studied him, then raised her Campari in a toast. "You know, for a priest, you're pretty okay."

"You mean most priests are not?"

Maria put down her glass. "Not the ones I've met. They

want sex just like any man. All men are born with an open fly."

"We are all sinners, Maria, in one way or another. None of us escapes life's impulses. Not even Jesus himself. But the important thing is that we try with all our heart to live our lives with truthfulness, dignity, and respect, and to follow his example. If we all did that, we might even live in a near-perfect world."

"Hey, don't tell me you're one of these do-gooders who want to clean up the streets. Next you'll be asking me if I believe in God."

"Do you, Maria?"

"See? I stopped a long time ago."

"What do you think of those in the Vatican?"

Maria snorted. "Half the world starves and they live like princes in their ivory towers. Will I tell you why I stopped believing? Because I always wanted to ask God why he allowed so much suffering, poverty, and injustice in the world."

"He might ask us the same question."

"How do you mean?"

"Don't we allow it, Maria? Each of us. In our hearts and minds. In the way we ignore the suffering of others and close our ears to their cries of pain. The way we disrespect our fellow man and are selfish for our own needs. Much of human suffering is avoidable. But a righteous path has a high price, and many are not prepared to pay that price."

Maria frowned. "You've lost me, Padre."

Becket placed a hand gently on hers. "Maria, I could give you the deepest theological thought on the subject of human suffering. I could even explain how pain and torment bring us closer to God."

"How?"

"Because our own suffering causes us to feel pity. And

pity makes us more human. And being human allows us to truly experience the joy of love. I could explain our purpose for being here, the reason for our existence in this universe. It's the most profound and yet the simplest reason of all: to enlighten our souls and to redeem God's gift to us—His eternal love. And make no mistake, Maria, the gift of love is truly eternal. But do you have the evening free to discuss it all?"

"Not unless you're paying me by the hour."

Becket was tempted to smile, then suddenly froze. Across the street he noticed the man in the nylon Windbreaker, jogging pants, and sneakers looking casually in a darkened store window. His head was still covered by the woollen hat but he was closer now, close enough for Becket to feel a tingle of recognition. His heart pounded. He was almost certain it was Sean Ryan. "Maria, I need to get away from here urgently."

"Is my company suddenly that revolting?"

"No, Maria, I have a problem. I have an important appointment to keep, but there's a man following me. He's across the street."

"Which man?"

"Be careful. If you look back don't make it obvious. He's wearing a dark blue rain slick, a woollen hat, sneakers, and running pants."

Maria took a few more sips of Campari before risking a casual glance. The man was peering into the darkened storefront. She turned back with a scowl. "Why's he after you? Did you steal from the church collection?"

"I wish it were that simple. But I need to get away from him."

Maria considered. "Your best bet is a door at the back of the café, past the toilet. It leads to an alley. Don't worry if the guy tries to come after you. I've been stopping men for years. One more shouldn't be a problem."

"Thank you." Becket placed a generous handful of notes on the table. "Please keep the change. Maybe it will stop you being beaten again."

Maria picked up the banknotes and raised an eye. "Maybe you did steal from the collection after all?"

"No, Maria, but I hope we meet again." Becket wrote a number on a bar napkin and slid it across. "If anyone ever threatens to harm you, or if you're afraid of them, I want you to call me at this number. If I can help you, I will."

Maria frowned. "You know, it's killing me where I saw you before. Were you ever a regular at the massage parlors near the main railway station?"

Becket suppressed a smile and gave the rim of his hat a sharp tug to ensure it covered much of his face. "I'm afraid not. You're a good woman, Maria."

She laughed. "Not for at least ten years. Now, get out of here or you'll be late for your appointment."

50

An hour later, as Cardinal Umberto Cassini was about to leave his office for a late appointment, his cell chirped and Ryan's name and number appeared. Cassini answered urgently, "Where are you, Sean? What's the news?"

"I just got back to the Vatican. I'm afraid uncle managed to evade me. The last time I saw him he was enjoying a drink with a tarty-looking lady in the red-light district."

"You're—you're joking."

"I wish I was. I saw uncle give her a handful of paper money. After that he disappeared and I lost him."

"So we don't know where else he's gone?"

"No, but he's back. Security on the east gate spotted him climbing out of a taxi five minutes ago."

Cassini said irritably, "This cat-and-mouse game is becoming ridiculous. Did security get the cab's license number? Maybe we could question the driver and find out where he made the pickup?"

"I'm afraid not."

"It's time I put a stop to this and demand an explanation from the Holy Father for his behavior. It's absurd."

"You think such a confrontation is wise, Your Eminence?"

"Wise or not, it needs to be done. I won't have his reckless behavior bring the church into disrepute."

51

Five minutes later Cassini walked the long corridors to the papal chambers. They were vast, with floor-to-ceiling oak doors, red carpet, polished marble tiles, and sparkling chandeliers. Even the intricate ceiling roses were finished with solid gold leaf.

Passing a Louis XIV writing bureau, Cassini knew it was worth a small fortune, like the many antiques that decorated the chambers; or the exquisite paintings that draped the walls. He recalled that a recent audit disclosed the Vatican's net worth to be in the region of $100 billion. Cassini thought that the figure was probably on the conservative side; after all, the Vatican was the single owner of Rome's most prime real estate.

He was just about to knock on the double doors when one of them was yanked open and John Becket stood there, wearing his plain white gown. "Umberto, I was just about to summon you. Come inside, please."

Caught off guard, Cassini felt a little anxious as he stepped into the gilded, exquisite papal rooms.

The pope slammed the door shut and struck an unfamiliar pose, his hands on his hips. "I'll get straight to the point, Umberto. I have been followed by Sean Ryan this evening. I demand an explanation. Was this your idea?"

Despite the tables being turned, Cassini bristled with indignation. "Holy Father, I confess it was. But there were safety concerns. And may I make a point? You were seen entering the red-light district, and offering a woman money. What if a press photographer recognized you and took your photograph? Think of the scandal. I mean, with all due respect, you were seen in the company of a *prostitute*."

"I seem to recall that so was Jesus. Would you have criticized him for that too, Umberto?"

Cassini was stuck for an answer and his face reddened. "Holy Father, I simply don't know why you had to visit that area—"

The reproof was instant and sharp. "That is my business. Even though I am pope, my privacy is my own. And please don't ever question who I keep company with, Umberto. Not ever."

Cassini still bridled with frustration. "Very well, but I can assure you that what was done was for your own good and the Vatican's. It's normal to have security in the background, to watch His Holiness wherever he goes. There are hundreds of Vatican security officers whose sole task is just that."

"Then it's time I made some changes."

"Holy Father?"

The pope spread his hands wide, indicating the opulent room. "Do we really need all this, Umberto? This gilded prison."

"I'm not sure I follow."

"All these trappings of power. All this material wealth. This vast, endless, often petty bureaucracy. As pastors, we should have no need of such distractions."

"I don't see where this is going, Holy Father."

"This church was founded in the name of a Nazarene carpenter who owned nothing, not even a bed he could rest his head on. Yet we who inherited his mission are surrounded by accumulated riches, by vast wealth. All over the world are barefoot, hungry men, women, and children with empty bellies. Yet we hoard our riches like misers and I am crowned with pomp and ceremony and live in gilded rooms. I am ashamed that the carpenter's successor should live like a king."

"Holy Father, the church has a reputation to preserve. Status and traditions to maintain."

"No longer." From behind his desk, Becket plucked a cheap canvas bag, the kind you might buy in one of the backstreets where he had fled. "I am leaving the Vatican, Umberto. I have packed the few belongings I will need."

Cassini felt as if he'd been electrocuted. *"Leaving?"*

"As of tonight the Vatican is no longer my residence."

52

"Okay, Pierre, make sure the men are careful. Some of the stuff in these boxes is pretty fragile."

"But of course, *mon ami.*"

Buddy Savage wiped sweat from his brow and jumped down off the back of the Fiat truck. He watched as one of the crew, a small, cheerful-looking Frenchman with an earring and a ponytail, began to supervise a group of Bedu workmen as they loaded packing crates onto the vehicle.

As Savage stood there wearing his grubby NYPD baseball cap, a voice said in accented English, "You look busy, Mr. Savage. I hope I'm not interrupting your work."

Savage turned and saw Sergeant Mosberg. "Busy enough. The dig finishes this week. We're getting ready to close down the site. We could probably close it down a lot quicker if we didn't have the media sticking its nose in our face. They're still buzzing around here when the mood takes them, asking questions."

"You're in a hurry to go somewhere?"

"No, but unless everything's properly catalogued and the paperwork in order for your Department of Antiquities the dirt's going to hit the fan."

"No more digging for scrolls?"

Savage lit up a Marlboro Light and blew out a mouthful of smoke. "Our work's done for the season. By spring, it gets too hot to dig, but a few of the crew will stay behind to tidy up. For the rest of us this tour of duty's over. What can I do for you, Mosberg?"

The sergeant rapped his knuckles on one of the packing crates. "What exactly have you got in here, Mr. Savage?"

Savage dangled his cigarette from the corner of his mouth. "Hundreds of pottery shards, a variety of bones and coins, personal artifacts and jewelry, almost all of it from the first century A.D. In short, three months' work. Why?"

Mosberg took a notepad from his pocket and flipped it open. "I'm afraid I need to ask you some more questions, Mr. Savage."

Savage sighed and tipped back his baseball cap. "I can give you ten minutes, Mosberg, then I've got to get back to work. Want a Coke? I sure could do with one."

"Very kind. I won't say no."

Savage flicked away his half-finished cigarette. "Follow me to my humble hacienda and excuse the mess."

"One thing you might like to know. Forensics had the flakes of parchment from the floor of Professor Green's tent analyzed. It's definitely the same material found in other Dead Sea scrolls. They also had the flakes and the ink carbon-dated."

"And?"

"There's no question that they're about two thousand years old."

53

Savage led the way to a cramped walk-in tent.

Mosberg said, "The experts said roughly between A.D. 25 and 50. You don't seem surprised, Savage."

"Why should I be? I never thought for a minute that the scroll was a fake. I've seen my fair share of parchments in my career. I knew it was genuine."

Mosberg picked his way past a folded camp bed, a dented travel trunk, and more piles of packing crates. One crate was open and contained a collection of small bones next to a large clay pot. A tag on the crate said L.I.E. "Are they animal bones?" he asked.

Savage grabbed a couple of chilled Cokes from a blue plastic cooler at his feet and tossed a can to Mosberg. "Actually, they're human. An infant, second century A.D. I'll let you in on a secret, Sergeant. Whenever archaeologists dig here they often come across human bones like the ones you're looking at. Thousands of years ago it was common practice to bury dead infants in clay jars. Even though they've been interred for millennia your Jewish religion still requires that we stop digging and perform a full and proper burial service. If they're from a more recent period than the one we're digging and they don't interest us, we label the bones with a tag that says L.I.E."

Mosberg arched an eyebrow as he plucked open his can. "What does that mean?"

"It's short for late intrusive element. We classify them as animal bones so that way we can keep going with the dig and focus on the period we're dealing with."

"Isn't that deceitful?"

"Sure, but the benefits outweigh the cost. And your Antiquities Department turns a blind eye. If they didn't, things would grind to a halt."

Mosberg examined what looked like a tiny, weathered rib bone. "To think this infant lived soon after the time of Christ. Remarkable."

Savage gulped a mouthful of Coke. "Make any progress, Sergeant?"

Mosberg looked up. "I'm afraid not. You know what makes me curious? Why did Cane choose to dig at that particular site where he found the scroll?"

"In field fourteen? Simple. Rodents."

"Pardon?"

"Creatures like rats and gophers, even wild dogs, burrow deep into the earth for shelter. That can be a blessing to archaeologists because they leave behind a mound of debris after they dig. Sometimes we get lucky and the mound contains coins and pieces of pottery shards, or other stuff of interest. A mound that Jack discovered at field fourteen contained pottery shards, first century A.D., so we decided to dig."

Mosberg jotted some notes. "Interesting. And may I ask where Mr. Cane is right now?"

Savage slumped into one of the chairs. "Your guess is as good as mine. The last time I saw him was here at the camp, yesterday afternoon."

"You have no idea?"

"Sometimes he drives into Jerusalem to visit friends."

"Which friends?"

"You've got me there. But I can only guess that's where he's gone."

Mosberg eased himself into the chair opposite. "I hope you're not withholding information from me, Mr. Savage?"

"Now why would I do that?"

"How long have you known Jack Cane?"

Buddy Savage raised the dented travel trunk, grabbed an old photo album, and tossed it on the table. "Does that answer your question?"

Mosberg flicked through sheaves of photographs in the album: many were of Savage and Jack Cane working on digs. Both men looked much younger in some of the snapshots, which obviously spanned many years. There were others of Savage with a man who resembled Cane, and some of the shots included an attractive, smiling woman, her arms around both men.

"The couple you see were Jack's parents. They died twenty years ago in an auto accident near Qumran. I guess that's why he keeps coming back here to dig. For years it's been like a pilgrimage for Jack."

"Why?"

"Are you familiar with the work of the Irish writer Oscar Wilde, Sergeant?"

Mosberg sipped more Coke and shook his head. "I can't say that I am."

"There's a line he wrote. 'The heart always returns to wherever it is most hurt.' Or words to that effect. I think the same applies to Jack. This place, Qumran, was a watershed in his life. It scarred him. And shaped him, made him the man he is."

Mosberg slapped the album shut and replaced it on the table. "Interesting. So you know Jack Cane a long time."

"His father and I were buddies for years. We worked digs together, Jack too, ever since he was a kid. He's a good man, Mosberg, not a murderer."

"You sound very sure of that."

"I am. He's not the professor's killer. Finding that scroll meant everything to Jack. It's like a vindication of his parents' life work."

"You're saying he really wanted to find a scroll?"

"Sure he did. Like everyone else on this site."

"And he did find a scroll but now it's missing. Then there's the small matter of Cane's own knife buried in the professor's chest."

"Listen, Mosberg, Jack wouldn't jeopardize himself by getting involved in murder. He's completely innocent. As for the knife, that's a weapon more familiar to Jews and Arabs, so I'd look elsewhere if I were you."

"We'll see, Mr. Savage. Perhaps if I dig deep enough, I can find his motive."

Savage tipped back his baseball cap and shook his head. "If you really believe that, then you're a big dummy, Mosberg. But good luck to you, because you're sure going to need it."

Mosberg's face flushed red with annoyance. He spread his arms and looked toward the excavation site, his tone icy. "Tell me, who pays for all this, Savage? The expense of the dig, the crew salaries?"

Savage sipped another mouthful. "The crew are mostly volunteers. Some, professionals like me, get a basic salary that's nothing to write home about. As for the costs, most digs have sponsors. Ours are a number of wealthy international businessmen and a religious trust that pick up our tab."

"And what do they get in return?"

Savage shrugged. "I'm sure there's maybe a tax break or two in there for some of the sponsors. But mostly they just want to contribute."

"To what?"

"Our knowledge of religion and of humankind's history."

Mosberg jotted more notes in his pad. "All very noble, but I'll need a list of your sponsors, Mr. Savage."

"Hey, I'm up to my plums in work right now, Mosberg, but you'll get it, rest assured."

"Today, please." Mosberg handed over his business card. "You'll see my e-mail and fax number at the bottom. May I ask what religion you are, Mr. Savage?"

"What the heck has that got to do with anything?"

"It's a simple question."

"There was a time when I could say Roman Catholic, but I'm afraid I fell from grace. These days I'm happy to settle for agnostic. What does it matter?"

"Where do you live when you're not working on digs, Mr. Savage?"

"A bachelor pad in a small upstate New York town."

"You find your work rewarding?"

"I'm not sure where this is going, Mosberg, but yeah, sure." Savage held up his calloused, clay-stained hands. "Would I work these fingers to the bone if I didn't love it? I've been doing this job for well over twenty years and with little reward except for the pleasure it gives me."

"Really?"

"Really. Though at this stage in my life I'd probably settle for a condo in Florida, a Mustang convertible, and an accommodating lady. Now, if you've finished scraping the barrel, I still have work to do." Savage stood and tossed his empty Coke can into a bin.

Mosberg rose. "When you found Professor Green you said he was already dead. Did you see anyone nearby or leaving the tent? Did you witness anything at all, no matter how insignificant it might seem? It could be important, Mr. Savage. Please think."

"I already answered that question for Inspector Raul."

"Please answer it again."

"I saw nothing. Not a soul. I heard nothing. Now, are you done?"

Mosberg flipped shut his notepad. "For now, Mr. Savage."

Savage watched Mosberg climb into a Nissan SUV and drive off in the direction of the Bedu village. He heard a noise behind him and turned.

Jack Cane stood facing him, his face drawn, his clothes crumpled and stained. "Hello, Pops."

"What the heck?" Savage stepped forward and his arm went around Jack's shoulder. "Boy, am I glad to see you. Sergeant Mosberg was just here, looking for you. Don't worry, I told the guy nothing."

"Has he any leads?" Jack's face was beaded with sweat, his voice hoarse.

"You ask me, the guy's as lost as a dog in long grass." Savage noticed a rip in Cane's inside right trouser leg, revealing a gauze bandage. The clothes' stains were caked patches of dried blood. "What happened? And where are Yasmin and Josuf? What have you been up to?" he demanded.

Jack was barely able to stand, his face racked with pain. "I've lost some blood. Yasmin's gone to find a fresh dressing in the first-aid kit. I need to sit down, Buddy."

As Savage went to help him toward his tent, Jack collapsed into his arms.

54

"Here, drink some of this, it'll settle your nerves." Buddy Savage splashed Wild Turkey into two glass tumblers and handed one to Yasmin.

Yasmin's clothes were dusty, her hair mussed as she sat in one of the canvas chairs and accepted the glass. "Thanks. Though the condition I'm in, I probably look like I've had a few already."

Savage grabbed another chair. "If you want my opinion, you all need your heads examined for crossing into Syria illegally."

"It was a spur-of-the-moment thing, Buddy, something we got caught up in. Jack was desperate to try to find the parchment." Yasmin looked behind her. "Does Pierre really know what he's doing? Shouldn't we just fetch a doctor?"

Savage followed Yasmin's gaze to the room at the back of the tent. Jack sat in a canvas chair, one leg of his trousers cut away. Seated in front of him, the cheery Frenchman was engrossed as he worked on Jack's wound, a first-aid kit open, next to it a plastic basin filled with steaming water.

"If we call a doctor he'd probably inform the cops. Don't worry about Pierre. Believe it or not he was once a medic with the French Foreign Legion. He's treated a few bullet wounds in his day, which is why he's in charge of our first aid. He gave Jack a morphine shot, so he can't feel a thing. How about you finish your story?"

"After the men set the monastery on fire they forced us to drive out into the desert. I had to drive Josuf's truck and he followed me in his Mercedes. Then the weather started to turn, a sandstorm blew up, and after about five miles we were made to halt and get out of the vehicles."

"Go on."

"We thought we were all going to be executed. The man named Pasha aimed at Jack's head. But at the last moment he deflected the pistol and shot Jack in the leg instead. That's when I blacked out. To be honest, the sight of blood freaks me out."

"Go on."

"Pasha slapped me awake. He said, 'Let this be a warning to you all to keep your noses out of this business and forget about the scroll or you'll regret it. If you come after me I'll hunt each of you down and kill you.' Or words to that effect, but we got the message. He scared the life out of me."

Savage's brow creased. "I'm astonished he released you all after you witnessed him killing the priest."

"We didn't understand it either. But we were grateful to escape with our lives. Then Pasha tossed away Josuf's pickup keys and he and his bodyguard drove off. Josuf had a basic first-aid kit in his pickup and managed to put a dressing on Jack's wound. It took us over an hour to find the keys in the dark before we drove back here."

"Any difficulty crossing the border?"

"The Jordanians didn't bother us but the Israeli guards seemed suspicious. They searched Josuf's pickup before finally letting us through."

"Did you learn anything useful from this priest, Novara?"

"Jack thinks he found some translations from the scroll. He spent most of the journey working on the notes he'd made in his notebook."

Savage said eagerly, "Tell me more."

"You better wait until you speak with Jack. He can fill you in better than me."

Pierre came in, wiping his hands on a towel. He immediately helped himself to the Wild Turkey, splashing a generous measure into a glass.

Savage said, "So what's the verdict?"

The Frenchman raised his glass to both of them before he swallowed the liquor in one mouthful and shook his head. "You know, it sometimes amazes me."

Yasmin got to her feet. "What does?"

"Some people have the devil's own luck. If Jack's wound had been a few centimeters to the right the bullet could have severed an artery and we might be nailing him down in a box."

"He's going to be okay?"

The Frenchman smiled at Yasmin and slapped down his glass. "I'm not a doctor but I believe he'll recover. It's really just a bad flesh wound."

Yasmin stood on her toes and kissed Pierre's cheek. "Thank you."

The Frenchman winked, then handed her two plastic vials of pills he'd taken from the first-aid kit. "Painkillers, if needed. The second vial contains antibiotics to prevent infection. Have Jack take one a day for the next four days. He's sleeping now, thanks to the morphine, but I'll be back later to check on him."

Savage and Yasmin peered in at Jack. He was sleeping soundly in the chair, his hair flopped to one side, his leg dressed with a fresh cotton bandage. Savage watched as Yasmin knelt beside him. She gently patted his forehead with a damp cloth. "He looks exhausted. I'm not surprised. He didn't sleep at all during our drive last night. He seemed totally preoccupied."

Savage looked down at her. "Because of his wound?"

"That too, but he was preoccupied by the stuff he recorded in his notebook. No doubt he'll tell you all about it once he wakes up."

"Has Josuf gone back to his village to grab some sleep?"

"Yes. Why?" Yasmin answered.

"I've a feeling he won't get much. Sergeant Mosberg was here earlier, asking questions. When he left, he drove toward the Bedu village. I hope Josuf keeps his mouth shut."

"Don't worry. We all agreed not to tell anyone what had happened, except you. Jack said you had to know."

Savage nodded down at Jack. "How about we let him sleep it off and you and I step outside. We need to talk, Yasmin."

She looked up. "About what?"

Savage was grim. "I think I know who took the scroll."

55

"Who did it?" Yasmin asked expectantly.

They stepped outside the tent and strolled for several yards toward the Qumran ruins. Savage lit a Marlboro and took a drag. "Before I answer that, do you mind if I make a nosy remark? I saw the way you tended to Jack. It's obvious you care."

Yasmin blushed. "What's that got to do with anything?"

"Maybe a lot. Don't look so embarrassed. You like him, don't you?"

Yasmin's brown eyes rose to meet Savage's stare. "I've liked him since the day we met. What's it to you?"

"You met Jack only a few months ago. I've known him most of his life. And in my own way I've tried to be like a father to him. When his dad died, I lost a good friend."

"He never talks much about himself after his parents died. Did anything else bad happen to Jack?"

"You bet it did. Think about it. He was parentless at nineteen. After he flew back to the States things went downhill. For a long time he tried to numb the pain with alcohol and pills. How he didn't wind up dead I'll never know, but there came a turning point."

"What happened?"

"I tracked him down, got him cleaned up. It took him a while to stitch his life back together but he did it. Archaeology was his first love, really all he wanted to do. He worked a bunch of lousy part-time jobs to pay for college fees—flipping burgers, night watchman, pumping gas—and got himself through. A teaching post followed, along with digs in Mexico, Egypt, Rome, and Israel. I really don't mean this to sound like a cliché, but in some ways I like to think he's the son I never had."

"You don't have family of your own?"

Savage smiled gently and nudged a rock with the toe of his desert boot. "The dice never rolled that way. I guess I never found the right woman. But then twelve years spent in the Catholic priesthood didn't help either."

"You were a priest?"

"A long time ago. After two years of serving in Vietnam and seeing hell on earth, it seemed like a pretty good idea at the time."

"You were a soldier too?"

"For a time. But that was then and this is now. What's important for you to know is that I couldn't bear to see Jack harmed. I want to see him happy and loved. I want to see him mend his soul before it's too late and he . . ." Savage broke off.

Yasmin looked into his face. "Ends up like you? Is that what you were going to say?"

Savage shrugged ruefully. "Maybe. Just know that I care about him, Yasmin. He's a man worth caring about. He's passionate about what he does. In a way, it's a continuation of his parents' work, don't you see? His way of honoring them. That's why I'm asking you to do something for me."

"What?"

"His father was a good and decent man, but boy, he could be a strong-willed character if he got an idea into his head. Jack's cut from the same cloth. He'll follow this business to the ends of the earth if he has to, no matter how dangerous the threat. That's why I want you to do your utmost to convince him not to."

"Why do you think he'll listen to me, Buddy?"

"It has to be worth a shot. I don't want Jack to wind up dead. Try to convince him to let the police handle it."

"If you really think it's worth trying." Yasmin looked at Savage. "You said you knew who stole the scroll."

He turned his gaze toward the stony ruins littering the dig site. "My instinct tells me it's an Arab or Israeli criminal gang that was responsible."

"Why do you say that?"

"Because as long as archaeologists have been finding precious artifacts in the Holy Land, criminals have been trying to steal them. The black market is full of vicious crooks and it's easy to understand why. One precious discovery could make them very rich."

"Any particular Arab or Israeli gang?"

Savage took a last drag and flicked away his cigarette. "Take your pick. There are dozens. And I'm guessing this guy Pasha's connected to them in some way. That's why I need you to convince Jack to leave it to the cops. I don't want him winding up dead. It would break my heart."

"Any more talk like that and you'll have me in tears, folks."

They both heard Jack's voice and turned. He was standing unsteadily and Yasmin went to take hold of his arm. "Pierre said you needed to rest."

"Hey, I'm not done for yet. Just a little lightheaded after the morphine." Jack hobbled over to sit on a boulder.

Savage said, "How long had you been standing back there?"

Jack smiled. "Long enough."

Savage said, "Good. Then maybe you'll think twice before making any more dumb trips like the one to Syria."

"You're wrong about that, Buddy." Jack patted his injured leg. "It wasn't a mistake. In fact, it was even worth the blood and the pain."

Savage frowned. "Are you crazy?"

"Maybe, but I found a clue at the monastery and your suspicions are way off the mark."

56

"Wake up, Lela. Rise and shine."

Lela felt someone patting her face. She blinked and came out of a deep sleep. Ari stood over her with a big smile. "Sorry to ruin your siesta. How do you feel?"

Lela struggled to awaken. She was in a single bed, the overhead light was on, the bedroom curtains closed. "Half dead. How long have I been sleeping?"

Ari crossed to the window and flung open the curtains. "Three hours. I left a cup of fresh coffee on the nightstand. Hot and black, the way you always liked it."

Lela sat up and squinted as sunlight exploded into the room. As she sipped the steaming coffee she looked around the apartment. The Mossad safe house was half a mile from headquarters. Ari had brought her there at 3 A.M. after they landed back at Tel Aviv. An hour's debrief followed and then Ari showed her to the bedroom and told her to get some rest. Then he disappeared into one of the other rooms and minutes later Lela heard him snoring.

The apartment was spotlessly clean but the decor was lousy: straw-colored walls, threadbare dark curtains, and a suite of well-worn furniture that looked as if it was ready for the dump. Lela had lain under the fresh sheets for at least an hour, her mind racked by the previous evening's events until she had been sucked into a coma by a wave of exhaustion.

Now Ari came out of the bathroom and tossed her a fresh white bath towel and a tube of shower gel. "For you. In the great Jewish tradition, when it comes to spending on nonessentials Mossad is as tight as a rusty nut. The soap's cheap and the towels like sandpaper. But at least the water's hot enough for a shower."

"Thanks." Lela climbed out of bed, pulling the cotton bath towel around her to cover her nakedness. "Any particular reason why you deprived me of eight hours' sleep, Ari?"

There was a sound of footsteps outside the door and Ari smiled. "I think you're about to find out."

A sudden rap came on the bedroom door, then it yawned open and Julius Weiss stood there. He wore a fresh blue shirt, khaki trousers, and the same old sandals. "So, you're awake, Inspector Raul. Have you told her yet, Ari?"

"I thought I'd leave that to you, sir."

Weiss jerked a thumb toward the door. "Outside, in ten minutes. Something's come up and we need to talk."

57

QUMRAN

"Before this goes any further, I've got some news you might like to hear," Savage announced.

"What's that?" Jack asked.

"Mosberg said his forensics people had the parchment flakes and ink analyzed and carbon-dated. It's the same material used in other Dead Sea scrolls, and in all probability dated between A.D. 25 and 50."

Jack slapped a fist into his palm. "I never doubted it for a second, Buddy."

"Neither did I. But don't keep us in suspense, tell us what you found," Savage demanded.

"I think Father Novara was trying to decipher some kind of message contained in the scroll. I saw jottings and lists of Aramaic words and characters lying on his desk, as if he was in the process of decoding something. I even found a couple of sentences he appeared to have translated and they're pretty remarkable indeed."

"Let's see them."

Jack reached for his notebook in his back pocket. "Over fifty years ago one of the translators working on the original Dead Sea scrolls, Professor Schonfeld, discovered a recurring cipher in some texts. A hidden language, if you like. He called it the Atbash Cipher. Ever heard of it?"

Savage nodded. "Sure. I thought it was found in scrolls written in Hebrew."

"It seems it may occur in Aramaic texts too."

"I never really paid much attention to Schonfeld's work. Didn't folks think he was a crackpot?"

"Some did. But a number of respected academics eventually recognized that Schonfeld had stumbled across something highly unusual."

Yasmin said, "Why would the Essenes want to devise a hidden code?"

Savage shook his head. "Nobody's ever come up with a credible answer, except that they were an eccentric cult and inclined to be secretive, which is probably one of the reasons why they hid their scrolls in the first place. It's probably also why the Essenes stashed their scrolls in local caves for safety when the community was destroyed by the Romans as part of a crackdown on Jewish insurgents, some time between A.D. 66 and 73."

"So what was Father Novara trying to decode?"

Jack said, "You're asking the million-dollar question, Yasmin. Some of the code had a biblical reference and Schonfeld suggested that certain of the parchments may have been encrypted with a prophecy or revelation. But Schonfeld died years ago and afterward his work became a sort of curiosity, not always taken seriously."

"What kind of prophecy or revelation are we talking about?"

"No one knows. But Schonfeld's study of the codes led him to believe that it was significant."

Savage put a hand on Jack's shoulder. "You're talking pure speculation, Jack."

"Am I? Have a read of this. I found this sentence jotted on one of the pages I discovered beside Novara's desk . . ."

Savage studied the lines Jack had recorded in the notebook:

> *When the messiah's corpse was removed from the*
> *cross, it was placed in a tomb in the burial caves*
> *outside Dora, on the road to Caesarea.*

Savage raised an eye. He looked totally flummoxed a moment, then he said, "What the heck have we got here? Are you sure you didn't make a mistake transcribing the words?"

"No, Buddy, I made sure of it."

Savage stared at the lines and shook his head. " 'When the messiah's corpse was removed from the cross, it was placed in a tomb in the burial caves outside Dora, on the road to Caesarea.'" He looked up, stunned. "If it's meant to be the messiah Jesus, biblical history records he was buried near Jerusalem."

"Exactly."

Confused, Savage studied the lines again. "It's a pretty explosive statement, but what exactly does it mean?"

Jack said, "Buddy, believe me, this is one conundrum that's only going to be solved by a complete translation of the full text."

Savage scratched his head. "You've sure got my attention. Still, I meant what I said. Don't be dumb enough to go tearing off and getting mixed up with criminals like Pasha, not unless you've got a death wish. Tell the police everything you know and leave the rest to them."

"Do you really believe the cops can move quickly enough to stop the scroll from disappearing into some private collection? Let's face it, all they've come up with so far is to suspect *me*."

"You said I was way off the mark about a criminal gang. Explain."

"Buddy, if Father Novara was decoding the text, then this has got to go much deeper than just a bunch of murderous thieves. Criminals are interested in cash, not codes or translations. Maybe thieves took it, but if they did they stole it to order. Novara said that the scroll was destined never to be seen, along with the others, which maybe implies it's bound for a private collector."

Savage frowned. "Others?"

"Novara suggested he handled other stolen parchments, not just ours."

"You mean from Qumran?"

"Who knows? In Novara's study I saw a drawing of a Roman inscription containing animals, monsters, and sylphs. I've seen a similar inscription before. I've been racking my mind where, but I can't figure it out."

Savage raised an eye. "Okay, Inspector Poirot, tell me more."

Before Jack could reply Pierre reappeared, clutching a newspaper under his arm. "The Antiquities Department just called, Buddy. They want you at their Jerusalem office right away."

"What for?"

"The guy didn't say, except it was urgent. You're to ask for the investigations unit when you arrive." Pierre winked at Jack. "How's the patient?"

"Feeling a lot better since the morphine."

"Wouldn't we all? Remember, no gymnastics, you don't want to open up that wound of yours. By the way, have any of you seen the local rag?"

Pierre handed Jack a local newspaper. The headline read:

BRUTAL MURDER MYSTERY AND THEFT AT QUMRAN
KILLER SOUGHT BY POLICE

Pierre said, "It gives all the grisly details of the crime and speculates about black-market thieves."

Buddy took the newspaper from Jack, scanned the article, and raised an eyebrow. "I'm glad I'm not the only one who thinks so." He looked up. "If this keeps up, you're going to have more media crews crawling all over this site like flies over camel dung."

Buddy handed the paper back to Pierre and patted Jack's cheek. "We'll continue this talk when I get back. Meantime, rest, okay?"

Savage disappeared toward the office trailer, following Pierre. Jack watched him go, then turned to Yasmin and shook his head, half smiling. "I don't think Buddy realizes that he sometimes acts like he's my old man."

"He means well, Jack."

"I know." Jack looked at his watch. "Listen, Yasmin, I need you to do me a big favor and drive me to Tel Aviv."

"What for? You're in no condition to travel."

"You heard Pierre. I'm on the mend." Jack held up his cell phone, excitement infecting his voice. "While you and Buddy were talking I made a few calls to Italy. There's a guy in Rome I intend to talk with who's an authority on Schonfeld's code. And there's someone in the Vatican I'd like to see."

"About what?"

"I'll explain later. I called the airport. There's a one o'clock flight from Tel Aviv to Rome."

Yasmin said with concern, "Rome? But you heard Buddy."

"By the time Buddy realizes the call from the Antiquities Department was phoney, I'll be on my way to the Eternal City."

"*You* made the call to Pierre?"

"I had to. I feel guilty about it but if I told Buddy what I was up to, he'd tie me down. I'll call him when I get to Rome. Besides, if I hang around here and the media heats up and starts mentioning my name, I may not be able to travel anywhere."

"What about Pasha's threat?"

Jack's voice sparked with resolve. "That's a risk I'm going to have to take. Besides, Rome's a long way from Syria. How's anyone going to know?"

"I have the feeling that Pasha's the kind of psycho who'd make it his business."

"Don't worry, I'll be careful. Well, are you going to drive me to Tel Aviv airport or not? I'll have a quick shower, a change of clothes, and pack an overnight bag. But I'll need to make a brief stop on the way."

"Where?"

"At my parents' grave."

"Why?"

"I'd like a private moment. Well, are you going to drive me?"

Yasmin's gaze met his. "On one condition, Jack."

"What's that?"

"You take me with you to Rome."

58

Twenty minutes later Yasmin pulled the Land Cruiser up near the side of the road.

"I won't be long," Jack said, and climbed out.

Yasmin watched him cross to the gravestone as a puzzled look erupted on his face. Jack kept his back to her as she saw him kneel and spend a few minutes tidying the grave, tossing away the remains of flowers and smoothing out the gravel chips. Finally, after a private moment of reflection he stood, walked back to the Land Cruiser, and jumped in. He stared out at the Judean desert, as if searching for something or someone.

Yasmin said, "What's wrong? You look shocked."

"My parents' grave was vandalized."

"You're kidding!"

"Someone crushed the flowers I'd left there the other day. They were a mess. They stomped them all over the gravel and scattered the stone chips."

"Why would anyone do that? Unless it's meant as some kind of warning."

"If someone thinks a cowardly act like that's going to stop me, then they've got another think coming."

59

TEL AVIV

Lela clutched her seat in the back of the wailing ambulance. She stared out past tinted windows and saw a white paramedic station wagon with a siren and flashing blue light speeding through the traffic in front of the ambulance. Julius Weiss's bodyguards riding shotgun, Lela guessed.

Ari sat next to her, clutching a leather attaché case on his lap. His boss, Weiss, was sprawled opposite on a red leatherette seat, next to an array of medical equipment. Beside him was a pale-faced man wearing a Jewish skullcap, a worn black suit, and scuffed brown shoes. One side of his glasses was held together with blue insulation tape. He was stonily silent—Weiss had not introduced him when they boarded the ambulance—but every now and then his myopic eyes darted shyly at Lela.

The Mossad chief said with an impish grin, "What do you think of my transport, Inspector Raul? It's the perfect cover. Who'd suspect the head of Mossad of traveling in an ambulance?"

Lela saw the whitewash sprawl of Tel Aviv rush past as they sped along the roadway. "Do I get to know where I'm being taken?"

Weiss snapped his fingers. Ari Tauber handed him a

bulky, mustard-colored envelope from the attaché case. The Mossad chief removed a sheaf of color photographs. Lela saw that they were the ones Ari had taken at the monastery.

Weiss examined the images and let out a sigh. "It seems that you and Ari had an interesting evening at Maloula, Inspector. Everyone in the monastery is dead and there's no sign of Cane or the scroll." The Mossad chief looked up and fixed Lela with a stare. "The plot certainly thickens, doesn't it?"

"I think you could say that."

Weiss pursed his lips in thought. "An interesting snippet of information that you ought to be aware of: Cane crossed back into Israel at seven this morning, along with the Bedu and Yasmin Green."

"What?"

"I had their passports flagged with border security and was alerted as soon as the three showed up at the Allenby Bridge crossing. The pickup and its occupants were searched but the scroll was nowhere to be found. Cane, however, had a noticeable leg wound."

Lela's face creased with concern. "What happened to him?"

"He claimed he'd had an accident. On my direct orders the border security guards didn't pursue the matter and risk making Cane suspicious. They allowed all three back into Israel."

"So we're none the wiser about what happened at the monastery?"

Ari said, "Lela, Professor Feldstein here thinks he may be able to help enlighten us."

Weiss added, "Inspector Lela Raul, meet Professor Feldstein. I should point out that the professor's a Harvard graduate and a Dead Sea scrolls expert. Go ahead, Paul."

Weiss handed the clutch of photographs to the black-suited Feldstein, who held up a snapshot for Lela to see. It was of Father Novara, lying in a pool of his own blood.

Feldstein pushed his glasses off the bridge of his nose and said in a soft, almost whispered voice, "This man, Father Vincento Novara, was a leading Aramaic scholar—an Aramaist. Many years ago he worked in the Vatican's archives as a translator and archivist. He specialized in the old Aramaic and the later dialect common at the time of Jesus. He was also an expert on the Dead Sea scrolls. It's my belief that the priest's job was to translate the stolen parchment."

Lela raised an eyebrow. "I think we've already figured that one out, Professor. The question is for whom? And what does the scroll contain?"

"This is no ordinary Dead Sea scroll, Inspector."

"What do you mean?"

"Many years ago, soon after the first Dead Sea scrolls were discovered at Qumran, an expert named Professor Schonfeld worked on their translation. He discovered a code hidden within certain of them. Have you heard of Schonfeld's work?"

"Never."

"It's a very simple code, one that Schonfeld called the Atbash Cipher. The letters of the Aramaic alphabet are completely reversed. The first letter becomes the last, and the last the first, and so on. It couldn't be simpler. Do you understand?"

"I think so. Go on."

"Not all of the Dead Sea scrolls contain a code, but a select few certainly do." Professor Feldstein removed a pen and notepad from his pocket, flicked open a fresh page, and drew two short dashes:

— —

"Only scrolls that contain two dashes in the upper-right-hand corner of the parchment contain code. It was a simple indicator to those who had knowledge of the code's existence that a secret message was contained within the text."

Lela said impatiently, "And the significance of all this is, Professor?"

Feldstein met her stare. "We believe that the scroll found by Jack Cane contains a similar marking, suggesting the document has an Atbash code."

"What kind of message are we talking about?"

"Schonfeld's work led him to believe that a number of Dead Sea scrolls contained important announcements meant to be passed down to future generations."

"How do you know this?"

"Because at least two others already found contain an important revelation. One is held by Israel. The other by the Vatican. Held in secret, I might add. In locked vaults and accessible only to those in the highest authority."

"What for?" Lela asked.

Feldstein looked at the Mossad chief, who nodded his approval.

"Tell her, Professor."

60

The Professor's face was grave as he took out a handkerchief, re-moved his glasses, and began polishing them vigorously. "It's a very remarkable revelation that would certainly stun the world. The description 'earth-shattering' definitely applies in this case."

"I take it that you know exactly what the revelation is, Professor?"

Before Feldstein could reply, Weiss addressed Lela. "The professor works for Mossad and is a keeper of state secrets. The answer to your question is yes, he knows, just as I do. And before you roll your eyes in doubt, Feldstein isn't talking bull. The code is real. The revelation is real. And we now know that the scroll Jack Cane discovered has been carbon-dated to between 25 and 50 A.D."

Lela smiled, sat back, and looked from Feldstein to Weiss. "You two are really serious, aren't you?"

"Of course," Weiss answered flatly.

"Forgive me, but I've heard nonsense like this before."

Weiss looked affronted. "What are you talking about?"

"It's the stuff of fiction, age-old myths, and bad movies and comes in various shapes and forms. You know the kind of thing I mean. The incredible Bible secret that will change the world. Or the cipher hidden in Scripture that suggests God has a secret to reveal. Or maybe newly discovered evidence that claims Jesus Christ never existed, or that Mary Magdalene was his wife or his girlfriend and that they produced a bloodline."

Professor Feldstein said confidently, "This is no myth, Inspector. And I can assure you that the revelation would have far-reaching consequences."

Lela sat back and folded her arms. "Really? And just what kind of revelation are we talking about? That Scientology got it right? That creatures from outer space seeded the earth? Or that there was no Jesus Christ? Or proof that God does or doesn't exist? At least tell me if I'm in the ballpark here, or am I so way off beam I'm starting to sound crazy?"

The professor looked worriedly to Weiss again as if for guidance, and Weiss answered. "You'll have to take my word, Inspector, that it's certainly a bombshell, and that's all I can say. Our hope is that when we find the missing scroll it will illuminate our knowledge of the revelation."

"You said *when* we find it. Why so confident?"

"Because failure is not an option I can contemplate. The scroll simply *must* be found. Jack Cane may know more than anyone about its disappearance. That's why you and Ari will stick to him like glue. You'll use every means at your disposal to discover what he does, knows, and learns."

"Will the revelation be made public if it's found?"

Weiss said, "You want my honest opinion? I doubt it."

As the Mossad chief went to replace the photographs in the envelope, Lela said, "What about the symbols Father Novara wrote on the wall in his blood? Do they have a significance?"

Weiss shuffled through the snapshots and plucked out the photograph of the blood-drenched symbols and held it up. "Good question. But I'm afraid that's something of a mystery right now."

Lela stared at the images. "It looks like it could be a pair of crosses to me."

Weiss said, "Professor Feldstein, do these symbols mean anything specific to you?"

"The old Aramaic *t*, pronounced 'taw,' was in the shape of a cross, because that's what it meant, cross or an X. But that was eighth to ninth century B.C. And to be honest the combination of two *t*'s suggests nothing to me except gobbledygook."

Weiss shrugged. "It's hard to say what the priest was trying to convey, or if his mind was simply confused close to death. But it's a mystery I'm hoping we'll solve."

Lela looked at Weiss. Her sixth sense told her he knew more than he was saying.

The ambulance siren died. Lela looked out the window and saw to her surprise that the driver had reached Tel Aviv airport. He drove in through a pair of manned security gates toward a line of private aircraft hangars and braked to a halt.

An unmarked gleaming Lear jet waited. Airsteps led up to the cabin and in the cockpit a uniformed crew was busy performing a preflight check. Weiss put the photographs away, pushed open the ambulance doors, but remained inside with the professor. "Step down, Inspector, the Lear jet's for you. This time you'll be traveling in comfort. Forgive me, but I'm already late for a meeting so I'll say my good-bye now."

"Traveling to where?" Lela asked as Ari ushered her out of the ambulance. She heard the jet's auxiliary power unit start up with a whine.

Weiss said, "To the Eternal City. Rome to you and me."

"But why?"

Weiss was a man in a hurry as he pulled the ambulance doors shut. "Ari will brief you. Good-bye, Inspector. Or I should say, *Arrivederci*."

PART SIX

PART SIX

61

At thirty-six thousand feet above the Mediterranean, the Al Italia Airbus 320 began its descent into Rome's Leonardo da Vinci Airport.

Jack felt tense and excited as he drained his scotch and stared out of the window while Italy's rugged coastline drifted below him in slow motion. His notebook and pen lay open on the fold-down table in front of him. An air steward came by and removed his empty plastic drink cup. Jack slumped back in his seat and stared at the notebook.

Yasmin sat beside him, her head over to one side, her eyes closed. He couldn't help but look at her. Her sleeping face was really quite beautiful.

He was unable to relax despite the scotch he'd sipped during the last two hours of his flight from Tel Aviv. His body felt racked by stress and excitement. He knew that any of his fellow passengers could be one of Pasha's people. *What if we're being followed? What if the Syrian means to kill us?*

He stopped looking at Yasmin and for the umpteenth time in the last two hours he studied the other passengers nearby. They were mostly Jews and Arabs, with a sprinkling of Africans and Europeans. A few looked suspicious. A restless Middle Eastern man in the opposite aisle caught his eye.

All during the flight the guy had shot nervous glances across the cabin in Jack's direction. Jack told himself his mind was working overtime. *The guy's probably just scared of flying.*

But Jack's anxiety didn't go away. At the airport, Yasmin had insisted on joining him even when he'd steadfastly refused. "Yasmin, the last thing I want is for you to be caught up in any trouble. It's best that you stay in Israel."

She was dressed in jeans and a pastel blue blouse and carried a worn leather travel bag over her shoulder. "We're in this together, Jack."

Then, in the middle of the crowded airport she leaned across, kissed his cheek, and said playfully, "Now be a good boy while I go book a ticket."

There was no arguing with her. He went to a currency exchange counter, bought some euros, and an hour later they boarded the Al Italia flight together. Now he looked again at her sleeping face, her generous mouth. He leaned across, kissed her forehead softly, and could smell the almond scent of her hair.

He turned his attention back to his notebook. As soon as Yasmin fell asleep he had switched on his phone—illegal on board, he knew—but his curiosity was eating him alive. He had scrolled through the photographs he had taken of the parchment, found one complete Aramaic sentence that he could make out that did not show signs of damage or wear, copied it down, and immediately switched off his phone again.

Then he set to work, applying the simple rules of the Atbash code, reversing the order of the alphabet. Aramaic wasn't his forte, and it was a slow process. Over an hour later, he was still trying to make sense of the remarkable sentence he'd decoded. He felt blown away.

I've discovered another explosive translation.

His heart was racing but he wanted to translate the sentence all over again just to be absolutely certain he'd made no mistakes.

Moments later the pilot announced that they were completing their descent. Yasmin blinked awake, rubbing her eyes sleepily. "Are we already there . . . ?"

"Just about. We ought to be landing soon."

"You sound wide awake and excited. Me, I'm still trying to recover after Maloula. Wake me after we've touched down." Yasmin snuggled into him, clutching his arm, and went back to sleep.

Jack went back to work, full of enthusiasm, but soon he heard the jet engines change pitch and felt a sinking sensation as the pilot began his approach into Rome. He kept working until ten minutes later when he put away his notebook, just as the Airbus kissed the runway at Rome's Da Vinci Airport.

Yasmin awoke, a catch of excitement in her voice as she stared out at the airport. "I can't believe we're in Rome. What now? Where do we go?"

"First, let's get through immigration, then we'll grab a cab and I'll tell you on the way to the Vatican."

Twenty minutes later, carrying their overnight bags, they passed through EU immigration and customs without any hitches and headed toward Arrivals.

The Serb carried a newspaper under his arm and wore a black leather jacket. He stood in the Arrivals terminal scratching an old scar under his chin as he observed the arriving couple.

They stepped out of the terminal building and walked over to a taxi stand. The Serb followed them from a safe distance, watching as they stepped over to a white cab. They handed their luggage to the driver, who loaded the bags into the cab's trunk. The Serb promptly crossed to his silver Lancia parked at the curb, jumped into the driver's seat beside Nidal Hassan, and grinned. "It looks like we're in business. This is where the fun begins."

Nidal watched as Cane and the woman finished stashing their luggage and climbed into the cab before it screeched away from the curb. "What are you waiting for? Follow them, don't lose them," Nidal ordered.

The Serb hit the ignition, gunned the engine, and swung the Lancia out after the taxi.

62

The chauffeured Mercedes slid to a halt outside the gates of a crumbling old sandstone monastery in the Aventino Hills.

Cardinal Liam Kelly from Chicago—a bull of a man with a craggy face, penetrating eyes, and wearing a priest's black suit and collar—didn't bother to wait for his chauffeur to open the door but maneuvered himself out of the car. The wrought-iron gates at the villa entrance were opened by two plainclothes armed guards who beckoned Kelly inside and scanned him with a handheld metal detector.

Steps led up to a pair of oak doors, above them a plaster image of the Virgin and child with a marble inscription underneath: "White Fathers. Monastery of Aventino." One of the doors opened and a cheerful bearded man appeared.

"Abbot Fabrio." Kelly smiled, noticing more armed guards inside the hall. "It looks as if this place is sealed tighter than Rome's central penitentiary."

The abbot beamed, showing a handsome face and perfect white teeth behind the beard. "Cardinal, it's good to see you as always. Come inside."

Kelly was led down a hall to a cluttered office and the abbot closed the door behind them. "Can I get you some coffee or tea?" Abbot Fabrio asked.

Despite being third-generation American Irish, and having a reputation as one of the Vatican's heavy hitters, Kelly had cultivated a charming Irish lilt while lecturing in Ireland's Maynooth College. He dabbed his brow with a handkerchief. "To tell the truth, Fabrio, in this heat I could really murder a cold glass of Guinness. But water's fine."

The abbot laughed and poured a fresh glass from a pitcher on his desk. "The monks are busy at their work. You'll have privacy in the garden at the back."

"That's excellent, Fabrio." Kelly drank the water in one swallow.

Beyond the open windows lay a garden full of palm and olive trees, and a small circular pond with an ancient stone fountain. Despite the presence of three additional plain-clothes guards wandering the garden, Kelly sensed an air of tranquil calm. He put down his glass, his expression more sombre. "How is the Holy Father?"

"He spends his time praying and reflecting. He sleeps little, no more than five hours a night. When I rise each morning at four-thirty A.M. for prayers he is already awake before me and praying in the chapel. He looks troubled, I will say that. He seems to have much on his mind."

"Has he talked at all?"

The abbot's face lit up. "Sometimes he joins the monks and myself in the gardens for prayer and discussion. It's really quite remarkable."

"What is?" Kelly enquired.

"The monks devour every word the Holy Father says about this new era he promises for the church. We are deeply moved by his wisdom and his biblical knowledge. And I've never seen my colleagues so impressed. They sit around listening to him like wide-eyed schoolboys. It's almost as if—"

"As if they were sitting at the feet of Christ himself?"

"Why—why, yes."

Kelly nodded. "I've known the pope ever since we were friends in the seminary. I knew even then he was destined for greatness. He's always been one of the most remarkable men I've ever known. Tell me, Fabrio, has he left these walls since he arrived?"

"Not that I'm aware of. He requested a simple cell, no frills, just a hard bed and coarse blankets, and that's what I gave him. Why?"

Kelly pursed his lips and shook his head. "Just curious. We may have to take special measures to ensure he doesn't leave the monastery unguarded."

"Special measures?"

"It's a delicate matter. I'll try to explain later, Fabrio."

"As you wish. Come, I'll take you out to the garden and then I'll tell Pope Celestine you've arrived."

63

ROME

"Rome's an incredible, madcap place. A hundred years ago they called the Eternal City the biggest open-air lunatic asylum in the world." Jack peered out the cab window as the *autostrada* traffic into Rome slowed to a thick stream of hooting horns and impatient drivers. "And that was before all the traffic problems."

Yasmin checked her watch. "We've hardly moved and it's been an hour."

Seconds later the taxi driver—a small, middle-aged man with sad, hound-dog eyes and a two-day stubble—weaved away from the chaos by turning off onto a slip road. He drove up through a series of narrow cobbled streets and soon they were in the hills above the city. The driver grinned back at them and said in Italian, "A shortcut. We get there faster."

The driver made a severe right turn. Yasmin held on to the seat as the swerving cab sent them sliding across the backseat. They got their balance back and Yasmin giggled and sat upright. "Is this your first time in Rome, or are you a seasoned veteran?"

"I was here on digs a bunch of times. In fact, most of ancient Rome has been buried, but parts of it can still be seen. There's almost an entire city thirty to sixty feet below street level, and I'm talking almost every street."

"I've read about it."

"Even under the Vatican there are deep subterranean passages, tunnels, and sewers that traverse Rome. They lead down to crypts and catacombs, baths and palaces, prisons and brothels. It's pretty incredible."

The Fiat continued to strain upward through a maze of narrow streets. Then the car nudged to the right and they were hurtling downhill, the sad-faced driver jabbing the brakes gingerly. Another five minutes and they drove past the vast splendor of St. Peter's Square.

Jack studied the ancient plaza, peppered with flocks of pigeons, as the taxi driver halted near the side entrance to a Vatican courtyard. It was protected by a barrier pole manned by Swiss Guards. The cheerless driver scratched his stubble and looked back at Jack for guidance, his eyes asking, *Is this where you want me to stop?*

"This is fine," Jack said, and paid the man from a wad of euros that he'd exchanged at Tel Aviv airport. The sad-eyed little man started to babble something.

"What did he say?" Yasmin asked.

"That his name's Mario. That he's got five kids who never stop opening his fridge door. That business is slow and if we need a driver he doesn't mind waiting for us. He says he'll show us Rome or take us wherever we want to go and his charges are very reasonable."

"I almost feel sorry for him."

"We could be a while."

"Tell him you've got a meeting and to wait right here but that we don't know how long we'll be."

Jack told the driver. The man was so pleased he stepped out of the cab and gallantly held open the rear door. "Take your time, *signore, signora.* Mario will wait, no problem."

As they strolled toward the Swiss Guards at the barrier, Jack said suddenly, "I have a confession to make. I took the scroll from Father Novara's study."

Yasmin stopped walking and stared at him, her mouth open. She felt too stunned to talk.

"It's the truth, Yasmin. When I discovered the original I switched it with one of the other old parchments I found in the study."

"You mean Pasha has a *fake*?"

"He sure has."

She laughed, but then her face began to darken as the reality set in. "Pasha's not going to like you duping him."

"It's a risk I took."

"How did you smuggle it into Israel?"

Jack patted his injured leg. "The guards never checked my dressing. I'd slipped it into a clear plastic bag from Josuf's first-aid kit and covered it with more gauze. After we crossed the border and I had a moment to myself I tucked it inside my shirt."

"Wasn't the parchment damaged?"

"More like roughed up a little."

"Jack, this could cost us both our lives."

"Now you understand why I wanted to come to Rome alone."

Yasmin was tense. "It's a bit late to be telling me that now. But where's the scroll?"

"In a safe place. Don't ask me any more."

"You're not going to tell me?"

"It's got to remain my secret for now. No exceptions. I'm sorry."

"Are you serious? After all we've been through? Thanks a bunch for trusting me, Jack."

"It's for your own good, believe me. Maybe at a later time. You're the only one who knows I've hidden the scroll. I didn't even tell Buddy. I don't want anyone else getting roughed up or killed on account of what they know. But I can tell you that I believe I've decoded another line of text."

"You're kidding."

"While you were asleep during the flight I worked on a complete sentence I'd jotted down. I think I've cracked it."

"Don't keep me in suspense."

Jack flipped open his notebook. He pointed to a sentence he'd written in block letters.

ON LEARNING THE TRUTH, JUDAS NOW BE-
LIEVED HIS MASTER TO BE A FALSE MESSIAH
AND NOT THE TRUE MESSIAH, THE ONE COME
TO CHANGE THE WORLD.

Yasmin said, puzzled, "What's it supposed to mean?"

Jack said excitedly, "I wish I knew, but it's another incredible statement, like the last one. Judas believing his master to be a false messiah. That's an astonishing revelation."

"Could you decode any more?"

"Sure I could, but it would be slow progress. To make any significant development we're going to need expert help. Parts of the text are missing, others are damaged, you see."

"So there's no way some of the text can be translated?"

Jack folded away his notebook. "Actually, that's not true. Some years ago unique software programs were written to help patch together and make sense of damaged Dead Sea scrolls. The programs can sometimes help fill in any missing gaps in the text by using mathematical projections. Don't ask me how it works, but if the stories I've heard are true it's been a terrific help to translators. The guy I know who's an authority on Schonfeld's code ought to be able to help in that regard."

"Are you at least going to tell me who you know in the Vatican?"

"An old contact of my father's I haven't seen in years."

"Who?"

"Someone high up I called before we left Israel. I figure he's got the clout to get us into the Vatican Archives."

"You're joking," Yasmin answered. "Are we talking the *pope* here?"

Jack smiled. "Not this time, even if I do know him."

Yasmin said wide-eyed, "You *know* the pope?"

"He was one of a Vatican delegation that joined my father's dig at Qumran."

"You certainly know how to impress a girl. What do you want to see in the archives?"

"Something I've never had the opportunity to see."

"What?"

"When my parents died, Father Kubel, one of the priests who arrived at the accident scene, wrote a confidential report. I'd like to read it."

"Why?"

"Call it a gut feeling, or call it a sixth sense if you want, but something's telling me there could be a connection between what happened then and what's happening now."

"Explain, Jack."

"People die at Qumran and a precious scroll goes missing. It's happened twice—to my parents and to your uncle, twenty years apart. Those kinds of feelings I can believe in, trust me."

"Everything I've heard suggests that the Vatican's archives are off-limits except with the permission of high-ranking clergy. What makes you think your dad's contact can help?"

Jack took Yasmin's arm and guided her toward the security entrance manned by the Swiss Guards. "Because I'm making him an offer he can't refuse."

The silver Lancia pulled up sixty yards behind the white taxi. Nidal and the Serb observed the couple climb out and approach the Swiss Guards at the checkpoint. They saw the couple being led to one of the security lodges.

One of the guards spoke into a telephone and then pointed them toward the Vatican. The taxi waited. Nidal scratched his beard. "It looks like they have business inside the Vatican."

"What now?" The Serb slid a MAC-10 machine pistol from under his seat and lay it on his lap, then grabbed a canvas travel bag from the backseat and slipped the weapon inside.

A look of steel flashed in Nidal's eyes and he took a Beretta pistol from his inside pocket. "We wait. They can't stay in there forever. But just remember, when there's killing to be done, Cane's mine."

64

It was very peaceful in the sunlit garden. The pond was covered with huge water lilies, a stone fish spewing water from its mouth. Kelly sat there in the noon heat, wiping his brow with his handkerchief. He heard soft footsteps and turned to see the tall figure of Pope Celestine approach.

He wore scuffed leather sandals and a simple white cassock. Kelly rose. "Holy Father, it's good to see you, as always."

Becket extended both his hands and gripped Kelly's warmly before kissing him on the cheeks. "Liam, old friend."

As Kelly went to kneel and kiss the papal ring, the pope protested. "Please, we know each other a long time, you embarrass me. Do you like my hideaway? Abbot Fabrio is an old acquaintance and spoils me, of course. Wine with dinner and clean sheets every day. I'm ruined for kindness."

Kelly stood and admired the garden. "It's certainly peaceful and quiet, and you can't hear the traffic, a miracle in itself. The Romans drive like they're still competing in an ancient chariot race to the death. Yesterday a madman tried to run me over as I crossed near the Colosseum."

The pope chuckled. "Poor Liam. And what did you do?"

"I called him an ignorant *eegit* in my best Italian."

The pope laughed warmly and gestured to the bench facing the pond. "Let's sit. We'll be out of hearing of the guards and can talk in private."

They sat by the bubbling pond. "Tell me what's so important you wanted to talk about, Liam."

Kelly sighed and stared at the bubbling water. "Holy Father, with every passing day your cardinals and bishops hear stories about your inspectors burrowing away like mad beavers in the archives' vaults."

Kelly's good-humored lilt had disappeared. The pope said patiently, "What else do they hear, old friend?"

"That they are discovering all kinds of material. Much of it a terrible embarrassment to the church and best consigned to history. They have also heard that *all* records of church financial dealings are being prepared for public scrutiny."

"This is simply as I promised, Liam. How can we speak of truth and then hide from truth ourselves?"

Kelly turned red-faced. "Then there was an episode with a prostitute. And now this, Holy Father. You leave your Vatican quarters for . . . for a monastery. Permit me to be frank."

"Haven't we always been, with each other?"

"John, all this may impress the young bloods in the church who seem to consider you a second messiah, but to the gray hairs among us, this is pushing it a bit far. I've heard the fearful whispers too. Antipope. Antichrist. For some older, more conservative cardinals, these controversial decisions of yours only seem to confirm it. And now to top it all you've left your official Vatican residence, for heaven's sake."

There was no trace of anger in the pope's reply. "Am I less of a pope because I choose to live here, Liam?"

"That wasn't what I meant." Kelly's face flushed again. "The Vatican press office has managed to keep it a secret so far, but surely when the media gets hold of this story it might appear to some that you're either choosing to live like a hermit or losing your mind. Or both. And then there's the suggestion of reaching out in friendship to other Christian churches. What next? Even other religions, perhaps?"

"Christians share many core beliefs and values, Liam. And may I remind you of a favorite saying of yours in the seminary—that the face of God can be seen from a thousand different angles?"

"Fair enough, but your mission may be too much for some of my fellow cardinals. The fact that you want to embrace *everyone* might be seen as being overzealous."

"I thought that's what Jesus wanted us to do—to embrace everyone."

"Well, yes, but the point is, there may be those among the Curia who will see your mission as threatening."

The pope stared back. "Who put you up to this, Liam? Was it your fellow senior Irish-American clerics? The ones we often jokingly called the 'Murphia'? Have they sent one of my fellow countrymen to change my mind?"

"I came here simply as a trusted friend, Holy Father. And out of concern for both you and the church." Kelly leaned closer, his voice a fierce whisper. "For the love of heaven, John, can you not see that all this will set the church back centuries?"

The pope met Kelly's stare. "No, Liam. This is what the flock has been waiting for. A fresh start. A renewal. A return to the simple values that Jesus professed."

Kelly's voice took on a bitter edge. "You mean there'll really be a chance of that *after* the Italian tax authorities have torn us asunder by suing the Vatican for billions because of past finan-cial misdeeds? And after half the flock have disowned us for some of the revelations made public from the archives?"

"Liam, I must tell you that some of the archives my in-spectors hoped to find have gone missing. Deliberately, it may seem."

Kelly blushed. "Are you suggesting that I, one of your most trusted cardinals, had something to do with that?"

"No, Liam, of course not. I will put the matter in Mon-signor Ryan's hands. I am hopeful he'll get to the bottom of it."

"Then what are you saying, Holy Father?"

The pope put a hand on Kelly's arm. "Simply that the church must bear the responsibility for its sins, Liam. Just as we ask our flock to bear responsibility for theirs. My plans will go ahead."

"I see." Kelly ran a palm across his face again, as if in de-spair. Then he slowly reached under his gown and removed a newspaper clipping. He placed it on the bench space between them. "I wanted to show you this."

A headline announced in Italian:

BRUTAL MURDER—MYSTERIOUS
TWO-THOUSAND-YEAR-OLD SCROLL FOUND
IN ISRAEL VANISHES

Kelly tapped the cutting. "Another scroll has been found at Qumran. A renowned expert, Professor Green, was mur-dered there. It seems the Israeli police have so far not yet ap-prehended anyone for the crime."

The pope scanned the page, his face bleak. "Yes. I've read this."

"The Holy Father is better informed than I thought."

Becket met Kelly's stare. "It seems there's no end to the misfortune that follows the scrolls, is there, Liam? It's like a curse."

Kelly folded the clipping and put it away. "I know of another curse. Your intention to open the archives. It could mean ruin for all of us who know what really happened at Qumran twenty years ago. What if some smart researcher reading the files pieces together the truth? It could be the nail in all our coffins."

"Yes, I know."

"You, me, Cassini, Father Kubel. We know what Robert Cane found and why it had to be kept secret. Just like the other scrolls were kept secret."

The pope bowed his head in shame, his hands clasped together, as if he were silently offering a prayer. "What happened to Robert Cane was a terrible tragedy."

Kelly said anxiously, "May the Lord have mercy on our souls for what was done back then in the name of the church, but had Robert Cane had his way and exposed his document to the world, the tragedy would have been worse."

"Your point, Liam?"

"The threat is no less great now than it was twenty years ago. Can't you see what will happen if we divulge the truth about the scrolls? We both played a part in the crime that was committed back then. It could ultimately destroy your papacy, the church, all of us."

The pope ran a hand over his grim face in a gesture of anguish. "You don't think I have considered that? My conscience has been wrestling with that dilemma."

"And?"

"It still wrestles with it. Part of me believes that telling

the truth will be our finest hour. But sometimes, just sometimes I confess I have my doubts about revealing this one
dark secret we share, Liam. Pray for my guidance. Will you
do that for me?"

"I always do, Holy Father. Just as I pray that you will at
least keep *our* secret to ourselves. We don't need to scratch an
old sore. You can still open up the archives, you can still reach
out to other Christians, but without sacrificing the fates of
your oldest friends. And consider your own position. A revelation this epic, along with everything else, could ruin the
church."

"Liam, you know where I stand on truth—"

"*Please*, I merely ask you to consider it again. For an old
friend. Just to reflect a little longer."

"I can promise nothing, Liam."

Kelly pleaded, "Just reflect some more, it's all I ask. What
harm is there in that, John?"

The pope stared back at Kelly, mulled over the request,
then finally nodded reluctantly. "Very well, I will give it con-
sideration."

The relief was evident on Kelly's craggy face, as if a small
victory had been won. "Thank you for that. Thank you sin-
cerely." He glanced at his watch and rose to his feet. "Excuse
me, Holy Father, but I'm afraid I have an appointment. Robert
Cane's son, Jack, is in Rome."

The pope paled. "What are you talking about?"

"It's ironic, I know. But he's the one who found the latest
Qumran scroll. The newspapers didn't mention him by name
but he's an archaeologist, like his father."

The pope sat there, baffled. "How—how do you know
this?"

"He called me from Israel. He flew to Rome this afternoon

and wants to meet me urgently and talk. I'm already late."

The pope's face sparked with a look close to fear. "Talk about what, Liam?"

"Jack Cane has a special request. One I will need your permission to grant, Holy Father. But in return he's made an intriguing offer."

65

The Lear jet carrying Lela and Ari touched down at Da Vinci Airport and taxied to a halt outside a commercial hangar. Ten minutes later, escorted through customs and immigration, they entered a private airport lounge.

Ari got on his cell phone to check his messages, then flicked it shut. "I'll go meet our local Mossad contact; he's waiting outside. He'll take us to Cane and the woman."

"Rome's a big city. How can you know where they are?"

"Because we've been watching them since they landed. Right now they're heading for the Vatican."

"Why there?"

Ari smiled and slid his cell phone back in his pocket. "I don't know, but it's interesting, isn't it? Let's go."

"Give me a couple of minutes to freshen up, Ari. I need to find a restroom."

"Okay, but try not to be long. I'll meet you by the exit doors."

Lela spotted the restroom sign down a hallway. A public pay phone sign was next to it.

As she stepped toward the bank of phones she recalled Julius Weiss's order not to involve herself further in the murder investigation until he ordered to do so. But she had a desperate need to know the investigation's progress.

She didn't want to use her cell phone in case Mossad was monitoring her calls back in Tel Aviv. One of the pay phones took credit cards and Lela found her Visa in her purse and swiped it through the slot. She punched in the number from memory, adding the international prefix for Israel, 972.

The line seemed to ring forever until it was answered by a blunt male voice. "Sergeant Mosberg."

"It's Inspector Raul."

"Inspector. This is a surprise. I was told you were on sick leave and couldn't be contacted."

"I am, but just between you and me, Mosberg, I wanted to find out if you've made any headway."

"I certainly have, and I'm glad you rang," the sergeant said brightly.

Lela glanced back over her shoulder. She was horrified to see that Ari hadn't left the terminal but was lingering by a vending machine, fifty yards away. He had his back to her as he clinked some coins into the machine. Lela felt a stab of panic. If Ari looked her way he'd see her making the call.

Mosberg went on, "First of all, the scroll's been carbon-dated, and it's genuine. Between A.D. 25 and A.D. 50. Second of all, Jack Cane has disappeared."

Lela was about to say *I know* to both statements when she caught herself. "Really?"

"We're not sure where he's gone but I haven't put out a bulletin just yet. I'm still looking for him."

Lela kept her eyes fixed on Ari's back, praying that he wouldn't turn round. She watched him reach down and retrieve a Coke from the vending machine. "You're right, he may turn up. You said you'd made headway."

"Yes, there's something important. It's kind of bizarre and it muddies things."

"In what way bizarre?"

Lela observed Ari crack open the Coke. He sipped from the can and started to turn round, idly surveying the terminal. She felt her pulse quicken.

Mosberg said, "I checked out Yasmin Green, like you asked me to. I called her uncle's relatives in New York and here's the weird thing . . ."

"Go on." Lela's heart pounded as Ari turned around and spotted her. Their eyes locked. Ari frowned. Lela offered him a limp wave. She'd been caught. But her mind was focused on Mosberg's next words.

"According to the professor's relatives, his niece Yasmin Green was killed ten years ago in an auto accident."

66

"I'll have to help you find the file myself, Jack. I'm afraid our archivists are being kept terribly busy."

Jack and Yasmin hurried alongside Cardinal Kelly as he led them toward the Vatican courtyard, Cortile del Belvedere. Despite his bulk the American was quick on his feet and rushed them along. Jack asked, "Why so busy?"

Kelly sidestepped a marble statue of the Virgin and child. "Thousands of scholars and visitors are welcomed each year in the Vatican Library. However, visits have been suspended while certain historical documents are being studied. But because your father was a good friend, I spoke personally with the pope. In fact, he remembered you and your parents very well."

"I'm impressed. It's been a long time."

"How could he forget their terrible tragedy? The pope greatly admired your father's work and gave permission for me to help you in your task."

"Father Becket's come a long way."

"He certainly has. Now, about this archive document written by Father Kubel that you wanted to see."

"Kubel told me he was asked to write a report. About the circumstances surrounding my father's death and the scroll's destruction."

Kelly nodded. "As you well know, Cardinal Cassini and myself occasionally visited our fellow clergy working at Qumran. Our Vatican superiors asked us to have Kubel write the statement."

"Why?"

"They naturally had an interest in the scroll. It would have been normal procedure to investigate its destruction. Nothing was found amiss, I can tell you that. What happened to your parents and the scroll was simply a cruel accident."

"Have you read the report?"

"Soon after it was written. But that was a long time ago." Kelly hurried them to the opposite side of the courtyard, toward a granite building with a pair of tall oak doors. "Forgive my haste. But I have an important church appointment to attend later and don't want to be delayed. Tell me more about this scroll you found. Do you think it may be important?"

"I think so. But first it has to be recovered by the police. Then we can ascertain the entire contents. However, we do know that the parchment's been carbon-dated to the second quarter of the first century A.D."

"Do you have any idea as to the contents?"

"No," Jack lied. "We didn't want to risk unraveling the parchment for fear of damage. The few lines that were legible I could barely make sense of. I'm arranging expert help with the translation."

"Could I see the lines in question?"

"I'd prefer to wait until the experts have had a look."

Kelly looked disappointed. "I see. Your discovery may be of great interest to the Vatican's scholars. Don't forget you promised me a copy of the translation in return for allowing you to see the archive files."

"You have my word."

Kelly put a hand on Yasmin's arm. "Your uncle was a much respected scholar, my child. I'll offer a mass for his soul."

"That's kind of you."

"Here we are." Kelly halted outside the oak doors, pulled one open, and they moved into a hallway with shiny oak floors that smelled freshly of wax polish. Two plainclothes guards stood just inside the hallway, next to a metal door.

Yasmin said to Kelly, "Tell me about the library, Cardinal."

"It was first established in the late fifteenth century, to preserve the culture of the Catholic Church and to catalogue its documents. The archives contain over fifty miles of shelves. Some precious Latin, Greek, and Hebrew texts go back thousands of years."

One of the guards shifted his eyes to a nearby table and the open pages of a visitor's ledger. The man silently offered his guests a ballpoint pen and Kelly said, "If you'd sign the book, please."

They signed the ledger but when Jack offered the pen to Kelly, the cardinal said bluntly, "There's no need. The duty archivist will record my presence. Besides, cameras placed inside and outside the building record all comings and goings. You look distracted, Jack."

"To tell the truth, I'm awestruck. Now I can imagine how Carter must have felt."

"Carter?"

"When he entered King Tut's tomb for the first time."

Kelly produced a plastic card and slid it along a security scanner by the metal door. It sprung open a few inches with a hydraulic hiss and a long hallway lay beyond. "Believe me, this is a privilege that's granted to very few. Follow me."

67

They followed Kelly to the end of the hallway and climbed a flight of steps. It led onto a landing and another steel security door. Kelly's face was red from exertion and he paused to catch his breath, saying with a hint of pride, "The Secret Archives lie beyond this door. Or to give them their full and correct Latin title, Archivum Secretum Apostolicum Vaticanum. They are one of the largest and most guarded document depositories in the world."

Above the door the Cyclops eye of a security camera watched them.

Kelly inserted his security card and pushed open the door. A vast chamber stretched below them, much of it divided up into cubicles made of glass or Perspex. Each cubicle was lit by blue lighting. The chamber itself was lined with shelves, stacked with ledgers and box files and bundles of parchments with wax seals.

Kelly gestured to the enormous hall. "This is the main section of the Vatican library. The blue light is to preserve the ancient documents from harmful rays while they are being studied."

He moved down a flight of marble steps. "Actually, this part is simply the nonpublic archive, it is not 'secret' in the modern sense. In the Middle Ages, every potentate had a public and a private archive. This would be considered the private part and is easily accessible if you happen to be an approved scholar."

Jack was suddenly conscious of the controlled, dry air and could almost feel his veins contract in response. They descended the stairway to a bank of vending machines selling snacks, bottled water, and Coca-Cola. Kelly pointed to a pair of tall doors where a young guard sat at a desk. A plastic sign on the door said in Italian, ACCESSO LIMITATO.

"The section we want is behind those doors—the so-called 'secret' archive, as the public knows it. It's also where all material relating to the scrolls is catalogued, including Father Kubel's report."

"Why is the report stored here?"

"Because, Jack, originally the Dead Sea scrolls were kept highly confidential. It was feared that some of the translated material could be misinterpreted, or that it might muddy Christian teaching. However, the day may not be far away when all scroll material will be made available even to the public."

"What makes you think that?"

Kelly said, "Let's just call it insider privilege. Our new pope is a great believer in truth and honesty. However, for now the usual rules apply. The report you wish to see must be read within the confines of the library. No document may be removed."

Kelly crossed the chamber toward the tall double doors. What surprised Jack was the activity: the great hall was buzzing. Dozens of clerics, young and old and wearing priestly garb, toiled like worker bees.

Some sat at tables or in blue-lit kiosks. A few glanced up

briefly out of curiosity at their visitors. The hub of their activity looked as if it was directed toward six priests who sat at trestle tables covered with ledgers and computer laptops. They appeared to be making records of documents.

"I see what you mean about being busy," Yasmin remarked.

Kelly halted outside the double doors. "In my younger days I was an archivist here, so I know my way around. Sign the book, then come with me."

The guard handed Jack and Yasmin a pen to sign their names in his ledger. Kelly pushed open the doors and escorted them into another enormous room, their footsteps clicking on the marble tiles.

This room was softly lit and smelled of age, with oak-paneled shelved walls stacked to the ceiling with parchments, boxes, and ledgers. Several more priests studied aged-looking documents or stood on ladders, searching files.

Kelly consulted a slip of paper he removed from his pocket. It contained a handwritten series of numbers and letters.

The cardinal seemed in a rush as he gestured beyond a bronze statue of the Madonna, toward a blue-lit glass alcove with a bare table and two chairs. "The section we need is over there. Now, let's try and find Father Kubel's report."

68

Lela Raul clutched the door rail as the gray Fiat taxi sped toward Rome. She sat in a rear seat behind Ari.

The traffic was manic but the Mossad taxi driver wove in and out of the traffic lanes like an expert. He had introduced himself as Cohen—a handsome young man with a three-day stubble and Ray-Ban sunglasses perched on his head.

"This traffic is crazy," Ari commented.

Cohen grinned. "You should see it on Friday when everyone's trying to get out of this asylum. You'd be tempted to cut your wrists."

Ari said bluntly to Lela, "Who were you calling from the airport?"

When she didn't answer fast enough, Ari said, "We're old friends, Lela. No lies between us. Who'd you call?"

"If you must know, Sergeant Mosberg."

"Lela, you know what Weiss said—"

"I needed to know how the investigation is progressing. I'm a cop and it's still my case. You of all people ought to understand that."

Ari said fiercely, "A word of advice. You should never cross Julius Weiss. If he gives an order he expects you to obey it, or he'll haul you over hot coals, Lela."

"I'm not Mossad. I'm here at Weiss's request, but he's not my boss."

Ari grimaced. "What did Mosberg say?"

"To tell the truth, it's just as well I called. Something very weird's going on."

Ten minutes later the Fiat swung into a street next to St. Peter's Square. It slid to a halt near a busy kiosk selling newspapers and religious trinkets: rosary beads and miniature plaster statues of saints dangling from every nook and cranny.

Ari finished speaking on his cell phone and flicked it off. "Weiss is at a meeting right now and can't be reached. I left him a message to call me back the moment he's free." His face creased with worry. "Is Mosberg a hundred percent certain that Yasmin Green died in an auto accident?"

"Mosberg's a meticulous man. He wouldn't make a mistake about that."

Ari scratched his head. "If it's true, then who's Yasmin Green and what's she up to? Why her subterfuge?"

"I have no idea. It's got me stumped, Ari."

"We'll pull her photo from her visa application and run a check on it. There's obviously something more going on here than we can figure. What if she and Cane have been together on this from the start? Did that occur to you?"

"For no more than a second. I know Jack Cane, Ari—"

"How could he be the same person you knew twenty years ago? Me, I wouldn't trust him any more than the woman. What if they planned the theft, but somehow it all went wrong and Professor Green got killed and now they're on the run?"

"That's nothing but wild speculation."

"Is it, Lela? It wouldn't be the first time an archaeologist conspired with criminals to steal priceless finds."

"I can't believe Jack's a willing criminal."

"You can think what you like, but my money's on Cane being tied up in all of this. I know Weiss thinks the same. Get real, Lela."

Cohen, the driver, looked up as his cell phone suddenly jangled. He flipped it open and spoke in Hebrew. "We're here, Mario. Where are you?" Cohen listened and peered beyond the windshield toward St. Peter's Square. It was crowded with hoards of Vatican tourists. "No, I can't see you yet. But stay put and we'll find you."

Cohen rested his cell phone on his chest. "My partner's across the square, near one of the Vatican entrances, waiting for Cane and the woman."

"Have they reappeared yet?" Ari asked.

"No, but guess what? He says they're being followed by two men."

69

Kelly slipped on a pair of reading glasses and consulted the slip of paper that contained a handwritten series of numbers and letters. He ran his finger along a shelf and selected a box file. A faded white sticker was glued on the spine. Written on it was a date and a couple of lines in indelible black ink.

Kelly said, "This is what you're after. 'A report compiled by Father Franz Kubel concerning the Qumran archaeological dig.'"

In front of them was an old beech desk and on top lay a magnifying glass with a worn wooden handle. Kelly placed the box on the desk and opened the lid. A smoky aroma of aged balsa wood wafted out.

Jack's attention was drawn to what looked like a list that lay on top of the thick batch of documents inside. "What's that?"

Kelly plucked out the page, studied it, and began to sift the papers. "An index of the file contents. It lists mundane details of the dig, the financing, the finds discovered, along with Kubel's report."

"I'd like to have some time to study all these documents alone."

Kelly looked taken aback. "All alone? I hardly think that's possible, Jack."

"Don't you think I'm due that right? Father Kubel's report was only written because of what happened to my folks."

Kelly shook his head vigorously. "I can tell you now, Jack, there's nothing new or startling among these papers. I must also remind you that Vatican archives are only permitted to be handled by authorized experts."

"I'm an archaeologist. I'm used to handling delicate and valuable documents."

Kelly's face flushed. "Well, it may do, but there's bureaucratic protocol to consider. And that would require high authority."

"Cardinal, we both know that you have the authority."

"Well, perhaps, but—"

"The report's twenty years old. If there's nothing in there I don't already know, is it really such a big deal? All I'm asking is an hour to look through the material. And think of what you're getting in return."

Kelly removed his reading glasses, considered, and sighed. "Very well. But you must confine yourself only to this file." He consulted the wall clock: it read 5:15.

"You have forty-five minutes. Not a minute more. I have an important church appointment and I can't delay, Jack."

"Done."

Kelly slid over the box file. He pointed past the bronze Madonna statue to a coffee machine. "I'll be sitting over there. Call me the second you're done."

Jack and Yasmin stood alone in the glass-walled alcove. Yasmin studied the arrays of security cameras. "They're not taking any chances, are they?"

"You can say that again." Jack could almost feel the heavy silence in the chamber. The only noise was an occasional cough from one of the archivists or feet softly crossing the carpeted areas of floor. He looked past the bronze Madonna statue. Kelly had slumped into a chair by the coffee machine and was restlessly flicking through the pages of a magazine.

Yasmin said, "He seems eager to be out of here." She stared down at the file. "Can we start? The suspense is killing me."

Jack stacked the paper bundle from the box in a neat pile on the table.

Yasmin looked at the thick wedge of papers. "There's no way you'll get through all of this documentation in forty-five minutes, Jack."

"You take one half and I'll take the other. Try to speed-read."

"What am I supposed to be looking for?"

Jack next separated the documents into two equal piles, keeping Kubel's document for himself. "I wish I knew. But if you notice anything unusual, anything that stands out or seems intriguing, holler."

"In a library?"

"Bad word choice. Whisper. Now let's get started."

70

Jack curbed his mounting curiosity and placed the report by Father Kubel aside for now. He separated his documents into neat stacks.

They consisted mostly of official Vatican letters inquiring after the dig's progress and querying expenditure. Nothing stood out. Next, he scanned Kubel's report—eight neatly typed pages—and then read it twice.

After ten minutes, Yasmin broke off from what she was reading. "Any luck?"

"The report's pretty basic. Kubel gives a testimony of the accident and states the police investigation concluded that the deaths of my parents and Basim Malik were an accident."

"Who's Basim Malik?"

"The driver who died with my folks. He worked on the dig, much like Josuf. Kubel reported that foul play wasn't suspected, and that the scroll was vaporized in the accident. But he makes no mention of the scroll's content. That's strange."

"Why?"

"My dad allowed Kubel and Father Becket a good look at a small portion of the scroll he'd managed to unravel, before we headed off in the pickup to the Israeli Antiquities Department in Jerusalem. Kubel and Becket were familiar with Aramaic.

It just seems weird that Kubel didn't mention whatever they'd read that day."

Puzzled, Jack handed the document to Yasmin and said, "Take a look for yourself. Have you come across anything?"

Yasmin put aside some pages. "Not yet. Trawling through a bunch of correspondence from Vatican bookkeepers doesn't exactly ring my bell."

"Here, let me check your stuff."

"You're welcome to it." Fifteen minutes later Yasmin had examined all the file material. "You're right. Kubel's report is bare-bones. It reads more like a back-covering exercise than a testimony."

Jack finished checking Yasmin's documents. He scanned the wall clock: thirty-seven minutes had passed. He rummaged in the files. "Do you have document number nine?"

Yasmin checked her pile. "No, why?"

Jack's fingers traced words on some notepaper pages in the stack. "The index says that document number nine is titled 'Father John Becket's statement.' Except it's missing. Look for yourself. But another note here says: Refer to file number QUM121B. Could that mean it's been replaced in another box file?"

Yasmin studied the shelves. "I see file number QUM121B." She pointed beside where Kelly had located their file. "It's written on the spine of that box."

"I'm going to take it down and have a quick look."

"But Jack, Kelly said—"

"Tell me a rule that hasn't been broken." Jack saw Kelly shoot a brief look in their direction before returning to his magazine. Jack whispered to Yasmin, "I'll keep an eye on him. You pluck down the file. Situate yourself in front of the Madonna statue so that Kelly doesn't spot you."

"Why *me*? And what about the cameras?"

Jack smiled. "You're slimmer and can hide behind me and the statue. The people who man the security cameras won't know Kelly's conditions. And if he spots what you're up to, all he can do is have security throw you out."

"Funny."

"Get the box down. Lay it flat on the table so that Kelly won't see it." Jack turned and studied a document from the file, placing himself beside the Madonna bronze. Kelly was still reading. "You're all clear, Yasmin."

Jack heard a scraping noise behind him, then a slapping sound as something hit the table hard. "What the heck happened?" he hissed.

"I—I dropped the file," Yasmin said.

Jack saw Kelly's head jerk up, as if he'd heard the noise. He stared over. Jack gave him a silent wave, then continued to pretend to study the document in his hands. Kelly returned to his magazine.

Jack said without turning round, "We're okay, Kelly's reading. Have you put the file on the table?"

"Yes."

"Try to keep an eye on Kelly from over my shoulder." Jack turned back to the table, flicked open the second box file, and the same balsa wood scent hit his nostrils. A typed page lay on top of a thin pile of papers. It said: *"Qumran dig, Additional documents from Fr. Franz Kubel."* Jack searched in the paper pile. "It doesn't look like Becket's statement is—"

He stiffened, his gaze fixed on a roughly made drawing in front of him in the shape of a Roman scroll—embellished with vivid pen-and-ink engravings, dramatic images of animals, monsters, and sylphs.

Yasmin asked, "What's wrong? What have you found?"

"Something pretty remarkable indeed."

71

"You ask me, those guys are definitely on a stakeout. What do you think, Lela?"

In the back of the Fiat, Lela handed the binoculars back to Ari and said, "Where's your agent who tailed Yasmin and Jack?"

Ari flicked his head to indicate the white Fiat taxi parked near the security gates. The middle-aged, unshaven driver stood by his cab, chewing on a toothpick as he watched the Vatican entrance. "Actually, he's the cabdriver, Mario, who picked them up at the airport."

"How did you manage that?"

Cohen answered, "We've had half a dozen people keeping tabs on Cane since the moment his flight touched down. We chose our moment at the taxi stand to try to get him to pick one of our cabs. Even if he hadn't it wasn't a big deal; we could still have tailed them."

Ari peered through the binoculars and said to Cohen, "Did Mario overhear anything they said during the drive?"

"The couple kept their voices low but he definitely heard the word *scroll* mentioned."

Ari sounded excited. "Good stuff."

Cohen added, "Mario offered to be their guide for the day

and take them wherever they wanted to go. They took the bait and had him drive them to the Vatican for an appointment. Then they left Mario at one of the entrances, saying they'd be back."

Ari looked toward the busy St. Peter's Square and rubbed his jaw. "Question one is, what are they doing in the Vatican? Question two is, who are the guys on their tail?"

Lela studied the men from the silver Lancia. One wore a dark leather jacket. He had stepped out of the car and moved across the square. A brutal-looking specimen, he had a broken nose, his body muscled by too many steroids. Lela thought that his high cheekbones gave him a Slavic appearance. He stood near the Vatican entrance, a carry-on bag draped over his shoulder, trying to look like a tourist as he studied a guide map.

The driver was Arab, slender and with a trimmed beard, in his twenties. Lela said, "Any ideas who they could be?"

Ari laid down the binoculars. "No, but it might be worth downloading their pictures to Tel Aviv and running a check on them, like we're doing on Yasmin Green. Get your big ugly head out of the way, Cohen."

The Mossad driver shifted in the front seat as Ari raised a zoom-lens digital camera and clicked off at least a dozen shots. When he finished he studied the results in the camera's viewing window. Satisfied, he connected a short coil of black cable from the camera to his cell phone. "I got a few good ones."

Ari pressed a series of buttons on his cell phone. As he waited for the data to transmit he was deep in thought and tapped his lips with his forefinger.

Lela asked, "What's the matter?"

"I've been thinking. Why would they come to Rome? There's an obvious answer."

"What?"

"This city's got a reputation as a hub for black-market antique dealings. What if Cane came here to offload the scroll?"

"We don't even have a shred of evidence that they have it, Ari."

"My gut instinct's screaming at me that Cane's here to sell the parchment."

"Ari—"

"He and Yasmin aren't here as tourists. They're up to something."

Before Lela could reply, Ari's cell phone flashed a message and he said, "The pic data's downloaded. We'll see if our people can get lucky by matching those guys and Yasmin Green to any criminal or terrorist in Israel's data banks. We can trawl even wider if we need to."

"How long will it take?"

Ari disconnected the cable, coiled it up, and replaced it in the camera case. "Depends on how busy they are." He reached under his seat and pulled out a Sig 9mm automatic pistol. "It's time we grabbed Cane and his girlfriend and interrogated them. We make our move as soon as they show their faces."

72

"Are you going to keep me in suspense?" Yasmin asked impatiently.

Jack's face sparked as he plucked the drawing from the box and studied it under the magnifying glass. "It's a rough drawing that represents an inscribed Roman slab. What they call a bas-relief. The reliefs were made to decorate a wall or building in an artful way, or to record important events."

"I know what they are. What's the big deal?"

"I saw a similar drawing in Father Novara's study."

"You mean depicting the exact same images?"

"I believe so. Both drawings were alike, with dramatic images of animals, monsters, and sylphs."

"What's the significance?"

Jack carefully shifted the drawing under the reading light, a burst of excitement infecting his voice. "When I first saw the drawing in Novara's study, I had a feeling I'd seen these images before but couldn't recall where. Now that I've seen the scroll shape the images are drawn within, I remember."

"Remember what?"

"During the middle of the first century A.D., when the Emperor Nero ruled, Rome was a vast city with a population of about a million. It had many of the trappings of a modern society—apartment blocks, an intricate sewage system, fire brigades, a rudimentary police force, and law courts. One of the digs I worked on explored parts of underground Rome that are still intact from that period. Guess what?"

"I'm past guessing, Jack, just cut to the back end. The suspense is torture."

"I've seen this same relief before on several marble slabs. These images of animals, monsters, and sylphs are very distinctive. The slabs themselves were about six feet long, shaped like massive unrolled Roman scrolls, and had chiseled inscriptions."

Jack studied the drawing more closely. "There was a whole bunch of them on the wall of an enormous round room, what the Romans called a rotunda. Many commemorated deeds by Roman commanders. Archaeologists called the slabs the Nero marbles because they were in a huge villa, part of which dated from the period."

"What did the inscriptions say?"

"There were too many to recall exactly. And many of them had been damaged by subsidence and rockfalls. But I remember one in particular documented a list of plundered gifts presented to Nero by one of his commanders in Palestine."

Yasmin frowned. "So what's the drawing doing in this box?"

Jack tossed down the magnifier and scratched his head. "Another inscription we found nearby commemorated the defeat of the Jews at Masada, near Qumran, in 78 A.D., during the Roman occupation. But apart from that, I can't really see any great relevance. Except the drawing's got to have some if it's in a Vatican file. Novara also had a rough copy of it."

Jack slipped out his cell phone and Yasmin said, "What are you doing?"

"Taking a picture of the drawing. Move that reading lamp over here."

"What about the security cameras?"

"Shift yourself over here. If I hunch my shoulders I can cover up what I'm doing."

"Kelly will go crazy if he finds out."

"Too late." There was a soft click, followed by several more. Jack checked the recorded images he'd shot before he flipped shut his phone and tucked it back in his pocket. "It's not exactly high-quality photography, but I think I've got what I need."

Yasmin's mouth opened as she stared past Jack's shoulder. "We've got a problem. Kelly's seen us and he's on his way over."

Jack had just replaced the second box on the shelf when he heard footsteps and turned. Kelly stood there with a sour look. Beside him waited a tall, lanky man with a dour expression like a sad bloodhound. Dark rings under his eyes suggested he hadn't had proper sleep for days.

Kelly said bluntly to Jack, "What were you doing? Did you touch one of the box files?"

"I found a note that referred to a document in another box, right there. I was almost tempted to take a look. How about it?"

Kelly appeared suspicious as he checked the box file on the shelf for himself, then pushed it back into place. "Absolutely not, you know the rules. Besides, your time's up."

Kelly clicked his fingers at the lanky man. "Father Rossi, one of our senior archivists, will check the file to make sure it's all there. Proceed, Father."

"Yes, Excellency."

Jack said, "There's a document missing from our box."

Kelly's eyes narrowed. *"What?"*

"According to the index there's supposed to be a document number nine, titled 'Father John Becket's statement,' but it's not in there."

Kelly was suspicious. "Is this some kind of trickery?"

"No way. Look for yourself."

Kelly searched the pages and frowned. "He's right, it's not there."

Jack said, "We haven't got it. We've nothing to hide."

The archivist was ashen, at a genuine loss to explain. "Excellency, we haven't got around to working on this section yet, so I can't explain why the document's missing. I'll check to see if anyone signed it out, but I'm sure I would have noted it in my records."

Kelly was grim. "This is serious, Father Rossi. Deal with it personally."

"Of course, Excellency." The archivist flushed, tucked the box file under his arm, and crossed back to his work area.

Kelly regarded Jack with a skeptical look. "Under the circumstances, you and your lady friend will have to submit to a full strip search before you leave."

73

They followed Kelly into a chamber manned by two well-dressed security guards, one male and one female. The cardinal spoke to the guards in Italian. "Check them both. A document is missing. Do a full and thorough examination, if you please."

The woman led Yasmin through a nearby door while Jack was escorted by the male guard into a windowless room with a doctor's couch and several chairs. A number of electronic devices were laid out on the table, looking vaguely like torture implements, and the guard said in English, "Please remove everything from your pockets, signore."

Jack removed his notebook, wallet, and cell phone and the guard checked each in turn before he picked up an electronic scanner. "Arms wide, please."

Jack did as he was told and the guard ran the scanner over his body. "What does the scanner check for?" Jack asked.

The guard smiled. "Paper or parchment of any kind. In case you have stolen documents."

"You mean people actually try and steal items from the Vatican Archives?"

The guard raised his eyes in amusement. "Over the years I have caught respected priests and senior clergy trying to smuggle out priceless church papers. But nothing escapes our eyes, or our fingers."

"Fingers?"

"Bend over, signore."

"You've just got to be kidding."

"I must check all your body's *orifices*."

The guard's pronunciation of the last word was a little askew but Jack got the message. "Now hold on a second—"

A smirk flickered on the guard's face as he tugged on a pair of latex gloves and picked up a jar of lubrication jelly. "Cardinal Kelly gave strict orders. Refuse, and his next step would be to involve the Vatican security police. Believe me, you don't want that nightmare. Actually, you'd be surprised how many people have been caught trying to hide papers in intimate places."

"What surprises me is that I've agreed to this."

The man picked up a penlight and flicked it on. "Like thieves, prisoners often hide objects inside themselves in slim containers. Lean forward, elbows on the table. This check I am about to carry out is just like the one a doctor does. You know, when he checks the *prostate* by putting his finger up your—"

"Yeah, I get the general idea." Jack sighed, took a deep breath, and tried to steel himself against the humiliation and discomfort that were about to come.

"Spread your legs, signore, and bend over."

"And to think you never even bought me lunch."

Minutes later Jack buckled his trousers and followed the guard out of the room. Apart from mild discomfort, he felt violated and said to Kelly, "That was a bit extreme, don't you think?"

"A document is missing; extreme measures are called for. We can't be too careful, Jack."

"I guess the good news is I won't have to visit my urologist this year."

Kelly offered a tight smile. "My apologies, but security really is paramount."

"Has Father Rossi had any luck finding the document?"

"Not yet. But trust me, he's like a hound after a scent in such matters. I'm sure he'll get to the bottom of it, or kill himself in the process."

The female guard gave a silent nod to Kelly when she appeared moments later, an unhappy-looking Yasmin behind her.

"It seems you're both in the clear," Kelly offered. "Now, let me show you out."

As Kelly hurried them toward the exit, Jack said, "Have you ever heard of the Nero marbles?"

Kelly frowned and looked up and to the left, as if at some imaginary spot above his eyeline, then shook his head. "No, I haven't. Why?"

"You're sure?"

"I haven't the faintest idea what you're talking about. What are they?"

"Maybe my other questions are more important. What about the Atbash code, Cardinal? Have you heard of that?"

Kelly arched an eyebrow. "Yes, I have. Professor Schonfeld, one of the original Dead Sea scroll translators, claimed to have discovered such a code hidden in some of the texts. Why do you ask?"

"The scroll I found contained part gibberish. I've been wondering if it's written in some kind of code."

Kelly's eyes sparked. "How incredibly interesting. *Any*

help the church can give, you only have to ask, Jack. Such a document could prove of great interest to our scholars." He handed over a card embossed with a golden Vatican seal. "My private cell phone number is on the front. Call me day or night if I can be of help."

Jack tucked the card in his pocket as they followed Kelly down a flight of steps. "I appreciate that. You said you read Father Kubel's report."

"Many years ago."

"What about the missing file titled 'Father John Becket's statement'?"

Kelly looked up and into the distance a few seconds, then shook his head. "I never even knew it existed. But I can always ask the pope about it. If he recalls having written it, and I feel the contents may be of help to you, I assure you I'll get back to you at once."

"One last question, Cardinal."

Kelly glanced at his watch as they came out into the Belvedere Courtyard. "May I remind you I have an urgent appointment, Jack?"

"Then I won't waste your time. Do you know Father Vincento Novara?"

Kelly frowned and gave that look again, toward some imagined point right above his eyeline. "Vincento Novara? Who's he?"

"A Catholic priest and Aramaic scholar who lived at a monastery at Maloula, in Syria. I believe he was translating the stolen scroll when I met him yesterday and that he was involved with black-market thieves who stole it. Novara's been brutally murdered."

"I—I'm sorry to hear. That's dreadful. But I've never heard of Novara."

"Could you do me another favor? Check out Novara for me? I'll take whatever you can find. He's bound to be in your church records."

"I can't promise anything, but I'll see what I can do." Kelly sounded noncommittal. They reached the door and the cardinal made a point of consulting his watch. "I'm afraid I'm already seriously late for my appointment."

"Just one more question. Is Father Kubel alive?"

"Why do you ask?"

"I'd like to talk with him."

Kelly held open the door. "I'm afraid that's impossible. The last I heard, Father Kubel was at death's door, if he hasn't passed away already." Kelly offered his hand. "I really must be going. I'll hold you to your promise of a copy of the translated scroll, Jack. A pleasure seeing you again. And to meet you, Miss Green. *Arrivederci.*"

———

The Serb had the patience of a hunter. He remained across the street from the security barrier manned by Vatican guards. He wandered around the square but stayed close enough to observe the barrier and the waiting taxi. Every now and then he played his role of tourist and used the video cam but eventually he folded his tourist map, stuffed the camera in the travel bag hanging from his shoulder, and strolled back to the Lancia. He leaned his elbow on the open window, grumbling to Nidal, "There's still no sign of the couple."

Nidal's eyes glinted as he stared past him. "You're wrong. Our wait's over."

The Serb spun round to see the couple stroll out of the Vatican. He clutched the bag on his shoulder. Tucked inside he felt the firm outline of the MAC-10 machine pistol next to the video camera. "Get ready. This is where the fun starts."

Cardinal Liam Kelly hurried along the corridors to his Vatican office. He stepped into a room with high ceilings and decorated with exquisite antiques.

A young priest-secretary was at a desk and as he started to rise, Kelly said, "I need to make an urgent private call and don't want to be disturbed."

"Of course, Excellency."

Kelly entered his sumptuous office. He closed the door behind him, sat at a polished teak desk, and dabbed his brow with a handkerchief as he picked up his desk phone. He hastily punched a number. A soft voice answered, "Yes?"

Kelly recognized an anxious quiver in his own tone. "It's Liam. We need to meet and talk. Cane visited the archives as arranged."

"And?"

"Bad news. He knew about the marble. He also talked about the Atbash code and about what happened in Maloula."

"What's your opinion, Liam?"

"I think we're looking at dangerous trouble. It's a cancer that needs to be cut out or this thing is going to destroy us all."

74

Ari peered through the binoculars. "We're in business. Here they come."

Lela observed Cane and Yasmin exit through the Vatican security hut. They talked briefly with the cabdriver, then crossed the square toward a café. Ignoring the tables on the pavement, they moved inside and sat by a window.

At that precise moment Cohen's cell phone rang. He answered and turned to Ari. "That was Mario. Cane just asked him to wait another twenty minutes while they go have a coffee."

Lela concentrated on the two men. The brutal-faced, leather-jacketed one now wandered closer to the café, clutching the travel bag hanging from his shoulder. The Arab was still seated in the silver Lancia and facing in the café's direction, his eyes hidden behind dark glasses.

Ari swept the scene with the binoculars. "My gut tells me we're going to see some action pretty soon. The Arab and his buddy are circling like buzzards, waiting for their chance."

"What do you think's going down?" Lela asked.

"Who knows? Maybe they're potential buyers and want Cane's scroll."

"What should we do?"

Ari tossed aside the binoculars. "Play the cards as they fall. You and I will try to move a little closer to the action, see what goes down. If we notice anything being exchanged, we move in."

"And do what?"

"Snatch Cane and the woman. The Arab and his buddy are not our concern at this moment. Unless it looks like they're taking possession of the scroll, then it's a different matter."

"Making a snatch in broad daylight is crazy, Ari."

"We've no choice. Cohen has a safe house ten minutes away we can use for the interrogation. Mario and Cohen will stop the Arab and his buddy from leaving if we think they're in possession of the scroll or if they try to follow us."

"We're spreading ourselves thin, Ari. There are only four of us."

Ari grinned. "Cohen and Mario might not look it, but they're trained Mossad professionals. I've every confidence in them." He reached under his seat and handed another Sig pistol and three loaded magazines to Lela. "Just in case."

Lela took the pistol and magazines.

They saw the leather-jacketed man casually walk back toward the Arab, lean in the driver's window, and engage him in conversation. Both men stared in the direction of the café, and Jack and Yasmin.

Ari racked the Sig's slide to chamber a round before he tucked the weapon in his jacket pocket. "Pay attention, everyone. I've got a feeling the Arab and his pal are debating a move. Cohen, you know the drill. Keep your engine running and follow close behind us. Lela, you come walk with me. What's up? You look worried."

"I—I'm fine." Lela cocked her Sig and slid the pistol inside her jacket. "I just don't want to see anyone get hurt."

Ari moved to open the car door. "If Cane doesn't make a fuss that shouldn't happen. Okay, let's get in position. Cohen, call Mario, put him in the loop. And caution's the word, everyone. I don't want any of us going home in a body bag."

The busy café smelled of espresso and delicious pastries. Jack and Yasmin each ordered coffee and sat by a window with a partial view of the Vatican. When the waiter brought their coffees, Jack took a sip. "Sorry about the indignity back there. How do you feel?"

Yasmin stirred sugar into her cup and looked as if she was trying not to break a smile. "I never thought I'd find myself being searched from head to toe in the Vatican, of all places. That woman probed me everywhere. And I do mean *everywhere*. What did you make of Kelly's answers?"

Before Jack could reply, Yasmin stared out of the window and said, "I hope I'm not being paranoid."

"What's that supposed to mean?"

Her gaze was fixed beyond the glass. "I think I saw a man following us just before we entered the café. I just saw him again."

Jack frowned and stared past the glass at the crowds toward St. Peter's Square. "Where is he?"

"He disappeared into the crowd."

Jack smiled, trying to make light of it. "You're sure he wasn't just an admirer? I've known guys to traipse behind women for miles just to admire their legs. Remember, we're in Rome, testosterone capital of the world."

"Jack, I'm deadly serious. I had a problem with a stalker

once. I know when I'm being followed. This guy wasn't check-ing me out. He was too intent."

"What did he look like?"

"Eastern European. He was about forty, wore jeans and a dark leather jacket and had a boxer's flattened nose. He carried a travel bag over his shoulder. At one point he went to talk with a thin Arab-looking guy, seated in a silver Lancia."

Jack picked up his coffee, scanned the crowds on the square, and felt a rising anxiety in the pit of his stomach. "De-scribe the Arab."

"He had a trimmed beard and looked young, in his mid-twenties. What if they're Pasha's men?"

Jack's cell phone suddenly rang. He checked the calling number. "It's Buddy. He's got lousy timing. I'll have to call him back." He silenced the cell, finished his coffee, and got to his feet. "Stay here."

"Where are you going?"

Jack slipped on his sunglasses. "To see if I can spot anyone on the street who resembles either guy. Keep watch from the window but put on your sunglasses. I don't want you mak-ing eye contact with them if they reappear. They may suspect we're on to them."

She touched his hand. "What if it's dangerous?"

Jack winked down at her and slapped some euro banknotes on the table. "Relax. Have more coffee. I'll be back."

Yasmin looked up at his face. "You never told me what you thought of Kelly's answers."

"The questions I asked were deliberate. Especially about Father Novara and the Nero marbles. I needed to see Kelly's reaction."

"And?"

"He looked up and to the right when he gave his answer and focused on an imaginary point above eye level. Some behavioral psychologists might tell you that kind of look is a clear pointer."

"Of what?"

"That someone's lying through their teeth."

75

When Jack stepped outside the café it took him only seconds to spot the man in the leather jacket. He was standing across the street and had high Slavic cheekbones and the broad, broken-nosed face of a boxer. He wore sunglasses and carried a canvas travel bag over his shoulder. The moment Jack locked eyes on him the man looked away.

Jack felt a hand lightly touch his arm and he tensed. Yasmin stood beside him, wearing her sunglasses.

"I said to wait inside, Yasmin."

"I thought it might help if I tried to help you spot the men."

Jack didn't protest but took hold of her arm and linked it with his. "See the guy wearing the leather jacket? He's across the street."

"Yes, that's him," Yasmin whispered.

"Let's take a walk. Try to make it appear as if we're taking a casual stroll."

Jack started to walk. "You see the other guy near the lamppost?"

He felt Yasmin's grip tighten on his arm. "That's the Arab I saw watching us. Do you think they're Pasha's accomplices?"

"It's always a possibility. We'll make a dash for the cab

and try to lose them. Whatever happens, stick close to me." Jack looked to the right and saw their cab still parked near the Vatican side entrance. "Ready?"

Before Yasmin could reply, a gray Fiat drove at high speed toward them, scattering tourists and pedestrians in its way. It screeched to a halt and Jack got the shock of his life as a man and woman jumped out. The woman was Lela Raul.

Yasmin said, stunned, "It—it's the inspector."

"What the . . . ?" Jack felt riveted to the spot. While the Fiat's driver remained in the car with the engine running, Lela and her companion approached Jack. He locked eyes with Lela but suddenly she raised her hand as if in warning and screamed, "Behind you, Jack, look out!"

Jack saw that the leather-jacketed man with the brutal face was pushing toward him, wrenching a compact machine pistol from his travel bag. The man spotted Lela and her companion drawing weapons.

He raised his machine pistol. The weapon stuttered, raking a burst of gunfire across the ground in front of Lela and her companion, sending chunks of asphalt flying as screams erupted from the scattering crowds.

Lela's partner managed to draw his gun but the Serb fired another burst. As the crowd went wild to escape, Jack lost sight of Lela and her partner, who were masked by fleeing tourists.

Jack felt his pulse race and sensed danger all around, his fear surging as he tried to catch sight of Lela. Then another two shots rang out somewhere in the crowd and more screams erupted. Yasmin grabbed hold of his arm. "Run, Jack."

But Jack's eyes were on the brutal-faced shooter who

struggled out through the mob. He was joined by the bearded Arab who burst through the crowd, an automatic pistol in his hand as his eyes locked on Jack and Yasmin.

"For heaven's sake, run before we're killed," said Yasmin, and Jack dragged her by the arm and they darted into the nearest backstreet.

76

They ran for fifty yards before Jack shot a glance back over his shoulder. The Arab pushed his way through the crowds, trying to keep up. Jack glimpsed the man's companion, concealing his machine pistol under his coat.

Jack kept running, dragging Yasmin through the crowds. Rome's streets were packed but there wasn't a police uniform in sight. They turned a corner and Jack saw that they were in a dead end. "Turn back."

By the time they turned round and reentered the street, the Arab was barely seventy yards behind them. Jack ran faster, his lungs ablaze as he clutched Yasmin's hand. She said breathlessly, "We can't just run blindly. Do we know where we're going?"

"I've got a rough idea." Jack scoured the street signs and steered a sharp right into an alleyway, the cobble shiny and worn. He wiped sweat from his face. "The street I'm looking for is around one of these corners. I can't remember which one but I'm pretty sure we're almost there."

"Almost *where*? What street?" Yasmin began to panic.

"The place I'm looking for is off the Via Varrone."

They entered the next turning and came to a wide cobbled street lined with tall, centuries-old residential homes with wrought-iron balconies. Their yellow stone façades were soot-streaked by pollution.

Yasmin said, "Is that supposed to mean something to me?"

"Trust me, it will."

Soon they came to a building with a basement entrance. A short flight of granite steps led down to a barred metal gate with a rusted padlock. Jack hurried down the steps and called back to Yasmin, "Keep an eye out and let me know if we've been followed."

Yasmin caught her breath and looked over her shoulder. "I can't see anyone."

"The Arab and his friend have probably taken a wrong turn. Come down here."

Yasmin joined him at the bottom of the stairwell. Jack rattled the bars. "It's locked solid."

Yasmin saw tarry blackness past the gate. "Where is this place?"

Jack probed between the metal bars with his left hand, fiddling with something on the inside wall. There was a soft *click* and a sparse string of lightbulbs popped on, revealing a rock-strewn passageway. Bulbs strung along the granite walls illuminated a stone pathway that inclined down. "I spent two years here, working on an excavation. It's still going on in fits and starts." Jack got down on his knees, slipped his arm between the bars, and felt along the lower wall inside the gate.

"Just tell me where we are."

Jack wiggled his fingers, trying to touch something. "What we've got down here is not exactly another Pompeii but it comes close. It's an entrance to underground Rome I told you about. The ancient city's right below our feet."

"Except the gate's locked."

"Right." Jack smiled as he removed his hand and revealed a worn metal key, patched with rust, dangling between his two fingers. "The dig caretaker, Rocco, always left the key here. Old habits die hard."

"Where does this passageway lead?"

"You'll see." Jack twisted the key in the lock and pushed in the creaking gate. The air chilled as they moved inside. He closed the gate after them, locked it again, and tucked the key in his pocket.

"Is it safe down here?" Yasmin appeared frozen by fear, a stale smell wafting up from the staircase.

"It is if you know what you're doing." A trio of dented tin oil lamps hung from hooks on the wall and Jack grabbed one.

"How are you going to light the lamp?"

"I've got a lighter somewhere but we'll keep going for now. The lightbulbs ought to be on for a good part of the way." Jack moved down the path. Fifty yards on, it curved downward into pitch darkness. They heard racing footsteps and looked behind them.

Jack put a hand to his lips to silence Yasmin. The footsteps halted. A pause followed, then a rush of feet moved down the basement stairwell.

The Arab appeared behind the gate and he spotted them in the passageway. He tried to rattle open the gate but when it refused to budge he stepped back and fired his pistol at the lock. The shot exploded, ricocheting off metal and stone. It zinged past Jack's head like a supersonic bee. A second shot ricocheted off the walls but already Jack was charging deeper into the passageway and dragging Yasmin after him.

Nidal saw the couple scurry away. Frustrated, he rattled the gate but the lock hadn't completely shattered. He covered his face with his arm, carefully aimed the Beretta, and his second shot blew apart the lock, sending shards flying.

The Serb hammered away the metal remains with the butt of his machine pistol, then dragged open the creaking gate.

Nidal stepped inside and spotted the oil lamps hanging on the wall. He grabbed one and raced down the passageway, the Serb following.

77

Jack and Yasmin hurried on. The air became cooler the deeper they went. After about two hundred feet the string of light-bulbs ended. Another metal gate blocked their path, this one with a heavier lock, an unlit passageway beyond.

This time Jack saw a key hanging from a hook in the wall and he inserted it frantically in the lock. The gate was slow to budge but when he slammed his shoulder hard against the metal, it creaked open in protest. There was barely enough room for them to squeeze through into the blackness and as Jack relocked the gate, they heard the echo of footsteps. "They don't give up, do they? Stay close to the wall and hold on to my coattail," he urged Yasmin.

The passageway they entered looked dark and forbidding and the air smelled stale. Jack slipped the key into his pocket and they pushed on ahead. The ground was smooth beneath their feet, the walls slimy to their touch, and they were mostly in darkness apart from the dying glow of the pathway lighting behind them.

Jack whispered, "I don't want to make us a target, so we'll wait as long as we can before we light the lamp. I ought to warn you that some of the passageways around here have open shafts that drop down to another level, so be extra careful where you step."

Tension edged Yasmin's voice. "As if being chased by a couple of armed madmen wasn't enough excitement for one day, I get to risk breaking my legs as well."

Jack's cell phone rang, the keypad illuminating, and he startled. "What the . . . !" He hit the mute and checked the caller ID. "It's Buddy again. Talk about bad timing."

Jack flicked off his cell as the footsteps on the slope grew louder. "I'd suggest you switch yours off too, in case it rings and gives us away."

Yasmin flicked off her phone. They moved deeper into the passageway and she kept a firm hold of Jack's coat as he felt his way along the walls.

Jack listened, and noticed that the echoing footsteps had halted. He looked back and saw moving shadows. The Arab and his companion had reached the second gate. It rattled fiercely and then came a muzzle flash as a ricochet exploded.

"Get down." Jack squatted, pulling Yasmin after him. "Crouch as low to the ground as you can."

Yasmin hunkered beside him, alarmed. "What happens when they come through the gate? We've nowhere to hide."

"There ought to be a corner up ahead. Then we can light the lamp and try to lose them in the tunnels."

"Are you sure we're even in the right passageway?"

Jack kept feeling his way forward, dragging her deeper into the tarry darkness. "I'm sure of nothing except that this part of Rome's underground is a maze of tunnels and it's easy to stray off course. That's why I'm hoping we can try and lose them."

Yasmin's voice hoarsened with panic. "You mean *we* could get *lost*?"

"That's a distinct possibility."

___

Nidal rattled the gate but it didn't budge. The single shot from his Beretta had ricocheted off the iron lock. "Take care of it," he ordered.

The Serb examined the rusted lock. The cast iron looked solid. He shook his head. "I'm not sure we can shoot out the mechanism. This one's much sturdier than the last. Step well away."

Nidal took a dozen paces back. The Serb aimed toward the gate, squeezed the trigger, and the MAC-10 stuttered.

Jack groped along the moist walls, moving as fast as he could. He felt a sharp right angle. "I think we've found our corner."

He rounded it, clutching Yasmin's hand, then fumbled in his pocket for a cheap plastic lighter and removed the oil lamp's glass cover. He struck the lighter and touched the flame to the wick. It lit at once, yellow light flaring in the darkness to reveal a massive veil of spiders' webs.

Yasmin staggered back in terror as the air in front of them came alive with colonies of huge black spiders. Their hairy bodies sprang through the air in wild panic, some of them landing on their clothes before they vanished into the shadows between the wall cracks. "What . . . what are those?" Yasmin was livid with fear.

Jack waved the lamp, tearing the veil of webs. "They're called *saltericchi*. A species of jumping spider that live in the darkest, most humid areas underground. At the first sign of light they start hopping around like they're on crack." He smiled. "They can scare the life out of you the first time you see them, but they're really harmless."

The distant rattle of the metal gate echoed behind them, then came the sound of a short blast of sustained gunfire. Yasmin said, "It won't be long before they break the lock."

"I'm not so sure. It looked pretty robust to me."

Yasmin brushed away the remains of a cobweb in her hair. "Are there any other shocks in store for me that I ought to know about?"

Jack held up the lamp. In every direction he looked was the unmistakable herringbone brickwork of ancient Rome, a barrel-vaulted ceiling rising high above them. "Quite a few."

When they turned the next corner they came to an ornate two-story mausoleum fronted by two huge marble entrance pillars. They stepped through and the lamplight washed over a collection of what looked like tombs.

One was topped by a stone carving of Christ and the Apostles. On another tomb was a figure of Apollo. Yet another showed Bacchus, the Roman god of wine and revelry, surrounded by rampaging, evil-looking satyrs with horns on their heads. "Where are we . . . ?" Yasmin asked in horror.

"Part of a Roman burial site called the City of the Dead. It came to light hundreds of years ago when the Basilica was being rebuilt. The necropolis dates from the second to fourth centuries A.D. A strange mix of the pagan and the Christian, from a time when Rome was caught between both camps."

Jack dangled the lamp as they passed a stream of pagan shrines, some of them defaced with cement or overlaid with Christian memorials of stone or marble. Yasmin asked, "What happened here?"

"Christians made a habit of trying to destroy the symbols of pagan gods, but they still had their followers."

A chill wind whistled through the passageway, making a haunting noise, and Yasmin rubbed her arms in the cold air. Jack waved the lamp toward the bend up ahead. "Just wait until you see what's around the next corner."

78

They rounded the corner into an ancient cobbled road. On both sides lay footpaths and ruined buildings, complete with mosaic floors and faded wall frescoes.

Jack scratched his head and tried to get his bearings. "If my intuition's right, the Nero marbles are somewhere near the end of this street."

"Where are we now?"

"Standing in the middle of what was once a sprawling complex of apartment homes, shops, and villas."

Yasmin looked around her in awe. "This is truly incredible."

"It's Rome as it existed more than two thousand years ago. It even had many of the trappings of a modern society. See that metal rod?"

As they passed a huge stone water fountain that had been scalloped out of solid limestone, Jack pointed to the remains of a blackened metal rod that protruded from the basin. Yasmin touched the rod. "What is it?"

"A lead pipe that once formed part of Rome's plumbing system. Fresh purified water was delivered to every doorstep from aqueducts. Over two hundred and fifty gallons a day per citizen, more than most modern cities provide these days. The problem was the Romans didn't know that they were slowly killing themselves with lead poisoning."

Yasmin turned her head and listened. "I can't hear anyone. Maybe they got lost in this maze."

"I wouldn't count on it."

"Do you know of another way out of here?"

Jack nodded. "I think so, unless it's been blocked up. Better keep moving."

Farther on they came to the portal of an impressive villa. The floor was littered with pottery shards, the remains of wine jars. One side of the villa's entrance contained a pagan shrine with the grotesque face of a stone-carved god.

"Mithras," Jack explained. "An Iranian god of truth and salvation. He was pretty popular, and one of Jesus' main rivals during the later empire."

"Rivals?"

"Jesus had hundreds of pagan contenders that the Romans believed were important gods. Under the polished floors of almost every ancient church in Rome, including St. Peter's, you'll find shrines to Mithras, because Christian builders wanted to eradicate the sacred places of any competing religions and replace them with their own symbols."

Beyond lay a courtyard, the cracked stucco walls painted in rich colors clouded by time. Jack swung the lamp to reveal faded murals: images of naked men and women, frolicking and drinking wine. He jerked his thumb at a half-ruined building across the street. "Where we're standing is what was once a rich pimp's villa. Right over there is the brothel he once owned."

"How do you know all this?"

"From the graffiti we found on the villa's walls. Etched outside the brothel was an à la carte menu of sexual services on offer."

Yasmin peered into the brothel ruins. A limestone wash-basin and toilet area occupied one cubicle. Others were fitted with what looked like concrete-made beds that would have once been topped with straw-filled mattresses. Frescoes of naked women and men in various sexual positions adorned the walls. Yasmin studied the images and smiled. "An erotic bunch, the Romans."

"They had no hang-ups about sex, that's for sure. Pretty much anything went. That's historical fact. The morality of the average Roman citizen was probably lower than a snake's belly. See that signpost out in the street? It's what I'd call down-to-earth advertising."

Jack pointed to a stone wall. Inset in the brick was a pro-truding piece of carved stone. At first Yasmin thought it was a carving of a finger. Then she realized that it was a chiseled symbol of an erect penis. It pointed toward the brothel. She raised an eye. "I guess people's vices haven't changed, have they?"

"You said it. But the city's immorality had a heavy price. You'll see what I mean straight ahead. And it's pretty grue-some."

They came to a flight of stone steps that led under an archway. Jack said, "The steps lead down to part of the Romans' sewer system. We found lots of infant bones down there during our dig."

"Why infant bones?" Yasmin asked.

"The brothel women often drowned their unwanted new-borns. Ordinary citizens were in the same habit if their off-spring were handicapped, or unwanted females."

Yasmin recoiled. "That—that's horrifying."

"Roman society didn't exactly cultivate the virtue of pity.

Clemency, sure, if a gladiator fought bravely in the arena then he might be allowed to live. But the cradle of modern society was a brutal place where life was cheap."

Yasmin marveled as the lamplight's yellow glow picked out ancient Latin graffiti still scrawled in faded black above the arch. "What does it say?"

"'Peaceful are the dead and the living will soon join them.'"

Yasmin shivered. "Let's hope it doesn't turn out to be an omen."

A huge rat scurried past and disappeared down the sewer steps. Yasmin staggered back, stifling a scream. "Did . . . did you see that?"

"I ought to have warned you. The rats down here are as big as lapdogs." He raised the lamp. "We've arrived."

Thirty feet past the archway was a wall at least six feet high, almost completely covered with a mound of building rubble.

Yasmin said, "I thought you said the marbles were here."

Jack wiped his brow, confused. "They were. You entered this archway to get to them. I remember the location exactly because of the sewer nearby."

He held up the lamp to study the debris mound. Then he knelt, placed the lamp beside him, and began grabbing handfuls of debris and tossing them aside. "There could have been a rockfall, but the roof looks solid enough. Or maybe someone deliberately covered up the marble with rubble."

"Why would anyone want to do that?"

Perspiration dripped from Jack's face as he stopped to tear off his jacket, then began tossing aside armfuls of stones. "That's a good question. Come on, give me a hand. If we can shift enough of this junk, we'll find the entrance."

79

"Slow down, Ari, or you'll bleed to death."

Ari slowed his pace as they ran through the narrow back-streets near St. Peter's Square. The crowded press of bodies was behind them as Lela ushered Ari into a deserted alleyway and they both caught their breath.

She released her grip on the Sig pistol in her pocket. "Let me see your hand."

Ari leaned his back against a wall, clutching his left wrist, his face glistening with sweat. Lela examined the gunshot wound. Blood seeped from the back of Ari's hand where a bullet had scored the flesh, exposing the wrist bone. "Does it hurt?" Lela asked.

Ari nodded and wiped sweat from his face with his sleeve. "I think the bone's chipped."

"You'll need something to ease the pain. Maybe a morphine shot."

"No time for that. You'll find a necktie in my right-hand jacket pocket. Use it to stop the bleeding."

"Shouldn't we just call Cohen and have him take you to the safe house?"

Ari winced. "No way. First, I'm going to find the creep who shot me. He and his Arab buddy can't have got far. Cane too."

"Meanwhile you'll bleed to death. Get sense, Ari."

He snapped back, "Who's in charge here, Lela? Find the tie, dress the wound, and let's get moving before they get away. We're losing time."

"Okay, have it your way." Lela fumbled in Ari's pocket and found a colorful necktie. She pulled up his sleeve, tightly bound his wrist, and let out a sigh of exasperation.

The confrontation on St. Peter's Square had turned into a nightmare. The Arab's companion had managed to shoot first, hitting Ari in the hand. Then the shooter and the Arab had disappeared into the panicked crowds, chasing after Jack. Ari and Lela had followed Cohen's dash back to the car and drove at high speed into the backstreets after them. Sirens had sounded and Swiss Guards and Vatican plainclothes security flooded the square.

When the backstreets became too narrow for the taxi, Ari ordered Cohen to circle the area but keep his cell phone on. Ari and Lela clambered out and caught a brief glimpse of the Arab and his partner darting down an alley but by now they had lost them.

Lela finished knotting the tie and the bleeding stemmed. "That's the best I can do."

Ari gritted his teeth, rolled down his sleeve, and scanned their surroundings. "Where the devil have they disappeared to?"

Distant, arguing voices drifted from a nearby alley. Ari said, "Let's try this way."

They came out onto a centuries-old street of tall houses decorated with wrought-iron balconies. A couple of the front doors were open wide and a nosy-looking elderly woman stood outside one, talking heatedly with two elderly men who appeared to be her neighbors.

Ari spoke to them in Italian. The woman replied in a

heated burst and pointed across the street toward a cellar stairway, protected by iron railings.

Ari had another brief exchange with the woman before he translated for Lela. "The old lady says that a couple of minutes ago she saw a man and woman go down those basement steps over there, followed by two other men. She and her neighbors heard gunfire soon after and called the police."

"Does she know what's down in the basement?"

"She says it's an entrance to some Roman tunnels that run under the city."

Almost on cue, the wail of a police siren shrieked in the distance. Ari ignored the neighbors and hurried down the basement steps, beckoning Lela.

"But the cops are on their way," she protested.

"Our job's to catch Cane. Besides, I want that creep who shot me. Now get down here, Lela."

She followed him down the steps. A gate swung open on its hinges, the lock shattered, and a stone stairway led down. From somewhere below came a *crack* that sounded like gunfire.

"Did you hear that shot?" Ari asked, alarmed. He stepped cautiously onto the stairway, his face still covered in sweat. He nodded back to Lela and cocked his pistol. "Stick close to me and keep your weapon ready."

Nidal raced through the underground passageway and came to a sudden halt. He swore.

In front of them were five Roman archways going in different directions.

The Serb's face was enraged as he ripped the magazine from the MAC-10, reloaded a fresh one, and slammed it home. "Which one do we take?"

Nidal clutched the lamp in one hand, his Beretta in the other, and cocked an ear. "Quiet. Did you hear that?"

"Hear what? We're lost. This place is like a rabbit warren. You know they found a tourist's skeleton somewhere in the city's tunnels a while back? He'd been dead for years—"

"Shut up," Nidal hissed, raising a finger to his lips.

The Serb fell silent. Nidal listened, then moved toward the mouth of the archway on his left. "I heard a noise. It sounded like rocks falling."

The Serb shook his head. "I heard nothing. You're imagining things."

Nidal ignored him and raised his Beretta, his eyes alive, like a bloodhound scenting his prey. "They're near here, I'm sure of it," and with that he swung the lamp high and plunged into the passageway.

80

"Are you *sure* this is the spot?" Yasmin removed another pile of rubble. She sounded breathless and irritated. "We're getting nowhere fast, Jack."

He dumped an armful of bricks on the pile, his face drenched in sweat. "I'm pretty sure we're in the right place."

"Then why haven't we seen the marbles? Face it, there's *nothing* here, Jack."

"Don't speak too soon." He worked feverishly, tossing away more rubble until a couple of brick stairs were exposed. A waft of foul-smelling air blew up, but disappeared just as quickly. "Give me a hand here."

They cleared away enough of the remaining debris to reveal stairs leading down into a darkened passageway. Jack grabbed the lamp. "Stick close and watch how you go."

They stepped down into a broad brick corridor draped with cobwebs. An army of *saltericchi* spiders jumped ahead of them, vanishing into darkness. Yasmin said, "Our friends are back. Where does this lead?"

"You'll see."

The flickering oil lamp threw eerie shadows around the walls. They fumbled on until the corridor ended at a plastered archway, pitch darkness beyond. "Let's have some light on the situation." Jack raised the lamp and they moved under the archway.

Yasmin gasped as they entered an enormous round room. It appeared about sixty feet wide and almost as high. All across the floor massive blocks of barreled limestone were scattered in total disarray, the remains of Roman columns. Debris from the partially collapsed roof had spilled into the room.

But it was the circular walls that were most impressive. Decorated with at least a dozen six-foot-high and three-foot-wide marble slabs that were set into the plaster, the slabs had been chiseled by stonemasons to resemble colossal unrolled scrolls. Half depicted battle scenes; the other half were inscribed in Latin. Most were cracked and had huge chunks missing, as if damaged when the limestone columns had collapsed into the room.

Jack stepped back to get a proper look, lamplight flickering over the marble. He ran his fingers over portions of the chiseled inscriptions, the borders decorated with theatrical images of wild animals, monsters, and sylphs.

"Is this the rotunda you talked about?" Yasmin asked.

Jack nodded. "This one's part of a luxury private villa. It's an exercise in vanity, really."

"What do you mean?"

"The marble scrolls are a sort of historical tapestry, depicting glorious past deeds, some of them a record of the villa owner's and his ancestors' achievements." Jack moved closer to study the marble, using his sleeve to remove a thick layer of dust. "According to this inscription, he was a man called Cassius Marius Agrippa."

"Was he someone famous?"

"If he was I've never heard of him. The ancient Romans loved the grand gesture. Their city was full of monuments, statues, and plaques to the movers and shakers of their world. Important figures liked to blow their own horn."

"So he could have been famous."

"Well, maybe not, Yasmin. Anyone worth their salt or with an ego complex had a bust made of themselves, or a statue commissioned. Some just liked to have their personal achievements inscribed for posterity, like Agrippa here."

"What did he do?"

"A whole bunch of things, according to this. Agrippa was a man of many parts. Roman army general, consul, businessman."

A portion of one of the inscriptions drew Jack's attention and he put the lamp on top of one of the limestone blocks and climbed up. He grimaced in pain as he reached the top and gripped his leg. "Ouch, that hurt."

"What's wrong?"

"A twinge in my thigh."

"Your wound?"

"Yep."

"Be careful, take it easy."

Jack used his elbow again to wipe off dust from the marble. He carefully ran a finger over the stone as if he were reading Braille. "I also think this guy Agrippa may have been in love."

"With who?"

"Himself. His list of his achievements seems endless. On top of everything else Cassius Agrippa was—"

"Was what?"

Jack held the lamp closer to the marble, light flickering over the inscription as his brow creased with shock. "There's something amazing up here. Come and see for yourself."

81

Lela stumbled over a hill of rubble. She felt totally confused as she halted in the middle of a cobbled Roman street, the remains of shops and villas on either side. "Where are we? This place is a total maze. Why do I have the feeling that we're lost, Ari?"

They were far past the entrance passageway, the string of lightbulbs had ended, and Ari used his lamp. Ahead, half a dozen passageways led in different directions. High above them was a metal trellis set in the roof, the hint of street light filtering down, the vague sounds of traffic and a distant church bell.

Ari swung the lamp to create a bigger spread of light, then peered up at the metal trellis above. "I read about these tunnels. They crisscross Rome. So there have to be other exits."

"I hope so. We can't go back the way we came with the police around."

Ari moved left but as he did his balance went and he teetered on the edge of a huge shaft, the lamp swinging in his hand to reveal that it dropped away into bottomless darkness.

"Ari!" Lela grabbed his arm and managed to pull him back in.

He wiped perspiration from his brow. "That was pretty close."

A second later, Ari's cell phone rang and he flicked it on, heard a voice, and said, "Go ahead." He covered the mouthpiece and said back to Lela. "It's base, in Tel Aviv."

"What do they want?"

"They've got a positive ID on the Arab."

Yasmin gripped Jack's hand and he pulled her up to join him on the limestone block. She found her balance and held on to him as he read from a damaged section of the marble. "What does it say?" she asked.

Jack touched the chiseled lines with his forefinger. "According to this, Cassius Agrippa was a commander in Roman-controlled Syria. It doesn't say where in Syria but it does mention it was at the same time as the governorship of Pontius Pilate, who controlled Palestine."

"Go on."

"Cassius Agrippa claims a long list of personal achievements. But what's particularly interesting is this one: *'Portavit sicco suus officium quod sentio quod neco Nazarene notus ut electus vir.'*"

"Give it to me in plain English, Professor."

"It says: 'He carried out his duty and judged and put to death the Nazarene known as the chosen man.'"

Jack took a worn, leather-bound notebook from his back pocket and jotted down the Latin words inscribed on the marble. "That's all I can make out. After that there's a big gap where the inscription's been damaged. The 'chosen one' was another term used to describe the messiah at that time. By 'chosen man' I've a feeling they mean the same thing."

"Is this the same commander who carried out the execution in Dora?"

"I've a gut feeling it may be. Father Novara and Father Kubel were both archaeologists and must have figured out some sort of connection to the Nero marbles inscription. Why else would the drawing be in the file?"

"Does it say where the execution took place?"

Jack followed the inscription with his finger. "No. Big chunks of the writing are missing here too."

Yasmin frowned as she looked around the rotunda scrolls. "Why do you think Cassius Agrippa wanted all this mentioned in his inscription?"

Jack thought about it. "Probably simple vanity. In the years after Jesus' death his name would have spread as Christianity grew. Jesus' legend would have been well-known in Rome. Judging by Agrippa's long list of triumphs the guy had a big ego. Maybe he wanted to stake his claim for posterity and suggest he played a part in the drama of Jesus' death."

"I don't get it. Why isn't a significant piece of history like this well-known, Jack?"

"Newly discovered Roman sites are being uncovered almost every day by construction workers. References to Jesus' followers are a dime a dozen. This one doesn't even mention Jesus by name. Let's face it, if someone translated the inscription it probably wouldn't make a whole lot of sense without some kind of context." Jack finished writing in the notebook and flipped it shut.

"Isn't there any more?" Yasmin asked.

"Nothing worth talking about. And the rest of the inscription is destroyed forever." Jack frowned as he climbed down off the limestone, careful not to strain his leg.

Yasmin said, "You look like you've got something on your mind."

"If we're talking about the same messiah that the world knows as Jesus—and remember, we're talking about the same time period, so it's probable—then this poses a huge question. Everyone knows that in the gospels Jesus was sentenced to death and crucified in Jerusalem by Pontius Pilate."

"Go on."

"So how could a commander, Cassius Agrippa, serving almost eighty miles away in Syria, have been responsible?" Jack offered his hand up to Yasmin.

She took hold of it and Jack added, "If my sense of direction's right, we're under or near the Vatican. Ease yourself down."

Yasmin slithered down into his arms.

Jack released her and then closely inspected portions of the shattered marble. "This area is probably normally out of bounds to anyone but Vatican officials with the authority to be down here."

"What are you saying?"

Jack slapped a hand over the damaged portion of the marble. "It all seems a bit convenient. What if someone deliberately defaced the marble to hide the full inscription? Some of this damage could just as easily have been inflicted with a hammer or chisel as by falling debris."

"Where does that leave us?"

"Nowhere, except with a bunch of questions. The big one being, how could Jesus have been crucified in two places?"

"Any suggestions that make any kind of sense?"

Jack considered, and then an excited tone crept into his reply: "Only this. What if two messiahs existed at about the same time?"

"Are you serious?"

"As weird as it sounds, it's about all I can think of. And

it poses a couple of mind-blowing questions. Did this second messiah have any relationship to the Jesus of history that we know of? Did their two stories connect in some way?"

A noise sounded behind them, of stones falling away. They turned and saw the Arab appear out of the shadows, his pistol aimed at them. "Move and I kill you both."

82

Nidal stepped into the room. Behind him the Serb appeared, armed with a machine pistol. Nidal said in perfect English, "Place the lamp on the ground and keep your hands away from your body."

Jack put down the metal lamp and it made a *clink* as it hit stone. He and Yasmin spread their arms.

Nidal's eyes darted restlessly. "You've led us both in a tiring dance, Mr. Cane. But no matter where you ran we would have found you."

His voice was laced with arrogance and he snapped his fingers. The Serb patted Jack and Yasmin for weapons, then stepped back.

Jack said to Nidal, "Who are you? How do you know me?"

Nidal glanced up at the marbled walls. "You'll find out soon enough. What are you both doing down here?"

"Trying to escape from you and the others following us."

Nidal aimed his pistol at Yasmin. "You. Tell me who are the others."

"Israelis. One of them is Inspector Lela Raul, of the Jerusalem police."

Nidal considered, and then without warning he turned and struck Jack a stinging blow across the face with the barrel of his pistol. Jack staggered back, clapping a hand to his jaw.

Nidal fixed him with a steely look. "Take that as a warning, Mr. Cane. You are not here just to escape, are you? I think you had a purpose when you dug a hole through that rubble back there. What did you hope to find?"

Jack wiped his mouth, stained wet with blood. "You probably wouldn't understand."

"I'll decide that." Nidal put the tip of the pistol to Yasmin's temple. "If I have to repeat the question you'll be scraping her brains off the walls."

"A clue led us here."

Nidal cautiously lowered his Beretta. Raising his lamp, he edged closer to the damaged marble. He studied the chiseled words with interest, touching them with his fingertips. "You mean here, to these inscriptions?"

"Yes."

"Which period are they?"

"First century A.D."

Nidal raised his gun again. "Translate the words. Whichever ones interested you. You're an archaeologist. Latin should not be a problem."

Jack interpreted the inscription.

"Interesting." A smile creased Nidal's face as he studied the marble, then he turned back to Jack. "But you know what I also find interesting, Mr. Cane? That despite warnings you persist in trying to find the scroll. That is admirable. Except you forgot one very important point."

"What's that?"

"The scroll doesn't belong to you. Where is it, Mr. Cane?"

"I've got no idea."

"Liar." Nidal struck Jack another blow across the face, this one even more vicious.

Jack reeled back, the blow stinging him like an electric shock, and clapped a hand to his jaw. "You mind telling me what I'm missing here? Who are you? What do you want?"

Nidal jerked his pistol. "Ultimately your life if you don't tell me the truth, Mr. Cane. Now move, you're both coming with us."

"Where?" Jack asked.

"To meet someone who's going to decide if you live or die."

83

Jack followed Nidal and Yasmin back through the passageway. The Serb covered them with the machine pistol and carried Jack's lamp.

As they mounted the steps from the rotunda into the ruined underground street, Nidal said, "It may not be safe going back the way we came. You've excavated in Rome, Cane. You have knowledge of these passageways. Find us another way out of here."

"You know a lot."

"Where's the nearest way out—or do I have to hurt the woman to force you to tell me?"

Jack studied the ruined street, trying to get his bearings. He pointed to a jumble of huge stone blocks. Another archway lay beyond, smothered in darkness. "There ought to be an exit somewhere that way."

"You had better be right, Cane."

"It ought to eventually lead us to a metal stairway. It leads up to street level on the Via Famagosta. Except the exit door is probably locked."

The Arab's partner waved his gun. "I'll take care of that. Get going."

"Wait," Nidal said, and traded his weapon with his partner. "Give me the MAC-10 and take my pistol."

The Serb took the Beretta and Nidal cocked the machine pistol. He aimed it at Jack and gestured for him to move. "If you're lying or attempt to escape I'm going to cut you down like a dog."

As Jack stepped forward to lead the way, a firm voice commanded in English, "Throw down your weapons. Nobody move or we'll shoot."

The order was immediately repeated in Arabic as Lela and her companion stepped out of the shadows and aimed their pistols.

Jack locked eyes with Lela a second before she told the Arab and his partner, "Obey the order. Throw your weapons down now!"

In an instant Nidal brought up the MAC-10 and fired. A burst of gunfire stitched across the chamber walls, gouging plaster and sending Lela and Ari diving for cover as Jack crouched for shelter behind a shattered stone column.

The Serb dragged Yasmin toward the jumble of stone blocks and disappeared under the archway. Nidal followed them, firing another burst back into the chamber.

The gunfire died but the echo seemed to go on forever as Jack moved from behind his cover. He saw that Lela's companion was already on his feet. The man raced toward the archway and fired a volley of shots into the passageway, the ricocheting rounds sparking off the walls.

A cry of pain erupted from somewhere in the darkness, then a ferocious burst of fire answered from Nidal's machine pistol, gouging the plaster walls and forcing Ari to throw himself to the ground for cover.

The instant the gunfire died Jack sprinted toward the archway. He heard another pained cry from deep in the shadows. *Has Yasmin been hit?*

As he went to plunge into the passageway he felt hard metal prod against the back of his neck. Lela appeared behind him. "Stop, Jack. Stay where you are."

"I've got to go after them, Lela. Yasmin's been abducted."

"I told you to stay—"

"Shoot me if you want, but I'm still going." Jack surged past her, darting blindly into the pitch-black archway.

"Jack!" Lela went to move after him just as Ari struggled to his feet, gripping his wounded arm, his face ashen.

"I think I shot one of the creeps. Why didn't you stop Cane? You let him get away."

"Let's hope you didn't hit the woman, Ari. Jack claimed she'd been abducted. And I couldn't just shoot him. We don't know the full story here."

"Just do your job and catch him, Lela." Ari was enraged, but as he staggered over to the archway in pursuit he came to a sudden halt, clutching his wound, his face twisted with agony.

Lela said, "What's wrong?"

"My wound's opened."

"Let me see." Lela held up the lamp. Blood streamed from Ari's arm. "It's gotten worse. You're losing more blood."

Lela tightened the tie on the wound, then checked the pulse on Ari's other wrist. "I think that might stem the flow. But your pulse is weak and you'll need proper medical help. Sit down or you'll bleed to death."

Ari slumped onto one of the limestone blocks. Lela fumbled in his pockets. "What are you doing?" he asked.

"Trying to find your cell phone."

"It's in my right pocket. Why?"

Lela found Ari's cell, examined the screen, and handed the phone back. "You've still got a reasonable signal strength. Call Cohen. Tell him where you are."

"How can I? I don't know where the heck I am."

"I heard Jack say we were somewhere near the Via Famagosta." Lela fumbled again in Ari's pocket and relit the remaining lamp with his lighter. Then she checked her magazine for rounds and slammed it home. "Have Cohen find the nearest underground entrance and come and get you. Tell him to bring a doctor. You ought to be okay until help comes. But if you start to feel worse, call me on my cell."

Lela readied her Sig in the two-hand position. She clutched the lamp's wire holder in her fingers and moved to the mouth of the darkened arch.

Ari's furious voice boomed around the chamber walls. "Just where do you think you're going, Lela?"

But she had already disappeared into the passageway.

84

Jack moved deeper into the passageway, feeling his way along the coal-black walls. Seconds later he banged his head and staggered back, pain jolting through his skull.

A rush of dizziness overcame him. He put a hand to his brow and his skull hurt like mad. He reached out his palm and touched something round and hard—a pillar, he guessed—thicker in girth than an oak tree.

Without light, he felt totally lost.

"Jack. Wait, please. I'm not going to harm you."

From behind him came the sound of someone stumbling over rocks. He looked back and saw a flash of light. Twenty yards away Lela was clambering over the rubble, clutching a lamp in one hand, her pistol in the other.

Jack froze. He could thrash on in darkness and get himself lost or hurt or both. Lela had a lamp. She also had a weapon. He needed her.

She reached him and caught her breath. "Are you crazy, going on alone?"

"No arguments, Lela, not now. I've got to find Yasmin and I'm losing time. If you want to stop me, you're going to have to use that gun." Jack peered ahead but the light from Nidal's lamp had disappeared.

Lela put away her Sig, brushed her hand across Jack's forehead, and showed him her crimson-stained fingers. "Do you know you've got a gash on your scalp? If you keep rushing ahead unarmed, all you'll do is earn yourself a slab in the mortuary."

They locked eyes and Jack said, "What would you suggest? That I borrow your lamp and gun?"

"Very smart. You've probably never used a firearm."

"Who are you kidding? That's a Sig nine-mil you're carrying. I was plinking cans with a twenty-two on my grandfather's farm when I was twelve. But I'm confused. How does an Israeli police officer go armed in a foreign country? Isn't that against the law?"

Lela reached for her Sig again as she stepped past him and moved ahead, swinging the light. "Explanations later. Be careful where you walk, this ground's treacherous. If anything happens that causes me to drop my pistol, find it fast and use it if you have to, okay?"

"Now you're talking."

85

Sixty feet on, Lela pointed to a trail of crimson splashes on the rubble. She knelt, touched one of the splashes, and withdrew her fingertip, red and wet. "It seems Ari hit someone."

"Your cop friend?" Jack's mouth tightened with fury. "What if it's Yasmin?"

"Don't blame me. And he's not a cop, he's Mossad."

"*Mossad?*"

"Like I said, explanations later. Did you hear that?"

"Hear what?"

Lela cocked an ear. "It sounded like rumbling. From somewhere up ahead."

They came to a winding metal staircase. The blood trail curved up the steps. Lela kept her gun aimed upward as she climbed the creaking metal, Jack behind her. At the top they found themselves in another passageway. This time the ground was smooth, no rubble in sight. Splashes of blood spotted the way every few feet.

"They went this way." Lela pressed on and stayed in front. "I need to know what happened to the scroll, Jack."

"Why does everyone assume I know where it is?"

"Who's everyone?"

"You. The two guys who abducted Yasmin."

"Who are they?"

"I don't know that either. But I have a feeling they may be connected to a very unpleasant Syrian I met recently."

"Where?"

"At a monastery."

"You mean in Maloula?"

Jack stared at her, incredulous. "How did you know . . . ?"

"Later," Lela answered simply.

"You've got a lot of explaining to do."

"All in good time. Go on."

"That's all I can tell you. I don't even know why you're in Rome, except maybe to arrest me for something I didn't do. I keep asking myself how the heck I got mixed up in this nightmare. Maybe I should have picked a less dangerous career. Like land-mine disposal."

Lela put a hand on his arm, her brown eyes searching his face. "Are you telling me the truth about the scroll, Jack? You didn't steal it from Green?"

"No, I sure didn't." Jack met her stare and felt the spark of attraction again.

Lela seemed conscious of it too but a second later she peered ahead and broke the spell. "The blood trail's gone."

Jack knelt and scanned the ground. The crimson spatters had disappeared. Lela said, "Whoever's been hit, I guess their wounds have been bandaged to stop the bleeding, so chances are they're still alive. If it's Yasmin the men won't harm her, not after going to the trouble of abducting her. At least until they get whatever it is they want."

"What makes you think that?"

"Gut instinct. I'm guessing they'll want to use her to get to you."

A distant rumbling noise sounded. Jack said, "You hear that?"

"It's like the noise I heard earlier."

"We've got to be near street level."

"It seems to be getting a lot louder. It's probably traffic." Lela swung the lamp. Ten yards away the wash of the light revealed a half-open metal gate set in the middle of an archway.

Jack said, "What's your plan now? Slap me in cuffs and drag me off to face a court in Israel?"

"Who said anything about dragging you anywhere? Except maybe to somewhere we can both clean ourselves up. First, I need you to help me find the scroll, Jack."

"And then?"

"*Then* I may arrest you."

They approached the gate. Jack pulled at the metal bars and they creaked open.

Lela went to step through first, her pistol readied, but the second she did so a thunderous roar exploded and a powerful blast of air almost knocked her off her feet.

Jack pulled her back as a thunderbolt of light streaked past. The earth shook beneath them, a metallic roar detonating in their ears as a train screamed past, its lights blazing. Jack felt the ground shake for at least ten seconds until the train roared away into darkness.

Lela was startled. "What was that? It felt like an earthquake."

"I ought to have remembered that some of the tunnels intersect near Rome's rail system." Jack moved cautiously past the gate and pulled a dazed Lela after him. A hundred yards to their left the lights of an underground station blazed. A few passengers stood around on the platform, near a pair of escalators. "They probably took Yasmin out through the station. We've lost her; they've got away, Lela."

She put a hand on his arm. "Maybe it's time I told you what I can, and why I followed you. There's something else you need to know, Jack."

"What?"

"It's about your friend, Yasmin."

PART SEVEN

86

John Becket knelt on the cold tile floor of his monastery cell.

He stared up at the crucifix on the wall, his forehead drenched in perspiration. The cell was simply furnished with a metal bed, a nightstand, and a plain wooden locker.

As Becket knelt in front of the crucifix, his sinewy hands were locked together in prayer. He knelt there for a long time, unaware of time passing, or of the pains in his knees from the hard floor. His lips moved in whispered prayer until finally he blessed himself and rose to his feet with a faint groan.

He rubbed his knees vigorously, then took a small hand towel from the nightstand and dabbed the sweat from his face.

Sometimes his praying became so intense that he lost all sense of time and place. Just like now. When he looked at his watch he saw that over an hour had passed. He rinsed the towel under a stream of hot water from the sink, then folded it neatly and placed it on the rail to dry.

As he sat on the edge of the bed, from somewhere far off came the echo of the monks' musical voices as they chanted their hymns. The sound of their voices always brought him back to those dark days after the desert of Qumran, to the remote monastery high in the mountains of northern Italy where he had chosen to atone for his sin. He prayed there earnestly for months on end for forgiveness. It was all many years ago now, but sometimes he felt that his sin had forever stained his soul.

Becket looked up again at the crucifix on the wall as if again to ask forgiveness. The simple cross of two pieces of wood symbolized so much. Once a brutal emblem of Roman injustice and savagery, it had been transformed into a blessed, enduring symbol—of hope and devotion, of justice, comfort, and peace. Proof, if proof were needed, that love and truth were greater than all the shadows.

He thought of the hard task ahead of him and sighed in despair, running a hand over his face. There was so much he needed to do, so many truths he needed to tell that had been kept secret. So many wrongs he wanted to make right, including his own grave sin. But in so doing, he knew he risked destroying both himself and the church.

The distant chanting that washed over him was suddenly interrupted by the jarring noise of his cell phone vibrating on the nightstand. It beeped twice, then twice again. Becket picked up the phone and saw he'd received a text message. When he read it, his face drained.

He had been waiting for this moment, and without hesitation he plucked a compact black leather bag from under his bed. Exiting his cell, he strode down the hall to the open door of the abbot's office.

The abbot was leafing through some papers, his reading glasses perched on his nose, and he jumped to his feet, his eyes darting to the black leather bag clutched in the pope's hand. "Holy Father. Is everything okay? You look pale. You're sweating."

"Fabrio, I need to borrow your car to make an important

trip. The red Fiat 500 I've seen you driving will do. Is it available?"

The abbot looked horrified. "Well, yes . . . but surely the Holy Father will have need of a driver and his bodyguards?"

The pope firmly raised a palm. "No driver, no bodyguards. The car, right away if you please, Fabrio. It's *extremely* urgent. Give me the keys."

"But Holy Father, I was instructed to watch over you—"

"And now *I'm* instructing you, Fabrio. Please, it's a matter of life and death. I haven't a moment to lose. The keys." The pope held out his hand.

The abbot opened a desk drawer and plucked out a set of car keys. "The Holy Father can't be serious about driving alone in Rome? The traffic's homicidal."

The pope grabbed the keys from his hand. "Sorry, Fabrio, this is no time for argument." He noticed a spare brown habit tossed on the back of a chair and threw the gown over his arm. "I'll need to borrow this habit. Not a word to anyone that I've gone, and that's a papal order."

"If—if you insist."

"I do. Now, have the guards open up the front gates, as fast as you can. Tell them you'll be driving out in a hurry, that you have an urgent appointment to keep and can't be delayed . . ."

"That *I'll* be driving out? You want me to lie to the guards, Holy Father?"

Something seemed to snap in John Becket just then, a strained look on his face as if he was under enormous pressure. "I've been living a lie most of my life, Fabrio. One more won't make much difference."

The abbot frowned, puzzled by the reply. "I don't understand what you mean, Holy Father. And where exactly are you going?"

"The less you know, the better."

The young man with the mustache was confused. Wearing jeans, dark glasses, a faded Levi's T-shirt, his corduroy jacket tossed on the passenger seat, he sat in the dark blue Lancia, parked across the street from the monastery.

He saw the guards open the electric gates and the tiny red Fiat erupt from out of the driveway. The tall figure of the monk who was cramped behind the wheel wore a brown habit, his face covered by the hood. He tore off down the road in the red Fiat, the car chugging a little at first, as if the driver was having difficulty shifting gear.

The young man frowned. *What monk wears a hood while driving?* It seemed a bit odd. He scratched his head and then picked up a notebook and pen from the seat next to him and jotted down the Fiat's registration plate. Next, he reached for his cell phone, punched in the number, and a voice answered on the second ring. "Ryan."

"It's Angelo Butoni, Monsignor."

"Good man, Angelo. What's the story?"

Butoni was a seasoned Vatican security officer and kept his eyes on the red Fiat as it drove away down the long avenue leading from the monastery. "You told me to call you if I saw Uncle leave the monastery. Well, I didn't, but I noticed something a little strange."

"What?"

"I just saw a red Fiat 500 come out of the monastery and drive off like a bat out of hell. The monk at the wheel was alone and I couldn't see his face. He had the hood of his habit up, which I thought was odd."

Ryan's voice flared. "Could it have been Uncle?"

Butoni rubbed his mustache. He saw the Fiat's brake lights illuminate, then the car turned right at the end of the avenue and disappeared. "Impossible to say, but my gut instinct told me to let you know. You think I should follow the Fiat?"

"Get after it, Angelo. We can't take the risk, not while we're still trying to figure out the shooting near St. Peter's Square. I'll call the abbot to find out what in heaven's name is going on. If it's a false alarm you can always turn back."

87

The Serb braked the Alfa Romeo to a halt outside Hassan Malik's villa. Beside him in the front seat, Nidal's head was lolled to one side, his eyes closed, a flood of crimson hemorrhaging from a wound to his stomach. A gurgling sound came from his mouth and there was blood everywhere—on his shirt, on the seats—and the car looked like the inside of an abattoir.

The Serb sweated as he tossed aside a used hypodermic syringe and handfuls of bloodstained paper tissues that he had discarded on the car's center console. He glanced over his shoulder.

The woman lay unconscious across the backseat. She was pretty, her tight jeans hugging her figure. The Serb looked back as the villa's front door burst open and Hassan Malik stormed down the steps.

He clutched a cell phone, two bodyguards accompanying him, and he looked ashen. "How is Nidal?"

The Serb jumped out of the Alfa and opened the passenger door. "Worse, Mr. Malik, he's lost a lot of blood. He was conscious until a couple of minutes ago but as I explained on the phone, he wouldn't let me take him to a hospital. But he was in so much pain I had to give him a tranquilizing shot I meant for Cane, just to calm him down."

Hassan Malik's eyes became wet as he held his brother's hand. "Dr. Forini's already here. He's one of Rome's best surgeons. I've got a bedroom set up with everything he needs, hot water, fresh towels."

Behind them, right on cue, a tall and distinguished middle-aged Italian, wearing a cashmere overcoat draped over his shoulders, hurried down the steps of the front porch. He carried a black medical bag and when he took one look at Nidal Hassan he snapped his fingers at the bodyguards. "Take him inside and be careful how you handle him."

Hassan grasped the doctor's arm. "Do your best, Francheso, he's the only brother I have."

The doctor nodded. "He doesn't look good, but we'll try to get him stabilized first, then see where we are. Have your helicopter stand by just in case." He noticed the unconscious young woman lying across the seat. "What the . . . is she wounded too?"

Hassan slapped a reassuring hand on the doctor's back. "No, she's okay, Franchesco. She fainted, that's all. Take care of Nidal, please, I beg you."

The bodyguards carefully eased Nidal out of the car. They carried him inside the villa, the doctor hurrying beside them, checking his patient's vital signs.

Hassan turned his attention to the woman as he snatched open the rear door. He leaned in, felt for a pulse, and then raised one of her eyelids.

The Serb wiped sweat from his face. "We were lucky to make it out of the tunnels alive with all the shooting, and that's the truth, Mr. Malik."

"Who shot Nidal?"

"The couple following Cane. They're Israelis."

The muscles in Hassan's face twitched furiously but

his focus remained on the woman. "Are you certain she's okay?"

"It was like I said when I phoned, things weren't too bad until we reached the car. Then Nidal took a turn and started to hemorrhage. There was blood everywhere and she fainted. It must have been the shock. But she'll come round soon enough, Mr. Malik."

"Help me carry her inside."

The book-lined study was at the back of the mansion. Hassan kicked open the walnut door as he and the Serb carried the woman in and sat her on a chair.

Hassan took her face in his hand and was about to shake her awake when the door burst open and one of the body-guards appeared, his expression drawn. "The doctor wants you, Mr. Malik."

When Hassan reached the bedroom, he saw the sheets were drenched crimson. The doctor was standing over Nidal, desperately trying to stem a faucet of blood from his stomach wound, a stainless steel pan with surgical instruments beside him on the bed.

"What's going on?" Hassan demanded.

The doctor looked under pressure, sweat glistening on his forehead. "The hemorrhaging has started again. He's even worse than I thought, Hassan."

As the doctor felt for a pulse, Nidal seemed to become conscious a moment, sweat drenching his forehead. He gave a low moan and Hassan saw to his horror a jet of blood gush from his brother's stomach.

The doctor ordered, "Give me a towel, quick. Before he bleeds to death!"

Hassan handed him a towel and the doctor pressed it hard

against Nidal's belly. The bleeding diminished but Nidal's body shook violently.

The doctor raised his voice. "We'll need to get him to a hospital at once, we're running out of time."

Hassan's face lost all its color as he shouted to one of the bodyguards, "Tell the pilot we're leaving right away."

"Yes, sir."

Hassan turned and saw the doctor let go of Nidal's hand just as his brother's head rolled to one side. The doctor said, "I'm afraid we're too late. He's dead."

88

The Hotel Anselmo—large and old-fashioned, with wrought-iron balconies—is in a quiet cobbled square near the Vatican. It was raining and just before midnight when Jack and Lela checked in.

The receptionist gave his guests a wary look as Jack tried to explain the mess they were in by saying they'd got caught in the downpour and he had slipped in the wet street, which explained his head wound. The receptionist kindly offered to call a doctor, but Jack politely refused. They registered as Mr. and Mrs. Cane and minutes later they were in a cramped room with a double bed, a minibar, and a view of one of Rome's noisy, cat-infested alleyways.

They dumped their belongings on the bed—two carrier bags packed with a fresh change of clothes and toiletries that they had bought in the tourist stores near the Piazza Navona.

Jack peered through the curtains at the rain-lashed alleyway. There was barely enough room to maneuver. "The Italians aren't exactly generous when it comes to hotel rooms. A man could get a hunched back in a room this size. I need to get rid of this grime."

"Me too. I feel like I've been crawling through a muddy

battlefield after those tunnels. You go first. I need to call our driver, Cohen, and see if Ari's okay."

Jack checked out the bathroom, grabbed a towel, and hung it around his neck. "I'm still waiting for you to explain about Yasmin."

"Have your shower first. Then I better take a closer look at that scalp of yours. The bleeding may have stopped but the wound will need to be cleaned."

Jack unbuttoned his shirt. "How do I know you're not going to tell your Mossad friends where we're hiding out?"

"You really don't trust me, do you?"

"Trust you? Considering we haven't seen each other in twenty years, I hardly know you, Lela."

A tiny smile creased her lips. "And here was me thinking that we were married."

Jack stood under the hot jets for several minutes, soaping his body clean. He toweled himself dry and checked the cut on his scalp in the mirror. The blood had congealed, but as soon as he touched the bruised gash an excruciating jolt of pain shot through him.

He examined his leg, unwinding the dressing until he came to the cotton pad stuck to the wound. The sutures were still in place. His leg didn't hurt as much as the ache in his skull. He still had a handful of painkillers in the plastic vial Pierre had given him. He swallowed two with a glass of tap water, then stepped into the bedroom wearing a fresh pair of Chinos and a T-shirt.

Lela was sitting on the bed, talking on her phone. "I've got to go, Cohen. No, I can't tell you where I am right now. But I'll speak to Ari just as soon as he's well enough. Meantime, take care of him." She had a worried frown as she flipped shut her cell and removed the battery. She saw Jack observe her and she said, "In case you're wondering, disconnecting the battery prevents a cell phone being traced."

Jack slumped into the only chair in the cramped room. "I know; I read it somewhere. I did the same to my phone. What's the story with your friend?"

"Ari's Mossad colleagues found him. He was barely conscious and had lost a lot of blood. They managed to get him aboveground and drive him to a safe house. A doctor's on his way."

"You told me that the Mossad chief gave you orders to find out what happened to the scroll and to return me to Israel."

"That was the general idea."

"You still haven't told me about Yasmin. It's killing me."

Lela put a hand behind her neck, undid a clasp, and let down her long black hair. "I'm going to take a shower first."

She stepped toward the bathroom, and Jack admired her long hair, her olive skin, the curves of her splendid figure.

Lela said, "While I'm gone, how about you crack open that minibar and pour us both a stiff drink?"

"And then?"

"You and I are going to have a serious talk."

89

Jack lay on the bed and replaced the telephone receiver as Lela came out of the bathroom. Her hair was wet and she had a white towel wrapped around her. She looked beautiful, her hair pulled back to the nape of her neck, exposing her high cheekbones. "Feel any better?" he asked.

"Much. I heard you talking on the phone."

Jack swung his feet off the bed and stood. "I had a call to make."

"To whom?"

He opened a couple of miniature scotches he'd taken from the minibar. "Someone I'm hoping can help me decode the scroll. There was no reply so I left a message for them to call me back. I also noticed at least a dozen calls on my cell from Buddy, but I switched off and didn't check the calls. I didn't want your Mossad friends to get a fix on me."

Lela toweled her hair. "That's wise. They could easily do that. Buddy's probably trying to find out where you've gone after you disappeared from Qumran. By the way, I'll have that drink now."

Jack poured her a scotch and splashed in soda.

Lela took her glass and went to sit in the chair and finish drying her hair.

Jack sipped his scotch, leaned against the window frame, and watched her.

She noticed his staring. "Why are you looking at me like that?"

"Honestly? I'm trying to figure out why you'd want to help me."

Lela blushed and put down her wet towel. "Because we were once friends. Because I cared about you. Maybe I even used to think that I loved you. I guess that had something to do with it . . ." Her voice trailed off.

"Tell me about Yasmin."

"Professor Green certainly had a niece named Yasmin. She was born in Lebanon and brought up in Chicago."

"I'm listening."

"She died ten years ago."

"Come off it, Lela."

"It's the truth. Sergeant Mosberg checked it out."

Jack put down his glass, stunned. "I don't get it. Who's Yasmin if she's not who she says she is?"

"I'm still trying to figure that out. But the professor had to be party to the deception. He went along with the pretense of her being his niece."

"Are you suggesting that Green was in some way involved in the scroll's theft?"

"Who knows? Something weird was definitely going on. There's something else you ought to know. The Arab who took Yasmin."

"What about him?"

"His name's Nidal Malik. He's the youngest son of your parents' driver, and the brother of Hassan Malik. You've heard of Hassan before?"

Jack nodded, and his face creased in puzzlement. "This

gets muddier by the minute. I didn't really know him well, but I recall seeing him around the dig when his father was working. Tell me about him."

"Hassan's the family's eldest son. His father's death made him a bitter young man. For a time, like you, his life spun out of control."

"How do you know all this?"

"My father learned Hassan was living rough in Jerusalem, caring for his family and having a hard time of it. My father helped him the little that he could. Arab or Jew, it didn't matter, my dad always said that we were the same blood. That we were like two brothers, quarreling for thousands of years."

"So what happened?"

"All I heard were the rumors. That Hassan eventually joined some of his Bedu relatives, scratching the desert for a living, searching illegally for precious artifacts. Rumors said he got lucky and found a bunch of valuable scrolls, sold them to private collectors, and made himself a fortune."

"Didn't the police investigate?"

Lela shrugged. "Sure, but they couldn't prove a thing. Before you know it Hassan's got a raft of legitimate businesses. He's also dealing in rare and precious artifacts and valuable paintings. Soon he's very rich. He's even got a villa outside Rome. If his brother Nidal's involved, it seems like a reasonable bet that Hassan's got a big interest in the scroll."

Jack's jaw tightened in anger. "And now there's a good chance he's got Yasmin."

"Whoever Yasmin is."

"Where's this villa?"

"A place called Bracciano, outside Rome."

"Tell me about the symbols you said you found on the monastery wall. Show me what they looked like."

Lela found a pen and sheet of hotel writing paper in the nightstand drawer and drew the symbols.

She said, "Blood splashes trailed from the symbol on the right and onto the floor, which probably doesn't signify anything except that Novara was bleeding to death. Apart from the fact they could look like a pair of crosses, do these symbols mean anything to you? Could they mean something in Aramaic?"

Jack scratched his jaw. "The letter *t* in an old version of Aramaic was in the shape of a cross. Which would give us a double *t*. Whatever that means. But that was eighth to ninth century B.C. I've absolutely no idea what the double *t* might suggest. Unless it's in some kind of code maybe?"

"There's no other significance you can suggest?"

Jack shrugged. "I'm afraid not. We might even be way off track."

"The symbols have to mean something, or Novara wouldn't have gone to the trouble of writing them on the wall in his own blood. I don't think he expected Pasha to shoot him. Maybe he was enraged and meant to leave behind some kind of evidence."

"But what does the evidence mean?"

"You've got me there. I'm no Aramaic expert, but the guy I rang earlier on the hotel phone is. I'm hoping he'll call me back." Jack moved over to the window and looked preoccupied.

Lela said, "What are you thinking?"

"Right this minute? That I'm exhausted. I haven't slept

in almost two days." He looked back and met her stare. "There's not a snowball's chance that you could be wrong about Yasmin?"

"I doubt it, Jack."

"Do you think Hassan might have had something to do with Green's death?"

"I can't say. But I don't think so."

"Why, Lela?"

"If he had, he'd probably already have the scroll, don't you think?"

"Good point." Jack suddenly faltered and put a hand out to grip the nightstand.

Lela grabbed him, giving him support. "What's wrong?"

Jack clasped a hand to his forehead. "I feel lousy."

"How's your leg?"

"It's okay. But I've got a throbbing headache and the room's beginning to spin. I took a couple of painkillers that made me drowsy. I guess I'm beat."

"Let me see that gash." She made him sit on the bed and examined his head. "I'll need to disinfect the cut with something. How does scotch sound?"

"A waste of good liquor, but go for it."

She smiled, dipped a finger in her scotch, and dabbed the liquid on his wound.

Jack felt a stinging pain and winced.

Something passed between them then, and as he looked into her eyes he saw a spark of concern. Lela brushed her hand against his face. "Try and sleep, Jack."

"Can I tell you something? It's good seeing you again after all these years."

"For me too." Lela leaned over and kissed him gently on the cheek. "Now lie back."

He lay on the bed. His eyelids felt like heavy weights. "Aren't you going to rest?" Jack asked.

"In a while. Close your eyes. Give in to it, please, Jack."

He sank his head into the pillow. The tremendous strain he had been under was finally taking its toll. His body was filled with an enormous fatigue and this time he didn't fight it. He closed his eyes and in an instant he felt himself being sucked into a soft cushion of blackness.

90

ROME

Anna Kubel was an undeniably attractive woman: buxom, middle-aged, her blond hair piled high in a bun. She tossed another log in the woodstove in the kitchen and wiped her hands on her apron. *Everything comes to an end,* she told herself. And the end was close now, she could sense it.

Anna wiped a tear from her eye and went to fill a cup of freshly brewed coffee from a pot on the hotplate, and then sat in front of the stove. The centuries-old house, like so many in Rome, was drafty and crumbling. It lacked a proper heating system and at 6 A.M. the tiled floors made the room feel as chilly as in winter.

Not that she was complaining. She had lived happily in this house for seventeen years since she had first come to Rome from Vienna as her brother's housekeeper. Sipping her coffee, Anna heard a wheezing intake of breath, followed by a familiar groan of pain.

She turned her head toward the room next door, the noise sending a rapier-sharp stab of anguish through her heart. She put down her cup and saucer, blessed herself, and hurried into the next room.

It was a cramped study-bedroom, the shelves lined with books on archaeology, religion, and history, and cluttered with old photographs. An untidy pile of newspapers lay scattered on a bedside table. It was in this room where her beloved elder brother Franz liked her to read to him from his favorite books and newspapers. It was also where he had chosen to die.

She felt moved to pity as she looked down at his sleeping form under the bedcovers, an oxygen bottle and mask by the bed. A wooden crucifix was clutched in Franz's bony, nicotine-stained fingers and his eyes were shut.

His once-strong, sculpted face was sunken, his cheeks hollow. The skin of his small, wasted body was the same color as the ancient parchments he had spent his life studying, and his sparse red hair—what few wisps were left after the chemotherapy—was plastered across his skull. Her brother would have been sixty-five next birthday if the cancer hadn't riddled his flesh.

A chain-smoker all his life, now Franz wheezed with every breath. He had endured another difficult night, Anna could tell, sweat drenching his brow. The pained look on her beloved brother's face was almost too much to bear. As she wiped away another tear, her eyes were drawn to the framed photographs on the walls.

Here was the other Franz she had known. The committed priest whom she and her Viennese parents had been so proud of. Snapshots of Franz as an altar boy and later as a young priest in the seminary at Graz. Images of him in Rome with at least two former popes and three eminent cardinals. Franz's religious zeal had from time to time led him to move in the Vatican's more rarefied circles.

Her brother had lived for the priesthood, and nothing had pleased him more than the praise or approval of his superiors. There were also several pictures of her brother in Jerusa-

lem, and on the archaeological digs that he loved so much—
"tracing the blessed footsteps of Jesus," as he liked to call his
many visits to Israel. At least one of the photographs was of
Franz and John Becket on a dig, smiling, their arms fondly
around each other's shoulders.

As Anna Kubel's proud gaze swept over the familiar
images she felt a stab of sadness. The photographs were all
taken a time long ago. Now Franz was nearing his end. On
the nightstand by the bed was a small enamel bowl filled with
melting ice cubes. Anna dabbed a flannel facecloth in the
bowl, wet her brother's parched lips, then folded the icy cloth
and placed it on his fevered brow. "Dearest Franz, can you
hear me? Would you like a glass of water to cool you?"

He wheezed another breath and his eyelids fluttered. The
feeble spark in his glassy eyes told her he was truly a man living on borrowed time. But then without warning he reached
out and clutched Anna's wrist, his fingers clawing her flesh
with surprising ferocity. "Remember, Anna? No—no more
morphine," his rasping voice reminded her.

Anna gently eased Franz's grasp and stroked his clubbed
fingers. "Yes, dear brother, I remember."

His head sank back and he erupted in a violent fit of
coughing. When it finally ceased, Anna wiped phlegm from
her brother's lips, then placed the oxygen mask over his face.
She heard the steady flow of rich air soothe Franz's wheezing
lungs. She knew for certain his time couldn't be long now. Her
brother's pain had to be excruciating, but Franz had insisted
on not taking painkillers. He wanted his senses to remain
clear until he spoke with John Becket.

Out in the street Anna heard a violent screech of brakes.
She peered past the lace curtain and saw the absurd sight of
John Becket's tall figure clutching a black bag as he pried him-

self out of a cramped old red Fiat 500. He strode toward the front door. A second later she heard the doorbell buzz, at least a half-dozen sharp, urgent bursts.

Anna forced back her tears as she looked down at her dying brother and patted his hand. "It's time, dear Franz. John is here."

91

Julius Weiss hated Rome.

Ever since he had first visited the city as a student many years ago, its history got right up his nose. The Romans had scourged the Jews almost into oblivion, and everywhere in this ancient capital's grandiose architecture was a reminder of that brutal past. To make matters worse, Weiss's own father had named him Julius. Talk about irony.

He crossed the road near the Colosseum that early morning as a white taxi pulled up at the curb. When he jumped in, the driver nudged out into the traffic and Weiss said eagerly, "Any more word from Lela Raul?"

Ari Tauber swiveled round in the passenger seat and nursed his bandaged hand. "She called me briefly some hours ago, sir. The call lasted less than a minute. She wanted to make sure I was okay. Since then, not a whisper. I've tried to have her cell phone located but her signal's completely dead. I don't understand. Was there really a need for you to fly to Rome?"

Weiss snorted. "Yes, there was. I have an important meeting."

Ari Tauber frowned. At first he couldn't see any of Weiss's personal bodyguards but then he spotted a powerful Mercedes and a BMW bringing up the rear.

Weiss asked, "What are the chances that she's no longer alive?"

Ari considered. "Jack Cane's known her a long time. I get the feeling they're still friends. I'd be surprised if he harmed her. My gut feeling tells me she's out there, helping him, for whatever reason."

Weiss's lips twisted in a grim expression, his tone urgent. "Find her, Ari. Use every means you have to."

"I already have, sir. My sources have turned up nothing."

"*Find* her. No excuses. I'll assign you extra men to tear Rome apart if need be. And keep calling her phone. If she answers, attempt to hold her on the line long enough for us to get a fix. Wherever she is, Cane and the scroll can't be far behind."

"One other thing, sir."

"What?"

Ari held up his cell phone. "I got a call minutes ago. We got a copy of Yasmin Green's passport photo from immigration. We couldn't figure out her identity until we scanned her picture into our computers. Dyed hair and a complete makeover can't fool digital face-recognition software. We know who Yasmin is, sir."

"Who?"

92

Jack was woken by the sound of screeching tires. He came awake groggily and stared at his watch: 6:45 A.M.

It still looked dark outside, a silver crack of streetlight flooding into the room through the curtains. When he put out his hand for Lela, she wasn't there. He climbed out of bed, flicked on the light, and saw her sitting in the chair near the window, wearing a hotel bathrobe.

He rubbed his eyes. "Some crazy Italian driver burning rubber woke me. Didn't you sleep?"

"I managed a couple of hours but tossed and turned."

"Any reason?"

She looked into his face. "You want the truth? I'm trying to figure out where we go from here, Jack. In case it hasn't registered, we're both in trouble deep enough to sink an elephant."

Jack crossed to the minibar and saw Lela's pistol on top. "Is that thing loaded?"

"Of course."

"How's your friend, Ari? Did you call again?"

"A couple of hours ago. Ari's recovering. A doctor tended to his wound. Don't worry, I kept it short, then I switched off my cell and removed the battery again in case the coordinates were traced. Ari will be fuming."

"You're right; you're going to be in big trouble." Jack twisted open a bottle of mineral water from the minibar. "Maybe it's about time I helped save your career and earned you some brownie points."

"What do you mean?"

Jack drank from the water bottle. "I have the scroll. It's in a safe place. I switched it at Maloula for another old parchment. Pasha must have realized afterward and he's probably out to kill me. For all I know, he could be working for Hassan Malik."

Lela stared disbelievingly at Jack. "But—you told me you didn't have the scroll."

"No, I didn't. I told you I didn't steal it from Professor Green."

Lela said angrily, "Don't play with words, Jack. Where's the scroll?"

"In a safe place." He held up his cell phone. "For good measure I have photographs I took of the parchment. I figured no one would think of looking in my cell phone memory."

Lela flushed. "Jack . . ."

"Don't accuse me of lying or twisting words. I had a valuable document to retrieve and preserve, and I was prepared to use any means to do it, Lela."

"But you did lie to me, Jack."

"Maybe a small white lie. But I had to keep the scroll safe at all costs. I just didn't know who I could trust."

"And you trust me now, is that it?"

Jack looked into her face. "Honestly? I'm not sure. But I obviously trust you enough to let you in on this."

"Where does that leave us?"

Jack drank from the bottle. "I wish I knew. But if you're

right about us hearing from Hassan, then he'll want to trade: everything I know about the scroll in return for Yasmin."

"Do you want her that badly?"

"I'd like to know who she really is. And why she's been lying to me." Jack took his notebook from his back pocket. "Now that we're being totally up-front with each other, how about I show you these?"

"What are they?"

"A couple of interesting translations. Another from the scroll I found and one I discovered inscribed under the streets of Rome."

Lela read the translations, and after Jack had explained, she stared down at the words. "You're certain that you interpreted them correctly?"

"They're accurate, Lela. My Latin's okay. I've translated enough Roman inscriptions in my day. And my Aramaic's pretty passable."

"They're . . . incredible."

"It makes me even more convinced that religion, history, everything could be changed by the scroll's contents. That's why I made the phone call."

"To whom?"

Jack snapped shut his notebook and put it away. "Dr. Alfonse Gati, to be precise, Harvard-educated historian extraordinaire. Fonzi to his friends. Fonzi's a little . . . well, odd, to put it mildly. But he's one of the foremost scrolls experts and he's familiar with the Atbash code. He worked with my folks in Qumran years ago and he's a friend of Buddy's. I'm hoping he may be able to help us decipher the code."

She sat there for a long time, looking at him, saying nothing.

Jack said, "What's up?"

Lela hesitated. "It's personal. I just wanted you to know something."

"What?"

"After your parents died, after you left Qumran, I thought about you all the time." Lela put a hand to his face, touched his cheek, let her hand fall away. "I've often thought that maybe I could have helped you heal back then."

Jack smiled bleakly. "It was something I had to go through myself. But there were often times when I thought of you. Wondered what had become of you. The truth is, I used to hope that we'd meet once more, that I'd have the courage to tell you why I didn't see you again."

Lela searched his eyes. "Kiss me, Jack."

Jack didn't answer but gently cupped her face in one of his palms. In response, Lela brushed a finger against his lips and then her arms went around his neck. Her eyes sparked, and he kissed her mouth.

A second later the bedside phone rang.

93

The ruins near the Colosseum were crammed with tourists that morning. Despite the rainy weather, hundreds had disembarked from tour buses parked along the curb.

Julius Weiss grunted as he handed some coins to a street food vendor. In return he received a hot slice of salami pizza. The Israeli spy chief bit into his snack as he watched across the street.

The café bar wasn't yet crowded with patrons, the polished metal tables outside mostly empty. Weiss recognized the small, scrawny Sicilian with bushy eyebrows. He sat alone at one of the tables, reading the *La Scala* newspaper. Like most clerics, he wore civilian clothes uncomfortably. His dark suit looked a size too big for him and at least twenty years out of date.

Weiss dumped the remains of his unfinished pizza slice in a garbage bin, dusted his hands, and crossed the street to the café bar. Cardinal Umberto Cassini looked up. "Julius, it's good to see you. What's it to be? Coffee? Tea?"

The Israeli eased his frame into the seat and grunted. "Something stronger. A grappa. Ice and water, a slice of lemon."

Cassini called the waiter and ordered a double espresso and the grappa. When the man had gone Cassini said, "It's been a long time, Julius."

"What made you pick this place?"

Cassini glanced around the café with tired eyes. "An old haunt of mine from when I was an archaeology student. The kind of bar where everybody's too busy admiring the Colosseum and the pretty girls passing by to pay attention to two old friends chatting."

Weiss removed his sunglasses and wiped them briskly with a handkerchief, his face mournful. "Acquaintances, Umberto. You and I have never been more than that. So, what's such a big secret that you have to drag me all the way from Tel Aviv to hear it from you in person?"

The waiter returned with their drinks. Julius Weiss sipped his grappa and studied Cassini's face. It was scoured with worry lines as deep as canyons, as if the cardinal was privy to too many secrets.

When the waiter had gone, Cassini ignored his espresso and said as quietly as a conspirator, "First, tell me what progress you have made, Julius."

"We've lost the woman. We think she may be with Cane and to tell the truth it has me worried." Weiss explained the details he'd learned from Ari Tauber. "It seems another party is interested in Cane's scroll."

"Who?" Cassini's eyebrows arched into twin peaks.

Weiss had dealt with Cassini for many years on matters of mutual interest. He grudgingly admired the Vatican's intelligence apparatus, considered it one of the best in the world. He took an envelope from his pocket and slid it across the table. "One of our agents took photographs of two men in St. Peter's

Square, the same pair they followed into the tunnels. There was also a shooting near the square. Our agents engaged fire with the men."

Cassini's eyebrows arched higher. "The Vatican security service is looking into the shooting. So that's what it was about."

Weiss tapped the photograph with the tip of his finger. "We identified the one on the left as Nidal Malik. A brother of Hassan Malik. Does that last name ring a bell?"

"Should it?"

"Hassan Malik's an Arab—of Bedouin extraction to be precise. He's an international businessman. His full surname is Al-Malik but the family is known by the shortened version. He owns a villa near Rome."

"Why do I get the feeling there's more?"

"Israeli authorities investigated Malik on suspicion of being involved in illegal digs at historical sites. There were rumors he had smuggled precious artifacts out of the country and sold them to black-market dealers in Lebanon and Syria. Whatever the truth, he became a rich man."

"Go on."

"Other rumors suggest he helps the Palestinian cause with generous gifts of money. And that he has brokered arms deals for the same cause."

"That's a lot of rumors."

"Hassan's a crafty fox who keeps a low profile. Nothing's ever been proven and no charges pressed."

"Why should I know him?"

"Hassan's father was a laborer who worked on several of Robert Cane's digs. In fact, Hassan's father died in the same accident twenty years ago."

Cassini put down the photographs, pursed his lips, and

tapped them with his finger. "How did Hassan learn about the scroll?"

"I've no idea. But he must want it badly if his own brother's involved. That kind of direct family involvement is unheard-of for Hassan. We also think Nidal may have been wounded in the tunnel shootout."

Cassini worriedly slipped the photos back in the envelope and slid it across the table. "I thought you had everything under control! This doesn't sound like it, Julius."

Weiss grimaced. "I'm doing my best, but right now we've hit a dead end."

Cassini's lips pinched thin as a razor. "You must try harder. Remember, we both have an agreement to honor."

Weiss didn't need reminding. Some years after the mammoth task of translating the scrolls had begun and extraordinary examples of Scripture material were revealed, some of it controversial, the Vatican and Israel had set aside their differences and agreed to a secret pact that sought to avoid the ultimate disaster. The core of that disaster was simple.

What if, among the rich mother lode of Qumran's scrolls, there was evidence that irrefutably revealed Jesus as the true messiah? Not just the messiah of Christian tradition but the true messiah expected by the Jews two thousand years ago? Such a revelation would have devastating implications for the state of Israel and its people. It would also rock the foundations of Islam.

Equally, what if a scroll revealed that the Jesus of history and the Jesus of faith were two different people? Or doubt was cast upon Jesus' resurrection, or his claim to be the Son of God? Such disclosures would destroy the Christian creed.

Israel and the Vatican had therefore agreed on a simple strategy: digs would be secretly monitored. Any discovered material deemed controversial to either religion would be withheld. It was a pact Weiss knew had worked well to date. "You don't need to remind me, Umberto."

Cassini's flinty Sicilian eyes glinted darkly. "Maybe I do. Our collaboration hasn't been needed in many years because there were no major finds. Otherwise your Antiquities Department would have confiscated Jack Cane's scroll on site. They would have confiscated it anyway and alerted you once they had translated the scroll."

"True."

"I have a confession to make, Julius."

"What are you talking about?"

Cassini scowled, his face troubled. "You already know my opinion that Cane's discovery may contain a coded revelation buried deep within the text. And that I fear this revelation can harm our status quo."

Weiss nodded. "I only have your word of that, Umberto. You said you'd provide solid proof. I'm still waiting."

Cassini whispered, "You will wait no longer. I am about to expose to you a dark secret."

94

"What dark secret?" Weiss demanded.

Cassini huddled forward, as if his bony shoulders were bearing a great weight. "You asked me how the Vatican knew that Jack Cane's scroll was a danger to the church. As you know, some of the Dead Sea texts have copies. We believe we have a replica of the same scroll."

Weiss frowned. "Explain."

"You will recall that when Cane's father died, his scroll vanished."

Weiss gave a tiny nod. "It was burned in the crash."

"The scroll didn't burn, Julius. The Vatican took it."

"What?" Weiss sputtered.

"John Becket and another priest, Father Kubel, were the first to arrive at the accident scene. They found the scroll in the wreckage and it was handed over to me. I decided that the scroll was too controversial and should be secretly transported to the Vatican."

Weiss's face burned red. "You're a thief, Cassini. And Becket is no better. You stole Israel's property. This breaches the spirit of our agreement."

"It breaches nothing. The Vatican kept to its word that no damaging material would be revealed. That's what was important. And believe me, it was certainly damaging, if not sensational."

"What did the scroll contain?"

Cassini removed an envelope from his pocket and held it between his thumb and forefinger. "Read for yourself. There is a revelation about a second messiah. A man who assumed the identity of Jesus and whose life and historical existence may cast great doubt upon the narrative of the Bible. And there are even more disturbing revelations almost too frightening to contemplate."

Cassini handed the envelope to Weiss. "What you'll read is not a complete translation of Robert Cane's scroll, because part of it was destroyed by fire. However, enough material exists to ignite serious religious controversy. And once the Holy Father opens the archives, that controversy will only intensify. We both know of several texts found at Qumran that could unsettle the Jewish and Christian faiths."

Weiss worriedly opened the envelope and read the single page. He ran a hand over his grim face. "Surely the pope knows the trouble he will cause by all this! Is he mad?"

Cassini plucked the page from Weiss, replaced it in the envelope, and tucked it back inside his pocket. "You want the truth, Julius? I suspect he is. That he even sees himself as another messiah sent to change the world. I also suspect that he is tortured by his theft and because—" Cassini halted in mid-sentence.

"Because what?" Weiss demanded.

"Robert Cane's death twenty years ago may not have been an accident."

"What makes you say that?"

Cassini sighed. "Sergeant Raul was in charge of the investigation. Privately, he told me something he never included in his report. That he had a vague suspicion the pickup's hydraulic brake line had been tampered with. But there was so much fire damage to the vehicle it was impossible to prove."

Weiss's face darkened. "That's the first I've ever heard of this. Who would have done such a thing?"

Cassini met his stare. "John Becket was one of the first on the scene."

"Are you saying he had something to do with Robert Cane's death?"

Cassini shrugged. "I could surmise a motive. Becket may have believed the scroll to be damaging to the church. Such a belief might have caused him to commit such a terrible crime out of a warped sense of loyalty. And the pope is tortured of late, of that I'm certain. I even began to wonder if he intends to make public his own guilt when he opens the archives."

Weiss shook his head, the folds of his rubbery face quivering. "This all sounds very troubling, Umberto. With so much at stake, isn't there any way to stop this madness?"

Cassini's face was carved in stone, every muscle taut as he leaned in close and gripped Weiss's arm. "Leave the pope to me. I believe I know how to solve that particular problem."

Weiss raised his brow. "How?"

"For my plan to work, first, we must find Jack Cane and retrieve the scroll. Then we must destroy them both."

95

In a city renowned for museums, with more per square mile than any other capital on earth, the private museum in the Villa Panaro is one of the smallest and most unusual of all. Located in a Gothic-style building that was once owned by the infamous Borgia family in the fifteenth century, it doesn't even have a nameplate.

That morning, with the rain lashing down and thunder grumbling in an ink-black sky, the arched entrance looked almost eerie. Two gas lamps on the walls either side of the entrance threw flickering shadows as Jack and Lela approached the building.

"Where exactly are we?" Lela asked as they halted below an elaborate array of stone gargoyles protruding from the roof parapet.

"Outside one of the most priceless private museum collections of Roman artifacts in the country, if not the world. I say private because it only opens to the public on certain days of the year, to avail of a tax break. If you're lucky enough to know about it you just may get to peek inside."

"Should I be impressed?"

"I think so. We're talking the personal effects of Roman

emperors and generals. As well as material unearthed at Pompeii—some really valuable gold and silver jewelry, town records, rare coins, and statues. There's even a marble wash-basin that once belonged to Julius Caesar."

They had stepped out of the taxi a block away and walked the empty streets to the villa, just as the thunder and rain erupted. Lela looked up at the black-painted double entrance doors. "If the collection's that priceless, where's the security?"

Jack smiled and pressed a button on a metal intercom box. "You won't see too many guards but the villa has a se-curity system second to none, linked to a local police station around the corner."

Lela shivered and rubbed her arms, feeling the chill in the morning air. "Are you sure your friend's home?"

"He's home all right. Fonzi doesn't call you back at seven-thirty A.M. just for the heck of it. His apartment is on the building's top floor. By the way, Fonzi's a dyed-in-the-wool ladies' man. So if you get the feeling he's checking out your assets, don't get offended."

"Assets?"

Jack pressed the intercom again. "He's got an eye for the feminine figure. But I hear the wheelchair's slowed him down."

"Wheelchair?"

"An Italian ex-girlfriend ran him down in her car for cheating. But that's the Latin temperament for you. Fonzi was lucky to escape with a bunch of shattered discs."

"I bet that put a stop to his gallop."

A metallic voice suddenly sounded from the intercom and a light sprang on to reveal a camera lens inset in the alu-minum box. "Actually, the back's on the mend and it certainly hasn't put a stop to my gallop. In another month or two, the surgeons say I can kiss the wheelchair good-bye."

The voice was cheerful and bright. Jack smiled. "Fonzi."

"Jack, greetings. I see on the screen that you've got female company. Word of her beauty has spread. The jungle drums have been beating."

"Who's been beating them?"

"Buddy calls me now and then for a chin-wag. He told me you'd been eyeing a certain woman on the dig. Said she was a stunner. Hello, Yasmin."

"Actually, this is Lela, Fonzi."

Without a beat, Fonzi said, "Well hello to Lela. Wasn't there a song called 'Lela'? Or was it 'Lola'? The Kinks maybe?"

Jack said, "A little before our time maybe."

"No matter, the lady looks wonderful." A buzzer sounded and one of the front double doors sprang open. "Advance, friends, and enter my lair."

96

Jack and Lela stepped inside the doorway. It revealed a short anteroom, protected by a security cage complete with thick metal bars. Beyond the bars lay a vast hallway, covered in checkered black-and-white floor tiles.

The entrance door behind them sprang shut. Moments later a squeaking sound came from somewhere and a man rolled toward them in a wheelchair, his hands clasping the rubber wheels. He wore a Paisley cravat at his neck, which gave him a rakish look, and his dumpling face grinned. "You know, I really need to get the oil out and lubricate this thing." He was at least sixty, oddly handsome, and had a mischievous spark in his eyes. "Terrific to see you, Jack."

"Hello, Fonzi. My apologies for disturbing you so early."

"No apology necessary. It's no morning for man or beast out there, so come on in. Let me get you out of the security cage." Fonzi slipped a remote from his pocket, stabbed some buttons, and the metal bars whirred open. Jack and Lela stepped into the checkered hall. The gates clanged shut behind them.

"What a great pleasure it is to meet *you*, signorina." Fonzi's eyes lit up with a playful glint as he grasped Lela's hand and kissed it.

Lela said, "Jack's told me a lot about you."

"All enticing and ubercharming, I hope?" Fonzi let go of Lela's hand, removed an embossed business card from his breast pocket, and presented it with a smile and a flourish. "Lela, if ever this primate mistreats you, is rude to you, neglects to romance you, causes you to grow tired of him, or simply reveals himself to be an unbearable ass, I want you to call me at once. I will offer you friendship, my brilliant intellect, all in return for the comfort of your companionship."

"I just might just take you up on the offer."

Fonzi grinned up at Jack and offered a firm handshake. "She's got eminent taste, hasn't she? Such a sweet and clever lady. Come, I've got some java blend on the brew that'll knock your teeth out. Then we can discuss this remarkable scroll of yours."

Across the deserted street from the Villa Panaro, a white Fiat van with dark tinted windows coasted to a halt beside the rain-lashed pavement. Thunder cracked and jagged lightning illuminated the dark clouds. The engine throbbed a few moments before it was switched off.

In the silence that followed, the passenger's electric window whirred down, just enough of a gap for a hand to squeeze through.

A moment later a pair of high-power Nikon night-vision binoculars slipped out between the window crack and pointed in the villa's direction.

97

Fonzi pushed his chair across the checkered hall. "I called Buddy when I saw the reports in the newspapers. He told me all about the professor's murder. A terrible tragedy. Not that Green and I were bosom pals. He could be overpowering when we worked digs together. Still, he didn't deserve to die like that."

"Buddy told you?"

"Every detail. Including that the police had you in their sights, Jack. Buddy said you were as innocent as a newborn and that's good enough for me. So when did you two arrive in Rome?"

Jack said, "Yesterday afternoon. I tried calling you after midnight but got no reply."

Fonzi grinned, pushing the squeaking wheels of his chair in through an open pair of polished, floor-to-ceiling doors. "The multimedia pics you sent kept me busy all evening, so I'd hit the hay by then, exhausted. You gave me a few interesting problems to solve."

"The images came through okay?"

Fonzi waved his cell phone. "Perfect. They got me so excited I was struck dumb. I never use the word *awesome*, but this is one time it certainly applies. I'm astonished, Jack. *To-*

tally. I take it you'd shot photographs of the scroll's text before the theft occurred?"

"I'll explain about that later."

"If what I've read in the text is true, this is going to have the world's media beating down your door. You'll wind up famous."

"This isn't about fame, Fonzi. I just want a reliable and true translation."

"And you shall have it. The first few lines of the parchment are in clear, by that I mean unciphered. The rest are in Atbash code, which is why they seemed unreadable. Such a technique isn't unusual in some Essene documents, but don't ask me why. The Essenes were a strange bunch, to say the least." Fonzi led them through an enormous room filled with rows of illuminated glass display cases. "Have you ever been to Rome before, Lela?"

"Never." Curious, she peered in at displays of coins.

Fonzi said, "Roman currency. Our collection includes gold and silver coins from the sixth century B.C., when the city was first founded. If we have time later, I'll give you the guided tour." He gestured to a nearby pair of floor-to-ceiling doors. "In there, if you're not too faint of heart, are collections of lewd Roman-era drawings, ornaments, and frescos. One of the collections was owned by an infamous Borgia pope, notorious for his shameless sex life."

"You're kidding me!"

"Actually I'm not. Did I mention what is perhaps our most important collection of all? Our records."

"What kind of records?"

"Examples of original Roman files, military records, accounts, and diaries. All kinds of writing on wood plate, parchment, papyrus, and inscribed on stone and metal."

Jack said, "What about the inscription I asked you to check?"

"The records suggest that a centurion named Cassius Marius Agrippa served in Dora, sometime between 27 A.D. and 36 A.D. The same man rose through the ranks to become a senior officer commanding Tyre, and later a general and a wealthy businessman and consul."

"That answers that. Have you got everything set up?"

"We're good to go. We'll use the basement projection room." Fonzi wheeled his way toward a pair of stainless steel elevator doors. He pressed a wall button and the metal doors swished open. "This thing's barely wide enough to take me and my wheels. The basement stairwell's through the doors to the right. See you both below." Fonzi pushed himself inside, turned his wheelchair round, and stabbed a button with his finger. "Arrivederci, kids."

The elevator doors whirred shut and it descended.

Jack said, "Fonzi once worked for the Rothschild Museum, which sponsored the dig that discovered the first Dead Sea scrolls. He's translated hundreds of Qumran texts, so if he says the scroll's astonishing, we're in for a treat." He pulled open the stairwell door for Lela. "Maybe at last we'll be able to understand why people are prepared to kill for this document. And what dark secret it's been hiding for the last two thousand years."

98

Anna Kubel checked her watch. She felt emotionally battered. Two hours had passed since John Becket arrived and by now her brother's wheezing sounded like a dying croak.

John Becket sat, silently holding Franz Kubel's hand and staring into his face. It was bone-white, the eyes closed, Kubel's wispy hair clinging damply to his forehead. "How long has he been unconscious, Anna?"

"He's been drifting in and out for the last thirty-six hours. Just as you arrived he came awake briefly."

The pope had anointed the dying priest with holy oils from his black bag, then he had raised his hand and pronounced the absolution. "*Deinde ego te absolvo* . . . I absolve you from your sins in the name of the Father, the Son, and the Holy Ghost. Amen."

Now he patiently held his old friend's hand as Anna spoke quietly. "You said to call you if he became lucid again. He did, several times, but slipped back into the coma."

"It's to be expected, Anna."

"Franz even insisted that I reduce his morphine because he wanted to keep a clear head when he saw you. But each time you arrived these last few days the pain seems to get too much to bear and his mind shuts down."

"I had hoped to speak with him. Franz's letter made it clear that he felt it terribly important."

Anna stared down at her brother. "It breaks my heart to see him so helpless."

John Becket grasped Anna's fingers. "In the end, we are all helpless. We are like children again before we are lifted up into the arms of our Father. Be strong. It will be over soon, Anna."

She wiped her eyes. "In the past, you and he were once such good friends. He so often talked about you. Yet he never told me why you fell out. Of course, that was Franz, always secretive."

Becket said, "We were the best of friends. Franz taught me so much. He was a kind and loyal comrade."

"But something bad happened in Israel, didn't it? Franz never wanted to talk about your time together there. I could only guess that something happened to sour your friendship."

"Yes, Anna, something bad happened."

"When I came across the article the other day about the newly discovered scroll and the professor's murder, I thought Franz might be interested, so I read it to him. The effect was alarming."

"In what way?"

"He became distressed and agitated. I never saw him in such a state. That was when he wrote you the note. He asked me to send it to you, along with the clipping from the newspaper. Then I found him searching through his old papers. He found a photograph. He kept praying as he held it."

"What photograph?"

Anna slipped open a drawer, withdrew a newspaper clipping, and handed it to Becket. "This photograph."

Becket saw that it was an old newspaper photograph of a couple and recognized Robert and Margaret Cane. "May I keep this?" he asked.

"If you wish. Franz told me he had to see you before he died. But he refused to say why. Do you know why, Holy Father?"

Becket slipped the photograph of the Canes into his gown. "Yes, Anna, I know why. It's because of a terrible secret your brother and I share."

"Secret?"

At that precise moment Franz Kubel's eyes flickered awake. It was as if he had been jolted out of his coma. His watery eyes tried to focus. His face looked tortured as he sucked a breath of air into his cancer-riddled lungs.

Becket spoke gently and rubbed the priest's scrawny hand. "Franz, it's good to see you again, old friend. I have given you the last rites. Soon you will be in God's loving embrace. Do you understand me, Franz? Nod if you do."

Franz Kubel seemed to make a supreme effort. He nodded and grasped at John Becket's hand.

The pope whispered, "Good, you understand. You are absolved now from all your sins, my dear friend."

Tears welled up in Franz Kubel's eyes.

The pope said quietly, "Franz, the time has come. We must share with Anna the secret we have both kept all these years. You must do the right thing for both our sakes, and above all for the sake of the church. Anna is ready to bear witness, to hear the confession of our crime."

A puzzled Anna Kubel stared at her brother, then at

Becket. "Crime? What—whatever are you talking about?"

"Anna, I will explain everything later. For now, please, just listen—"

The pope fell silent as Franz Kubel's bony fingers grasped his sister's hand, his wheezing voice as dry as sandpaper. "Anna, I . . . I need you to listen to what I have to tell you. And then dear sister, you must do exactly as the Holy Father instructs you . . ."

99

"Okay, here we go, guys," Fonzi said.

A blinding whiteness lit up the whiteboard projector screen. Jack and Lela blinked, their eyes stung by the powerful light explosion as they sat together on a couple of plastic chairs in a dimly lit basement room.

Fonzi operated the projector screen using a laptop computer he'd hooked up. He flicked on a study lamp, stuck a pair of half-moon glasses on the end of his nose, and consulted a sheaf of handwritten notes. "I transferred the digital images from my cell into the computer. I then had my software program decode and interpret the data three consecutive times to be certain I'd got it right. I've used this program before to translate Dead Sea documents and it's pretty reliable."

"What about decoding the text?"

"The program to decode Atbash text is very simple. Atbash is a basic substitution code that merely reverses the Aramaic alphabet. Are you with me so far?"

"Sure, I'm with you," Jack said.

Lela nodded.

"Good." Fonzi tapped the laptop keypad and the projector screen burst into life with scrolling Aramaic symbols. Seconds later the images blanked, a scroll segment appeared, then another, until finally eight segments filled the screen.

Fonzi's voice had an excited edge. "Okay, Jack, here's the complete scroll you sent me via eight photographs. Now I'm going to merge them into a single translated text, including the uncoded first few lines, in clear. This is where things get very interesting."

Fonzi hit the keyboard and a chunk of English text replaced the eight segments on screen. Then he flicked on a laser pointer. With a circling motion of its red dot he indicated the entire body of text.

"What you see here is about half the scroll contents. First I decoded and translated the text myself, then I ran it through the translation software and compared the two. What you see on the screen is as close to a literal translation of the original as I can give. Peruse at your leisure, and then we'll move on to the rest."

Jack and Lela looked up at the screen and read:

This story concerns the man known as Jesus the Messiah. Having traveled from Caesarea to Dora where his name had become well-known, he failed miserably to cure the blind and the sick, despite his promises to do so. Soon after, he was arrested in Dora by the Romans, tried and found guilty, and sentenced to be executed.

This story was told to the Chosen of God by our brother Judas Iscariot, who while visiting nearby Caesarea in the company of Jesus' brethren, learned of the Messiah Jesus' presence in Dora. Yet when he traveled there to see and hear his master Jesus preach, Judas found him to be a false messiah, a usurper who was misusing Jesus' name. On learning the truth, Judas now believed his master to be a false messiah, and not the true messiah, the one come to change the world. Judas Iscariot confessed that after discussing the matter with his brethren, it was decided that he would betray the false messiah to the Romans in Dora.

Indeed, this false messiah was believed to be a man who traveled the land widely, pretending to be the chosen one. He made use of Jesus the Nazarene's name and reputation, falsely promising to cure the sick and the possessed, and made claims to be the son of God. He is believed to have traded on the name of Jesus the Nazarene for his own ends, and to have gathered worldly riches in his name. But in truth, Jesus the Nazarene forbade the gathering of such riches. He believed that man should divest himself of all excessive possessions, and give alms to the poor, and help to the ill and the needy. But this false messiah's greed for eminence was to condemn him.

The text stopped there. As Jack finished reading, he felt an icy chill ripple down his back. He flicked a look at a confused Lela but before either of them could say a word, Fonzi broke the silence.

"What we've got here," he announced, pushing his glasses up the bridge of his nose, "is a story unheard-of before now. It's also one mountain of a mystery. As always the language used in the scrolls can be a little stilted, but what it seems to be saying is this: about the same time as the figure we know from biblical legend as Jesus the Nazarene—or Jesus Christ, *Christ* meaning 'messiah' in Greek—there was another Jesus, an alter ego, a con man if you like, pretending to be him. It seems this con man traveled the Holy Land while at the same time attempting to carry out miracles and hoping to profit by his pretense, financially, egotistically, or both."

Fonzi paused to take a breath. "That's what the text and subtext seem to be saying to me. Does it make sense to everyone so far?"

His excitement rising, Jack nodded his approval. "Go on."

Lela said, "Hold on a second. Doesn't the Jewish Talmud claim that Jesus is a false messiah who practiced magic and was rightly condemned to death? Our Bible, the Tanakh, is full of references to false prophets, deranged or not, who all claimed to be the chosen one."

Fonzi smiled. "True. Jesus even talks about it in Luke, for example. 'Be not deceived for many shall come in my name, saying I am Christ.' Except this is different. It's extremely specific. We're given details of someone who existed at the same time as Jesus. We're given exact incidents. And if you think about it, what's written about here is really a likely scenario."

"What do you mean?" Lela asked.

"Successful people always have their imitators. Pretenders who try to make money or achieve notoriety on the backs of others. Whether it's Elvis, a rock band, or a businessman with a brilliant idea, they've no sooner started to make a buck when there's a bunch of clones trying to cash in on their achievement. Would it have been any different in Jesus' time that someone might try to profit by imitating him?"

"Profit how?" Lela asked.

"Lots of ways. Jesus attracted a lot of attention, respect, and awe from his followers. He also attracted crowds, and gifts of alms and money, and was accommodated with food and lodging most places he went. Those are pretty tempting rewards to an impersonator."

Fonzi added with a smile, "In other words, he was a magnet for attention. No doubt women hit on him too. He probably resisted the groupies, but all that attention and reward is a pretty enticing cocktail for a con artist."

Fonzi paused a second before going on. "And it would have been easy to carry out a deception. Travel in the Holy Land back then was done by donkey or horse or cart, or in most cases, by foot. Roads were bad, and it took an eternity to reach anywhere and news spread slowly. No TV, no radio, no newspapers."

Jack said, "Even Judas's short journey along the coast from Caesarea to Dora, a distance of about ten miles, could have taken half a day. How many people would have known what Jesus looked like in a town where he'd never visited?"

Fonzi nodded. "Exactly. In those days nobody carried IDs. If someone shows up and announces that he's Jesus the Nazarene, there's a good chance folks are going to believe him."

Fonzi pointed the laser's red dot to underscore a portion of screen text. "Know what else is important? A couple of things appear to lend credibility to this text. The Chosen of God are the Essenes—they alone liked to refer to themselves by that name. And the mention of Judas Iscariot in an Essene document makes sense. The Essenes were known to be Zealots—fanatics if you like. The word *Iscariot* is thought to be a corruption from the Greek of the word *Sicarius,* which derives from the word *Zealot.* Some scholars believe that *Judas Iscariot* is a corruption of *Judas Sicarius,* and that he at some stage belonged to the Essene community. So it seems plausible that he'd confide in the Essenes. You know what else intrigues me, Jack?"

"What?"

"I've always found it incredible in the Bible that Judas has no valid motive to betray Jesus. Okay, he gets his thirty pieces of silver, but the money means nothing to him. He betrays Jesus because he betrays Jesus, and there's absolutely no good reason for his treachery. Judas always claims to be totally loyal to Jesus, so scholars might say that the betrayal was simply to fulfill a prophecy. But to me, that's bull, a total cop-out. Here, the text tells us that Judas's betrayal had a genuine motive. A con man was guilty of identity theft. Judas betrayed him to protect the real Jesus. The motive makes sense of a betrayal that up until now is often seen as a complete mystery. That's mega."

Lela said, "What are you trying to imply?"

It was Jack who answered. "I think what Fonzi means is that if the text could be verified it could throw the Bible into doubt."

Fonzi stabbed a finger on the desk. "Exactly. Scripture records only one Jesus the Nazarene. Now we have two. And two betrayals by the same disciple. Two trials in two different Roman provinces. Two sentences of death by different prosecutors, and two crucifixions. We're muddying the waters, creating a huge mystery that raises enormous questions.

"All that aside, even the message of the real Jesus the Nazarene forbidding the gathering of riches is of colossal significance. That he believed man should divest himself of all excessive possessions for the benefit of the poor, the ill, and the needy. There are churches out there that have accumulated vast wealth, and I'm not just talking about Rome. Still others encourage their followers to accumulate riches. This is going to blow a lot of their so-called values out of the water. This is dynamite."

Jack blew out a breath. "Is there *any* chance you got the decoding or translation wrong?"

"Are you kidding? I'll bet my baguettes on it." Fonzi replaced his glasses, his excitement rising. "And it's about to get even more explosive. This last part is guaranteed to blow both your minds."

100

Fonzi poised his fingers over the keyboard. "Question: what's the bedrock on which Christianity is built?"

Lela raised her eyes. "Don't look at me, I'm Jewish."

"Jack?"

"This is starting to sound like a quiz show."

Fonzi smiled. "It's a question most Sunday schoolers could answer. What's the *rock*?"

"I can think of several. For one, a belief that Jesus Christ is the son of God."

"Sure. But I'm talking about something even more fundamental, which supports that belief."

Jack considered. "The resurrection? Jesus had to have been the son of God if he was raised from the dead."

"Bingo." Fonzi stabbed the laptop keyboard with his finger. "Read on, be enlightened, and then we'll discuss."

The screen cleared and then presented another chunk of text:

The Roman commander in Dora, a harsh man known for his brutality, having heard of Jesus the Nazarene's deeds and that he was gathering crowds around him and that he had claimed to be the King of the Jews, promptly imprisoned the false messiah on charges of sedition.

A trial was quickly arranged. The prisoner was found guilty on Judas's evidence, and on the evidence of the brethren in Judas's company, who spread rumors about the prisoner and conspired against him. All this time the fearful prisoner had begged to be cleared of his charges, no longer claiming that he was Jesus the Nazarene. But the commander failed to heed him, the charges remained, and the sentence of execution was carried out by crucifixion.

When the messiah's corpse was removed from the cross, it was placed in a tomb in the burial caves outside Dora, on the road to Caesarea. On the third day, several of Jesus the Nazarene's disciples went to the tomb and removed the body, to prevent it becoming a false shrine to their master. And there the matter ended. All this was told by Judas Iscariot to the Chosen of God.

The text ended. As Jack read it again he felt as if his lungs had turned to stone. "It—it's astonishing," he said hoarsely.

"Astonishing doesn't even come close." Fonzi shook his head. "But right now, we don't know *when* exactly this other crucifixion happened in the timeline of Jesus' life. Was it in the same year he was crucified? Or before, or even after? But for various reasons, which I'll come to, I'd suggest that it's likely to be some time between 30 A.D. and 33 A.D., which is generally agreed to be about the time when the real Jesus was executed. And if this means what I think it means, then it may cast doubt on the most powerful core of Christian belief—the resurrection itself."

"How?" Lela asked.

Fonzi massaged his temple with the fingers of one hand.

"The pretender—let's call him the false Jesus—is caught, sentenced, crucified by the Romans, and then his corpse is removed from his tomb by the real Jesus' disciples. In effect, his body has disappeared. At some point, before or after this event, we assume that the real Jesus is caught, sentenced, crucified by the Romans, and then rises from the dead.

"But clearly this raises questions. One story mirrors the other. What if this second event is misrepresented? What if the two stories—the one concerning the real Jesus, and the other story that reflects the false Jesus—have essentially blurred to become one? Or even that one of them replaced the other?"

"You mean the resurrection may have never happened?"

Fonzi said, "Hey, I'm just throwing out thoughts, Jack. Like any sane, reasonable thinker would do if they read this material. And some of those thoughts might be adhesive enough to stick. It's even conceivable that this story we've just read may cast doubt on whether the real Jesus was crucified, and not a substitute, as many early Christian heresies and the Koran have claimed."

Fonzi paused, then added, "Something else that's worth considering—Bible experts have been known to suggest that there had to be some kind of collusion between Jesus and Judas for his betrayal to take place. This report makes you wonder if the collusion went even deeper. That Jesus might never have died on the cross in the first place. You get my point? The pretender's crucifixion was the only one that took place. Those are the kinds of speculations that might arise from this material."

"How come a story as controversial as this hasn't surfaced before now?"

A knowing smile twisted Fonzi's face as he addressed

Lela. "How do we know it hasn't? Lots of stuff got cut out of the Bible. It's not a book that's come down to us from history in one solid piece. It *evolved*, Lela. For example, do you know about the Council of Nicaea?"

"No."

"Jack, can you explain?"

"The Council of Nicaea was convened by the Roman emperor Constantine in 325 A.D. Bishops met to decide what writings should be considered Holy Scripture and included in the Bible."

Fonzi nodded and added, "Even the divinity of Jesus was up for discussion. Legend has it that Constantine got majorly cheesed off when the proceedings were going nowhere. So he threw a batch of papers he was to choose from on a table. Those that remained on the table were in, those that fell off were out. He ordered that the controversial material left out of the Bible be completely destroyed. When some bishops disagreed, Constantine had them murdered."

Fonzi sat back in his wheelchair. "You see, Lela, down through the centuries the Bible's been assembled and disassembled, edited and re-edited, had lines cut, words altered."

"You mean to reflect what the church's leaders, its cardinals and scholars, wanted it to reflect?"

"Exactly. Most of the gospel may truly represent what was written by its four authors, Matthew, Mark, Luke, and John, but as any biblical expert can tell you, other gospels and testaments have been left out. There were even rumors of a gospel according to Judas that was deliberately destroyed. Who knows, maybe this text is part of it? And something as contentious as this, if it *was* known by the church's forefathers, my belief is they would have left it out because it might seriously cast doubt on aspects of the Bible."

Fonzi grabbed a bottle of water from the desk, unscrewed the cap, and swallowed a couple of gulps as if to quench the fire of his exhilaration. "Do you realize what you've found, Jack? The echo of Jesus' drama has come to light in an ancient parchment preserved in the Judean desert. A drama that may now be called into question. So long as the scroll is original, so long as it's not a fake, then you've opened an explosive can of worms."

"I'd know if it was a fake, Fonzi. Professor Green would have known too. But he was certain it's original. So am I, and carbon-dating of some flakes from the scroll has proven it. We're talking sometime between A.D. 25 and A.D. 50."

Fonzi put down the bottle and turned to the keyboard again. "Then what we've got here is astonishing. And there's even one last cherry on the cake."

101

Fonzi jabbed the keyboard and the screen displayed a segment of the original scroll. He circled the red laser dot around a squiggle on the left of the parchment.

~

"See this? Something you ought to know. A number of Qumran scrolls had similar markings. It's believed to be an indicator that the writer made a copy. Often the more important documents were duplicated in case of damage or destruction."

Lela said, "You mean there could be a copy of *this* scroll?"

"Actually, there could be more than one. What's wrong, Jack? You're frowning."

Jack studied the screen. "I'm thinking about my father's scroll. He could barely unroll it a couple of inches because the parchment was badly damaged. But I remember seeing a similar marking on his parchment."

Fonzi said, "Which means it likely had a copy. When the original scrolls were found at Qumran, it wasn't unusual for copy scrolls and fragments to be found. Even in different caves."

Jack reflected. "One thing bothers me about the text we've read."

"Shoot," Fonzi answered.

"Would a low-ranking Roman commander have the power to authorize an execution on a serious charge of sedition? I thought only a governor could do that. In Jesus' case he was brought before the Judean governor, Pontius Pilate."

Fonzi nodded. "A good point. And it has to do with the final cherry on the cake. Actually, sedition would have covered anything from rabble-rousing to treason, which is a pretty broad definition. It wasn't unknown for Roman commanders to take the law into their own hands. In fact, in this case the commander's action makes perfect sense."

"Why?" Jack asked.

Fonzi peered over his glasses, consulting his notes. "I learned that the governor of Syria back then was a man called Lucius Aelius Lamia, a Roman senator. Ever heard of him?"

"No."

"Here's the cherry. What's interesting about Lamia is that the records say he was recalled to Rome between 27 A.D. and 33 A.D., and his governorship was left vacant by the Emperor Tiberius—in the last years of Jesus' life. In fact, his local Roman commander in Dora, Cassius Agrippa, would certainly have taken charge of such a trial and execution, because his governor was absent. It's perfectly feasible, so it lends credence to the text. And Pontius Pilate may never have even been informed because it occurred in another Roman province."

Lela said, "I want to show you a pair of symbols. Can you tell me if they have any significance for you? They may be Aramaic; I'm not sure."

Lela picked up an indelible black pen from the desk. She

crossed the whiteboard and stepped in front of the blazing projector light and drew the two symbols with the pen.

Fonzi wheeled closer to the whiteboard, studied the symbols, and shook his head. "I'm sorry, these mean absolutely nothing to me. Except that they look vaguely like two cruciform shapes. Why do you ask?" Without waiting for an answer, he twisted in his wheelchair and stared toward the door at the end of the room. "Did you hear that?"

"What?" Jack asked.

"I thought I heard a noise in the corridor."

Jack listened. "I didn't hear anything. Did you, Lela?"

"Nothing."

Fonzi frowned and spun his wheelchair to face the door. "Let me go check."

A split second later a *crack* sounded and the room plunged into darkness.

102

"What was that?" Jack tensed. He could see nothing, the entire room smothered by blackness.

Fonzi said, "I've heard that noise before. It sounds like the main circuit breaker in the switch room down the hall. It must have dropped out."

Lela answered from the darkness, "It could be the weather causing it to trip, there was lightning earlier."

Fonzi said, "Then why hasn't the emergency generator kicked in? It ought to kick in once the main power goes out. It controls the alarm system. I'll need to check the panel."

Jack stood. "I'll go. Do you have a flashlight?"

"There's a penlight in the desk, if I can find it in the dark, and there's a big torch hanging in the switch room."

"Use your laser light, Fonzi."

"If I can find the blooming thing."

Jack heard a fumbling noise on the desk for a few moments, then Fonzi said, "Got it."

He flicked the laser on, directing it toward the palm of his hand. The red-hot rapier sliced through the blackness, suffusing the air with a crimson blush. It was just enough for Fonzi to locate the penlight in a drawer and flick it on, and the beam sprang to life. "That's better."

Lela reached into her pocket, removed her Sig pistol, and racked the slide to cock the weapon.

Fonzi startled, his expression confused. "Why—why the gun?"

Lela said, "A precaution in case there's trouble."

"Trouble? Why on earth would—"

Jack interrupted. "It's complicated and now isn't the time. Let's just say that I've attracted a lot of interest."

"What kind of interest are you talking about?" Fonzi demanded.

"From the same kind of murderous thugs who killed Professor Green."

Fonzi studied their faces in the torchlight. "Gosh, are you for real?"

Jack said, "Now's not the time. Where's the circuit breaker panel, Fonzi?"

He pointed to the closed door. "The switch room's down the hall. Turn right at the end and it's the first door. All the circuit breakers on the panel ought to be in the up position."

Fonzi considered, then rubbed his jaw. "The alarm system really should have switched over to battery and the power-fail alarm should be going off by now. Maybe it's an alarm malfunction that's brought the power down."

Lela raised an uncertain eyebrow. "Who knows the alarm codes besides you?"

"The police and a few trusted employees."

"There's no chance one of them has come in early?"

"Italians? On a Sunday? Are you kidding? Besides, everyone's off today, we're closed."

Jack said, "Stay here, Fonzi. Lela and I will check out the switch room panel. Hold on to the laser, but we're going to need that penlight."

Fonzi handed it over. "Don't you want me to come along?"

"We'll find it. You'll have to stay here in the dark and keep your cell phone handy. You're our backup." Jack turned toward the door and Lela moved beside him, her Sig at the ready.

Fonzi said uneasily, "Backup? Now you've really got me worried."

Jack aimed the penlight ahead of him. "Don't be. But keep your cell phone at the ready. If there's any sign of trouble, call the cops at once."

103

Jack reached the door at the end of the room, Lela beside him. They listened for noise out in the hall but heard nothing.

Lela moved right of the door frame and whispered, "Yank open the door as fast as you can on the count of three. Then keep back against the wall, just in case we've got company."

Jack passed Lela the penlight. "Whatever you say. Here, you may need this. Ready?"

"On the count of three." Lela planted her feet firmly apart, her back against the wall. She clutched the Sig in both her hands, the light meshed awkwardly between her fingers.

Jack got a firm grip on the door handle. "Ready when you are."

"One. Two. Three . . ."

Jack yanked open the door and slammed himself back against the inside wall. Lela aimed her pistol and penlight into the hall but kept most of her body behind the cover of the door frame. Anxious moments passed before she finally said, "It looks all clear. You can come out."

Jack stepped out as Lela flashed the penlight down the hallway. It looked deserted. The light beam ended after about fifty feet with a blank wall. A hallway led off to the left and right.

Jack said, "What now?"

"We'd be sitting ducks once we're halfway down the hallway, so we'll move down one at a time, me first."

"Whatever you say."

Behind them, Fonzi's voice called out shakily, "Is everything okay?"

Jack whispered, "So far. Stay there. We'll be back as quick as we can."

"Hey, I'm not moving, guys."

Lela stepped cautiously into the hallway. She crouched low, swinging her pistol left and right as she moved forward, keeping her back to the wall.

When she reached the end of the corridor, Jack saw her peer round both corners, flashing the torch, searching for a target with her Sig. Finally, she beckoned Jack forward and he joined her. "Well?" he asked.

"I saw the switch room door. It's around the right corner."

"What are we waiting for?"

"The door's already open, Jack."

They approached the switch room. A warning sign was fixed to the open door—a black lightning bolt on a yellow background. Aiming her Sig, Lela poked a look inside the switch room. It looked no bigger than a closet.

Jack saw it was empty and smelled of cleaning fluids. A jumble of janitorial supplies, mops, and brooms were stashed on the floor. On the facing wall was a large gray metal panel with rows of black Bakelite circuit breakers. To the left was a security panel with a keypad and several arrays of miniature colored lights. All of them were extinguished. Jack punched the keypad with a finger but got no response. "This security panel's dead."

He turned his attention to the circuit breakers. Each had

a cardboard tag insert above it, written on in black pen, identifying which circuit it fed.

"You know anything about electricity?" Lela asked.

"I know it can kill you. That's about the sum of my knowledge. According to Fonzi, all the breakers ought to be up. There's our light."

A powerful-looking yellow work light was nestled in a charger unit fixed to the wall. Jack plucked out the torch and turned it on. The tiny cupboard flooded with light, drowning out the weak beam from Lela's penlight.

Jack studied the breaker panel. He noticed that a large, robust circuit breaker had tripped to the down position. All the other smaller breakers appeared to be up. "See there? It looks like the main circuit's dropped out."

"Can it be reset?"

Jack shrugged. "Maybe not if there's a short." He gripped the breaker between his thumb and forefinger and yanked it up. The breaker clicked into place and all the lights sprang on in the hall, including in the switch room.

"Let there be light. There you go. I guess the circuit wasn't shorted after all. Maybe Fonzi was right and the main breaker simply popped." Jack took a step back and dusted his hands.

Lela frowned. "Why was the switch room door ajar? And why didn't the alarm switch over to the battery circuit, like Fonzi said?"

Jack studied the security alarm panel, then gestured to a key inserted into a lock in the panel's side. "There's your reason. The alarm key's in the off position. Someone's totally disabled it."

A frightening scream erupted from behind them, and it stopped a split second later. Jack directed the powerful flashlight down the hall. "Fonzi!"

He raced back down the corridor, Lela following him.

104

They reached the basement. A blaze of light radiated from inside the door. Lela aimed her Sig as she moved cautiously into the room. She beckoned Jack and he joined her.

The room appeared empty. No sign of Fonzi.

The projector screen was on, the screen lit up and glowing. Fear pounding in his chest, Jack found a light switch by the door and flicked it on. A fluorescent light sprang on overhead. A darkened hallway was exposed at the far end of the basement. Beyond the hallway, an open exit door led to a short flight of gray metal stairs that rose up to ground level.

A breeze wafted in, the sound of heavy rain drumming beyond. When Jack looked back across the room he noticed Fonzi lying sprawled on the floor beside his upturned wheelchair. A horrific slash stained his neck, his throat cut from ear to ear, a growing pool of blood oozing onto the carpet.

"Jesus, no." Jack was ashen as he went to kneel beside the body.

Lela joined him. A gurgling sound erupted from Fonzi's lips. It sounded like a strangled cry and then he fell still. Jack felt for a pulse. "He—he's gone. What callous brute would kill—"

"Sssh." Lela put a finger to her lips, then aimed her Sig

toward the exit hallway, just as a bulky figure dressed in dark clothes started to move up the stairs.

"Halt!" Lela shouted.

A muzzle flashed in reply and two gunshots cracked.

Lela threw herself to the floor. "Get down!"

Jack crouched low as another two shots exploded, the rounds zinging above his head like crazed hornets and thudding into the wall. As the figure moved awkwardly up the stairs, pointing the weapon back at them, Lela aimed and fired twice from a prone position. The figure grunted, spun round, and collapsed back into the hallway.

Lela got to her feet, still aiming at the man sprawled on his back on the floor. Jack joined her and flicked on a light. They stared down at the man.

He was dressed in dark pants and a jacket and black leather gloves and wore a black ski mask. An automatic pistol was clutched in one hand and blood oozed from wounds in his upper shoulder and in the back of his head. Jack knelt and felt the man's neck through the bloodstained mask. "He's dead. You did the right thing. He could have killed us both."

Lela was gray with shock. "It's the first time I've shot anyone."

Jack leaned across and yanked up the dead man's ski mask. "Well, what do you know."

It was the Syrian, Pasha, his dark eyes glassy in death. As if to confirm it, Jack tore off the man's left leather glove to reveal the withered hand. He was about to tell Lela when she tensed. "You hear that? Someone's moving outside."

She shifted toward the exit door just as Jack heard a rush of footsteps. He wrenched the automatic from Pasha's fingers and hurried up the stairs after Lela.

They came out in a lit courtyard at the side of the villa.

It was decorated with flower beds, tall palm trees, and fountains. Fifty yards away a black metal railing protected the villa's perimeter and beyond it was a public street, the rain spilling down. A gate set in the middle of the railings yawned open. Jack spotted a figure climbing into a white van and tearing off a black ski mask.

He recognized the Syrian's companion, Botwan. The van roared away with a squeal of tires. Botwan fired out the window, making Lela dive for the cover of some bushes. The van screeched round a corner and disappeared.

Jack reached Lela and helped her to her feet. "You could have got yourself killed."

"I was going to try to shoot out their tires. Whoever they are, they came prepared."

"What do you mean?"

Lela walked back toward the gate. A box of tools lay scattered on the grass, a selection of pliers and screwdrivers and an electronic digital meter. She kicked at the meter with the tip of her foot. "They probably used this stuff to disable the alarm."

Lights sprang on in windows along the street. Raised Italian voices sounded irritated; people's sleep had been disturbed by gunfire and squealing tires.

"Let's get out of sight." Jack led the way as they descended the steps into the basement.

Lela stared down at the dead Syrian. "Who is he?"

"The killer named Pasha I told you about."

"What about the guy in the van?"

Jack looked down at Fonzi's corpse and felt sickened. "His accomplice." He moved over to the desk, held up a bundle of ripped-out wires, and said bitterly, "He grabbed the laptop, for whatever good it'll do him."

Lela knelt, searched in the Syrian's pockets, and removed a cell phone and wallet. "We can check these out later, to see if they tell us anything."

"I think I'd feel safer if I kept this." Jack slipped Pasha's firearm into his own pocket. Then he knelt, and using his finger and thumb he closed Fonzi's eyes before he stood and stared down at the body. "May he rest in peace. I should never have got him involved."

Police sirens shrieked in the distance. Lela put a hand on Jack's arm. "We have to leave. What's wrong?"

Jack stared at the blank projector screen, the empty whiteness blazing out at him. The black indelible marks that Lela had drawn on the side of the whiteboard were clearly illuminated.

Jack stared at the cruciform shapes as if the wheels of his mind were turning furiously. The sirens wailed closer.

"Jack, we better go, *fast*. Are you listening? What's wrong?"

He turned from the screen and met her stare. "I know who robbed the scroll and killed Green."

105

Dawn licked the horizon as Hassan sat grim-faced in the back of the black Mercedes S600. He stared out of the limo's smoked glass windows. His insides felt hollow as the car drove through a ragged sprawl of whitewashed mud brick houses that passed for a village.

Not a soul stirred, the occupants still sleeping, the only sound a barking dog. As the cortege of three black Mercedes drove toward the burial ground, Hassan Malik's eyes were fixed on the hearse in front of him. It carried Nidal's body, wrapped inside a simple white cotton burial cloth. The hearse bumped and settled as it hit a rut.

The image of his brother's body being tossed around made Hassan's heart stutter and he wiped his eyes. *We are all dust and to dust we will return.*

He reflected on the last five hours. After the doctor had falsely signed the death certificate, Hassan had laid out his brother in the private prayer room at the back of the villa. There he had respectfully washed Nidal's body with scented water before wrapping him in the simple white *kafan* shroud.

Then Hassan sat alone, praying over the body, grief like a dagger in his heart, his mind tormented, and then it came time to leave for Rome's airport and the two-hour flight to Amman.

The Lear landed at 2 A.M. but it took another hour for Jordanian customs to clear the paperwork for Nidal's remains, stored in the aircraft's hold, before the cortege drove to the Bedu graveyard near the Dead Sea, opposite the Israeli border. Now Hassan emitted an anguished sigh as the cortege turned into the burial ground and slid past granite tombs.

He had dreaded the finality of this moment as the cortege came to a halt near a bank of olive trees. A fresh grave was opened, uprooted earth piled by the plot. An imam appeared out of the first limo, and two gravediggers wearing white Arab gowns and carrying shovels materialized like ghosts in the twilight.

The Serb stepped out of the Mercedes and eased open the rear door. Hassan climbed out, choking back his tears.

It was time to bury his beloved Nidal.

The ceremony was brief. The gravediggers helped carry Nidal's body from the hearse and Hassan touched the cloth that held his brother, kissed it, let it go.

Then, in accordance with Muslim custom, the gravediggers placed the body in the open grave, lying on its right side, the eyes closed, the shroud removed from the face, the head facing Mecca.

The imam recited his prayers for the dead, and then each man present took a turn to pour three handfuls of soil into the grave while reciting from the Quran. *"We created you from clay and return you into it."*

Prayers over, the gravediggers and the others withdrew out of respect, the red taillights of the remaining two limos disappearing into the darkness.

Hassan went to kneel in front of the grave. He touched the earth, felt its coldness seep into his fingers, and he exhaled. Tonight and forever Nidal would be as cold as the soil. Hassan said his anguished prayers and when he finished, a violent crack of thunder sounded and he looked up. Storm clouds drifted, the Mediterranean sky the color of dark chocolate.

A thunderbolt sizzled and rain spattered the parched soil. Hassan looked back at his brother's resting place and his mind boiled with a rage so powerful it made his hands tremble.

He wiped his eyes. It was time to finish what he came to do.

106

"Who did it, Jack? Who stole the scroll and killed Green?"

They sat in the back of the taxi that Jack had flagged down. As it drove through the Sunday morning streets toward their hotel, Rome was no longer a traffic asylum.

Jack said, "My gut feeling tells me the Vatican. I still can't figure out exactly what Father Novara's twin cross symbols mean but I have my suspicions."

"Go on."

"Novara was an expert in old Aramaic, sure, but he could have simply meant to suggest that there was more than one messiah. I also think maybe he was trying to convey by implication that the Catholic Church had a hand in his death. That's what my instinct tells me. Novara was dying, his life ebbing away. He used the twin cross symbols as a kind of desperate shorthand, a clue. It's about all that makes sense."

Lela stared back at him. "That's a lot of supposition. You can't make such a bold statement without backing it up with evidence. The Vatican doesn't exactly have a reputation as a den of killers and thieves, at least not since the Reformation. What evidence have you got?"

Having spoken to the driver, Jack was certain that the man didn't speak English, which was just as well—he probably would have crashed the cab had he understood the conversation. "How about motive? Who stands to gain most by possessing the scroll? Some rich and powerful collector?"

"Obviously you don't think so."

"No collector, no matter how rich or fixated they are about possessing a Dead Sea scroll, would risk multiple homicide charges and a lifetime in prison just to add to their collection. They wouldn't be that dumb or desperate."

"What if they had someone steal it for them?"

"They'd still be putting themselves in jeopardy. When I was in the monastery at Maloula, Father Novara said something that made me think."

"What?"

"He said that the scroll was destined never to be seen, along with the others. Meaning, I can only guess, that other scrolls like the ones found at Qumran have been kept out of circulation. Only a very powerful and wealthy organization could afford to bankroll buying a whole bunch of scrolls. And the Vatican's got a powerful motive. A controversial reference to Jesus that could undermine the faith, maybe even destroy it. You want to know something else?"

"What?"

"Now that I've put my suspicion into words my mind's turning cartwheels. The first people to arrive on the scene of my parents' crash were two Catholic priests and that scroll also goes missing. How's that for a coincidence? Your own father had his suspicions that the pickup's brakes may have been tampered with."

"You're starting to sound angry, Jack."

"And the more I think about it the angrier I get. What if there *was* more to my parents' deaths than just a simple accident? If the crash was deliberate to gain possession of my father's scroll?"

"Except there was no solid evidence."

"You're the cop. You know as well as I do that evidence doesn't always turn up and that sometimes the guilty go free."

"True, but—"

"Can you even think of any other prime suspects who'd be prepared to kill to get their hands on my scroll?"

"I hate to admit it, but Mossad's been known to carry out assassinations in Israel's name."

Jack raised an eyebrow. "I've thought about that. But Mossad's the heavy brigade and usually deals with state security. This isn't exactly their territory. I mean, it's not like Israel's nuclear secrets have gone missing. It's a two-thousand-year-old scroll, for heaven's sake."

"But a controversial one. Mossad's boss said the scroll was vital to Israel."

"How could it be vital? The document's got to do with Jesus. He's not exactly center stage in Jewish religion." Jack slapped a fist in his palm. "We're missing something, Lela. We just haven't figured it out. Let me see the stuff you found in Pasha's pockets."

Lela fumbled in her jacket and handed across the cell phone and wallet.

Jack emptied the wallet on his lap. A few euro notes and coins fell out, but no ID. "Pasha wasn't taking any chances. Let's have a look at the phone." Jack stuffed the money back in the wallet and flicked on Pasha's cell phone. It played its opening theme tune and the window lit up, the cell going through its power-up sequence as the screen illuminated. "That's a bummer. He's got a pin code."

"There are always ways to crack a cell phone pin."

"We'll worry about that later." Jack flicked off the phone, stuffed it into his pocket, and found the embossed business card that Cardinal Kelly had given him. He waved it between his fingers. "Meantime, we need to bang a few heads together to get some answers. Talk to someone at the top of the Vatican totem pole. Someone who ought to know everything that's going on."

"Who?"

"How about we begin with our old friend, John Becket? The way my mind's been working, Becket's got a whole bunch of questions to answer. A couple of big ones in particular."

"What questions?"

"Did he steal my father's scroll and commit murder?"

107

The sky was still dark, rain hammering down as Hassan's Mercedes S600 turned toward the edge of the village. Minutes later it cruised into a lemon grove on the outskirts and halted. Ten paces away stood a ruined corrugated metal hut with filthy white walls.

The Serb held open the car door as Hassan stepped out into the drenching rain. He led the way into the hut, a goatherd's ruin that stank of urine and stale fodder. He recognized Josuf waiting inside. The Bedu wore a djellaba and carried an electric lantern, his curved blade stuck in his belt.

They kissed in the Arab fashion and Josuf grasped Hassan's arm with an expression of grief. "I am sorry for your loss, Hassan. May Allah protect your brother's soul. May his angels comfort him."

"You did everything I asked of you, Josuf. You carried out my plans and now you must have your promised reward."

The elderly Bedu's eyes glittered. "I thank you, Hassan. You are a man for whom I would do anything."

Hassan withdrew his hand. "Indeed, Josuf. Even betray me to the Israelis."

The words made Josuf freeze, his face gaunt. "What—what are you saying, Hassan? I took Cane to Maloula to try to recover the scroll, just as you instructed. You and I are old friends. I did everything you asked of me."

"And some things I did not ask."

"No—"

"I am no fool, Josuf. I have ears and eyes everywhere. You involved the Israelis, you took their money. You told them you were taking Cane to the monastery."

Josuf's brow sweated and he had a trapped look. "I—I only told them a little, Hassan. Nothing to compromise you, I swear. Just enough to wheedle some money from them. You know how it is. We only tell the Jews what we want them to know."

"You are their spy. You betrayed me and your treachery may have cost my brother his life."

"No, Hassan, I swear—"

Hassan clicked his fingers at the Serb, who tore Josuf's curved Arab knife from his belt.

Josuf recoiled. "In the name of mercy, Hassan, I beg you—"

The words died in Josuf's mouth as the blade flashed through the air and cut his throat. He collapsed in a heap on the floor, blood spewing from his gaping neck wound. The Serb tossed the blade on the body.

Hassan's face twisted with venom as he stepped over to Josuf's corpse and spat on it, then wiped his mouth, moved out into the rain, and climbed into the back of the Mercedes. The Serb slipped into the driver's seat, his clothes drenched in rainwater. "What do you want me to do about the body?"

Hassan stared beyond the limo's smoked glass as the two gravediggers appeared again from out of the downpour and moved into the hut. "Don't worry, it will be buried in the desert for the vermin to eat. Now let's get back to Rome. It's time to finish this once and for all."

108

Cardinal Liam Kelly had an anxious frown as he rose from behind his desk and crossed to the window of his Vatican office.

As he stared out at the throngs of tourists assembling on St. Peter's Square, the door behind him opened and Umberto Cassini strolled in, looking regal in his cardinal's red cassock and hat. He made a point of checking his wristwatch. "Ah, Liam. You wanted to see me. Can we make it quick? I have a meeting with the Bishop of Paris in ten minutes."

Kelly looked troubled as he came away from the window. "I think you're going to find this a lot more interesting, Umberto."

"How so?"

"I just had a strange phone call and an even stranger request from Jack Cane. He wanted me to arrange an immediate private audience with the pope. Demanded it—would you believe?"

Cassini riveted his attention on Kelly. "Go on."

Kelly's craggy face darkened. "Cane says he now knows the location of the stolen scroll. He also says that its contents will rock the church and the world."

Cassini's jaw twitched nervously. "Those were his exact words?"

Kelly nodded. "He said he would only discuss it with the pope. And that if we don't comply with his request within the next hour, he'll divulge what he knows to the newspapers. He says if that happens, then tomorrow's headlines would make for interesting reading."

"What else did he say?"

Kelly wrung his hands worriedly. "Nothing, but I got the feeling he was hinting that the Vatican could be in the firing line for some kind of scandal if his wishes aren't met."

"What kind of scandal?"

Kelly restlessly came away from the window. "I've no idea, Umberto. I told Cane that a papal audience can't be arranged just at the drop of a hat. Besides, his request was highly irregular."

Cassini slumped into the chair in front of Kelly's walnut desk and ran a hand over his face, his mind working overtime. "Did Cane say where he was calling from?"

"No. Why?"

"Just curious."

"He didn't stay very long on the phone either. I got the impression he was afraid his call might be traced."

"Did he now?"

Kelly added worriedly, "This has a bad feel to it, Umberto. I can sense it in my bones. What are we going to do?"

Cassini's mouth twisted in a scowl as he pushed himself up from the chair.

"Apparently the only thing we can do. Arrange for Cane to speak with the pope at once."

Angelo Butoni no longer wore his Levi's T-shirt and corduroy jacket, but a shirt and tie. As he ushered Sean Ryan into his office, the monsignor said expectantly, "You told me you followed the pope back to the monastery. So where exactly did he go?"

"As I explained on the phone, he drove to a house not far from the railway station, about a block from the red-light area," Butoni answered.

"Give me the details," Ryan demanded.

"He went in the front door, which was opened by an attractive middle-aged woman."

Ryan sighed deeply. "Don't tell me we've got the makings of a scandal here, Angelo."

"I checked. The house is registered to a Father Kubel. The woman in question was Kubel's sister and housekeeper."

"Was?"

"A doctor visited the house about half an hour after the pope arrived. It seems Father Kubel was terminally ill with cancer and passed away. I saw his body being removed by paramedics and got the gist of the story from his neighbors."

Ryan sighed again, this time with relief. "Kubel, you say?"

"Franz Kubel. I checked on him with the diocese. He was an archaeologist as well as a priest, and spent years working in Israel. Why, do you know him, Monsignor?"

"The name rings a bell."

"It seems the pope may have been privately visiting Kubel these last few days. The priest was on his deathbed."

Ryan wiped his forehead with his handkerchief. "Well, thankfully we've got a simple enough explanation, that's all I'll say. But why all the secrecy on the pope's part?"

A knock came on the door and a plainclothes Vatican security officer appeared. "The lab results you wanted, Angelo."

He handed a sheet of paper to Butoni, who read the contents, frowned, and looked up at the man. "You absolutely certain about this?"

"A hundred and ten percent, boss."

"Thanks, Rico, you can go."

The man left and Ryan said, "What was that all about?"

Butoni held up the paper in his hand. "The threatening letter to the pope that you asked me check for prints. The one that Cardinal Cassini received. And the videotapes of the Vatican archive building, where the secret archive documents went missing. You asked me to review all the security tape footage since the day after the pope's election."

"Go on, Angelo."

"We didn't find any fingerprints on the sheet, but I got samples of printed letters from every cardinal's office, going back several years, and checked them against the paper type and printer font in the original threat letter."

Ryan smiled and his ears pricked up. "Good man, Angelo, that's what I like to hear. Find anything interesting?"

"I think you could say that. And I'd like you to have a look at one of the archive's security videotapes while we're at it."

"Why?"

"I think we've found our thief."

109

The taxi pulled up outside the gates of a centuries-old sandstone villa and Jack climbed out. A marble inscription on the wall said: "White Fathers. Monastery of Aventino."

Jack approached the wrought-iron entrance gates, manned by two plainclothes guards, stern-looking men whose stare never left him. He presented his passport, told them his business, and one of the guards spoke into a walkie-talkie. When he received a reply, the man unlocked the gate.

The moment Jack stepped inside, the gate was locked again. He had left the pistol he'd taken from Pasha with Lela, which was just as well because the second guard used a metal detector and then frisked him before the front door opened and a cheerful, bearded monk appeared. "I'm Abbot Fabrio. We've been expecting you, Signore Cane."

Jack followed him inside. Two more cautious guards lingered in the corridor, keeping watch on the door and eyeing their visitor.

"This way, please." The abbot led Jack down the hallway to an open doorway. Beyond lay a lush garden full of palm and olive trees. A fountain resembling a stone fish spewed water from its mouth into a pond covered with water lilies.

Another pair of watchful plainclothes guards strolled in the far end of the garden. One of the men had his jacket open to reveal a holstered automatic pistol. His companion wore a Heckler & Koch machine pistol draped across his chest.

The abbot grimaced. "Guns, I hate them. But they're a necessary evil to protect the pope." He gestured to a bench facing the fountain. "Please, take a seat and I'll tell him you've arrived, Signore Cane."

It was peaceful in the garden and as Jack sat there he heard footsteps. He turned and saw the tall figure of John Becket approach. He wore leather sandals and a simple white cassock.

Jack waited as he approached. Becket had aged; his skin was more wrinkled and deeply tanned. But it was his eyes—piercing, the palest blue. Jack felt an odd shiver down his back. He rose from the bench.

Becket gripped his hand. "Mr. Cane, or may I call you Jack? It's been a long time."

His voice was deep and powerful but with a surprising gentleness for such a big man. Jack was dumbstruck. It was hard to believe he was addressing the pope. "Twenty years."

"The time has flown. I hear that you're an archaeologist like your father. I'm sure he would have been proud."

Despite his friendly manner, when Jack looked more closely Becket appeared under stress, his eyes swollen from lack of sleep.

Jack glanced toward the garden. The watchful guards never took their gaze off him. "To tell the truth, I was expecting to meet in the Vatican."

Becket gathered the folds of his cassock and sat on the bench. "The setting here is less formal. I hope you don't mind.

I'm afraid it's also partly the reason for all this security. Please, sit down."

Jack joined him on the bench.

Becket said, "I've often kept you in my prayers. The death of anyone's parents is a terrible loss. When you're young and an only child, it's an immense tragedy. I only wish I could have offered you more solace at the time."

There was a genuine look of sadness on Becket's face. He placed a hand gently on Jack's shoulder and his blue eyes seemed to bore into his soul. "But of some things I am certain, Jack. They are watching over you, and someday you will be reunited. They still love you, but from a different place."

Becket's intimacy was disarming and his voice had a powerful conviction. Jack tried to focus on why he was here. Shifting away, he caused Becket's hand to fall.

For a moment the pope seemed surprised by the gesture, and he said awkwardly, "Cardinal Kelly urged me to meet you. He says you had made a discovery of a scroll. That the text was highly controversial. He said that you wanted to make me personally aware of its contents."

"That's right."

"I admit you've stirred my curiosity. And I was struck by the curious twist of fate—your father also made a discovery at Qumran. But why do you think it may be so important to the Vatican?"

Jack met Becket's gaze. "We'll get around to that. But first, I want you to tell me the truth."

"I don't understand."

"I think you do," Jack said bluntly. "I think my parents' deaths were murder, not an accident. And that you stole my father's scroll."

IIO

ROME

It was very still in the garden, the only sound the gurgling fountain. Jack waited for Becket's reaction. He saw it immediately. A look of discomfort spread over the pope's face.

Jack said, "You haven't answered me."

Becket's eyes suddenly became wary. "You've made a serious allegation, Jack."

"Is that all you have to say?"

"You sound angry."

"I'm sitting beside the man who may have killed my parents. How do you think I feel?"

"You truly believe that I killed them?"

"You were the first person at the accident scene. And I've never known what you were doing there that day."

"I was on my way to Jerusalem."

"I think you're lying."

Becket bit back his response.

Jack said, "You remember Sergeant Raul, who questioned you?"

"Of course."

"He almost convinced himself the brake line in my father's pickup had been deliberately tampered with. But he couldn't prove it."

Becket paled a little and shook his head. "The sergeant never mentioned his suspicion to me, Jack."

"Then what about the missing scroll? There was no evidence to prove it was destroyed by fire. I think you know more than you're telling."

"Jack—"

"What happened to my parents ripped my heart out. I don't think I've ever found peace since that day. But this isn't just about burying ghosts or even solving a crime. It's not even about justice. It's about simple truth. Something you're supposed to believe in."

Becket fell silent. Beads of perspiration glistened on his brow. It appeared as if a great weight was pressing down on his shoulders, that he was under enormous stress. He tightly shut his eyes, then opened them again. As he sat there, rigid, his face set in stone, his breathing became more labored. He rubbed a bony hand over his face. There seemed to be an agony in that simple gesture, as if he faced a colossal decision.

He turned his head and fixed Jack with a penetrating stare. "Please understand one thing. I didn't set out to harm anyone."

"What's that supposed to mean?"

The sound of footsteps approached along the path. Abbot Fabrio appeared and bowed. "Holy Father, my apologies. The security detail says that your car will be here in ten minutes to take you to the Vatican. You are due to give your speech and blessing from St. Peter's Square after your meeting with the cardinals."

Becket waved a hand in dismissal. "Tell them to delay the car."

"Until when, Holy Father?"

"Until I say I am ready."

"But—"

"No arguments, Fabrio. And tell Cardinal Cassini that he is to assemble the Curia in the Sistine Chapel. I will have an important announcement to make."

"As you wish, Holy Father." The abbot left.

Jack looked up at Becket as he stood. The pope's face was suddenly tired and sagged. In the space of ten minutes he had aged ten years. He gestured to the path through the garden. "Will you walk with me, Jack?"

"Why should I?"

"Because I think it's time you knew the truth about what happened to your parents."

Lela studied her wristwatch as she sat outside the café. She sipped her espresso. The sidewalk table gave her a view of the monastery entrance at the far end of the street. Every now and then she could see the guards discreetly patrol behind the gate.

She put down her espresso and sighed. She felt confused. Her relationship with Jack went back such a long time. She still had feelings for him, and that troubled her. What right had she to think it might be rekindled? Besides, Jack still seemed more than a little smitten by Yasmin Green. And why shouldn't he? She was beautiful and young. *But who is she?*

"The rain's gone, the sun's out. Nice day for a coffee."

She turned, startled, and saw Ari standing behind her, his injured hand bandaged. He held a newspaper in his other hand. He pulled up a chair and indicated to the waiter that he wanted an espresso, the same as Lela. The waiter went to fill the order. Ari smiled. "Don't think of running, Lela. You wouldn't get far."

Across the street, she saw the Mossad taxi driver, Mario, leaning against his cab. Farther along, Cohen smoked a cigarette as he lounged next to a wall.

Lela felt the barrel of Ari's pistol prod her in the side as he leaned in closer with the newspaper. "Where's your pistol? Give it to me."

"Ari, please . . ."

"You've been playing hide-and-seek with me, Lela. I don't like that."

"Ari, there's been good reason—"

"Make a fuss and I swear, I'll have you bundled into our car in no time, screaming or not. Now, where's your pistol?"

"In my pocket."

"Any other weapons I should know about?"

"Another pistol, in my right pocket."

Ari reached into Lela's pockets, removed her own pistol and Pasha's weapon, and tucked them inside his jacket. "It looks like you were expecting trouble."

"I wasn't expecting you. How did you know where to find me, Ari?"

"Lots of state security organizations keep loose contact with each other. A case of 'you scratch my back, and I'll scratch yours.' Mossad and the Vatican are no exception, that's all I'll say."

The waiter came with Ari's espresso and left. Lela said, "Tell me how Mossad and the Vatican are connected in all of this."

Ari used his bandaged hand to add a sugar cube to his cup and stirred. "You can ask Weiss when you see him."

"That's where you're taking me?"

"Yes. Then onward to Israel. Along with your friend Cane." Ari gave a tight smile and sipped his espresso. He pulled his pistol back from Lela's side but kept it clutched in his good hand, tucked under his newspaper and out of view. "Just as soon as he appears from his private papal audience, we're going to finally bring this to a conclusion."

112

"For twenty years I've lived with a lie. I've kept a dark secret I chose not to speak about. Do you know why?"

Jack was frozen, not knowing what he was about to hear. "No . . ."

"Because I knew my secret would tarnish the church. My own destiny didn't matter, but the church mattered deeply to me. So I kept my silence."

"Did you kill my parents?"

The pope's mouth tightened as he said grimly, "I played my part in a conspiracy of lies, Jack."

"What's that supposed to mean?" Jack felt anger rise up in him like bile. He wanted to lash out, to strike Becket, but the man suddenly let out an anguished sigh and buried his face in his hands.

For a long time he remained like that. Then he looked at Jack again. "It means that I lied. That I was a party to a crime by remaining silent. But in the end, every one of our sins demands a price."

"Who killed my parents? Who stole my father's scroll? It *was* stolen, wasn't it?"

Becket nodded. "Yes, it was stolen."

"Why?"

"Because certain people believed its theft was for the good of the church."

"How can you say that? How can you condone theft and murder?"

"I'm not, Jack. I'm merely stating fact."

"Who killed my parents?"

The pope stared out at the fountain, then back again. "When your father discovered his scroll, he was baffled because part of the wording he read didn't make sense. So he permitted Father Kubel to see it, who realized immediately that it was a coded text. Such scrolls contained a certain marker."

"I know about the marker. Go on."

The pope said, "Kubel was aware of what the marker meant. As the Vatican's coordinator on the dig, his superiors had already made him aware that any coded scrolls could prove to be controversial. And that several had turned up at Dead Sea sites over the years and had been kept secret, with Israel's consent."

"Why?"

"For what seemed like perfectly good reasons. Neither the Vatican nor Israel wanted any controversy to rock the foundations of their religions."

"Some of the scrolls contained controversial material?"

"Yes. Revelations, mysterious predictions, references to Jesus' beliefs and the early church. Some of it with the potential to muddy the waters of religious dogma."

"Tell me what Kubel did."

The pope said, "Your father was incredibly excited by his find. He told Kubel that on his way to Jerusalem he intended to visit an old friend of his, a journalist with the *Post*, to show him the scroll. In Kubel's mind, alarm bells went off as soon as he heard that statement."

"Why?"

"He feared that by involving the newspapers there was a danger that the scroll's content would be revealed."

"What did Kubel do?"

The pope sighed. "He decided he had to gain possession of the scroll, no matter what the cost. It was all utter madness, of course, and went beyond all reason. But Kubel was always a hothead. There was no stopping him."

"Go on."

"He deliberately tried to loosen the pickup's brake fluid line. To cause a slow leak, hoping the brakes would fail on the way to Jerusalem and that your father would crash. Kubel intended to follow the pickup. In his urgency to get his hands on the scroll he truly didn't care if you all died. That was how reckless he was, a true religious fanatic."

"So when Kubel arrived at the accident scene he'd already been following us. But you turned up also."

The pope met Jack's stare. "I saw Kubel follow your pickup. He had a deranged look on his face, a look I knew spelled trouble. So I drove after him and later heard the explosion and came across him at the accident scene. I saw the army truck had exploded. Whether it was a genuine accident or not, I'm afraid we will never know."

"How did you learn about Kubel's part in all of this?"

"Weeks later he asked me to be his confessor. Only when I listened to his admission of guilt did I learn the real story. But as a priest, I was duty-bound by my vows not to divulge Kubel's confession, even to the police."

"Even if it involved murder?"

"It was unclear that Kubel had committed murder. He didn't know it himself. Theft, yes. But murder, it was uncertain. The police determined that the crash had been caused by the army truck."

"Except Kubel intended·to kill us all if he had to."

"I believed that. So I sought clarity from my superiors. I was told that Kubel had committed no provable crime in the eyes of the law. His action had evil intent, certainly. But the results of his action were unclear."

"That all sounds very convènient."

"You're right, of course."

"What did your heart tell you?"

The pope sighed deeply. "Kubel had handed over the scroll to the Vatican and his superiors wanted to cover up his actions. All of which was wrong. I made a written statement condemning their stance. My statement was suppressed."

"Why didn't you follow your heart and tell that to the police? Why help cover up Kubel's wrongdoing?"

The pope put the tips of his fingers to his lips as if in silent prayer. "I have wrestled with that question for the last twenty years, Jack. The answer I came to was that I should remain a priest. Only in that way could I one day try to change any wrongdoing from within the church."

"That sounds like a very convenient answer."

"No, Jack, it's not. I did not ask to be made pope. I never sought the papacy. But I believe that I was chosen for a reason."

"What reason is that?"

"To bring about a sea change. And that is what is about to happen. Very soon, the Vatican's archives will be thrown open to the public, along with details of all its private dealings. There will be no more lies. No more secrets or duplicity. The course of the church's future is about to be forever changed."

Jack heard the sincerity in Becket's voice and stared back at him. "You really mean that, don't you?"

"Yes, I do. One other thing. Father Kubel died this morning after a long illness. His sister was a witness to his deathbed confession of his crime. I can arrange for you to meet and speak with her, if you wish."

Jack considered. "Tell me this. Is the scroll's revelation true? Was there really a second messiah?"

"Yes, it's true. There are several other scrolls that mention this false messiah and cast doubt upon some of the real Jesus' actions."

Jack frowned. "How will you answer that? How will you stop the doubt from creating havoc?"

Becket didn't flinch. "I don't honestly know, Jack. I have been praying for an answer. But so far, one hasn't come."

"Has it altered your belief?"

Becket's voice was firm with conviction. "No, it hasn't. Every day I have witnessed God's love and goodness. I have felt His presence. How could I not believe?"

"You're a remarkable man, John Becket. I wish I had your faith."

The powerful gaze of Becket's blue eyes almost bored into Jack's soul. "You do have my faith. We all have it in us. In some it's simply buried deeper than in others. But we all hear the echo of God's voice. We are all remarkable creatures, Jack, touched by our Creator's love and greatness. And because of that we can do incredible things."

"Answer me honestly. Did the Vatican have anything to do with Professor Green's death and the theft?"

"You have my honest word, I know nothing about that."

"But if it *was* involved in any way, you'd have the authority to find out, right?"

"The Vatican has a reputation for secrecy and intrigue. If I have my way, that will cease. But in any large organization there are always groups who seek to have their way with power and cunning. I will try my utmost to find out for you, Jack."

Becket gripped Jack's hands in his. "I will pray that your soul finds peace. And that if you discover who stole the scroll, who killed the professor, you'll try to find it in your heart to forgive them."

"Why should I?"

"Because to forgive is the first step toward redeeming the sin."

"I'm afraid that's one pledge I can't give a promise to."

113

Lela sat in the back of the stationary cab, Ari next to her. He clutched a pair of palm-sized binoculars and studied the monastery at the end of the street. "Did Cane say how long he'd be meeting the pope?"

Lela replied, "No. Ari, take my word. Cane didn't kill Green. He's innocent in all of this."

"That's for Weiss to decide." Ari reached into his pocket for his pistol. "I have orders to take Cane back to Israel. Nothing's going to change that. A word of advice: whatever happens next is going to happen hard and fast, so let me give you a friendly word of warning, Lela."

"Meaning?"

"Keep your nose out of it and leave me and my men to do our job. Try to help Cane in any way and one of us is liable to put a bullet in you."

Jack came down the few short steps of the monastery entrance. Behind him, Abbot Fabrio closed the oak doors. One of the armed guards unlocked the security gate and Jack stepped out onto the sunny pavement.

As he started to walk toward the café where he had left Lela, his cell phone rang. Jack checked the number. It was unfamiliar to him. He decided to take the call.

"Yes?"

"Mr. Cane." A man's voice, full of authority.

"Who is this?"

"No questions. Just listen and obey the orders I give you."

"What—"

"*Listen*, Mr. Cane."

It sounded as if the phone was being manhandled, then Yasmin's voice came on the line, edged with fear. "Jack? Is that you?"

"Yasmin—"

"Jack, these—these people say they'll kill me."

"Which people?"

He heard panic in Yasmin's voice. "They want the scroll, Jack. They want to—"

Yasmin was cut off mid-sentence and the man interrupted. "Where are you, Mr. Cane?"

"In Trastevere."

"Do you know where the Trevi Fountain is?"

"Yes."

"Go there. Across the plaza from the fountain you'll see the Via del Lavatore. Stand on the corner and wait. Contact no one or the woman will be killed."

"Listen—"

"You have twenty minutes to get there, Mr. Cane."

"I can't make it to the Trevi that quickly."

"Twenty minutes, or don't bother coming. She'll be dead."

———

Ari kept the binoculars pointed toward the monastery and said, "Okay, Cane's on his way."

Lela saw Jack appear from behind the security gate, ushered out by one of the guards. He walked toward the café for a few moments, then suddenly took out his cell phone and put it to his ear.

Ari watched. "He's taking a call."

"What do we do?" Cohen asked Ari.

"Wait until he gets closer, then make our move."

Lela saw Jack finish talking on his cell phone. He halted, stood a few moments as if he was trying to make up his mind, then walked on again, disappearing behind a parked green van.

Seconds passed but he didn't reappear. Ari frowned, still watching with the binoculars. "Where's he gone?"

More anxious seconds passed but there was no sign of Jack Cane. A frustrated Ari tapped Cohen on the shoulder. "Start the car and cruise closer to the van. For some reason Cane's stopped behind it."

Cohen said, "Or else he's hiding."

Ari said, "We'll soon find out. Get ready to grab him."

Lela saw Ari remove a black silencer from his pocket and screw it on the end of the Sig's barrel. Ari said, "I want to make sure we don't alert the Vatican's security guards."

"I've got a funny feeling about this, Ari. This isn't you."

Ari ignored her, finished screwing on the silencer, and cocked the pistol. "Where the heck is he, Mario? Cohen, get closer to the van."

As they came alongside the green van, Lela saw that it concealed a cobbled alleyway that was completely deserted.

Ari clenched a fist and hammered it on the car seat. "Cane's suckered us. He's slipped away."

114

Jack ran until his lungs seared his chest. He figured that the Trevi was maybe a couple of miles from the monastery.

When he ran down the alleyway behind the van he came down onto an empty street. Five minutes of hard running and he was breathless as he reached the Via della Renella. He reckoned it could take him more than another twenty minutes to reach the Trevi.

"Twenty minutes, or don't bother coming. She'll be dead." The man's tone suggested that he meant what he said. Regardless of who Yasmin really was, he couldn't bear to think that he'd be responsible for her death.

He crossed the Tiber and came to a piazza. Halting for a few seconds to catch his breath, he checked his watch. Nine minutes had passed. Eleven minutes remained.

He'd never make the Trevi in time.

Traffic whizzed around the piazza. A rage of car engines, mopeds, and buses merged into a symphony of noise and choking exhaust fumes. Among the mass of vehicles Jack saw a couple of cabs whiz by. He stuck out his arm to hail one down. Not one stopped.

He sweated, panic taking hold now, conscious that with

every passing second Yasmin's life might hang in the balance. Another taxi sped past and Jack shot out a hand. The driver completely ignored him.

Jack felt drenched in sweat. Thirty yards to his right a tough-looking youth wearing a sleeveless wife-beater T-shirt dismounted from a Vespa scooter and put it on its kickstand. He removed his black motorcycle helmet, left it on the seat, and crossed to a kiosk next to a park. He bought a pack of cigarettes, lit one, and strolled over to chat with a couple of girls sitting on a nearby park bench.

Jack crossed to the scooter. The keys were still in the ignition. He looked over at the tough-looking youth, still smoking and chatting with the girls.

He grabbed the scooter by the handlebar and the seat and jerked it off its stand. The helmet rolled onto the ground and he at once heard a roar behind him.

One of the girls pointed to him and yelled at the moped's owner. The youth spun around and spotted what Jack was up to. A vicious scowl erupted on his face.

Tossing away his cigarette, he balled his fists and strode forward, shouting obscenities in Italian.

Jack ran with the scooter, jumped on, and twisted the ignition key as the youth raced toward him, screaming his lungs out.

The engine started the first time. Jack shifted into gear, revved the engine's handlebar controls, and released the clutch. He had barely moved ten yards when the youth caught up and reached out to drag him off the scooter.

Jack revved hard and flicked into second gear. The Vespa's engine snarled and it sped forward with a burst of power . . .

Ten minutes later, with barely a second to spare he turned the Vespa into a side street leading on to the Trevi Fountain.

He'd broken the speed limits in his rush to reach his destination, but this was Rome, where almost every motorist was deranged.

He removed the Vespa's ignition keys and stuffed them in his pocket.

The cops would eventually find the scooter and the youth would get it back, minus his keys, but at least no one else could steal it in the meantime.

Jack crossed to the corner of the Via del Lavatore. He saw no one waiting nearby except a couple of Japanese tourists clutching handfuls of shopping bags. Jack was still sweating, from anxiety this time, wondering what would happen next. *What if I'm walking into a trap?*

He stood on the street corner and turned in a slow circle. The place was busy with tourists and shoppers.

A second later someone brushed up behind him. Jack felt a sharp pain in his shoulder, like the hard stab of a hypodermic needle. He spun around but immediately his legs started to feel like rubber under him. "What the—?"

A powerfully built man gripped his arms. Jack couldn't see his face but he heard his voice. "Do as I tell you, Cane. Move to the edge of the pavement."

Jack felt lightheaded, his senses fading. When he didn't respond to the order, the man pushed him toward the pavement's brink. A dark-colored Toyota van drove up beside him and slid to a halt. The side door rolled open and Jack was roughly pushed inside, other hands grabbing him before he could fall.

The man jumped in and the door rolled shut. In the back of the van someone grabbed hold of Jack's hair, then dragged an eyeless woollen mask over his face. The last thing he heard as he surrendered to blackness was the sound of screeching tires.

115

Hassan Malik stood at the villa's study window, smoking a cigarette. He saw the headlights sweep up the gravel path and the Toyota van slide to a halt under some palm trees. The side door burst open and the Serb and two more bodyguards dragged a masked and unconscious Jack Cane from the back of the vehicle.

A look of vehemence erupted on Hassan's face as he crushed his cigarette in a crystal ashtray on the desk in front of him. He reached down and slid open one of the drawers. Inside lay a silvered Walther PPK pistol with polished ebony grips. Next to it was a fully loaded magazine with seven rounds.

Hassan removed the pistol and magazine as the study door sprang open and the Serb appeared. "Well?" Hassan asked.

The Serb grinned, as if he relished what was to come. "We've got everything set up in the back room, Mr. Malik. The blowtorch, the tools, the lot. I'm ready to go to work whenever you are."

Hassan slammed the magazine into the Walther's butt and tucked the pistol into his pocket. "The time has come for Cane to pay for his sins."

"Pull up here," Ari ordered.

Cohen halted the taxi and Ari jumped out like an angry bull. After driving in circles they ended up in one of the avenues leading to the Colosseum, hoping to catch sight of Cane in one of the maze of side streets, but there was no sign of him.

Ari slapped his balled fist off the car's hood. "Cane could be anywhere by now."

Lela climbed out of the backseat. Ari said, "Where do you think you're going?"

"We need to talk, Ari. What are you going to do with Jack? Tell me honestly."

"I told you. Take him back to Tel Aviv, like Weiss ordered."

"What happens to Jack then? Does he end up in some desert prison, locked up at Mossad's discretion? Weiss could do anything he wants with him."

"Probably. I don't know what Weiss intends back in Tel Aviv. But I can tell you this." Ari plucked out his cell phone and began punching in a number. "I know who Yasmin Green really is and right now that's the only lead we have."

116

"Wake up, Cane. Wake up."

Jack came awake with a jolt as a fist crashed into his jaw. A light blinded his face and he was strapped down, his hands and legs tied with rope to a chair.

Another blow struck him and Jack's head snapped back. He tasted blood in his mouth. His mind was a fog and it took a couple of moments before he began to come to his senses.

"Good. You're back in the land of the living."

Jack blinked and saw the Serb stand over him with two companions. One of them twisted the knobs on a portable blowtorch, rubber tubes running to an oxyacetylene tank. The Serb smacked a leather cosh in his hand. "Can you hear me, Cane?"

When Jack didn't reply, the cosh smacked hard against his injured leg. An excruciating pain shot up his thigh and he stifled a cry. He came wide awake, fear stabbing at his heart. "Who—are you?"

"Where's the scroll?"

Jack heard the question, expected it, but said nothing.

The Serb nodded to his companion. "Let's see if we can jog his memory."

The second man took out a cigarette lighter, touched it to the tip of the blowtorch, and the flame lit. The torch glowed red, then turned an intense blue. The Serb said, "Burn off his fingers, one at a time. That'll loosen his tongue."

As Jack struggled, the man stepped forward with the blowtorch.

"*Stop.* That's enough for now."

A figure stepped out from the shadows. Blinded by the light, Jack couldn't see the man's face but he heard the authority in his voice. "Leave us. I'll call you when I need you to continue."

The Serb nodded. His companion doused the blowtorch, hung it on a metal hook by the gas bottle, and the three men left.

Slowly, the man who had spoken emerged out of the shadows. He took a handkerchief from his pocket and dabbed blood from Jack's mouth.

"Who are you?" Jack asked.

The man ignored the question. "You've chosen to walk on very dangerous ground, Mr. Cane. My men mean to kill you. But if you do as I say, perhaps—just perhaps—I'll spare your life."

"Who are you?"

"My name is Hassan Malik. You've heard of me?"

"Yes." Jack blinked, his skull still on fire with pain. "It's been a long time."

"But I never forgot you, Cane. We have an appointment with destiny."

"I haven't the remotest idea what you're taking about."

Hassan took a pack of cigarettes from his pocket, laid them on the table, and selected one before he produced a gold cigarette lighter. "Then you're about to learn exactly why Professor Green was murdered. And most important, why I want my scroll back."

"*Your* scroll?"

Hassan lit a cigarette, touching the lighter flame to the tip, then blew out a cloud of smoke. "Yes. It belongs to me. I planted it at Qumran."

117

The polished black Mercedes with tinted windows silently turned the corner of the Via della Conciliazione. Two other dark-windowed SUVs drove in front and two behind—like the Mercedes, they were specially armored to withstand even a rocket-propelled grenade. Each SUV carried Vatican security guards armed with sidearms and Heckler & Koch machine pistols.

John Becket sat in the back of the chauffeured limousine, his armed driver and a bodyguard occupying the front seats. As the cortege approached the broad barrier-controlled streets leading up to the Vatican, the sidewalks were lined with crowds making their way to St. Peter's Square.

Becket glanced out of the dark-tinted windows that hid his identity from the throng.

Next to him, Ryan observed the legions of worshippers that crammed the sidewalks and the gaudy souvenir shops and kiosks. "As they say on Broadway, it seems we have a full house."

"You and your men will have a busy afternoon, Sean."

"They'll earn their money, that's for sure. According to the carabinieri, over a quarter million people are expected in

Rome for your blessing. Naturally security will be tight, but I'd beg you once again to reconsider the bulletproof vest, Holy Father?"

The pope waved his hand as if to dismiss Ryan's question. "You said you had important news for me, Sean?"

Ryan stuck his fingers inside a brown leather briefcase on his lap. He produced a plastic evidence bag containing a single sheet of paper, made up of cut-and-paste newspaper letters stuck on the page. "The threatening letter I told you about that I had checked for prints."

"I'm listening, Sean."

Ryan waved the plastic bag containing the letter. "I'm afraid we didn't find a single print. However, we had the page analyzed by a forensics lab." He turned the page over and pointed to an illegible line of black characters. "The lab discovered these faint print characters on the back of the paper. Perhaps it was an old sheet that was discarded when the printer ink ran out. But luckily for us, the perpetrator obviously didn't notice it when he decided to use the page to assemble his collage of letters."

"What does all this tell us?"

"First, the typeface matches a mass-produced Hewlett-Packard printer commonly in use in all the curial cardinals' offices. There's absolutely no doubt the source was someone who works in those offices."

"But can you tell who exactly the printer belongs to?"

Ryan seemed genuinely embarrassed delivering the news. "Microscopic differences in printer ink and character formation can sometimes discern minute variations, even in material printed by mass-produced printers. This one belongs to Cardinal Cassini's office, it's his own private printer. It could, of course, mean that someone deliberately used the printer to falsely lay blame. Or it could point the finger. Only further investigation will tell."

The pope considered, then sighed and nodded. "You have my authority to do so. Is there anything else, Sean?"

"You asked me to check all the security tape footage from the Vatican archives, from the day after your election until you discovered that the archive documents went missing."

"Why do I have the feeling that you're going to tell me they were stolen?"

"I'm afraid so. With over a hundred cardinals, some will abuse their rank and choose not to sign the Secret Archives visitor's book. That's a breach of protocol, of course, but many young archivists are reluctant to challenge their superiors."

The Mercedes and its cortege approached one of the Vatican gate entrances, manned by the Swiss Guard. There was a barrier down, three uniformed Swiss Guards on duty. The pope said, "Who's the thief, Sean?"

Ryan stuck his hand in his briefcase and removed a DVD stored in a clear plastic case. "We turned up a possible suspect on this security disc from several days ago. You can see a figure entering the archives. It's obvious that he knew the building layout because he tries to keep his head down and remain in certain camera blind spots, but there's a camera or two we more recently installed that—"

"*Who*, Sean?"

There was a momentary distraction as the Swiss Guards lifted the barrier and saluted, and then the pope's Mercedes passed into the Vatican.

Ryan said solemnly, "I'd stake my life it's Cardinal Liam Kelly."

Five minutes later the pope entered his private apartments, and Ryan followed. Two of the pope's staff were already waiting, an array of papal vestments laid out on a long trestle table, others hung from a metal rail with wooden hangers.

Gold-threaded gowns were made of the finest linen and silk. The papal hat was embossed with silver and gold and encrusted with sparkling diamonds.

Exquisite slippers lined with Siberian fur were inlaid with precious gemstones, every garment exquisitely tailored by Italy's finest craftsmen. A secretary bowed. "We are ready to dress you whenever you are ready, Holy Father."

"I have no need of these garments."

"Pardon, Holy Father?"

Becket inspected a richly embroidered gown inset with dazzling gemstones, then replaced it on the table and fingered the simple wooden cross at his neck. "In a world scourged by poverty, I should have no need of these expensive garments. I will wear a simple smock. The one I'm wearing will do well enough. Along with my cross and sandals."

The secretary was aghast as he stared down at the pope's ragged footwear. "But Holy Father, the international press, TV cameras, and photographers from all over the world will be watching—"

"Then they will see what they should have always seen— that Christ's representative on earth has no need of such robes. People starve and cry out for shelter in this world. Why should I wear dazzling robes and mock them?"

"But—"

"I have spoken." The pope turned to Ryan. "Delay the cardinals' assembly in the Sistine Chapel. I will tell you when to summon them."

"Is there a problem, Holy Father?"

"I'd like a few moments alone to phone Cardinal Kelly. Then I wish to pray in the Sistine. I will have an important announcement to make when the cardinals join me."

Ryan inclined his head. "Of course. What about Cardinals Kelly and Cassini?"

"Detain them both."

118

"*You* planted the scroll." Confusion spread on Jack's face. "I don't get it. The parchment I found is genuine. Carbon-dating proved it."

"Of course it's genuine, Cane. Just like all the others discovered at Qumran. That's where it was originally found, months ago."

"By who?"

"Josuf, the Bedu foreman. He saw a copy of the site areas you meant to dig. On my instructions he did his own digging secretly at night, the way the Bedu always do. Several of the guards the Israelis employ are Bedu and turned a blind eye. After Josuf found it, I had it partly translated."

"You realized how explosive it was?"

Hassan nodded. "I'd been waiting a lifetime for such a prize. So I chose my moment and carefully had it reburied, as if it had never been found."

"For what reason?"

"I wanted you to find it, Cane."

"Why me?"

Hassan drew on his cigarette and blew out smoke. "Because as an archaeologist you have credibility. And because I knew that you would do your utmost to make the message the scroll contained public, no matter what it took."

"But why would a Bedu want the contents made public?"

Hassan's dark eyes flashed with anger. "I could give you many reasons, Cane. The Israelis destroy Arab settlements. They kill and imprison my people. They steal land that has always belonged to the Bedu, long before the Jews or your Christian Crusaders ever laid claim to it. Even today, you Christians do nothing about their pillage but pay it lip service."

"So that's what this is about, simple revenge?"

Hassan shook his head. "There is nothing simple about it. It encompasses centuries of wrongs and occupations. And for those wrongs your people will pay. A two-thousand-year-old truth will shatter your beliefs forever."

"And your father's death. Don't tell me you've got that score to settle as well?"

Hassan spat. "You're wrong. I despised my father. He was a fool who did the bidding of the Jews and the Vatican priests. A traitor who helped them unearth treasure that rightfully belonged to his own people, in return for a few miserable shekels. But you and your kind are the real thieves, Cane. You and your kind come here to steal from us. And for that, I mean to make you pay."

Hassan took a final drag on his cigarette. "The revelations the scroll contains are not easily dismissed. The Israelis will pay a heavy price too, once the world learns of the other parchments. There's an old Bedu saying: The desert wind whispers the truth."

"What's that supposed to mean?"

Hassan crushed his cigarette in a crystal ashtray. "The Bedu have heard the whispers for decades. How the Vatican and the Jews have kept secret the damning revelations of their religions found in the Qumran scrolls. Revelations that compromise both their faiths. It will prove interesting when the evidence is revealed."

Cane considered. "It seems to me that no sooner had I discovered the scroll than your plan went wrong."

"Yes, it went wrong, Cane," Hassan said bitterly and picked up the silvered Walther pistol from the table. "My plans were ruined. But now I have different plans and I want the scroll back. I think you know where it is, so I'm not going to waste time."

Hassan stepped back and opened the door. Jack saw the Serb waiting outside with his men. Hassan said, "Bring her in."

The Serb and one of his men vanished and reappeared moments later, dragging Yasmin between them. The Serb shoved her into a chair and tied down her wrists with a couple of lengths of rope. Her head lolled to one side and she barely seemed conscious.

Hassan snapped his fingers, the men left, then he crossed to Yasmin. Her hair spilled over the edge of the chair and there was dried blood on her lips.

Hassan said, "She has already confessed that you hid the scroll in a safe place, so don't lie to me, Cane."

Hassan slapped Yasmin's face. She came awake with a moan, her eyes trying to focus. Groggy, she took in the room, then stared at Jack.

Hassan gripped her face. "Good, you're awake. Nod if you understand me."

Yasmin nodded, wide-eyed with fear.

Hassan's arm snapped up and the Walther's barrel touched the nape of her neck. He turned to stare at Cane. "Now, tell me where the parchment is. Tell me everything, or so help me I'll put a bullet in her."

119

John Becket stepped into the cool air of the Sistine. It was scented faintly with incense. As always, he marveled at the riot of Michelangelo's colors, at the beautiful splendor and anguish of the scenes. Then he slowly crossed the marbled floor, aware of the rhythmic slap of his sandals. He knelt, made the sign of the cross, and prostrated himself in front of the altar.

He needed to be alone in the silence of the chapel. To reflect and to pray for guidance. For he knew that in a small way this would be his Gethsemane. That the drama on Michelangelo's walls would soon be reflected in his own soul. And that apart from exposing the Vatican's darkest secrets, he was about to make another dramatic revelation that would shock his cardinals.

The words spilled hoarsely from his lips. *O Lord, I ask for courage in this my hour of need, as I struggle to find the right words to convey the disclosure that I must reveal to the world.*

Lying on his stomach, pressing his face against the cold marble floor, Becket felt the drenching sweat begin immediately. He closed his eyes and began to pray.

120

In Umberto Cassini's office, Cardinal Liam Kelly dabbed sweat from his face. His hands shook as he picked up a crystal glass and swallowed his brandy in one gulp.

He heard a soft click and turned, startled, the bookshelf swinging open on its hinges as a grim-faced Cassini entered through the secret passageway. He carried a thick red file stuffed with papers and bound with waxed string.

"Umberto, you frightened me. Do you have to use the back passageways?"

Cassini slapped the thick file on his desk. "It saves time and allows me to avoid unwanted visitors. So, John Becket definitely won't change his mind?"

Kelly poured himself another brandy. "He called me and told me the answer's no, and it's final. His tone sounded unusually cold."

Cassini slumped into his chair. "Go on."

"Then Ryan phoned. He said that the pope wants to see us both after his speech to the cardinals. From the tenor of Ryan's voice, I'd say we're in trouble."

Cassini's mouth twisted in a faint, odd grin. "Do you really believe that, Liam?"

Sweat began to glisten on Kelly's upper lip. "Of course I

do. The game's up. It's not even a case of our transfer to some mission house in darkest Africa. Once these revelations come out and the fact that we helped cover up Kubel's actions all those years ago, we'll both be forced to leave the church in absolute disgrace."

"As will the pope."

"He doesn't seem to care. Only the truth matters to him."

The little Sicilian pushed himself up from his chair. "Let's be honest, Liam. We've simply hoped in vain that we could change the pope's mind. Now that small shred of hope is gone, but no one's ruined yet."

"What are you talking about, Umberto?"

Cassini picked up the thick red file from his desk and waved it in his hand.

"These are the documents you took from the Secret Archives."

"At your request, Umberto," Kelly countered.

"Yes, but for the protection of the church." Cassini grasped his letter opener by the deer-antler handle and slit the binding string. Then he gathered up the papers and spread them in the fireplace. He opened a desk drawer, found a cigarette lighter, and touched the flame to the papers, turning them over with the letter opener's blade to catch the rising flames.

"What are you doing?" Kelly demanded.

"What any sensible bureaucrat would do under the circumstances—destroying the evidence." Cassini watched as the flames licked at the paper.

Kelly looked aghast. "But you said we'd remove them temporarily until this trouble had died down. Destroying them will only make matters worse. Are you mad, Umberto?"

"Only John Becket can make matters worse." Cassini examined the letter opener, the tip blackened from soot. He polished it with a paper tissue he took from his pocket until the steel gleamed. His mouth twisted with contempt as he held up the inscribed blade. "You see what it says? *'With great affection, to a loyal and dutiful servant of God.'* Our last pope knew my value. He knew the importance of loyalty. But Becket, he's a traitor to the cause."

Kelly went to pour another brandy from the decanter but changed his mind, his speech already slurred. "Our day is over, Umberto. I should never have listened to you all those years ago and become involved in your dirty little schemes. *Never.*"

"But you did and it served you well. Look at you now. A full cardinal."

"Served me well?" Kelly gave a derisory laugh. "In another few hours I'll be nothing, not even a priest."

"There's still a way to stop Becket if we're bold enough."

"How?"

"By invoking an age-old Vatican practice that hasn't been in fashion for years: kill the reigning pope."

A stunned Kelly stared Cassini in the face and saw something close to madness in the wiry Sicilian's eyes. "Have you totally lost your mind, Umberto?"

Cassini's mouth twisted bitterly. "You said it yourself. There's a cancer that needs to be cut out. Becket's insane. His mission to expand the flock by embracing all Christians of the world is misguided. He'll destroy us all—priests, bishops, cardinals, all for his own glory. Are we going to allow a fanatic to destroy two thousand years of our history?"

Kelly was horrified. "This isn't the sixteenth century. Or the Roman Forum where murder is just another political tool. How could I condone anything like that, Umberto?"

"The same way you condoned Robert Cane's death."

Kelly moved toward the door. "A grave mistake that I'll no doubt roast in hell for. Good-bye, Umberto."

"Where are you going?" Cassini demanded.

"To confess everything to Ryan and take my chances."

Cassini grasped Kelly's sleeve. "Are you a traitor too? Doesn't anyone believe in loyalty anymore?"

Kelly tore free from his arm. "Let go of me; you're insane."

The scrawny Sicilian exploded with rage, and in an instant his hand swung through the air, the bone-handled steel moving in a perfect arc before it was embedded in Kelly's back.

Kelly gasped, his body contorting in agony as he fell back, clutching at handfuls of air. "Oh my God . . ."

Cassini was in the grip of an uncontrollable frenzy and dug the knife in again and again. Kelly's red smock blossomed with darker crimson patches. Finally, Cassini stood there, his chest heaving as he fought for breath. In that brief instant he seemed to realize what he had done and stared in horror at the bloodied letter opener clutched in his hand.

A heavy pounding sounded on the office's double oak doors. "Cardinal Cassini? Open up, it's Monsignor Ryan."

The pounding became louder, and then came the sound of a heavy thud and the doors shook, as if someone was hurtling himself against the wood. Cassini heard a crack of oak splintering.

The Sicilian froze, a snarl on his face, like a wildcat caught in the glare of headlights, but only for an instant. Still clutching the bloody letter opener, he darted into the passageway and pulled the bookshelf after him.

121

Outside Cardinal Umberto Cassini's office, Monsignor Sean Ryan aimed his Glock 27. Behind him stood an array of security staff and Cassini's secretary, all looking worried as Ryan leveled the barrel at the door lock.

He had already racked the Glock's slide and chambered a round. "Stand well back, all of you. I don't want a ricochet killing anyone."

In front of Ryan stood a massive pair of double oak doors that seemed impregnable. After minutes of kicking and heaving against the solid wood, Ryan had barely created a few splinters. Now he aimed his Glock at the gap between the door frame and the lock.

Cassini's secretary was aghast. "But Monsignor, what if there's someone behind the door—?"

Ryan figured the relatively low-velocity .40-caliber round wouldn't completely penetrate the thick oak. He ignored the secretary and fired a single shot. The noise boomed around the room and splintered the door. It took another shot before the wood around the lock cracked, and then Ryan heaved his boxer's shoulders against the oak. It gave way and he crashed into the office, almost losing his balance.

Ryan saw no sign of Cassini. As the others rushed in after

him, Ryan's eyes swept the room and he saw Kelly's body lying near the fireplace, blood oozing from a wound in his back. A flutter of black motes floated in the fireplace, where some flames were dying.

Ryan raced over to Kelly and examined his wounds. The cardinal's red gown was punctured with slits that looked like the work of a knife. "Call an ambulance at once."

Angelo Butoni felt Kelly's pulse. "A waste of time. He's dead."

Sweat rising on his face, Ryan scoured the huge office but he knew instinctively where Cassini had gone. He crossed to the bookcase, pressed the red leather-bound book, and the shelf swung open. He stepped cautiously into the darkened chamber and pulled the light string, the Glock readied.

The secret chamber looked empty, the winding stone staircase leading up and down. "What's the chance that Cassini's disappeared into one of his rat holes?" he said back to Butoni, who joined him, along with two more guards. Butoni nodded. "Kelly isn't dead long and the secretary didn't see Cassini leave his office."

With such a maze of Vatican tunnels and passageways, Ryan was temporarily perplexed, his mind working feverishly. "Remind me again where this passageway leads, Angelo?"

Butoni found a switch on the chamber wall, flicked it on, and an array of small red-tinted guide lights came on, illuminating the spiraling passageway walls. "I believe to one of our old armories, several floors below. It also leads to the archives, and out to several courtyards. In fact, pretty much anywhere you want it to, even the Sistine. This is one of the main channels, Monsignor."

"The Sistine?"

"Yes."

Ryan felt sweat drench his face. "The Holy Father went there to pray. *Which* armory, Angelo?"

"The small one on the second floor. It contains a cache of weapons in case of emergency. Pistols, rifles, even Heckler & Koch machine pistols. Why?"

Without a word, Ryan pushed past Butoni, almost knocking him over, and dashed down the passageway's stone steps as fast as he could run.

122

Umberto Cassini raced down the hidden stairway, clutching the hem of his cardinal's crimson gown. The patter of his feet on the stone steps moved at a frantic rhythm. His body pumped adrenaline, his gown drenched with the stench of perspiration, his pounding chest on fire. He came to a landing and a solid door with a handle.

Cassini clutched the handle, pushed in the door, and found himself in the old armory. It was a room familiar to him, used by the Vatican's security officers to store caches of weapons in case of emergency. Three long, sturdy, black metal boxes, with heavy locks, were pushed against one wall.

Cassini knelt in front of the first box and slipped the letter opener's blade between the underside of the lid and the bottom frame. He grunted as he pried. The blade stressed, but the metal box didn't budge. Cassini rattled the padlock in frustration. The lock was solid.

He wiped sweat from his face with his sleeve and tried the other two boxes, but clearly the blade wasn't strong enough to pry them open. Cassini had managed to raise the last box lid open about an inch when he heard footsteps and voices from beyond the open passageway door.

Ryan.

Cassini darted back into the passageway and raced farther down the winding steps.

123

"It's completely empty. They could be long gone."

"Gone where?"

"How should I know, Lela? They've been here but now the place is deserted. There's not a soul."

Lela stood on the lawn in front of Hassan Malik's luxury mansion. It looked majestic, with colonnades and gushing ponds, Roman and Greek statues. A turquoise swimming pool at the back was all lit up, just like the villa.

Except that the mansion was hollow, echoing.

A furious Ari and his men searched the property from top to bottom after Cohen scaled the walls, then managed to admit them through the front gate after picking the lock. Prepared for trouble, Cohen and Mario were armed with Uzi machine pistols, but they met none, every room deserted.

Ari vented his frustration as he stood beside the pool. "Wherever Hassan and his men have disappeared to is anyone's guess. Maybe he expected trouble and just decided to wind things down and get out of here."

Lela said, "Is this the only Italian property belonging to Hassan that Mossad knows of?"

Ari kicked out at a pool chair and sent it skittering across the tiles and splashing into the water. "This is it. And we've no other leads."

He stormed over to the patio doors on the back of the mansion. They were thrown open, lights blazing inside. Cohen and Mario with their Uzi machine pistols and powerful flashlights wandered the gardens searching for any evidence.

Ari had found the room at the back, with the chair and discarded lengths of rope, the oxyacetylene blowtorch attached to a bottle, a few bloodstains on the floor. But no sign of Jack Cane.

"They probably brought him here and tortured him," Lela said worriedly.

Ari lingered by the patio doors, clutching his pistol and slapping it against his leg in nervous agitation. "They obviously think he knows something."

Lela fell silent.

Ari turned to her. "You look guilty."

"Jack has the scroll."

"What?"

"He's hidden it in a safe place."

Ari fumed. "How long have you known this?"

"Since after I escaped from the underground."

Ari's fury was instant. "And you never told me? Whose side are you on, Lela?"

"I'm telling you now."

"Withholding information like that could have cost us the scroll, never mind what happens to your friend Cane. Weiss will have your head for this." Ari yanked out his phone and began to punch in a number.

"Who are you calling?" Lela asked.

"Weiss. He's still in Rome and isn't due to fly back to Israel until tonight." Ari's mouth twisted ironically. "But I'm pretty sure he'll delay his departure to talk to you."

Cohen came running up. "I've noticed something. Take a look over here."

Ari stopped making his call and they all followed Cohen around the side of the property and onto a huge lawn.

"You see what I see?" Cohen first pointed with his Uzi toward a wide concrete pathway. At the end was an empty aircraft hangar of some sort. Then with the barrel of his Uzi, Cohen followed the line of the path toward the lawn's center.

Ari stared at where Cohen's barrel ended—at a large circular marking on the ground, with a giant H in the center. "Yeah, it's a helicopter pad. So?"

"Where's the helicopter?"

124

Cassini stepped out of the secret passageway onto cold marble tiles. A false wall panel swung shut behind him and clicked back into place.

Dripping sweat, he found himself standing in a massive corridor with soaring white plaster walls and stained-glass windows. A few feet away a wood bench was positioned beneath a magnificent window.

Cassini grasped hold of the bench and dragged it, scraping across the marble floor, to position it in front of the false wall panel and block it from opening.

It would stop Ryan exiting the passageway.

Slow him down, at least for a time.

Cassini stood there resting, catching his breath again, his chest still aching with pain. When he regained his stamina he moved along the soaring hallway and halted in front of a pastel blue door. He was outside one of the Sistine Chapel entrances.

He pressed down on the door handle and pushed it open on its hinges without a sound. Silence was the watchword in the vicinity of any of the Vatican's chapels. Every hinge was well oiled or greased.

Cassini took a couple of calming breaths before he

stepped into the fourteenth-century chapel. The air was infused with the fragrance of incense. He loved the peace and drama of this chapel, with its motifs of power and pain, heaven and hell, torment and redemption.

He feasted his eyes on Michelangelo's powerful wall and ceiling images depicting the terror of the Apocalypse, the Creation, and the Flood. Standing there in the calm of the ancient chapel he suddenly felt a strange peace, and the pains in his chest ebbed away.

The peace before the tempest.

John Becket lay prostrate on his stomach on the floor, praying.

Cassini couldn't hear his prayers, only a hushed whisper. He knew there was no going back now. This was for the sake of the entire church. Someday, the value of his selfless deed would be recognized. Perhaps he would even be elevated to sainthood.

St. Umberto. The church's savior.

As he stared at John Becket's spread-eagled figure on the cold marble tile, Cassini felt his anger rise again as he concentrated on his reason for coming here.

To scourge the church of the traitor who threatened to destroy two thousand years of history.

Cassini took a step forward and heard a soft click of shoe leather.

He halted.

John Becket didn't move.

Cassini hesitated and looked down. His black slip-ons had leather soles. He nudged them off with his toes, heel by heel, until he was in his stocking feet. He began to step silently across the silky marble.

Eight yards.

Seven.

Six.

Cassini quickened his pace, his eyes fixed on Becket's back.

Five yards.

Four.

Three.

Two.

He stood over John Becket.

The pope must have sensed his presence because his back arched and he began to raise himself from the floor. Becket halted in a kneeling position, blessed himself, and turned. His brow creased when he saw Cassini standing over him. The Sicilian offered him a twisted grin.

"Umberto, what—" The words died in the pope's mouth as he put up his hands to defend himself.

Cassini pulled the metal blade from under his gown and spat out his reply. "Traitor! Devil! You will destroy no more!"

And in an instant Cassini's blade flashed and he plunged the steel into Becket, again and again.

125

Ryan's chest heaved as he sucked in mouthfuls of air. He raced down the corridor, Angelo Butoni behind him.

They came to a landing. Ryan saw a paneled door, slapped at the handle, and gave the door a powerful kick. It burst open and he stormed into a room, his Glock gripped in both hands, Butoni and the other security officers behind him.

Ryan's face was drenched in sweat as he swung his pistol barrel in an arc, scanning the armory, seeking a target.

Three sturdy, black metal boxes with heavy locks were pushed against one wall.

Ryan checked the locks and saw scrape marks on the surrounding paint. He rattled every lock. They were secure. "It looks as if someone's tried to pry open the boxes to get at the weapons."

"Cassini."

"Who else?"

The other guards thoroughly searched the room and checked the doors before Butoni said, "Every door's locked. I don't think Cassini hung around."

But Ryan was already darting back into the secret passageway. "He must be headed for the Sistine."

And Ryan plunged frantically down the winding steps, Butoni and the guards hard on his heels.

Moments later Ryan came to another landing and a wall panel. He turned the handle on the panel and pushed. The panel didn't budge. He slammed his shoulder against it and saw a crack appear, light spilling in from a hallway beyond. Butoni and the others joined him.

Ryan said, "There's something shoved against the panel. Give me a hand here, Angelo."

Butoni pushed his shoulder against the panel and both men heaved. The panel opened another inch. Ryan peered through the crack. "Curse it anyway. It looks like a bench is wedged against the door. Get back."

Ryan gestured for everyone to step back and he took a short run at the door and kicked it with the flat of his shoe. He felt the wood tremor and the object behind the panel appeared to budge. Encouraged, he shouldered the panel again and again. "Come on, give me a hand, all together now, heave."

A sweating Ryan, Butoni, and the others pushed and shoved, until at last the panel scraped open at least a foot and a half. Ryan squeezed through the gap, followed by the others.

They found themselves in a corridor. Soaring white plaster walls and stained-glass windows. Across the hall was a pastel blue door, an entrance into the Sistine Chapel.

A muffled cry of agony rang out. It seemed to echo from the chapel.

"Oh no!" Ryan uttered, and sprinted across the marble floor toward the blue door.

126

Ryan pushed open the door and stormed into the Sistine, the others behind him.

Ryan's face was misted with sweat and as he scanned the room everything seemed to happen in a kind of slow motion. Afterward, he would recall that what he saw was so disturbing and absurd. In this wonderful place of peace and solitude with its fragrant smell of incense, here he was clutching a loaded Glock, his sights searching out a target, which he soon found.

A disturbing sight caught his eye near the altar.

Cassini.

He was kneeling over John Becket's body, which was spread-eagled on its back on the marble tile. Cassini clutched a blade in both hands. He stabbed it into Becket's chest, again and again, the pope's white gown awash with crimson.

"Cassini!" Ryan's alarmed cry echoed around the chapel like an explosion.

Cassini's head snapped around, his eyes blazing with a deranged look, something close to madness, his own gown spattered with blood.

"Cassini, for pity's sake, stop!" Ryan screamed.

But Cassini ignored him and raised his hands to again bury the blade in the pope's body.

In an instant Ryan squeezed the Glock's trigger once, then once again, and two powerful .40-caliber rounds thudded into Cassini's chest and head. The force sent his body flying back across the altar, the shots exploding around the Sistine like bursts of thunder, the shock waves rippling and dying over the dazzling visions of Michelangelo's Apocalypse, the Creation, and the Flood.

127

The Lear jet entered Lebanese airspace just after 3:30 A.M., skimming above the clouds at twenty thousand feet.

Sitting in a leather passenger seat in the luxurious private cabin, Hassan Malik wore an expensive linen suit and shirt, Italian handmade shoes, and his Patek Philippe watch.

On the tray in front of him lay the curved Arab knife that had once belonged to his father, and to Nidal. The thought of his beloved Nidal lying cold as marble in a desert grave sent a ghostly chill down Hassan's spine. His eyes moistened.

He slid the curved blade from its scabbard and the polished metal gleamed, the edge scalpel-sharp. An aide came through the cabin. "A call from Rome, sir. And the captain says we should be landing in thirty minutes."

Hassan slammed the blade into the scabbard. "Good. Tell Bruno to come in here."

"Yes, sir." The aide left.

Hassan took the satellite phone. He listened to the voice at the other end as it spoke for several minutes, and when the conversation ended, Hassan said, *"Mille gratzi.* I appreciate the news. *Arrivederci."*

The line clicked dead and Hassan put aside the phone

as the door to his private cabin snapped open. The Serb appeared. "You wanted me, Mr. Malik?"

Hassan picked up the curved Arab blade in its scabbard and tossed it to the Serb, who caught it. "Wake up Cane and bring him here. Then you know what to do."

———

Jack woke with a blinding headache. He felt a sinking sensation. He blinked open his eyes. He was covered with a blanket and seated in a large, comfortable leather seat in what appeared to be a private aircraft. The dimly lit cabin had similar plush seats on both sides of the narrow aisle. Darkness raced beyond the oval windows.

He had a faint recollection of telling Hassan everything, then the Serb jabbed him with a hypodermic before they had dragged him from Hassan's mansion to a helicopter. After that he blacked out. He heard a sigh and turned his head.

Yasmin lay on the seat next to him, a blanket draped over her body. He could hear her breathing softly, her dark eyelashes closed, her beautiful face angelic in sleep. He smelled the almond scent of her. He couldn't help but reach out to stroke her hair. She murmured in her sleep. He thought, *Who is she?*

Across the cabin, he recognized two of Hassan's bodyguards, tough-looking men in suits who lounged in their seats. One slept, his arms folded and his head thrown back, mouth open as he snored. The other man was awake and watchful, and stared blankly at Jack.

A cabin door behind him opened. The Serb appeared. "So, you've decided to join us again. How do you feel, Cane?"

"Like I've been kicked by a camel."

The Serb grinned and pulled away the blanket. "And the fun hasn't even started yet." He grabbed Jack viciously by the hair and dragged him up. "Move. Someone wants to talk with you."

128

Jack was pushed into another cabin. Hassan sat in a leather seat, his expression blank. The Serb forced Jack into the seat opposite and withdrew, leaving them both alone.

Jack said to Hassan, "What's happening? Where are you taking me?"

"Back to my homeland, Cane. We'll be landing shortly."

"You'll be arrested. Mossad will find you. They're not stupid—"

"I'm well aware of Mossad and their ways. We're not landing in Israel. But over the border in Jordan, at a private airfield."

"And the plan is?"

"To retrieve the scroll. The desert is the Bedu's home, Cane, and always has been. No Israelis or border patrols will ever stop that. But we'll remain near the border with Israel, for safety." Hassan held up the satellite phone. "The call has already been made to have someone bring the scroll to us."

Hassan snapped his fingers. Jack looked up. Behind him the Serb had reappeared in the cabin doorway, holding a savage-looking curved Arab blade. The Serb grabbed Jack by the hair, yanked back his head, and held the knife against his throat.

Hassan said, "Just a friendly warning. If you've lied to me about the location of the scroll, Bruno will slit your throat."

"I told the truth."

The Serb let go of Jack's hair and stepped back.

Jack said to Hassan, "Why does the scroll still matter to you if the Vatican opens its archives?"

Hassan tossed the satellite phone on the seat opposite. "So you claim. But I wouldn't count on that, Cane. The news I heard from Rome is that your friend Becket was stabbed by a knife-wielding madman and is not expected to live. Whoever succeeds Becket, I doubt that he'll be willing to be assassinated for the sake of revealing the truth."

Jack said in disbelief, "You're lying—"

"I have no cause to. No doubt it'll soon be in every newspaper in the world. Nothing will change in the Vatican now, not ever. You say you left the parchment hidden under the gravel at your parents' grave. It makes sense." Hassan nodded to the Serb, who disappeared a moment, then reappeared with Yasmin, who stepped into the cabin.

Hassan said to her, "Well? Has Cane told the truth about where he buried the parchment?"

Yasmin's face was pale with torment as she stared over at Jack, then turned to answer Hassan. "I was with him at the gravesite. For a time he had his back to me, so he could have hid something under the gravel."

"One good truth deserves another." Hassan forced a smile, stood, and put his arm around Yasmin, whose brown eyes never left Jack's face. "It's time I introduced you to my sister."

129

Monsignor Sean Ryan clutched his hands together in prayer and paced the corridor outside the emergency room in Rome's Gemelli Polyclinic Hospital.

He prayed with every step.

Prayer was a habit with him: he prayed every single morning, afternoon, and night. But at that moment, the focus of his prayer was John Becket.

Ryan felt a sickness in the pit of his stomach and looked down at his clutched hands. They were shaking. He had killed Cassini. The team of paramedics and doctors who came to attend to the pope had pronounced the Sicilian cardinal dead.

"He was probably dead before his head even hit the marble altar," a medic later observed, seeing the massive wounds the .40-caliber slugs had inflicted on Cassini's skull and chest.

Ryan still felt shaken. He had taken a life. His cloud of depression was made only worse by his knowledge that the pope was not expected to live through the night.

Ryan was drawn to a blaze of light beyond the corridor windows and paced over to the glass. The world had gone raving mad.

Powerful television arc lamps illuminated the hospital. The parking lot was a chaos of media crews, TV vans with satellite dishes, and heaving crowds, all eagerly awaiting news.

Ryan knew from the Vatican Press Office that more than a thousand carabinieri and police were drafted to keep back the surging masses. But still the crowds came, to gape, to pray, to wait—the fearful, the hopeful, the curiosity seekers, the doomsday mongers.

A mute TV hung from a corner ceiling of the corridor. It caught Ryan's eye for the umpteenth time in the last half hour. The screen spewed out file footage of Pope Celestine and the Vatican, live shots of the hospital, and interviews with every religious commentator on the planet giving their two cents' worth.

Ryan turned back as a surgeon wearing a blood-spattered green gown came out through the double doors of the emergency room. The man crossed the corridor and bought a coffee from a vending machine. Then he stepped toward an open window, lit an illicit cigarette, and inhaled deeply. Ryan noticed that about Italian doctors: so many of them had the nicotine habit.

He saw the surgeon pace the floor as he drew hard on his cigarette. The man's expression was bleak, edgy. Ryan recognized him as one of the ER team attending John Becket. Ryan saw the surgeon glance over at him. Their eyes met. No words were spoken, but Ryan raised an eyebrow in query. *How goes it?*

The surgeon gave a slight shake of his head—*it doesn't*—then he stubbed out his cigarette and returned briskly through the ER's swinging doors.

A rush of footsteps sounded in the corridor and Ryan looked round. A tall, unshaven priest rushed up, clutching at least three cell phones and looking harried. The Vatican press officer, Father Joe Rinaldi, asked anxiously, "Any more news, Sean?"

"I was told to expect the worst. He's in a coma. Clinging to life by a thread."

Rinaldi dabbed his face. "I better prepare the press releases. It's sheer madness outside. I had to switch off my cell phones for a few minutes, just for a break. Every TV and news editor in the world is jamming the lines looking for an update. What have the surgeons said?"

"He's got at least nine deep stab wounds. Two to his hands as he tried to fend off Cassini's blows, others to his side, head, and chest. They've pierced organs, severed veins, and he's lost blood by the liter. They've got him hooked up to life support but I've been warned that it might not be for long. It's bleak, Joe. I believe we've lost him and we just have to accept that."

Rinaldi's pallid face was a mask of confusion, his eyes suddenly moist. "Whoever would have thought? The best thing to happen to the church and now we're losing him. What are we to make of it all, Sean?"

Ryan clutched the press officer's arm. "I wish I knew. Do you believe in miracles, Joe?"

"Working in this business, I've got to."

"Then start praying for one, because that's the only hope we've got."

130

Buddy Savage pushed his baseball cap back off his head and wiped the gritty 4 A.M. tiredness out of his eyes. He tried to focus on the Land Cruiser's twin headlights as they flooded the dark desert road beyond Qumran.

Despite his tiredness, Savage felt alert, scared, and excited.

The tangerine dawn hadn't yet tinted the horizon and when he reached the rise in the road the Land Cruiser's beams swept over the gravestone. Savage halted, keeping the powerful beams directed at the grave, and snapped on the handbrake. He left the engine running and jumped out of the cabin.

The desolate landscape was bitterly cold. It would be another hour before dawn struggled behind the mountains of Edom. Buddy Savage shivered and felt an odd feeling of exhilaration rip through his veins.

A goat bleated in some far distant Bedouin camp. Savage ignored it as he knelt in front of the grave, using the wash of the headlights as he scrabbled madly at the gravel. Rummaging and digging below the pebble, he finally grasped the package under loose earth. It was wrapped neatly in a black garbage bag.

The scroll.

His heart raced as he opened the loose knot that tied the garbage bag. Inside he found the parchment, protected in a clear plastic bag. He carefully examined his find and noticed that some parts of the parchment were already crumbling. But it was still intact, which was all that mattered.

He crumpled the black garbage bag and tossed it away. His anxiety rose as he carried the precious parchment back to the Land Cruiser.

Carefully holding the scroll with one hand, he picked up a worn leather briefcase from the passenger seat and flicked it open. He gently laid the scroll inside the briefcase, holding it in place with two pieces of white foam, then he sweated as he picked up his cell phone and punched in the redial key.

The anonymous male caller answered. "Well?"

"I have the scroll. It's where you said it was."

"Good. You know what to do next, Savage. Any mistakes, any involvement by the Israelis, police or military, or anyone else, and Jack Cane is a corpse. Is that very clear?"

Savage's voice was flecked with a mix of fear and anger. "I'm pleading with you not to harm Jack."

"Do exactly as you've been told and he won't be. But disobey my instructions, and I swear he'll die. I've told you the rules. You come alone, Savage."

"I heard you the first time you called."

"And you had better not be armed."

"Do you think I'm crazy? I told you, I'll do whatever you say."

"We meet in an hour, the place where I said. I'll call you then."

"What about cell phone reception in the area? It can't be that great."

"Don't worry, Savage. There's enough signal coverage." The line clicked dead.

Savage's face twisted and he spat the words. "You better be sure about that, pal."

He punched in another number on the cell phone's keypad.

When a voice answered, he spoke for at least five minutes before he terminated the call and tossed the phone on the passenger seat.

Then he swung the Land Cruiser east, toward the Jordanian border.

131

The desert airfield was fifteen miles inside Jordan's border, near the Dead Sea. It had long ago been abandoned. Weeds grew on the cracked concrete, a perfect home to lizards, snakes, and scorpions, and camel thorn bush blew across it when the desert wind shrieked. But that early morning the wind was calm and the landing conditions near perfect, despite the darkness.

The runway had last seen service over twenty years ago by the Jordanian air force. Now the control tower was a derelict mess. Every window was broken, the doors and plumbing scavenged.

Two hours earlier a convoy of pickup trucks had drawn up.

At least two dozen Bedu men jumped down. A pair of the pickups kept their lights dimmed as they drove along the runway, the men working in front as they swept away gravel and rocks and removed any foreign objects from the concrete until the runway was clear of all debris.

A young man wearing spectacles and a Bedu headdress checked the wind direction. The air was still as a rock. Then he climbed into one of the pickup trucks and drove to the far end of the runway, reversing the truck a few yards out into the desert before he halted and jumped out.

An object in the back of the truck was covered with a rainproof tarpaulin and he ripped it away. Underneath was a radio transmitter dish hooked up to a portable power supply and a laptop.

As the young man switched on the laptop, his comrades in two of the other pickups drove along each side of the runway, stopping every sixty feet and placing plastic, battery-operated electric lanterns on the runway's edge, then adjourned to the runway's edge to brew tea on a battered portable Primus stove.

The young man watched the laptop's bright blue screen fill with data as the portable Instrument Landing System computer worked through its loading sequence. A motor whirred and adjusted the radio dish to transmit the glide slope at a perfect three-degree angle. Minutes later, the computer finished its setup.

Satisfied, the young man grinned to himself, jumped down off the truck, and then went to join his comrades making tea.

132

Jack felt a sinking sensation again as the Lear nosed down.

Yasmin peered out the oval starboard window. A few weak streaks of dawn's burnt orange light tinted the cabin. "We'll be landing soon."

They were alone. Hassan and the Serb had moved into the rear cabin. Yasmin sat back in her seat and looked over at him. "No doubt you want to know why I tricked you."

"I'd be lying if I said it hadn't crossed my mind. What's your real name?"

"Fawzi."

"I think I preferred Yasmin. In fact, let's keep it simple and I call you Yasmin."

She shrugged, her face even more beautiful in the cabin's soft light. "Can I say something, Jack? We both know what pain is. You lost your parents. I lost mine. Do you know how my mother died?"

"No."

Her eyes misted with pain. "I was five. The day my father died she went to Jerusalem on the pretense of being consoled by her sister. Instead, my mother hung herself. All because she couldn't stand the indignity of raising a family without her husband. My world fell apart that day."

"I never knew."

"Had it not been for Hassan, Nidal and I probably would have starved to death in some gutter. But Hassan was always such a good brother to us. He begged, he stole, his own belly went hungry so he could feed us. He did whatever he had to do to keep us together. Many evenings I saw the calluses on his hands and the exhaustion in his eyes from hard work. He was still not much more than a child himself."

"So you helped him out of a sense of duty."

"You make it sound so flippant, Jack."

"I didn't mean to. I'm just stating a fact."

She stared back. "Of course I helped him. He did so much for me. Washed me, clothed me, replaced the love I lost from my parents. And when he had crawled out of the gutter, he gave me the best education money could buy. Hassan isn't a beast, Jack. He's a good man. A good man with a lot of harm done to him—to his head, to his heart and soul, just like you. But no matter how hurt he was himself, he would always assure me that everything would be all right." Her eyes became wet. "And now with Nidal gone, Hassan's all the family I have left."

"How did Professor Green get to play a part in your little game?"

"Green was a ladies' man, easy to manipulate. Hassan wanted someone he could trust on site when the scroll was discovered. Someone to keep him informed. Who better than his own family? He had Josuf's help, of course, but he wasn't family, and Hassan didn't fully trust him, and rightly so."

"What do you mean?"

"He worked for Hassan. That's why he took us to Maloula, on Hassan's orders, to meet the black-market thieves his brother dealt with and to try to find out where the scroll had disappeared. Unfortunately, Josuf was also an Israeli informer when they paid him enough. But now he is no more."

"You mean he's dead?"

"It's the Bedu way, Jack. Deceit carries a heavy price. Josuf's family will be taken care of financially by Hassan. But Josuf betrayed his tribe."

"How did you manipulate Green?"

"I made it my business to bump into him in a hotel bar in Jerusalem. The rest, as they say, was easy."

"Sex in return for a ringside seat to keep watch on your brother's big plan?"

Yasmin shook her head. "There was no sex, I made sure of that, only the promise of it. Green was entranced by me, wanted us to spend time together. I told him I was fascinated by archaeology. With a little coaxing he came up with my cover story. As his niece, I'd have a tent nearby and he could see all of me he wanted to, without raising suspicion."

"Clever. Kisses and hugs for Professor Green when no one was looking, and his hopeful prospect of sex down the line."

"That about sums it up."

"I'm not surprised Green fell for it. I did too. You're good, I'll give you that. And here was me thinking you might have liked me. But there's something I don't understand. After we left the Vatican and sat in the café you alerted me to Nidal and his buddy. Why?"

"Hassan's plan was to abduct you, along with me. That's why I followed you out of the café, ultimately to make it easier. I had phoned Hassan, told him you'd confided in me and you'd hidden the scroll. Nidal was to take us to Hassan's villa to interrogate you and get the information from you. By me alerting you to the danger, it would help protect my cover."

"Then Hassan could use the ploy of threatening to harm you to make me reveal where I'd hidden the scroll."

"Yes."

"But then the Israelis appeared and ruined it all?"

She nodded. "Nidal thought it wiser if I disappeared with him into the tunnels. He didn't like the idea of leaving me with Israelis."

"I guess I really fell for it, didn't I?"

"I'm sorry that you've been used and hurt, Jack. But there was no other way."

The Lear jet lurched as the air brakes deployed, slowing the aircraft, lifting it slightly. Yasmin peered out. "Another few minutes and we'll be on the ground."

"And then?"

"Hassan has Bedu friends who'll take us close to the border but not over it—we don't want the Israelis interfering in what happens next."

"And what's that exactly?"

"An exchange. We get the scroll and you get your freedom."

"Somehow I doubt the latter. Who's doing the exchanging?"

"Hassan called Buddy Savage and told him where the scroll was buried. He gave him instructions to bring it to us, otherwise you'd die. But I promise you no harm will come to you, Jack, just so long as Buddy doesn't try any double-cross." Her eyes moistened. "I've lost Nidal. There's been enough killing. I don't want any more of it."

"So the bottom line is, Hassan wants the scroll back."

"It rightfully belongs to the Bedu. Just like all the other scrolls found at Qumran. Hassan now intends to release them to the public, along with dozens of other scrolls he's collected over the years. They will expose the Israelis and the Vatican for what they are, liars and thieves."

"Why didn't he do that long ago?"

"He had evidence but not enough. This scroll was the

solid proof that he'd always hoped to find. It was the jewel in the crown." She came over and took hold of his face. Leaning forward, she kissed him on the lips and looked into his eyes. "And just for the record, I did like you, Jack. I still do. If things were different, who knows what might have become of us?"

"That's a polished brush-off, I'll give you that."

She reached out and gently grazed his cheek with her hand. "A word of advice, Jack. Please don't meddle with Hassan. If you try anything that would jeopardize the exchange, I promise you, my brother will kill you."

"He'll kill me anyway, I'll guarantee you that."

A moment later the plane lurched and a cabin light chimed on. The cabin door opened and Hassan appeared, slid into the seat, and buckled his belt. "You made it clear to Cane what will happen if his friend Savage messes this up?"

"Yes, Hassan."

"Good." Hassan glared at Jack. "Remember the warning, Cane."

The Lear banked sharply and dipped again, the landing gear whirring into place. Jack peered past the window. A faint orange glow streaked the horizon. He thought he recognized the distant shape of the mountains of Edom.

Minutes later the knot of fear he felt in his stomach turned to steel as the Lear finally touched down with a wild squeal of rubber.

133

Three hundred miles away, another Lear jet was fifteen minutes from commencing its final approach into Tel Aviv's Ben-Gurion Airport.

Julius Weiss handed a satellite phone back to his aide, who immediately exited the cabin. Weiss sighed, made a steeple of his fingers, and turned to address Ari and Lela, seated opposite.

"It seems our intelligence was right. Air traffic control registered that the helicopter from Bracciano landed at a private airfield outside Rome. Fifteen minutes later the Lear jet owned by Hassan Malik departed the same airfield, with a flight plan bound for Beirut. However, they altered the flight plan midflight."

"For where?" Ari asked.

"Amman, Jordan. Except Amman air traffic control hasn't heard from them yet. Hassan Malik may well have used the Beirut and Amman destinations as a ploy. Which means he could be headed anywhere." Weiss's mouth tightened in a look of frustration. "What the devil is he up to? We logged another flight Hassan made yesterday to Amman."

Lela frowned. "I don't understand."

"He flew to Amman in his private jet, with his brother's

body on board. Where he went after that we couldn't determine. But less than three hours later he flew back to Rome, minus the body. It seems he may have buried his brother. And one of our operatives too."

"Who?"

Weiss addressed Lela. "The Bedu foreman on the Qumran site, Josuf. He was an occasional source who fed us tidbits of information when it suited him. It was he who told us Cane was headed for Maloula. Josuf was due to contact Mossad yesterday but hasn't been heard from. I have a terrible feeling that Hassan may have discovered his treachery and dealt with him."

Weiss fixed Lela with an icy stare. "Well, Inspector, any suggestions as to where we might find Hassan? Seeing as you helped to get us into this mess?"

"My gut instinct tells me he's headed to wherever Jack hid the scroll, which is probably somewhere near Qumran. There must be dozens of abandoned military airfields out in the desert where his aircraft could land."

"You have a point."

Ari said to Lela, "Maybe he's already killed Cane."

"Wouldn't it make more sense to keep him alive until the scroll's retrieved?"

Weiss considered, then ran a hand tiredly over his face and sighed again. "Maybe, but Hassan's a wily fox who has the advantage. And our big problem is that Cane really could have hidden the scroll anywhere, not just near Qumran."

Lela said, "What if Hassan finds it?"

"Then all hell will break loose. I do hope you have a good pension plan, Inspector." Weiss suddenly looked tired. "In fact, I'm going to need one myself. To be honest, I intend to hand in my resignation to the prime minister as of tomorrow.

I'm getting too old for this game, and I'm not sure I like it anymore. Maybe it's time to do something less stressful, like opening a topless bar in Gaza."

Weiss's aide came through the cabin again, still holding the satellite telephone. "Sorry to disturb you, sir, but it's urgent. Another call has come through and I have a feeling we may need to overfly Tel Aviv. Detour to one of our military air bases near the Jordanian border."

"What the devil are you talking about? A call from whom?" Weiss demanded.

"Sergeant Mosberg from the Jerusalem police. He wants to speak with Inspector Raul."

134

<hr>

Buddy Savage halted the Land Cruiser and killed the headlights. He was fifteen minutes from the Jordanian border.
Barren desert lay ahead, broken only by clumps of rocks
and a few palm-fringed wadis.

He knew that the nearest Israeli military outpost was five
miles away but their patrols diligently scoured the surrounding area. Savage worried about that. Just as he worried about
how the endgame was going to play out. He plucked a pair of
powerful Zeiss binoculars from the glove compartment and
swept the landscape, dusky with a faint murky gray.

Nothing.

Not even a light or a plume of dust to indicate that he
wasn't alone. His cell phone chirped. Savage's heart skipped.
He flipped it open. "Yeah?"

"Are you near the rendezvous, Savage?"

"Near enough. Maybe fifteen minutes away."

"Continue to drive southeast. After five miles you'll
reach a wadi, with a half-dozen palms. Halt your vehicle, step
twenty yards away from it, and wait."

Savage didn't reply.

The silence went on and then the voice said, "Did you hear
me, Savage?"

"Yeah, I heard you, but there's been a change of plan," he said matter-of-factly.

"There's only one plan, Savage. The one I told you about—"

Vehemence sounded in Savage's reply. "Listen, you piece of dirt, whoever you are. Just shut your mouth and hear what I have to say or you can kiss the scroll good-bye—that's a promise."

Savage heard the stunned silence down the line, and then the reply was pure fury. "Savage, you don't know who you're dealing with. If a man talks to me like that, he'd better be prepared to lose his life."

"Maybe you didn't hear me right the first time. I said shut your mouth. Now you're going to listen to *my* plan. Because if you think I'm going to walk into a trap you've got to be a total moron. I've got the scroll. And you want it. Are we at least clear on that? So from now on you do as *I* say."

"I've got your friend Cane," the caller protested, his voice still firm, but a slight waver there.

"Yeah, and his life obviously ain't worth a cent if you're prepared to trade it for the parchment. So this is how it's going to pan out, pal; this is how we're going to do our trade. But a word of warning: you try and mess with me and I swear I'll burn the scroll to ashes. Got that?"

There was a long pause. Savage could almost feel the white-hot anger on the line, and then the voice, suddenly calm and very composed, said, "What do you propose?"

"This isn't a proposal, it's an order. You come alone and you bring Cane. And now here's exactly how we're going to do it."

Savage sat for a moment, sweating, breathing deeply, thinking hard. His mind was ablaze as he removed his baseball cap and wiped his brow. He didn't like the sound of the caller's voice. Angry at first, then perfectly calm. A real pro, he guessed. Not someone you messed with.

But then neither was he.

Turning back to the briefcase, Savage hefted out a Browning 9mm pistol with polished walnut handles. The same gun Pasha had given him in case there were ever problems. The same gun he'd threatened Professor Green with before he'd used the knife instead and stabbed him to death.

Savage had stashed the pistol at Qumran behind a rock marker, ready to be retrieved if he needed it. And he needed it now. He needed it to put everything to bed, tie it all up in a neat bow, once and for all.

Nothing had gone the way he'd originally planned. The whole scheme was messed up, everything all over the place like a madman's mind. But then every dark cloud had a silver lining. And he'd just been handed one—a chance to resolve the entire mess.

Savage felt the solid weight of the Browning pistol in his hand and checked to see that the magazine was loaded before he snapped it home. Then he tucked the pistol inside the briefcase and clicked it shut. He turned the ignition key and the Land Cruiser's engine throbbed to life. He dimmed the lights and turned in an arc, heading for his new rendezvous.

135

The Serb turned the pickup onto the rocky desert track. Hassan sat in the passenger seat. Jack felt cramped between both men, his hands bound in front of him with thin, blue plastic rope. Dawn was still struggling to rise over the mountains of Edom.

Hassan said, "Pull in here."

The Serb halted and jerked on the handbrake. The second pickup following them pulled up right behind. Hassan jumped out, clutching a pair of night-vision binoculars and used them to sweep the dusky, rolling desert landscape. Behind him, Yasmin disembarked from the other pickup and joined him. "Do you see Savage's vehicle?"

"I see nothing." Hassan put down the binoculars, his usually composed face tight with concern.

Yasmin said, "I don't like this, Hassan."

"Neither do I. But then nothing ever goes as planned, does it?" He kissed her on the forehead. "You will remain here, sister."

"No, I want to go with you."

Hassan's hand came up and gently cupped her face. "No, you'll stay. I don't want you exposed to any more danger." He slipped out a thin flashlight and flicked it on and off before he returned it to his pocket. "No matter what happens, stay put in the second pickup unless I give the signal that it's safe to move, or I contact you on your cell phone. Otherwise, stay back at least a mile and keep the headlights off."

"What about Cane? He's not a bad man, Hassan, he's not—"

Her brother put up his hand to silence her. "This is not the time for talk."

Hassan clicked his fingers and the Serb jumped out of the driver's seat. One of the bodyguards tossed him a Heckler & Koch machine pistol. The Serb climbed into the back of the pickup, cocked the weapon, and made sure the safety was on.

"Remember," Hassan told him. "You don't move unless I tell you to."

"Of course, Mr. Malik." The Serb grinned, as if relishing trouble, then lay down flat in the pickup, out of sight.

Yasmin asked, "Are you certain this is wise, Hassan? Savage said you were to go alone and unarmed."

"Don't question me. I know what I'm doing. I know the area where Savage wants to meet. It's right on the border and there's more rock cover, which is to his advantage, but remember we have Cane." Hassan gestured to one of the other bodyguards from the second pickup. "Bring him here."

The man did as he was told and dragged Cane from the truck cab over to Hassan, who stared him in the face. "You'll do the driving, Cane. I'll tell you which direction to take to meet Savage."

Jack met his stare. "No doubt you'll kill him too?"

Hassan showed not a flicker of emotion. "That all depends."

"On what?"

"If he safely hands over my property, everyone can go on their way. But if Savage double-crosses me, or either of you tries anything, I swear, Cane, you'll both die."

136

Savage saw the pinpricks of headlights approach through the binoculars. They were at least a mile away, he guessed, the dawn light a murky gray.

He stood on a rugged outcrop of rock, the Land Cruiser parked nearby. The rocks would offer him solid cover if there was any shooting.

The headlights drew closer. He scanned the desert for any other signs of life but saw nothing, and heard only the faint throbbing of the approaching engine. It was too dark to distinguish the solid form of the vehicle just yet.

He stepped down off the rocks and moved back to the Land Cruiser, tossed the binoculars on the seat, and slid out the briefcase. He clicked it open again and removed the Browning pistol. He flicked off the safety and cocked the slide, chambering the first round. One thing he'd never forgotten from his stint in Vietnam was how to use a gun. He'd been a good shot, not a virtue he boasted about. He flicked on the safety again, lay the pistol down, and picked up the binoculars once more.

The headlights came closer.

Even in the poor light he was pretty certain it was a single vehicle.

He listened carefully and heard the low growl of an engine. He saw no trace of any other vehicles or movement in the murky landscape.

It was still cold out in the desert and he shivered, as much from the temperature as from a growing fear. He knew now what he was going to do, everything planned out in his head, or as much of it as he could.

Using one hand, he held on to the briefcase by placing four of his fingers behind the bottom part of the case, his thumb against the front part. Using his free hand, he slipped the pistol between his four fingers and the briefcase, keeping the weapon pressed hard against the leather so that it was out of sight.

The headlights came closer and turned in a slight arc.

Savage flipped open his cell phone with his free hand and thumbed the redial. It rang. The man's voice sounded when it picked up. "We're here, Savage. I can see you."

Savage said curtly, "Well, I can't see you. Turn on the interior light like I told you."

The cab light came on. Inside, Savage saw Jack in the driver's seat. An Arab was seated beside him. Arrogant-looking, wearing a pale linen suit and open-necked shirt.

Savage put up his left hand, indicating for the pickup to stop.

Jack braked and it came to a halt with a squeal.

Savage spoke into the phone to the Arab. "Kill the lights and switch off the engine."

The lights and the engine died.

"Tell Jack to get out of the car. You do the same."

Jack stepped out. Hassan followed.

Savage, close enough now to be heard, put down his cell phone and said to the Arab, "We meet at last."

"You have the scroll?" Hassan demanded.

Savage held up the briefcase, still concealing the Browning pistol. "Right here. So how about we get this dirty little business over and done with and we can all be on our way?"

137

Hassan was silent a few moments, then said, "You've caused me a lot of trouble, Mr. Savage."

"I'm not here to listen to your woes. Let's get this done with."

Hassan said, "I've kept my part of the bargain, now keep to yours."

Savage held out the briefcase, his thumb on top, his fingers below, holding the Browning in place. "Here, take it. The scroll's inside."

"Toss it on the ground, away from you."

"There's a two-thousand-year-old scroll in here. If it was me, I wouldn't want to risk damaging it. But that's your choice."

"Toss it on the ground," Hassan repeated.

Savage seemed to hesitate, and then some instinct in Hassan sensed danger and he stepped backward toward the pickup and called out, "Bruno!"

Jack shouted, "Look out, Buddy!"

At that precise moment, the Serb rose from the back of the pickup. He raised the Heckler & Koch just as Savage dropped the briefcase and brought up the Browning. He fired twice, and twice again, hitting the Serb in the chest, sending him flying backward, his body toppling from the rear of the truck into the sand. He lay sprawled and motionless, then gave a groan.

As the gunfire echoed across the desert a shocked Hassan raced to grab the machine pistol. Savage fired again, hitting him in the shoulder, spinning him round, knocking him off his feet. But Hassan struggled to his knees and crawled toward the machine pistol with a fierce determination.

Savage stepped over and put the Browning against the back of Hassan's neck. "Go ahead, try to pick it up. But it'll be the last thing you'll ever do."

Hassan turned and collapsed in the sand, clutching his bloody shoulder and staring up at Savage with a look of pure vehemence. "You've signed your own death warrant, American."

"I did that long ago." Savage picked up the Heckler & Koch.

Jack crossed to Hassan, searched his pocket, and pulled out his cell phone.

Savage said, "What are you doing?"

"Bringing this to an end." Jack tossed the phone to Hassan. "Call your sister. Tell her to come here alone. And I *mean* alone."

138

Moments after Hassan made the call they saw the headlights appear. Dawn's burnt orange painted the horizon. The approaching vehicle, a light-colored pickup, was visible in the distance. Savage looked worried as he went over to the Serb's sprawled body, felt for a pulse, and said, "He's gone. It couldn't be helped."

He crossed to Hassan, examined his bloody shoulder, and said, "I've seen worse. You'll live."

"But will you, Savage?" Hassan replied sourly.

"You're perky, I'll give you that." He turned to Jack. "Who is he?"

"His name's Hassan Malik."

Savage raised an eye. "I've heard stories about him. Poor Bedu boy turned rich. That the guy?"

"Yes." Jack saw the headlights speed closer. "Where did you learn how to shoot like that?"

"Once a marine, always a marine. Tell me more about Hassan. What's his angle in all of this?"

By the time Jack told him, the headlights were less than a hundred yards away. "Cover the pickup, just in case," he told Savage.

Savage leveled the Heckler & Koch and shook his head in disbelief. "What a story. He planted the scroll?"

"He wanted it found and the world to know about it, Buddy."

"I guess he succeeded. And destroyed us all in the process."

"What do you mean by that?"

Before Buddy could reply, the pickup halted thirty yards away. Yasmin jumped out, saw the Serb's body, and ran to her brother. "Hassan!"

Jack said, "He's lost some blood. Get him to a doctor as quick as you can."

Jack helped her maneuver Hassan over to the pickup and sat him in the passenger seat. "Let it end here, Hassan. Let it end and we both get on with our lives."

With that, Jack said to Savage, "Give me the briefcase."

"What?"

"Just give it to me, Buddy."

Savage picked it up, crossed to Jack, and asked, "What's going on?"

Jack tugged the briefcase from Savage's grasp. "The scroll's caused nothing but death and trouble. Maybe if he has it back that'll be the end of it." Jack thrust the case into Hassan's chest. "Take it and let's call it quits. Head back over the Jordanian border; they can't touch you there. Now get out of here fast."

Savage brandished the pistol. "Are you crazy? That's not the deal I made, Jack."

"What deal? With who?"

A second later a long string of headlights appeared and the faint rumble of engines sounded, moving fast across the desert, heading toward them at high speed from the Israeli border. Savage said, "The Israelis."

Hassan stared out at the approaching headlights with

no sign of fear and said, "You're a strange man, Cane. But an honorable one."

Savage brandished the machine pistol. "Give the briefcase back."

Jack said, "No, Buddy—at least this way the scroll stands a chance of being made public. If the Israelis get their hands on it, it may never see the light of day."

Hassan grunted, clutching his wound, the bleeding getting worse. "*Ma'assalama, Cane.*"

"*Ma'assalama.*"

Yasmin stared at Jack, their eyes met, and she started to say something, to touch his arm, but Jack said, "Move, before the Israelis get here or your brother bleeds to death."

"We owe you our gratitude," Yasmin said.

"You owe me nothing. Just keep your brother out of my life. And you try to live a long one."

Yasmin's lips trembled. She bit them, then she started the engine and turned in an arc, heading toward the Jordanian border at high speed, the tires kicking up dust.

The pickup drove off, the taillights disappeared, and then there was only the silence of the desert. The headlights from the Israeli side came ever closer.

Jack said, "What deal did you make, Buddy?"

Savage put down the machine pistol but kept the Browning. "Get in the Land Cruiser. We haven't got much time."

"For what?"

Savage's face tightened with fear. "I'm afraid you and I need to have a talk."

139

Jack moved inside the Land Cruiser. The cab faced away from the Israeli border, toward the mountains of Edom. Buddy sat next to him in the driver's seat and kept his eyes on the procession of headlights in the rearview mirror. "Who's coming?" Jack asked.

"Your friend Lela and the cops. Maybe the Israel Defense Forces for all I know."

Jack stared at the Browning pistol in Buddy's hand. "Where did you get the gun?"

Savage's face was blank. "I stole the scroll, Jack."

Jack's shock was total. He felt as if someone had cut his wrists and his blood had drained.

Buddy said, "I never meant to take it. All I wanted was a couple of fragments."

"I—I don't follow. What's that supposed to mean?"

"Sometimes on site I'd work for myself. I'd take artifacts. Nothing major that would attract attention. But I'd sell them, like the Bedu who work the black market. Make some money."

Jack was still thunderstruck. "Sell them to whom, Buddy?"

"Pasha. Some of his black-market stuff went to private collectors. The really important parchment material he sold to the Vatican by a special arrangement he'd had for years. I figured a few fragments of your scroll could make me a small fortune."

Jack said, stone cold, "Go on."

"A little after you left Green, I sneaked back into his tent. I'd been waiting for my chance all night. I got a smell of alcohol, saw him clutching an open bottle of Wild Turkey and lying on his bed. He looked to be asleep. So I went to work on the scroll, cutting off a few slivers. But Green was barely dozing and he woke and saw what I was up to. The guy went crazy. We scuffled, I pulled the gun. The rest you could probably figure."

"I want to hear it, Buddy."

"I couldn't bring myself to shoot. But then Green came at me like a wild bear and knocked the gun out of my hand. That's when I grabbed your knife from the table." Savage's eyes were moist. "I didn't mean to kill him, Jack. It just happened, out of the blue. But I know I did wrong and that nothing's going to put it right, not ever."

Savage began to sob, shaking his head as if he couldn't believe his own admission.

Jack touched his arm. "Why steal, Buddy? It's not you."

Buddy tipped back his baseball cap, wiped his eyes with his arm, and looked out at the headlights as they drew even closer. "I could give you a hundred reasons."

"Give me one."

"Because at my age I got tired of scratching for a living, and for nothing much more than my board and keep. I got tired of traveling coach class and busting my guts with not so much as a decent pension to show for it. I got tied of hearing stories about some dirt-poor Bedu making a fortune for themselves digging our sites."

"Is that what it was about, Buddy, money?"

"I figured I'd set myself up for retirement. Except I never reckoned on getting in way over my head. After I killed Green I decided to take the scroll. Make it look like a proper murder and theft. That way the police might think it was a criminal gang. I'd arranged to give Pasha the cuttings, but I gave him the entire parchment just to get rid of it. I didn't want a cent from it."

"You stopped Pasha from killing me, didn't you?"

"He called and told me you were on his tail at Maloula. I warned him that if he killed you I'd tell the Israelis everything. That's why he tempered it with a warning and shot you in the leg instead."

Savage paused, closed his eyes tightly, then opened them again. "There was no talking to Pasha. He was a nasty piece of work who probably would have killed us all in the end, especially after you did the switch. He went crazy, wanted your blood. Your friend Lela did everyone a favor killing him."

Jack said, "You told him I was in Rome, didn't you?"

"He said if I didn't give him some leads, he'd kill us all. He said all he wanted was the scroll back. If he got that, he'd leave us alone. I figured I had to tell him my suspicions that you'd gone to see Fonzi."

"Why did you think that?"

"He was a scroll expert and familiar with the code. I reckoned he'd probably be one of your first ports of call. I warned Pasha again that if he harmed you, I'd tell the Israelis everything. He swore he wouldn't kill you."

"And you trusted him?"

"I never trusted him, but I figured he'd be smart enough to keep his word or risk being hunted down by the Israelis. I tried to call and warn you to be careful, left lots of messages, but you didn't answer my calls."

"Pasha killed Fonzi, Buddy. Cut his throat."

Savage's eyes were wet again, and he ran a hand over his face. "Oh, no . . ."

Jack glanced in the rearview. He guessed the headlights were less than a hundred yards away. "How could you be so dumb, Buddy? *How?*"

"We all do dumb things in life."

"Why all of a sudden tell the Israelis?"

Savage looked back at him. "To square things. Make sure they didn't put you behind bars. After I got Hassan's call, I phoned Sergeant Mosberg. I told him I wanted to make a deal. The cops get me and the scroll and you walk free. I told him you were innocent. But now if Hassan has his way, the world's going to know about the scroll anyway. The Israelis aren't going to be able to deny its existence."

Savage nodded toward the rear mirror and the approaching headlights. "You better get out, Jack. Any second now and the cops are going to be swarming all over this place like ants on a dung pile."

Jack flicked an anxious look in the mirror. The cortege roared closer.

Buddy said, "Keep your hands in the air when you get out. I don't want any misunderstandings and you getting hurt. My deceit's caused enough of that."

"Pops . . ."

Savage shook his head. "I want to face them alone, Jack. But I'm truly sorry for what I did. For letting you down."

Jack's eyes filled with emotion. He stepped out of the Land Cruiser and looked back at Buddy. "I forgive you."

Savage wiped his eyes. "Love you, Jack. Always have."

The rows of headlights appeared to spread out until they half circled the Land Cruiser and halted. Jack felt frozen to the spot.

Savage said, "Jack, listen to me, get your hands in the air. The Israelis don't mess around."

"What about you?"

"Don't worry, they'll come for me. Lela knows the drill. Just do as I say and play it like she told me to."

Jack raised his hands. A metallic voice spoke over a loudspeaker, in Hebrew, then English: "Step away from the vehicle slowly and keep your hands high."

Buddy urged, "Do it, Jack. Just do as they tell you."

Jack moved slowly from the Land Cruiser. "Don't shoot!" he called out.

When he had gone thirty yards he saw an armed Lela step out of one of the police SUVs. Their eyes locked.

A bunch of other uniformed cops and plainclothes jumped out. Jack kept his hands up. He recognized the Mossad guy named Ari. He and Lela stepped forward, their weapons outstretched, then Lela swept her gun in the direction of the Land Cruiser's rear.

"Where's Buddy, Jack? *Where is he?*"

"In the Land Cruiser."

A split second later Jack heard the loud crack of a gunshot. Lela crouched, the cops ducking low and taking aim at the SUV. But no more shots came and when the echo died the desert came alive with barked orders.

Jack's heart crumpled. "Pops, no!"

Ignoring all caution, he ran back toward the Land Cruiser.

140

John Becket awoke on the third day. There would be some who saw it as an omen.

Just as there would be those who saw a powerful sign in the suffering inflicted upon his body: bloodied cuts in both his hands—the defensive wounds from Cassini's attack—and the stab wounds in his chest. Gashes to his forehead, not caused by a crown of thorns but by the sharp slashing of steel.

To some, the wounds resembled stigmata. They would be endlessly talked about by those who believed in such manifestations, part of the miracle of John Becket's survival, though the skeptics would put it down to the pope's hardy physique and to the determined surgeons at Gemelli hospital.

But no one would deny that John Becket's survival was something close to miraculous, and if God had played a part in it, then so be it.

It was very still in the hospital room that evening when Becket awoke. But moments later the air came alive with a flurry of noise and muted whispering. The medical team at Gemelli went to work immediately. More monitors were wheeled in, doctors arrived, and charts were consulted. Life signs and senses were checked, the pope's blood pressure and breathing endlessly monitored.

It was another four hours before Monsignor Sean Ryan was admitted into the softly lit private room, and even then just for a few minutes.

"Holy Father . . . " Ryan began. He sat by the pope's side, clutching his hand, feeling the weakness of the man's grip. He noticed his skin was as sallow as parchment, his arms stretched outward as if he had been crucified, connected by drips and tubes to a bank of electronic monitoring equipment.

Becket's voice was hoarse and frail. "Sean. The doctors tell me it was you who helped save my life."

"It wasn't only me, Holy Father. The doctors have been working day and night."

"So the nurses tell me."

"The streets of Rome and churches in every corner of the globe are filled with people praying for your survival. Every avenue approaching the hospital is crowded with well-wishers. Some have even slept out in the streets at night. I couldn't tell you how many acres of flowers I've had to wade through on my way up here. Presidents have sent their ambassadors; everyone wants to offer their good wishes." Ryan wiped his eyes and added, "It seems all our prayers have been answered."

"Is it true what the doctors tell me? That I was dead to the world for three days?"

"No one believed you would make it. No one except those who wanted to believe."

Becket's frail hand gripped Ryan's with a sudden strength. "Then my work must not be over yet. Tell me everything, Sean."

Ryan explained all that had happened in the last three days. "The newspapers are full of reports of your intentions to open the archives, and of Cardinal Cassini's attack."

"Umberto died instantly?"

Pain etched Ryan's face. "Yes, Holy Father."

Becket's blue eyes filled with grief and he squeezed Ryan's hand more tightly. "I know that the burden of having taken a human life is a terrible one to bear. I know too that Umberto was a troubled soul. I want us to pray that he will be blessed by forgiveness, just as we must forgive him, Sean."

"Yes, Holy Father."

There were other words, some private, others just nods and hoarse whispers from the pope, his body still feeble, but even so his powerful presence filled the room, and Ryan knew that it was only a matter of time before the man's spark of life returned.

And then the pope's medical team came back in and the meeting was over. Ryan rose to leave, still clutching the pope's hand, and Becket said, "I need you to deliver a message for me, Sean."

"Of course."

"Tell the deputy camerlengo that he is to convene a special meeting of the Curia."

"When, Holy Father?"

"Just as soon as the doctors allow me to walk out of this room. I have important words to say. There is a revelation they must hear. Not just the Curia, but all the world."

141

The place John Becket had chosen for his meeting with his cardinals was the Sistine Chapel. Not because it was the place of his election or on account of the beauty of Michelangelo's artwork, but because of all the other papal elections that had taken place there.

It was an anchor to the church's past.

There was no more suitable a place to end that past.

That morning, the sun spilled through the Vatican's stained-glass windows, the air in the Sistine Chapel tense and expectant.

John Becket had chosen not to sit in his magnificent cano-pied chair but to stand in the center of the chapel. He wore his plain white cassock and a cross around his neck. Unlike the night of his election, this time his voice didn't falter as he stood to make his address. All eyes in the chapel were fixed on his towering figure.

"My brothers in Christ, I am happy to be alive and to see you all assembled here today. You are all aware of my inten-tion to open our archives. What you are not aware of is the news that I am about to reveal to you."

The majestic chapel was silent, every pair of eyes focused on the pope.

"But first, I will address the matter of the scroll. The historical evidence it discloses of a second messiah is true. Other such secrets have been kept from many of you in the past. These secrets, once revealed, will gravely wound the church. They will make skeptics of priests and lay alike, and create an enormous test for all of us. For some, it will shake the very core of their beliefs, or crush them entirely.

"How will we answer our critics? How will we rectify the lies that were told, the seeds of doubt that will be sown, the wrongs that were done? Yet we know that this scroll, by revealing the existence of a false messiah, also confirms the reality of the true Jesus. We who walk in His footsteps need no such confirmation. We have willingly given our lives to the work of delivering His message.

"But this message has become corrupted. The church has been embroiled in scandals. It has too often failed to practice what it preached. It has quoted God's words, and yet too frequently failed to live up to them."

Becket paused, but only long enough to draw breath. "We all know this, just as we all know that we cannot ignore our legacy from Christ—to plant the seed of His kingdom in the hearts of all men, that they may create an earthly order based on love and truth, charity and justice, and an ethical law.

"As human beings, our senses are acutely aware of the memory of the echo of a voice, as if someone is speaking to us, whispering in our ear, reminding us that we and this world are made for a greater purpose. But we have too often ignored that voice.

"Recently I met with a woman, a prostitute like Mary Magdalene. When I asked her what she thought of those in the Vatican, she said, 'Half the world starves and they live like princes in their ivory towers.'

"My brothers, I know that she spoke the truth. I know that what she said is thought by many. And I know that what I am about to say next will shock many of you. But I believe God has sent me here for a greater purpose, and that purpose is to prepare this world for a second coming."

Gasps filled the Sistine Chapel, cardinals exchanged glances, with questions written on their faces as if to say, *Is this man insane?*

Becket carried on. "Yes, I see the questioning stares. But before each of you begins to doubt my sanity let me say this. The last night Jesus broke bread with his disciples, he left us a solemn legacy. But often I have to ask myself: Did we ever correctly interpret that legacy? Did we remain true to Jesus' words?

"And many times, I have to answer that I feel we did not. The world suffers and starves, and yet still we sit here in our gilded prison and pray. Our scientists have conquered the moon yet we cannot conquer the wrongs that crush men's spirits.

"In two thousand years it is true that we have achieved much. But is the symbolic pinnacle of our achievement meant to be a city of beautiful chapels and priceless works of art with walls around it? Truth and love do not need walls. Christ did not build walls. He tore them down. And he prayed, not in lofty, beautiful churches but in people's homes, in the countryside, in the streets. He led by example, and now so must we.

"My brothers, you may doubt my sanity even more when I tell you that the second coming we must prepare for is our own. I believe that all of us who take up the torch to carry light into the dark corners of the human heart are Christ returned, His second coming. For in truth, I believe this is the complete fulfillment of the meaning of Christ's presence on earth. He planted the seeds and it is up to us to cultivate and gather the harvest, or else it will wither.

"So from this day, we must decide not only our fate but our faith. Do we wish to be bureaucrats and remain behind these walls? To sit here and debate the finer points of theology while the sick are untended, the hungry go unfed, or children are left unloved? Or do we go out as priests to the people, just as Jesus and His disciples went out two thousand years ago, with nothing to call their own, nothing but honest belief in His words?

"From this day, I want us to divest ourselves of all our wealth and worldly goods. To divest ourselves of every stone and brick. I want us to use that wealth to alleviate the wrongs we witness, the poverty and injustices all around us.

"I want us to go forth in peace, to pronounce the brotherhood of all men, without exception of country, creed, or race, and in the belief in one God. And to those who will criticize us, we will answer them with the same answers Jesus answered with, and if need be, we will suffer the same wounds.

"My brothers, my authority as Supreme Pontiff is absolute. No matter how many arguments are railed against me, my word is law. But I will give you each a choice. To remain behind, or to walk with me as true disciples and step out from behind these walls to fulfill Christ's promise."

Becket stared out at them all and said, "So now I must ask you, *Mos vos insisto mihi?* Will you follow me?"

John Becket stood waiting and looked around the chapel. For a moment there was a silence so intense that it almost felt like a crushing weight. No one spoke. Some of the cardinals looked at one another awkwardly, as if uncertain what to do. Becket knew instinctively that he could not count on these men, that they would waver.

But one by one, a number of red-robed cardinals rose, some of them moved to tears, others fearful. Some were empowered by his words, others aware of their own weaknesses in the face of such an enormous challenge. Yet it was one elderly cardinal who raised his frail voice above the uncertain crowd and spoke first. "Yes, I will follow you!"

Another man next to him repeated the cry.

And another. A chorus of voices rose to give their answer, and then one by one, in a single procession, they came to kneel before John Becket and kiss his ring in a token of commitment.

It was very still in the Sistine. In a single procession the cardinals had left, until finally John Becket was alone.

He was aware of two things: the terrible weight upon his shoulders, as heavy as a cross, and that the most difficult journey of his life was about to begin.

He was conscious also that many of his cardinals had been carried away by his noble words and by the consensus of the crowd. That in the days ahead some of those men would change their minds. Some would consider the task too challenging. Reflecting on their decision, others would choose not to join him.

But many would, he was convinced of that. The ones who mattered, the ones who shared his honest intent.

Was it too difficult a path that lay ahead?

Was it too ambitious a plan?

Would it succeed, or would the process destroy the church?

But with his candid questioning came a deep sense of purpose. Becket knew at that moment he was intensely alone, except for the presence before him now, within the golden tabernacle.

That presence would be all he would ever have to guide him in the days and years ahead, yet he knew that it would be enough.

He dropped to his knees in front of the altar. He felt something brush against his cassock. He reached into his pocket and drew out the worn newspaper photograph of Robert and Margaret Cane. In the coming days he would publicly reveal his part in their tragic deaths and the theft of the scroll, and he would face those consequences. But for now, racked by guilt, he held the photograph in his palm, touched the image of their faces. As it always did, his memory flooded with pain for all the hurts and wrongs that had been done in the name of God. As always, he would pray for forgiveness and the redemption of that pain.

As was his habit in these personal moments, Becket laid himself prostrate in front of the altar, his pained and wounded body outstretched, and the words that spilled from his lips were spoken with deep and honest conviction. "Our Father, who art in heaven . . . I beseech you to bring peace to Jack Cane's soul. That you quench his pain. That you allow him to glimpse the eternity of your love, your reason for our being . . ."

142

The Toyota Land Cruiser bumped over the desert trail and where it ended Jack cut the engine and jerked on the handbrake.

He stared over at the grave, the gravel chips a mess where Buddy had dug up the scroll. The heat of the desert drifted in through the open windows. Beside him, Lela handed him the water bottle and the flowers from the backseat.

Jack said, "My father told me once that the ancients believed the spirits of the dead lingered near their tombs. That he'd always be here for me, when I needed to talk." He looked out over the rugged, desolate landscape. "It's why I keep coming back. To be near them."

She touched his hand. "Can I tell you a secret? I used to drive out here too. Sit here and remember that day and how close I felt to you." Lela smiled. "You probably think I'm a sad case, don't you?"

"What I'm thinking is, would you have dinner with me tonight? Somewhere in Jerusalem that serves good food and a half-decent bottle of wine?"

Lela's fingers brushed against his face, and swept his hair off his forehead. She looked into his eyes and shook her head. "Not unless I can let you in on another secret."

"There's more?"

"I've been waiting a long time for you to ask me a question like that. Maybe part of me has always been waiting. Hoping that we'd meet once more. Of course, it can never be the same as it was and it's foolish to expect it to be so. But I'm just glad that we've seen each other again."

A smile broke on Jack's lips. "Is that a yes or a no?"

She smiled back and moved her mouth over his, kissed him, gently at first, then more hungrily, until she slowly pulled away, and stroked his arm. "I think you already know the answer to that. Go talk to them, Jack. They'll be waiting."

The still desert air was dry as a bone as he stepped in front of the grave. The sun beat down. No murmur of wind disturbed the solitude, no hawk overheard to desecrate the silence.

He tidied the gravel chips, then went to sit on the boulder. He laid the flowers where he always did and filled the parched oasis from the plastic water bottle. Then he sat back and studied the words on the chiseled granite that inscribed his pain. *Miss you always, love you forever.*

Today he had so much to talk about. But as always, out of habit the same whispered questions echoed in his mind: *Do the ghosts of the dead hear the words of the living?*

Timeless questions that came from the core of him. *Do we meet again? Does the love we nurture on this earth go on forever, beyond this universe, for all eternity?*

No answers came, they never did, but that afternoon something strange happened.

Something that he would remember to the end of his days.

His questions had barely passed his lips when he felt a powerful current of air sweep in from the parched Judean desert.

It erupted out of nowhere, brushed across the sands, sending balls of camel thorn brush tumbling in its path. He closed his eyes, felt the wind's breath on his face, as cool as a balm.

He opened his eyes again. They filled with water, reacting to the hot, gritty air.

The whistling wind had sent a swirl of dust across the sands. It raced out into the wilderness and then it was gone.

Silence once more filled the desert.

He felt it then, a presence at his shoulder. It went beyond anything natural. But it felt so real that the shock of it made him turn.

There was no one there.

His heart quickened.

The incident, coming out of nowhere, caused the hairs on the back of his neck to rise. At the same time he felt a strange, inexplicable feeling of calm, an intuition that he wasn't alone. That in this desolate patch in the middle of the Judean desert, he was being watched over. It made him think of that day long ago with his father beneath the pyramids of Cheops.

You won't see or touch us, but we'll be standing next to you.

Was the spurious gust a sign? An answer to his questions? Had it merely been a trick of nature? Or had some willful spirit caused it so?

In the deepest recess of his soul, in the void that we all know, the place where each of us alone meets with God and where we hear the echo of a voice, somehow he already knew his answer.

AUTHOR'S NOTE

It took well over forty years for authorities to make public the bulk of the translated texts found at Qumran. While many scholars believe that all of the texts have been revealed, others assert suspiciously that the Vatican has secretly held back explosive material of a disturbing and prophetic nature.

Despite their statements to the contrary, this assertion has never been properly or openly addressed by the Vatican.

Excavations in the hills and caves at Qumran continue to this day. As for the account of a second messiah, it has existed since the time of Jesus. Numerous references survive in Scripture, along with dire warnings of a false prophet walking the land. Jesus himself made some of these warnings.

Two thousand years ago in the Holy Land, identity theft was an easy matter and no doubt many such deceivers existed—some of them mad, some of them fraudsters—claiming to be the true messiah.

As for a pope who will return the church to its true and simple course, without pomp and possessions, we all await that day.

In the meantime, two things are certain. All of the Dead Sea scrolls have yet to be discovered, and all of their secrets have yet to be revealed.

The Second Messiah
Readers Group Guide

TOPICS AND QUESTIONS FOR DISCUSSION

1. In *The Second Messiah,* the idea of a second coming is proposed by the author. Do you think that the world needs a second coming? If so, why? Do you think it's necessary for mankind? What do you think the effects of a second coming would be worldwide? What effects would it have on you personally? If a second coming were to occur, how do you think it would manifest itself?

2. The new American pope, John Becket, decides to renounce all the trappings of a wealthy and bureaucratic church, to leave the pomp and circumstance of religion behind and to embrace the simple ways of Christ by going out to the people, much as Christ's apostles and disciples did. How practical do you think such an act would be if a church leader did likewise? Would it be popular and embraced by Christians? Would it spur them on to stronger faith? Would they admire such an act or consider it reckless?

3. John Becket wishes to unite different faiths to a common purpose. Do you think that's feasible? Are different faiths really more alike than unalike in their belief in the idea of one God? Have we enough in common to find a shared ground that will help us to work together with a shared purpose in mind of spreading Christ's word? What are the likely barriers to this shared purpose? How could they be overcome?

4. Do you think our society has become too materialistic, too caught up in our needs, wants, and pleasures? Or do you believe that God wants us to enjoy our time on this earth and indulge ourselves with our financial and material successes? How does the pursuit of wealth help us/affect us?

5. What did you enjoy most about the story? The thrilling action sequences? The characters and their relationships? The unraveling of the enigma of the second messiah?

6. John Becket offers us reasons for our existence. Do you agree with his reasons? What do you think is the true purpose of our existence on this earth?

7. The Dead Sea scroll that archaeologist Jack Cane discovers contains a dramatic revelation. From what you've learned in the book about the Dead Sea scrolls, do you think it likely that such a scroll will ever be discovered at Qumran? What kinds of secrets, revelations, or prophecies do you imagine it might contain?

8. If such a scroll containing the revelation of a second Jesus were actually found, how do you think it would affect the church and the faith? Would it harm it? Help it in any way?

9. Do you think that the important messages and teachings of Jesus Christ have been corrupted in any way since they were first communicated to us? If so, in what way? Is there anything we can do, individually or collectively as church members, to clarify those messages?

10. Jack Cane makes a habit of visiting his parents' graves, where he prays and speaks to them. He likes to believe that

his departed hear his words. Do you think the spirits of our loved ones have the ability to listen to us and watch over us? Have you any experiences of sensing departed loves ones close to you, in times of crisis or otherwise? Does this suggest to you another dimension of existence?

A CONVERSATION WITH GLENN MEADE

Most of your other books have been about political intrigue and murder in the twentieth century. What made you decide to take up the topic of archaeology and the Vatican in *The Second Messiah*?

Sometimes, stories find the writer and not the other way round. I think that happened with *The Second Messiah*.

Archaeology and religion have always interested me—I've written about both before, though in a minor way—but I guess mulling over my own life kick-started me into combining both subjects in a novel.

At certain milestones in your life—once you have children and mature, once you lose a parent or a loved one—your own mortality smacks you like a billy club. For me, at least, I started to dwell a little more than usual on the eternal questions: *Do I really believe that there's a God and why? Is there definitely an afterlife, or am I gone for good once I exit stage left? After all these life experiences, what do I truly believe in?*

Truthfully, I think I wasn't just looking for answers to important questions—I was also looking for a subject for another book and somehow the two combined.

Big subjects interest me, especially topics that have a major influence on our lives. And there didn't seem any bigger a topic than Jesus Christ, whose presence has had such profound consequence for the world.

It struck me that I had never read a novel or seen a movie that explored the premise that there might have been not just one messiah in existence at the time of Jesus, but two (apart from the absurd movie *The Life of Brian*). It occurred to me that if such had been the case and two messiahs had existed side by side at the same time—and the Bible is peppered with references to false saviors and prophets—then the pillars of faith might just stand on shaky ground.

Then the "what ifs" started. What if, at the same time as the pillars of faith are being shaken by this revelation, a new pope is elected in Rome, a figure whose true motives are uncertain, who could wind up either being an antichrist or even a second messiah . . . ?

As I set about exploring the premise I knew that in many ways I would be stress-testing my own faith, or lack of it, and all those beliefs I had been brought up to accept as given without ever really questioning their veracity. The notion both intrigued and troubled me—and made for a very interesting journey.

Your books have been translated into more than twenty languages and distributed throughout the world. How do you feel *The Second Messiah* will resonate with Middle Eastern audiences as opposed to European and American audiences?

The Second Messiah has recently been published in the Middle East. It sold surprisingly well and received very good reviews.

As always, stories are principally about characters and plot, but by taking readers on a journey into unfamiliar but interesting territory—in this case, one in which they learn about dark dealings and subterfuge in the Vatican and in the world of archaeology—you're hopefully going to stimulate their interest, regardless of their religious beliefs.

Of course, Middle Eastern audiences are very familiar with the life of Jesus—considered an important and respected prophet by Islam—so they're not entirely on unfamiliar ground.

The Second Messiah is both an impressive work of fiction and research. How much of this book is factual? Where and how did you do most of the research for The Second Messiah?

Although I like to think that my premise could be feasible, the story is of course fiction, braided with a lot of historical and contemporary fact. Even the Roman commanders and officials I mention by name in the course of the book existed. (We're all prone to errors, even the experts I consulted with, but I like to think I did my research pretty thoroughly.)

Also, the background details I used in the various scene settings and locations, whether an ancient monastery, a location inside the Vatican, an archaeological site in Israel or Syria, or just a restaurant in Rome, these places exist in reality.

Most of my research was done in Rome and the United States, with sources in the Middle East helping me with research there.

The vivid descriptions of many scenes in The Second Messiah, such as those set in the ancient Roman remains or the monastery in Maloula, suggest that you personally visited these sites. How many of the locations in the book were you able to visit, and how did these visits translate into what takes place in The Second Messiah?

I earned some air miles, for sure. I didn't get to Maloula but I've visited places like it, and I did visit the Vatican and Rome on several occasions. As part of my research I stayed for many weeks in a monastery in Rome run by Armenian monks, where I had the smallest room in the cloister and the hardest mattress in the universe. Most evenings, while I was stuck in my closet-sized room mulling over research material, the Armenian monks drank wine with dinner and had their girlfriends over—when the latter made my eyebrows rise I was told by one of the monks that lucky for them the Armenian religious have an opt-out clause in regard to celibacy . . .

I kept this monastery setting in mind as the kind of refuge Pope John Becket flees to when he decides to leave the Vatican for good. But as tempting as it was to weave all the original details into the story, the monks were not Armenians who had their girlfriends come visit . . .

I also spoke to archaeologists and scroll and Bible experts in the United States and the Middle East and took several private and public tours of Rome's incredible underground ruins, which feature in some of the book's action sequences.

While you were doing your research, how helpful or reticent did you find the Vatican Press Office to be? Did this influence how the Vatican is represented in your book in any way?

To be honest, I didn't find the Vatican Press Office all that helpful. I did thank them in the acknowledgments and they were certainly courteous in their dealings with me, but typical of most Vatican offices it often proved bureaucratic and guarded with its answers.

I felt that the press office dodged getting its teeth into any questions I posed dealing with controversial subjects. Wander into that minefield and you began to feel like you'd gotten typhoid—they avoided you.

It was my experience that many Vatican officials were ever busy trying to protect their rear. (I'm reminded of the lifelong bureaucrat who famously wanted inscribed on his tombstone: "Am I covered?")

By far the most helpful were individual Vatican priests and senior clerics who spoke to me off the record.

There are some wonderful, hardworking men and women serving the church. But for sure the Vatican seems to have its share of the disaffected—quite a number of clerics I spoke with appeared unhappy with the church's direction and its past failings in dealing honestly with various scandals and their victims.

A priest I met mentioned graffiti painted on one of the Vatican's walls, allegedly by a disgruntled padre: "The Church believes in truth and justice—but obviously not for the faithful or for Vatican employees."

What was the most surprising thing you discovered during the course of writing *The Second Messiah*?

That I managed to both pose and answer for myself a lot of deep and troublesome questions that had rattled around inside my head for much of my life. In fact, no other book I've written has made me think so long and hard about my own existence and my faith—or why at times I've had a lack of it—and to try to figure out what's really important in my life.

The writing of a book is always a journey—it sounds so clichéd but it's true. Often, too, it's an emotional release, a way to pressure-valve emotions and feelings. Fortunately for me, by the end of the journey I knew that I had answered many of my own difficult questions, or at least as best I could. I also encountered some of the most interesting minds I've ever met.

Even more happened in the process of writing but I think it's too private to share in public. It's enough to say that I feel the better for the experience of writing *The Second Messiah*. And grateful for the important truths that I learned along the way.

There seems to be a critique of the secrecy of the Vatican and the general atmosphere of mystery within the Catholic Church in *The Second Messiah*. Do you wish there was a real-life John Becket who could take similarly courageous risks?

I sure do—a hope I'm pretty certain many of us would harbor. I think we all long for a messianic-type Christian figure to appear again who would set us to rights once more, reinvigorate our religious beliefs, and reset the world's moral compass.

It's often such a powerful motif—a longing for a savior who will administer justice and moral guidance—and such a recurring theme in our storytelling that I wonder if the seed of its yearning is in some way planted in our DNA.

The church wasn't founded on secrecy, intrigue, and bureaucracy, but rather on love, truth, and justice. Those bedrock virtues are so often ignored by the Vatican when it faces public and legal scrutiny during investigations into its various sexual and financial scandals.

As you were crafting and developing your narrative, how present in your mind were the recent scandals in the Catholic Church? Did they play a part in your decision to write this book?

To be honest, they didn't. I was certainly aware of the powerful worldwide media attention they generated, but I really just saw them as another symptom of a seriously dysfunctional Catholic Church.

Scandal in various forms seems to be a constant—and incredible harm has been done to the Catholic Church over the years by pedophile priests in particular. (Though I dread to think of the harm that was done before the media age, when victims had little or no voice and the church's authority went unquestioned.)

I also think that the pedophilia priests' scandals have harmed as many good clerics as they have their victims. There are so many earnest men and women in the Catholic Church who dedicate their lives to Christ and who are sullied by the behavior of errant colleagues.

You mention in your author's note that the account of a second messiah "has existed since the time of Jesus." Can you elaborate on this?

Numerous references and warnings exist in scripture regarding false prophets and false messiahs. Jesus himself made some of these warnings. In Luke, for example, Jesus says: "Be not deceived for many shall come in my name, saying 'I am Christ.'"

Acts 13:6 refers to the Jewish false prophet Bar-Jesus, encountered by Paul. Matthew 24:24 also refers to false messiahs and false prophets "who will appear and perform great signs and wonders to deceive." Mark 13:22 says much the same.

And the Old Testament is peppered with warnings of false messiahs.

The Jewish Talmud claimed that Jesus himself was a false savior, and the Jewish Bible, the Tanakh, is full of references to false prophets, some of whom claimed to be the chosen one.

Regarding the premise of *The Second Messiah*, I think it's highly plausible that Jesus had his pretenders and that such people existed in biblical times—some of them deranged, some of them fraudsters motivated by personal gain.

Two thousand years ago in the Holy Land, identity theft was an easy matter and Jesus would have attracted a lot of attention, adulation, respect, and awe from his followers. He also attracted crowds, gifts of alms and money, and was accommodated with food and lodging most places he went. Those are pretty tempting rewards to an impersonator.

Successful people have always had their imitators, pretenders who try to achieve notoriety on the backs of others. Whether it's an Elvis impersonator or a businessman cloning a product idea, there's always someone ready to cash in on achievement. Would it have been any different in Jesus' time that someone might try to profit by imitating him? That you might have a Jesus alter ego, a con man, traveling the Holy Land and hoping to profit by his pretense, financially, egotistically, or both? It's possible. And it would have been easy to carry out such a deception.

Travel in the Holy Land back then was done by donkey or horse or cart, or in most cases, by foot. Word traveled slowly and nobody carried IDs. How many people would have known what Jesus looked like in a town where he'd never visited before? In those days if someone showed up and announced that he's Jesus the Nazarene, there's a good chance many folks are going to just accept it.

What's next for you? Are you interested in continuing with archaeological thrillers or is there another project in the works?

I'm glad to say that my next book also has an archaeological backdrop.

Some years ago I wrote a novel entitled *Snow Wolf,* much of it set in Russia. It proved very successful internationally and was translated into more than twenty languages.

Russia intrigues me—the stoicism of its people; its vast, dramatic landscape and tumultuous history. And for all its legendary past enmity with the west and, in particular, the United States, I have found that the average Russian holds the U.S. and the American people in very high regard. Many Russians also remain deeply religious people—communism never managed to purge their faith. (I've visited the homes of old guard communists where I saw lit-candle shrines to Lenin on one side of the living room and religious icons on the other.)

My interest in Russia goes back years. I can vividly recall as a young boy sitting in front of the TV and seeing my parents enthralled by David Lean's movie *Doctor Zhivago,* based on Boris Pasternak's sprawling novel of the same name. It was a wonderful story—powerful, dramatic, touching, and rich with many layers. As for the book, you either loved or hated it; technically it's all over the place but it does capture the extraordinary essence that is Russia. For my next work, I decided to revisit that country and research a story that I've been interested in writing—like *Snow Wolf,* much of it is set in Russia and based upon truth.

I'm almost finished writing the book, but for me, talking publicly about stories I'm working on is a no-no. I feel that a writer can easily talk his story to death and dissipate his own need to write about it. So I'll just say that I believe it to be a powerful, emotional tale and I hope that readers will feel the same way.

Turn the page
for the next thrilling ride
from Glenn Meade

THE ROMANOV CONSPIRACY

Available August 2012 from Howard Books

I believe that the greatest secrets lie buried and only the dead speak the truth.

And in a way that was how I came to be in the woods that morning when we found the bodies. It was raining in the City of Dead Souls, a heavy downpour that drenched the summer streets.

"Traffic isn't bad this morning. Thirty minutes, no more," my Russian driver said as our Land Rover skirted imposing granite buildings, the remnants of a grander civilization long since past.

I sat back and watched the old imperial city flash by. Founded by Catherine the Great in 1762, Ekaterinburg lies in the shadow of the Ural Mountains. The landscape resembles the rugged beauty of Alaska—thick woods filled with wolves and bears, deep ravines and snow-capped peaks. Rich ore mines contain the greatest treasures in the world; platinum and emeralds, gold and diamonds honeycomb the soaring mountain ranges that lie beyond this sprawling Siberian city.

As my Land Rover left Ekaterinburg behind and drove past heavily forested birch slopes, I snapped open the leather briefcase on my lap and plucked out a blue-colored file. The cover said:

I reviewed the thick clutch of pages, the results of my work for the past three months. The brief of our cooperative venture was simple—to dig in the forests for evidence of mass executions during the Russian Revolution's Red Terror.

Many thousands perished, not least the Romanovs, the Russian royal family—the tsar and tsarina, and their four pretty daughters, and their youngest child, fourteen-year-old Alexei—shot and bayoneted to death, their skulls smashed by rifle butts and their corpses doused with sulphuric acid.

The Ipatiev House where they were held captive was known locally as the House of Dead Souls. But the Reds executed so many victims, their bodies dumped in mine shafts and unmarked graves in the vast forests outside Ekaterinburg, that the locals gave their city a new name: the City of Dead Souls.

The rain stopped as my driver turned onto a narrow, worn track, rutted and muddy from the movement of heavy vehicles. The Land Rover headed toward a collection of temporary huts and heavy canvas walk-in tents erected in the middle of a clearing in a birch forest. A painted wooden sign said in English and Russian:

THIS SITE IS
PRIVATE PROPERTY
NO UNAUTHORIZED ENTRY

Something else I hadn't counted on that summer's morning as we pulled up beside one of the tents. I came to these resin-scented woods to exhume the ghosts of the past. Yet absolutely nothing could have prepared me for the bizarre secret that I was to stumble upon when the frozen Siberian earth offered up its dead.

For with the dead came truth.

And with truth came the first whispers of the most incredible story I have ever heard.

I stepped out of the car and opened the entrance flap into my tent. I went to sit behind my work desk as my dig supervisor, Roy Moran, came in. "Hey, baby."

"Memphis Roy" we call him, and he always called me "baby." In Memphis, everyone calls everyone else "baby." The fact that a woman was in charge of the dig didn't make any difference—if I'd been a man, Roy still would have called me "baby."

Roy's a big, bony, no-nonsense guy and one of the best in the business. I tore open my briefcase, ready to attack some paperwork, and said, "I thought you were supposed to be digging shaft number seven this morning."

"Baby, I sure am." Roy stood there, hands on his hips and a little out of breath. The look on his face was a cross between excitement and puzzlement. He raised the grimy Tigers forage cap he always wore, wiped sweat from his forehead, and grinned. "Turns out, seven may just be our lucky number."

"Spit it out."

"We went down as far as we could and hit a peaty layer of near permafrost. But we've found something, Laura. I mean, *seriously* found something."

I threw down my pen. Roy wasn't a man to get wound up about anything. But at that moment he seemed energized, delight bubbling from him like an excited twelve-year-old. "Tell me," I said.

"Hey, baby, you really need to see this for yourself."

I followed Roy through the scented woods. He walked slowly, his muscled legs picking a way through a path of rain-drenched ferns and old fallen trees. He said, "The shaft mouth goes down about sixty feet. It's pretty deep."

The entire clearing was crammed with mining equipment, wooden staves, and scaffolding and dotted with a bunch of trucks and SUVs. "Why do I feel an *and* coming on? You still haven't told me what you've found."

Roy grinned, not changing his pace, his excitement infectious. Beads of sweat glistened on his forehead and his eyes sparked. "Baby, it's a woman. We believe there may be another body down there, too, but it's too deeply buried to see what we've got. Who knows? There might even be more."

I felt excited as we moved between clumps of silver birch trees and halted at the mouth of a mine shaft. I smelled the rich, earthy brown scent of peat. The shaft was a hole in the ground, about eight feet square, the sides buttressed with thick wooden planks. It was one of several mines we explored during the dig, looking for any evidence we could find of artifacts from the Romanov era, when much of this region was a killing ground.

On the night of July 16/17, 1918, in Ekaterinburg, the Romanov family—then the world's wealthiest royals—vanished. Eyewitness accounts suggested that the entire family was massacred.

But for whatever reasons the Bolsheviks chose not to confirm their deaths and rumors persisted that some, if not all, of the family had escaped execution. There were even suggestions of secret plots to rescue them from imprisonment in Ekaterinburg.

Reports flourished for years that one or more of the tsar's daughters, most likely Anastasia, and her brother, Alexei, had escaped.

The family had sewn precious stones—diamonds and other gems—into their underclothing, in the hope that such valuables would prove useful in the event of their escape. It was believed that those same precious stones had impeded or prolonged their deaths.

Those stories had held me spellbound in childhood. No matter what the truth, and like so many others fascinated by the mystery, I *wanted* to believe Anastasia and Alexei escaped.

The mystery deepened when decades later on separate occasions digs outside the city uncovered the remains of six adults and among them were believed to be the tsar, his wife, and two of his daughters. DNA tests affirmed the likely identities by a possible blood connection to the British royal family.

But the discovery was shrouded in some controversy. Many experts believed the bones belonged to the Romanovs. But just as many didn't, citing among other reasons the fact that countless royal relatives were executed in the region and that the bones could have been theirs.

A later dig in a forest pit west of Ekaterinburg discovered two more sets of human remains. DNA tests suggested that they belonged to the tsar's missing daughter and son, Anastasia and Alexei. But one of the sets of remains was never completely proven to be that of Anastasia—a *probability* existed, but it couldn't go beyond all doubt. And so the tests were branded as being inconclusive by some scientists and hardened doubters within the Russian Orthodox Church. It left a nagging feeling that the mystery persisted, that the puzzle was somehow still unsolved.

Above the shaft mouth our engineers had rigged up a motorized winch with an old harness chair, driven by an electric generator. The smell of earth wafted up. I said to Roy, "You mean bones, or a complete skeleton?"

"I mean a woman. She's complete, mummified in the permafrost, and she's perfectly preserved by the bog peat and the cold."

I felt a raw tingle of excitement down my spine. I leaned my hand against one of the silver birch trees, the bark bleached white by the sun. "How old?"

"At an educated guess and from the way she's dressed, we're talking the Romanov period."

Roy went down first. He descended with a wave of his hand as the motorized harness whirred him down into the dark pit. A few minutes later the harness returned empty. I climbed aboard and strapped myself in.

For the last month working at Ekaterinburg we'd unearthed a bunch of material: rust-covered Mosin-Nagant rifles, green-corroded copper coins, spent ammunition cases, a pair of eyeglasses, even several caches of silver and gold tsarist ingots, along with personal effects and jewelry. So many wealthy families with tsarist connections had fled here during the revolution, hoping to escape the bloodshed, but the Reds caught up with them.

Not all the victims were wealthy. My own past lies buried in these woods. Long before I saw Ekaterinburg I knew about this city by the snaking, broad banks of the Iset River, where my grandmother Mariana lived as a young girl. She was eleven when the October revolution's Red Guards invaded her city. Her family were hardy *mujiks*—tough Russian peasants—who worked back-breaking hours digging ore from the icy permafrost, the rock-hard peaty Siberian earth that remains frozen even in summer.

Three of Mariana's brothers were executed in the forests beyond the town, including her beloved Pieter, barely fifteen. Their crime? They protested when the Reds seized their small mining company, a ragged enterprise that barely fed their family of twelve. Lenin didn't believe in personal ownership.

Everything a man possessed now belonged to the Soviets. If anyone protested, he was imprisoned. If he protested still, he was shot, all part of the brutal Red Terror that swept Russia once Lenin seized power.

Fleeing for their lives, my grandmother's family traveled across Siberia one malignant winter and boarded a rusty steamship in St. Petersburg, bound for America. The only memories they carried in their cloth bags were some faded sepia family photographs and postcards of imperial Ekaterinburg, the brittle pages yellow with age and smelling of wood smoke. I still recall that peaty wood smell when as a child I would leaf through the family album, filled with the faded images from another world.

And now here I was, part of an international archaeological dig, spending my summer in jeans and grubby sneakers in a walk-in tent on the outskirts of Ekaterinburg. Absurdly, it seemed as if my family's past had come full circle.

My curiosity eating me, I pressed the harness control block. The motor whirred. The harness lowered me into the pit and I was devoured by shadows.

At first I descended into blackness, but after about twenty feet the shaft's sides were lit by electric lightbulbs. Here and there, I kicked against the walls with my worn Reeboks to keep from hitting the sides.

Below me I saw a blaze of light and suddenly Roy gripped the harness. "Okay, baby, you're at rock bottom."

I let go of the rope and my feet hit a floor of muddied wooden planks. I maneuvered out of the harness and shivered. It felt intensely cold. I rubbed my arms. A cube of aching blue light shone down from the shaft mouth.

Nearby, a couple of powerful halogen lights illuminated the chamber floor, which expanded for at least twelve feet in all directions, wider than the shaft. Some of the chamber was lost in deep shadow and it felt eerie. Joe had engineered a lattice of struts and beams to prevent a cave-in, but that didn't comfort me—I hated enclosed spaces, especially tunnels, which in my profession didn't help.

A heavily built man with a thick gray moustache and wire-rimmed glasses was busy working away on one of the chamber walls, hacking into the hard-packed permafrost with a lump hammer and a broad chisel. He stopped hammering and grinned. "Hey, Laura, how're they hanging?"

Tom Atkins, from Boston, had a toolbox open at his feet, and his breath clouded in the chilled air. He wore a thickly padded Columbia ski jacket, heavy woolen gloves, and earmuffs. Next to him was a trestle table covered with an assortment of tools and brushes, as well as a couple of powerful electric torches. He removed the earmuffs.

"You came prepared, Tom." I nodded toward a pile of unopened Budweiser and Red Star beer cans stacked in a corner.

"Hey, don't knock it, this place is better than my refrigerator."

"So what have you two found besides the perfect place to chill beer?"

Tom jerked a thumb toward the opposite side of the chamber. "Better take a deep breath, Laura."

"Why?"

"It's kind of uncanny. Macabre almost."

I picked up one of the flashlights from Tom's table and

moved deeper into the chamber. I shone a powerful cone of light onto the frozen soil and experienced a moment of pure terror. A human hand protruded from the permafrost. The flesh was intact, bleached white, the fingers lightly caked in mud, the fist tightly clenched. It appeared to be clutching something. "What the . . . !"

"You ain't seen anything yet. Look right there." Roy pointed to the permafrost wall.

And then I saw it. Connected to the hand was a body—a woman's face stared out grotesquely from the peaty earth. Her clothes were exposed, some kind of pale-colored blouse and a dark woolen top that looked from another century. "*Jeepers.*"

To the left I saw the remains of a dark, coarse jacket protrude from the rich brown earth, about a foot of the cloth exposed, and what appeared to be the vague shape of a small human torso underneath the fabric.

Roy said, "There's another body in there. We can't be sure if it's a child or an adult, but it'll take us some time to get it out. We'll concentrate on the woman first."

I turned my attention back to the woman, shivered, and peered closer. The preserved head was plainly visible. Her eyes were closed. I could see her nose and lips, ears and cheeks, locks of dark-colored hair curled across her features and forehead. She had good cheekbones. I shone the torchlight on her alabaster face and it was a disturbing experience. I knew I was looking at one of the most remarkable finds ever discovered at Ekaterinburg. "It's incredible. I wonder who she was."

"God only knows. But there's something else," Roy offered.

"What?"

"Take a look at what's in her hand."

I shone the flashlight on the still-clenched bones, held

firm for how many decades? It appeared that she was clutching some kind of metal chain. "Anyone want to try to pry the hand open?"

Roy grinned at me. "We thought we'd leave that to you."

"Thanks a bunch."

"You're the boss, baby." Roy handed me a pair of disposable surgical gloves.

"Here, hold the flashlight while I try."

Roy held my light and shone it on the clenched hand. I slipped on the gloves, steeled myself, closing my eyes a moment, and then I went for it. I gripped the index finger and the wrist and pulled gently, trying to open the hand.

The flesh felt marble cold and solid.

I was afraid that I might tear the skin apart or the entire hand would shatter like delicate porcelain. To my surprise, the bones uncoiled silently, just a fraction, but enough to see what they held.

In the palm's bleached white furrows I saw a chain and locket.

It didn't look extravagant or expensive like some of the jewelry found at Ekaterinburg, hidden away by royal relatives or the wealthy merchants who were executed here. I lifted out the locket and wiped it gently with my fingers. I could see it had some kind of inscription, but the locket was partly covered by peaty earth, the chain fragile.

Roy offered his penknife. "Here, try this."

I took the knife and scraped away caked dirt. There was no mistaking the raised Romanov family seal in gold, inlaid on front. It showed the double-headed imperial eagle—the Romanov family seal. I could make out an inscription on the locket's rear, but it was obliterated by corrosion. My heart skipped.

Tom said, elated, "You think we've got lucky?"

I didn't reply, just stared at the locket, mesmerized.

Tom rubbed his frozen hands as if trying to set them on fire with friction. "Who knows? But we better inform the Russians. We'll have to cut her out of the permafrost. Hopefully a closer look can tell us if her body suffered any trauma and how she likely died."

The Russians had control of the dig. An inspector came out every other day from Ekaterinburg to check on our progress. But that was barely on my mind as I stared at the locket, my mind on fire. "*No,* don't do anything, or inform anyone officially. Not just yet."

Tom frowned, and Roy said, "Why not?"

I stared again at the remains of the two bodies and I felt stunned, filled with excitement. I looked up toward the gaping mouth of the shaft. The blue light that shone down at me that moment felt like an epiphany. I clutched the locket. My heart raced.

Roy must have seen the excitement on my face and said, "What's wrong?"

I crossed back to the harness and strapped myself in. "Someone get me photos of the body. I want them from every angle. And get a hair sample, we need to carry out a DNA test. I want to know if this woman could be a Romanov, or a blood relative." I pressed the motor control switch and the seat began to ascend.

"Hey, where are you going, baby?" Roy asked, confused.

"To book a flight. And don't ask me to where. You'd never believe me."